CW01511014

Contents

Snowed Under

JULIANA SMITH

"If I could live anywhere, it would be in Cooper and Madeline's dates." – Julie Olivia, author of Off The Hook

"Snowed Under is the coziest holiday romcom of the season!" – Kelsey Whitney, author of In The End

"Cozy and delightful...I adore Madeline and Cooper." – Madison Wright, author of Off The Beaten Path

"Snowed Under is charming in a way that you'll think of these character far beyond the page." – Beta reader

Books also by Juliana Smith:

Stand-alones:
I Can Fix That
Baggage Claim

Wells Family Series:
Per My Last Email
Signed, Sealed, Delivered
Rock and a Hard Place
For the Record
A Fine Line

For my very own half pint:
You shine brighter than the sun, Saylor girl.

Sensitivity note:

I always love to keep my books fun and cozy but there are a couple of heavier topics in this book such as: loss of a sibling (off page), absence of a father, hospitalization of a side character, and a touch of alcoholism. As always, take care of your heart while reading.

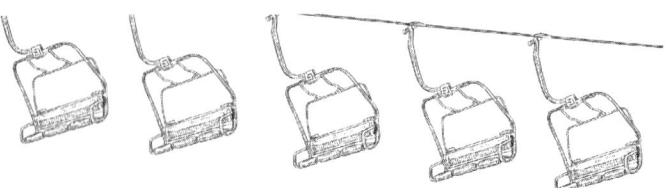

Chapter One
COOPER

What a disgusting day. For most people, anyway.

The freshly fallen snow from last night's unexpected storm provided a blanket of cloud-like crystals that trickled down from the mountaintop toward the lodge. For an average local, this would mean a day of staying inside. A day of reading by a fireplace or sitting on the couch and binging an entire season of a beloved sitcom. Having their face pressed to the window, watching as the sky poked hundreds of holes in itself and let the snowflakes fall like tiny gifts to the earth. A day to take everything slowly, a minute at a time.

For me, it meant speed. Heart-racing, blood-pumping, wind-chilling speed. Post-snowstorm days like this meant empty slopes, fresh powder, and adrenaline like you've never felt. This weather was a skier's dream. A mountaintop stretched out before you, a vast expanse of pristine snow shimmering under the winter sun. Even if you'd seen something similar fifty times, the sight still had your heart pounding with a mixture of excitement and apprehension. Below, the hill dropped away sharply, a steep slope disappearing into the distance. This raw anticipation would bubble, a thrilling mixture of nerves and adrenaline. That was what I lived for—the rush of flying down the mountain, the sharp wind in my already messy short hair, relishing the freedom only speed could bring me.

I looked up at the mostly empty hill, finding only the workers in hi-vis vests at the top where the lift was being tested. I momentarily imagined how I had done it a million times before. Pushing off with a powerful thrust of my poles, feeling the snow crunch beneath my skis, controlling the earth beneath me, or feeling as though I did, at least. My chest expanded with a deep breath, and I closed my eyes. My feet were at the top once more. Instantly, gravity took hold, and I pictured hurtling down the hill, faster and faster with each passing second. The wind whipped past my face, roaring in my ears like a symphony of exhilaration. The more speed I gained, the sharper my senses became, every nerve tingling with awareness. The world around me became a white and baby blue kaleidoscope, the snow fading into streaks as I carved a path through the mountain, leaving scars of travel in my wake. My muscles tensed with each turn, responding instinctively to the shifting terrain beneath me.

Despite the breakneck pace, it brought me a sense of control, a connection to the mountain that was both primal and profound. Every twist, every turn, was a dance, a delicate balance between speed and precision, power and finesse. It brought me to life in a way solid ground never could. My whole being thrummed with energy. The rush of wind, the sting of the cold, the burn in my muscles, the heat in my thighs as I pushed myself further—

"Mr. Cooper?"

The tiny Minnie Mouse voice broke into my vision. Like a picture catching fire, it burned slowly in one corner, consumed by black smoke. Then, all at once, it dissipated into thin air like it had never existed in the first place.

I ripped my gaze from the vast mountain before me and settled it on the pink-covered three-foot-nothing human wearing Elsa skis. Her goggles stared right up at me, reflecting my own goggles in the blue and purple lens.

"Are we starting soon?" she asked with a head tilt, making her helmet bob a little to the side, a sign that it wasn't on tight enough.

I knelt, adjusting my own skis, and lifted my hands to Abigail's white helmet. I grabbed the strap and pulled it tight, leaving no slack.

Skiing down the mountain would have to wait until my shift was over in another six hours. When all that virgin snow would be packed down and probably smothered in ski lines. That was the only thing I didn't love about my job: being so close to home and yet never being able to fully reach it. It was the purest form of torture, and yet I wouldn't trade it for any other career out there. It spoiled me.

"Yeah, kiddo. We're about to start." I patted the top of her helmet with my glove and smiled at her. She looked out at the snow like it was calling for her. A feeling I had known all too well since before I was her age.

I could see it in her gaze, the connection to the snow. Certain people picked up the art of skiing like they were just walking. Like every movement came naturally to them. Years of teaching these classes allowed me to point them out almost instantly. I could see it before they touched a hill. It was the way they buckled their gear like they'd done it a hundred times before. How there was no hesitation when they locked their boots into the skis. They may stumble a bit when they get settled, testing the weight of their skis, but for the most part, they took to it like a duck takes to water. I would know because I was the same way the first time I came out here.

Besides working for my family, it was the best part of my job at the resort. I got to see this raw talent, to mold and shape it like pottery until they were almost as good as me. Almost.

Abigail turned to me with expectant eyes. I snorted. Impatient. Every single one of them was. "We've got one more joining us today."

A giant relief on my end, considering all three of my classes had dwindled over the last month. Ever since a smaller, albeit much newer, resort opened up on the other side of Aspen on Ajax Mountain, I was losing students left and right. And it wasn't just in my classes. The café inside the lodge's lobby was less busy too. I should be relieved, considering they used to sell out of my favorite bacon cheddar scones before I could make it up there on my breaks. Still, I only felt the weight of stress on my shoulders as, each day, more of the treats sat in the display case.

It wasn't that our resort was terrible; it was just no longer new and exciting. I guessed the same way people became after being married for twenty years.

You get familiar with every slope and curve, every dip and turn in the hills. Before you know it, you've gone hundreds of miles on your skis without genuinely going anywhere. I got it. I understood the whole seven-year itch thing. But what was so bad about consistency? What was wrong with knowing a place like the back of your hand? A place you could step into and breathe in the deep pine smell and brisk cold air and feel comfortable. Like it was a second home. But no. Apparently, everyone and their moms needed something exciting and new. So, the little traitors had turned their backs on our mountain and headed straight for another. I didn't care if Timmy Silbeck was six years old and his mom was the one who pulled him out of classes. They were both dead to me. Not really. Maybe just a little, though.

Point being, any kind of new skiers, even in a seven- to nine-year-old class, meant traction as a whole for the resort. Finn, my coworker and best friend, had the new kid in his classes for a while apparently—but new to me meant new in my mind. I wasn't going to fret over technicalities.

I checked the fitness watch on my right wrist. We still had three minutes till class officially started. My students were lined up beside an array of tiny orange cones, five sets of eyeballs staring at me, just waiting for me to say go.

"Three more minutes, guys. Just stretch for a little bit."

I turned back to the main exit, the one with yellow signs that read Ski Lessons—> Class B. My class. The best class—despite how much Finn swore his were better.

We technically held the same positions at the lodge. It was how we became best friends over the years. But I knew my kids were on another level. One of these days, we were going to bring all of these kids out here to battle and watch them fall until only one was left standing. Just to see whose group of kids was superior. What were they going to do, fire me? Good luck, considering I'd be seeing their unfortunate asses every Thanksgiving and Christmas.

Soon, a woman with curly dark hair and gray roots strolled through the exit with a short blond-haired boy in all black ski gear. I lifted my gloved hand to wave them toward me, and when the woman caught sight, her chest seemed to fall in relief, and she grabbed the boy's wrist and pulled him toward our group.

Shit, what had Finn said the kid's name was? Carson? Calvin? Christopher? I shook my head. It didn't matter. Names didn't stick with me. Never had and probably never would. It was exactly why I kept a Rolodex of nicknames in my head that could be applied to any and every situation. Sport, kid, man, etc. Easy money was another recent favorite.

As the woman and boy approached our group, he lifted his goggles.

I shortened my height by bending my knees. "What's up, man?" I stuck my gloved hand out for him to shake, and he did it with a small smile. He didn't respond with a hello or anything, but he looked behind me at the line of kids, who were less of a line and more of a mosh pit of sugar-hyped Bluey-loving monsters, but he smiled at them, nonetheless.

"I'm Cooper. I'm glad you're here." I smiled back at him. "We're gonna have some fun today."

The boy looked to the woman who'd brought him in, and she nodded. "Go on."

He listened and bounced to the side, sitting on a nearby bench to hook his boots into his skis as two of the other kids in my class approached him. I felt a pull at my chest and turned to the source. The woman—who, from this distance, looked like she was probably the boy's grandmother—was holding my clearance badge. It said Instructor at the top, just above my name. Below it was a picture of twenty-year-old me with floppy brown hair that desperately needed a cut.

She eyed the picture before looking at my face and squinting skeptically. I raised both hands in defense.

"I know, I know. The hair got better with age."

"Charlie can't have peanuts. He's not allergic, but they're not good for his digestion. He has filtered water in his backpack and will need breaks regularly. Finn usually lets him rest every half hour—"

I smiled at her, trying my best not to stare at the wrinkles in her forehead.

"We all take breaks every thirty minutes, and water is heavily encouraged. I always bring the kids oranges or beef jerky as snacks, and they can have them whenever they want, and I have a 100 percent accident-free guarantee. Been teaching for nine years and never had an incident." Other than some minor scrapes and bruises, but those were essential for a good childhood. It was character building on their end.

Still, the woman eyed me and glanced over at...what's-his-name, who was smiling at the two kids beside him as he listened intently to whatever nine-year-old phrases they were using. I stopped keeping up after yeet became a thing a few years ago. I was too old for that shit now.

"He is a special boy. Keep him safe."

I nodded. They were all unique in every parent's or grandparent's eyes. "Yes, ma'am. I promise he won't want to leave when you pick him up."

I'd been known to have a kid or two stuck to my leg, begging to stay longer.

"Unlikely. My daughter will be coming to get him, but I am always near."

I shuddered as the lady walked away, occasionally glancing back at her grandson and over at me with those menacing eyes. Freaky.

"All right." I clapped. "Who's ready to get started?"

One hour, two snack breaks, and at least five Mr. Cooper, I have to pees later, my first set of lessons was over. As was the prospect of skiing on a mostly empty slope with that fresh blanket of snow staring seductively at me from the mountain.

I sighed, leaning against the nearby bench and twisted my back to the left, then right, searching for relief. I may have not gotten any solo steep hill skiing done today, but I did get to witness something pretty incredible.

About ten minutes into our standard lesson—discussing pizza feet or how to control your speed going down a hill—I noticed something click in the new kid. His feet moved naturally with the snow, shifting and gliding with it like he had a personal connection with the earth itself. It was like magic to watch, how I'd demonstrate a certain movement, and he'd follow, nailing every skill with talent that a nine-year-old with little experience shouldn't possess.

I had to imagine it was like watching Aaron Rodgers tossing a football around as a kid, or maybe seeing Elton John perform live before anyone knew his name. It felt like I was watching history unfold before me. Or like I was looking back on my old self, back before I gave up on going pro. It was like everything moved around this one kid, and all the other students knew it too.

At one point, one of the younger girls' skis kept getting tangled together, resulting in her tripping over herself where the hill curved to a flat spot. Before I could even rush over to help, little man was already there, speaking low to her.

"See? Like this," he said in a gentle but direct tone. Next thing I knew, everyone was watching him teach her. I couldn't even be upset that the whole class was distracted because I think we all knew one thing: his grandmother was absolutely right; this kid was special.

Everyone slowly trickled off with their parents, leaving the new kid and a few others who were talking by the bench where they'd removed their skis.

I craned my neck, looking around the crowd of people near the back entrance of the lobby. Most of them looked like they were together, so I doubted any of them were parents. But then one of them stood out.

A woman looking down at her phone and then back up, head turning from side to side like she was looking for something. Someone.

I felt a strike to my chest when she looked up. Long chestnut-brown hair cascaded over her shoulders and down her back in soft waves, catching the light off in the distance and settling over her in a warm glow during this freezing morning. It framed her face delicately, accentuating her features with a touch of elegance. My eyes trailed downward to the shapely figure, studying the curves in all the right places. Hips swaying, she moved with such fluidity that it was both captivating and effortless. Like the snow she walked on was a stage, and she was a dancer. There was a hint of a smile on her face. Not a big one, but a reserved, permanent closed grin. Resting happy face, I thought.

Everything about this screamed out of your league. I didn't care. And I was out of practice when it came to talking to pretty women. I didn't care about that either.

Her eyes stopped on me before her lips tilted up farther. She took a few steps closer to our setup, her smile growing. Completely forgetting about my job, I glanced over my shoulder to the small group of kids behind me, where she kept her attention fixed.

The closer the woman got, the more her face came into view. Her long, slender nose seemed to favor the right side of her face. Her smile was a little crooked, with these full pink lips. On her left cheek, there was a faint smattering of freckles, reminiscent of constellations scattered across a night sky. Like God had taken a paintbrush and speckled her with them on that one side. The other side was a blank canvas, minus the smallest beauty mark above her lip.

My breathing picked up speed as she walked closer to us, and heat followed directly behind it, spreading down my abdomen. Don't do it. Don't do it. Do not do it. You didn't work to avoid women for an entire year only to toss it all aside for a random one who doesn't even know your name.

Only I did, because when she was a few feet away, I lifted the goggles from my face and let them rest on my head in the mess of hair 'on top. The kid next to me—Mini Coop, I settled on—stood and began gathering his things. Before I could process the idea fully, I was reaching for his shoulder and tapping the back of my knuckles to it.

"Hey, Mini Coop. Let me borrow you for a sec."

The kid shrugged and lifted his bag, but he left his skis and goggles behind him before following me to where the woman was approaching.

I murmured out of the side of my mouth to the kid who was already wearing a half grin, like his factory setting was pure happiness. Or maybe it was just being out in the snow.

"There's a girl over there. All you gotta do is stand there and be super quiet."

He glanced at the brunette and chuckled a bit, but he followed right alongside me until we were face to face with the woman. She looked down at Mini Coop and right back at me, with my crossed arms and messy hair.

"Can I help you?"

She smiled politely. Scholarly, I thought. Like the kind of woman who knew how atom bombs worked or why, when you pursed your lips and blew, the air was colder than when you opened your mouth wide and blew. Like she knew all of life's greatest wonders. Shy, smart, beautiful. Each word was practically painted on her forehead.

Looking down at the kid beside me, she replied. "Yes, actual-ly—"

"I can help," I said, ignoring the tiny crack in my voice that escaped, as if this was the first time I'd so much as seen a woman. As if I were an alien in disguise and had to pass myself off as an actual human. I cleared my throat as I settled an arm on Mini Coop's head, wrist settling on his helmet as he giggled below me. "You know, having a kid, I completely understand the struggles of getting them to and from practices and whatnot."

She quirked a brow at me, and the freckles on that side of her face lifted with it, stretching. "Oh, you do?"

"Yeah, I mean"—I tapped on the helmet below me, causing him to chortle—"me and Mini Coop are always swamped. But I'm not too busy this weekend if you aren't."

It wasn't the worst pickup line I'd ever used, but it wasn't the greatest. I was on a year-long hiatus, and it turned out that talking to pretty girls was not like riding a bike. Finn called it helmet confidence. For some reason, in my work outfit, with half of my face covered up, I felt more invisible than when I was in day-to-day clothes.

The woman's eyes volleyed between me and the kid, and her smile grew, sending a rush of pride through my veins. I was ready to make up for lost time. If I nailed this, nailed another single moment with her, then this kid was my good luck charm for sure.

I opened my mouth to speak again when the woman turned to the kid beside me. "Ready to go home, squirt?"

"Yeah, let me get my stuff." He giggled again, his shoulders shaking and his helmet bouncing.

I stood entirely still for a moment, my jaw tense and eyes wide. His mom. Of course she was his mom. And, of course, that meant on the rare occasion that I got a new student, I went and screwed it up by flirting with his mother, who was more than likely married to a buff, tattooed construction worker who would torture me, kill me, and put my body under wet cement, never to be seen again.

Walking back with his bag, the kid latched his arm around his mom's, and they made their way to the lodge. The sun bounced off the reflection of his helmet to blind me. I quickly glanced over my shoulder to double-check that the kids were all there before I followed the two, taking long strides in my steps.

"Wait!"

Both the mom and her son stopped in their tracks, turning to look back at me. I expected a form of rage. Some kind of I'm not bringing my kid back to this place ever again face or a My review will be posted all over Yelp scowl. But I was met with only amusement. A sly smirk resting on her lips.

"I'm not some creep," I explained, hunched over and slightly out of breath, exactly like a creep. "I was just—"

The woman spoke before I could finish. "I know exactly who you are, Cooper Graves."

My back straightened at that. It meant one of two things: she knew that my relatives owned the place, or I had made a fool of myself somehow in front of her before without realizing. My younger self hadn't exactly appreciated the value of what little time we had here on earth, much less the value of learning to keep my mouth shut when the time was right. Something I was still learning as of two minutes ago.

"You do?"

Her chin dipped in a nod, the dark brown waves around her temples falling to surround her face. "Exactly who you are."

"Why do I feel like that's not a good thing?"

That foxish grin gave me nothing more, not a sliver of information, before she turned right back around, hips swaying and shoulders perked up, and headed to the lodge.

The kid beside her laughed again, the sound nearly identical to the one the woman beside him had let out.

"Bye, Mr. Cooper."

I watched the two of them open the door to the lobby and took the last opportunity I had to shout with both hands wrapped around my mouth. "Your kid is really special."

The woman turned her head back to me, still with that smirk on her face. Her lips were full and expressive and slightly asymmetric, with the upper lip slightly fuller than the lower. That tiny birthmark was visible, even from this distance. Every part of me fought the desire to see more of her just as she shouted back at me.

"I know."

Chapter Two
Madeline

I practically fell into the driver's seat when we reached the car.

Charlie bounced up and down behind me as he buckled his seat belt, holding enough energy for the both of us and practically pinging off the walls of the vehicle. Behind my eyes, a sharp, yet dull ache was forming. That mixed with the unsteady shakiness in my fingers was a dead giveaway. I was running on too little sleep, and I'd pumped too much caffeine, courtesy of Mr. Dunkin himself, into my veins.

I forced my back straight as I started the car, pulling every bit of energy left in me from my mostly sleepless night. The knot forming at the base of my spine tightened. Looking back, signing up for an extra cleaning shift after spending half my night studying for an upcoming exam wasn't my brightest idea. But money talked, and I had never been known to ignore it.

To be fair, signing up for night classes in nursing school wasn't my brightest idea either. Especially with two small children whose lives rested in the palm of my Pine-Sol-soaked hands.

Looking back at Charlie, who was looking down as he played with the buckle on his ski helmet, I reminded myself of the two affirmations that would never leave me.

You are valuable.

He left them for you.

A deep breath resonated in my chest as I pulled air in through my nose and let it out through my mouth. In one sentence, out the next.

You are valuable.

He left them for you.

I turned over my shoulder, mustering every inch of a smile I could, and directed it at the nine-year-old who read me like a book.

"Did you have fun?"

He looked back up at me, and it felt like sunshine itself was pouring through the car. This kid lived his life on bare necessities and smiled like he ruled the world.

"Yeah, Mr. Cooper was really cool."

"I'm glad you liked it."

"Mr. Finn is cool too," He was quick to add on. "But I think I like Mr. Cooper better. Don't tell him I said that, though. It would probably hurt his feelings."

"All right, kiddo." I smiled back at my sensitive little guy. He was always so aware of everyone's feelings. I used to joke that he would be a therapist one day. But judging by his natural talent, I had a tiny Olympic skier in my hands.

We pulled out of the half-full parking lot, turning down the highway still covered in the snow from last night's storm. When I'd clocked in this morning, the other cleaning ladies around me were complaining on and off about the weather from the night before. Talking about the pain of shoveling and salting their driveways or how they should have just called in sick. The I am so over this weather discussions would make you think they weren't local to Aspen. I smiled to myself the whole time and kept quiet. I loved a good snowstorm.

It felt like nature's way of wiping away the old and setting a blank slate right on top. Out with the old, in with the new. A renaissance, if you will. The beginning of a new era. One I was desperate to enter.

Ahead, the road stretched out before us like a ribbon of asphalt, disappearing into the horizon where the snow-capped peaks of the Rocky Mountains loomed in the distance.

Despite the bustling traffic of tourists, the view from the windshield would have been serene enough to put me to sleep if I was still long enough. Or maybe I was just that tired. Snowflakes fluttered, slow and delicate, against the glass, leaving behind intricate patterns that shimmered in the soft mid-morning light. Trees lined the highway, tall and proud. Their branches bowing under the weight of winter's embrace, with fresh snow lying right on top of them.

"Can we get an ice cream on the way to Gram's?" Charlie cut in.

"Nope." I popped the P and passed a couple of cars, then turned toward my mom's house, which was thankfully only a few minutes from the lodge.

A mixture of a whine and a groan erupted in my back seat in tandem with a long "come on."

Oh, this was Will's kid, all right. It felt like he was laughing down at me every time I heard that whining. It was like his way of peeking down from the clouds in heaven and pointing a finger at me, always needing the last word.

"No, 'cause Piper is going to want one and I"—am counting change to get us to the next paycheck—"don't feel like cleaning up after her."

That part wasn't exactly a lie. Charlie's two-year-old sister was a menace with anything that melted. I could already envision spending my afternoon with a carpet cleaner, removing the chocolate essence that had soaked into the soft material of my car seats. I cleaned enough in my day job. The last thing I needed was to add to the list.

Charlie crossed his arms, unsatisfied but not fighting it. "Fine."

Pulling into my mom's driveway always felt like God was tossing a coin up there, trying to decide which side of her he was going to pull out today. Heads for serenity, tails for chaos. My bet was always on tails.

I knocked on the door twice before opening it, only to be met with the booming strains of the Pocahontas soundtrack coming from the kitchen speaker. We were currently on week three of four of Piper's Pocahontas phase, and I had painted with the color of the wind at least fifty times this week. My guess was that we were going to either circle back into Elsa territory after this or take a turn and go straight to A Bug's Life. There was really no way to tell. Seasons changed, leaves fell, snow melted. But no matter what, our two-year-old movie critic was known for her four-week-long obsessions that led to car karaoke. Even if she couldn't say a majority of the lyrics. Or the movie names themselves. Nicknames such as "pokey"—for Pocahontas—were a staple in her limited vocabulary. Still, we'd endure four weeks of border-line addictive watching, then her movie obsession would die out, and she'd be on to the next thing.

Two tiny pink-sneakered feet tapped the floor, pausing for a moment before pounding against the hardwoods. She inched closer until a thirty-inch angel came into view. Crooked blond pigtails, a wide-open grin, red-stained lips—presumably from the popsicle stick in her hand, and a pink sweat suit with Everyone's favorite written across the top. A spitting image of her mother, of my best friend.

"MayMay!" she shrieked before throwing the half red popsicle stick to the side and sprinting to me with open arms.

I loved a lot of things about this kid, about both of them, but if I had to pick an absolute favorite, it would be this. The way they acted like every time I appeared, it was the first time they'd seen me in years. The way Piper's sticky hands clung to my legs as she wrapped her arms around my thighs. Or how, even when he wanted to be too cool for me, Charlie never passed up a hug or an offered arm. No matter how big they grew, these two were always proud to be considered mine. And most days, I needed that kind of blind faith.

"Pipes!" I shouted back, bending over at the waist to squish her, planting a kiss on the top of her head, right next to the loosened left pig tail. "How was your morning?"

I pulled back from the hug and crouched down to her height. Piper spoke with her hands, waving them back and forth as she mumbled a bit of her own language. A stranger wouldn't know it, but after a year of speech therapy, she was making some remarkable progress. She wasn't up to par with most almost-three-year-olds, of course. We had a while to go for that, but she was no longer entirely silent. She had a voice. It just wasn't one everyone understood yet. She was getting there, and we were meeting her halfway. Every so often, I could pick up a single word such as pay—play—or nack—snack—and that was progress enough for me.

"Oh, you painted with Gram?" I smiled down at her, mostly picking up on that one by the dried orange paint I was going to have to scrub out from under her fingernails tonight.

She nodded with wide, excited eyes before looking over my shoulder and taking off in her brother's direction. Charlie grinned at her. "Hi, squirt." Then he dipped down and picked her up, settling the princess on his hip and bouncing her.

"We did paint, and she got it all over my great grandfather's mahogany desk." My mom hobbled into the living space with a wet gray cloth in hand, favoring her left leg again.

God ended up with tails today. Noted.

I stood to my full height and straightened my back. "You could just tell her no when she asks to paint. Or let her do it somewhere else."

My mother scoffed, as if the idea of telling Piper—the same toddler who tried to throw herself down the stairs when I suggested we change her diaper—no was up there with snorting cocaine and robbing a bank.

"Well, all right, then." No need to stay here longer than we had to.

It wasn't that I didn't appreciate my parents. They were great. Most days...some days...days. But a majority of the last two and a half years had been centered around whether I was managing parenthood well enough and whether I was giving these two the lives they deserved whilst maintaining my own. The answer to both of those would be a resounding no. But at the very least, the universe had to reward me for my efforts.

I turned back to Charlie, who was blowing raspberries at Piper, causing her to erupt in excited giggles. "You guys ready?"

Charlie set down his sister. "I'll go grab her bags." He turned away and walked back to the kitchen without hesitation, and my lips curved up. Your kid is special. Cooper Graves had one thing right, at least.

"Thanks, bud." I watched him walk away before turning to Piper and picking her up. "What do you think about McDonald's and movie night? Does that sound good to you, little bug?" I tickled the inside of her neck with my nose, and my heart grew at the sound of her laughter.

Piper nodded in excitement before shouting. "Pokey!" and I laughed. "Yes, of course, Pokey. Because what else would we watch? Go grab your boots, and we'll head out."

Piper slid down my body to the floor, rushing to grab her little snow boots—that she had yet to grow fully into and were probably causing more harm than good. I figured by winter she would fit into them, but whereas her speech had grown, she was still our short and tiny girl.

"Madeline." My mother said it with a sigh, in the same way she had when I was caught kissing my boyfriend in my car at seventeen or when she found out I was friends with a girl who smoked medical weed one time to help with a migraine.

I sighed right back, and any ounce of energy that these kids gave me left my body in an instant. I forced my chest to lift in preparation for whatever was coming. It could be the usual, the kind of lines she masked as concerns and questions but were more like distrustful accusations. The Well, are you feeding her enough? or Is cleaning the best job you can find now? Then there was How about quitting nursing school and finding something steadier for the kids? I'd heard it all, and to each one, I had a default answer.

"Yes?" I asked.

"Are you sure McDonald's is the best meal for them?" Because fast food chains were up there with the devil's lettuce or public debauchery.

My default answer came into play before I really had time to update the settings. My brain just took over. "I've cooked dinner every day this week. It's the best meal to keep them happy and my sanity straight."

"If you insist. I just—"

"You just what, Mom?" I cut in. From lack of sleep to the weight sitting on my shoulders daily, the last thing I needed was one more thing on my to-do list, because satisfying my mother's high standards and buying more Pull-Ups were not exactly on the same level.

And because it was that kind of day, both kids came running back into the kitchen before I could finish the sentence full of words that I typically muted on TV shows for their sake. I twirled the keys in my hand before dipping to pick Piper up again. "Say bye to Gram." I smiled and picked up Pipe's hand, forcing it in a wave, as Charlie gave her a quick hug.

We turned to walk outside, and Charlie said, "Did I hear McDonald's?"

My mom's voice popped into my head. Is that the best for them? I looked down at both of these kids—like I was looking into my brother's eyes—before nodding. "Absolutely."

You are valuable
He left them for you.

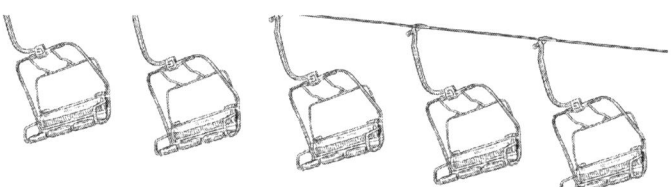

Chapter Three
COOPER

I t was edging close to the best time of day.

When the afternoon started to wane at the ski lodge, which meant five o'clock, since it was November and the moon visited us early, the sky transformed into this canvas of yellows, golds, and oranges. The sun dipped low behind the snow-capped peaks, casting a glow across the horizon and dancing on your skin.

The blanket of snow glistened in the fading sunlight, a temptation itself. The open hills started to die down, calling your name. Only thirty minutes left to ride them. Thirty minutes to get that adrenaline rush that my veins cried out for.

As the sun slipped below the horizon, the first twinkling lights of the lodge began to illuminate the landscape, soft and inviting. They emanated from the windows, a warm contrast against the cold mountain backdrop.

It was my one time to ride the way I wanted to. To cut through the snow, slicing my legs back and forth down the mountain like an artist painting a picture on my way down.

It was the best way, the only way, to end the day before going back to an entirely empty house. The silence there seemed so loud that I'd started leaving the TV on all day just so that, when I got home, there would be voices around. It felt kind of pathetic when I started, but now it was almost a game. Guessing what channel 132 was going to have on each day. Would it be reruns of Oprah, or are we spicing things up with something like a Spanish murder drama? A mystery was always waiting for me when my feet crossed over the threshold.

Gliding down these slopes was like a last-minute treat before having to go to the nearly dead place I called home, where it was just me, an eight-year-old Xbox, and leftover Thai food to keep each other company. It didn't seem as pitiful before Finn had met his wife. Most days after work, we'd head to my place and drink a few beers, or we'd go downtown, sliding in and out of bars with trails of tourist that we knew we'd never see again.

I used to think it was cool. I assumed everyone around me did too. Running into random guys I graduated with that told me I was "living that dream life," or the odd "hey, have a little fun for me" from a married man here and there. But now that I've…grown, I guess, I see how pitiful that life truly was. How time was so quick to leave us, and once it was gone, you don't get an ounce of it back. Time was really selfish in that way, and after my grandfather had died, I realized I wanted to keep all of it to myself. So, the drinking stopped, the women stopped, and the skiing picked up.

It made me kind of sad for my past self. Poor guy didn't know how rough he actually had it. Made me wonder if the people closest to me realized it too. Pops warned me, telling me that just 'cause I was young didn't mean I had to be dumb. Or Ma always trying to set me up with a sweet girl from her work. Telling me to settle down, that a life in the fast lane wasn't a life worth living. They were both right, but still, I learned some lessons could only be taught through grief.

And somehow in those snowy hilltops, time slowed. It turned snaillike, and my movements, fast as they were, felt more like I was the one in control. I was taking back those countless youth-wasted hours one by one. It gave me a connection to Pops too, like he was in those slopes and curves, in the dips and divots of the hills. In the sketchy spots too, the ledges that snuck up on you and had you feeling like you were inching toward death as your heart fell to your ass. Gotta keep you humble, kid. You could practically hear it in that voice that sounded more and more like Morgan Freeman's the older he got.

After the last kid had been picked up, I was going to have almost an hour on the slopes. Maybe longer if I hightailed it out of here. I lunged for my bags, ready to shove them into my designated locker and race back here to get on the lift. I've only got des, and I'm going to make every single one count.

The strap of my backpack—which, truthfully, was full of snacks and "prizes" for the kids, for when they did well or accomplished a new skill—dug into my shoulder, all but begging to be tossed to the side and forgotten for the next adrenaline-packed half hour. If my keys and wallet weren't in there, I probably would have listened.

My legs took off, and I rushed toward the side door that would lead me into the employee only area.

"Mr. Graves," a voice called from behind me. I almost considered stopping. But then again, there were a lot of people with the last name Graves, weren't there? And a vast majority of them worked at this resort, so it was possible they weren't calling me in particular.

"Cooper?"

There...were also a lot of Coopers in the state of Colorado. I wasn't exactly sure how many, but more than ten, right?

"Cooper Graves."

All right, fine. I give up.

I turned my head as my fingers dug into the tight strap on my shoulder. A couple not much older than me were on my tail. The woman in a blazer and heels, despite the icy walkway, and the man in a suit that looked similar to what I'd rented for Finn and Olive's wedding.

"That's me." I clicked my tongue and smiled halfway, trying to keep eye contact and not look at the glorious hills behind them screaming my name.

The woman spoke up. "Sorry to catch you if you were in a hurry, but our niece, Makayla, is one of your students, and she's always going on about you."

Makayla...I racked my brain.

"Curly red hair. Says the word literally every two minutes, but she has a lisp, so it sounds like widawee."

Ah, Rusty. The five-year-old who could barely even stand in skis. She was adorable and liked to frequently tell me I was intredabeel. I think she meant incredible, but sometimes I just nodded along with her. My smile unzipped a little wider.

"Yeah, she's a good kid."

The husband spoke next. "I did say your last name correctly, right? Graves? As in Alex Graves?"

I wasn't too shocked at the question. It was something I got a lot since my family owned the lodge. I never wanted to bring it up first—it was kind of a dick move—but I loved my family, and I was never going to be ashamed of who they were or what they owned.

"That's my uncle. Most of the family works around the lodge," I confirmed.

Pops had this place for as long as I could remember, expanding it into what it was today until his passing. My uncle and his wife took over from there. One of his cousins helped work the lift, and another ran the social media page. My other aunt managed the café in the lobby, and her husband oversaw finances. Essentially every family member of mine, except my mom, had worked here my whole life.

We always joked that Ma wasn't cool enough to work with us, when in reality, we all knew it was the exact opposite. My mom was the kind of free spirit who wasn't going to be tied down to a certain jobsite just because her family was involved in it. So instead, she was a pediatric travel nurse for years. When she had me, she settled here, switching over to speech therapy and worked her way up until she eventually opened her own office. Officially—and not so humbly—she received an award for Colorado's top speech therapist for the last three years in a row. She was pretty great at what she did.

So, again, denying my incredible family was never going to be an option.

"We assumed." The husband nodded before pulling out a card to hand me. I glanced down at the fancy card covered in matching fonts and monotone colors. Brandy and Chase Smith.

"We work for Family Matters Magazine."

I wasn't exactly sure what this had to do with me, but the title sounded somewhat familiar. I rarely picked up magazines, and if I did, they certainly weren't Family Matters.

"Oh," I nodded and glanced again at the lift behind them. Time would win this battle if I didn't wrap this up now. "Cool…"

Brandy, I assumed, snorted and shook her head at her husband. "We've been doing columns on local businesses. We've tried to get in touch with your uncle, but—"

"He's a busy man," I cut in with a chuckle, remembering Thanksgiving a few weeks ago. My uncle was on the phone outside the entire time, eventually coming in to cold turkey. He had no kids, and his wife was just as busy, so I guessed it didn't matter to them how many hours they racked up.

"Right, of course. Would you be interested in meeting with us for the column instead?"

I almost glanced behind me to make sure there wasn't another Cooper Graves sitting in a bush, waiting to take my spot. But no, they knew me. They knew little Makayla and not so little Alex.

Technically, there was no reason to say no, other than the fact that these two were cutting into precious slope time. But I was also just a children's ski instructor. Not exactly magazine material. And I still wasn't 100 percent positive they'd meant to ask me the question.

My answer came in spurts between puffs of forced laughter. "I, uh, don't know if I'm your guy for that, but I could maybe hook you up with one of my younger cousins?"

There was Danielle in marketing or Tanya, who worked on the lift every few weekends. I was quite literally the last Graves family member that should be included in this.

"Well, the thing is, we're focusing mostly on skiing. Since the lodge is hosting the upcoming ski competition in January, we were wanting to find someone who knew a lot about the sport, and since the magazine focuses most on family, and you're a children's instructor, it would be perfect."

Our annual ski competitions had been prevalent for the last ten years. A staple here at the lodge. The first weekend of every year, we held one of the largest competitions in Colorado. People from all over the states and even other countries would fly in for it. It took months of training and prepping. Everything really added up to that final moment. Each year, Finn and I would train one kid from our classes and sponsor them—which mostly meant teaching them a little outside class and placing bets on our skier being the number one racer. It was what the lodge was counting on during the transition. Last year performed well, but not as well as the year before. Or the year before that. Numbers were shifting, sliding, as the new lodge in town built up its credibility among social media sites. Any added publicity was a dire need. Be that as it may, I was far from a family man who should be featured in a magazine called Family Matters.

Her husband bumped in next. "We have a pretty good following on social media. This coverage would be seen by a lot of local people and tourists too. It would be great for your family's lodge."

That had my attention. Ski event. Tourists. Great for lodge.

The words replayed over and over, a broken record. I doubted a magazine column would flood the place with new guests, but we were getting desperate for exposure. The slower business was becoming more and more apparent, and every time I drove home, I passed by the newer lodge, whose parking deck was packed to the brim. So, I shrugged and was about to say sure, why not?

But before I could, Brandy spoke, a hand on her husband's bicep. "Two million followers is more than pretty good in my opinion."

"Two million...?" As the words left my mouth, I sounded like I was closer to the moon than on solid ground next to these two strangers. Famous strangers. Kind of, anyway.

They both nodded, and I imagined the results for a second. How many people would that bring in? How many more tourists, skiers, professional snowboarders? Social media influencers? Families? Family reunions? Parties? Famous people? Ryan Reynolds? The list was never ending. Expansive marketing that was specifically made for a skiing event would be incredible for our family. For the lodge.

Two million...

I pictured Pops hearing that number, imagining the creases around his eyes deepening as they widened. His mouth, once curved in a knowing smile, would gape in disbelief. Then he would break out into that rusty belly laugh.

Even if it brought the numbers up to cushion the blow we were feeling from the new lodge, it would be enough. Enough to make me feel like I'd done my Pops proud. Enough to make me think that yeah, maybe I'd wasted all of those years when I was young, but I could make up for it here. I could make up for it with an interview and an event that would at the very least get some social media traction.

"All right, yeah." I nodded a little too enthusiastically, bobbing my head up and down and letting go of any idea of skiing this afternoon. "Actually, that would be great."

The husband smiled before handing me a business card. "You can text me at this number, and we can set a date to meet with you and your wife and kids."

"Wife and kids?" I tilted my head.

"Right, since it's a family magazine, it would be about you and your family specifically," Brandy explained.

Don't do it. Don't do it. Do not screw this up.

"Oh. Um, I..."

"Or husband," she shouted, clasping her hands and doing little jazz fingers. "Husband and kids. Either way, we are entirely open and considerate of—"

I shook my head. "No, no. Wife. Not a husband."

"Either way." Chase smiled at me directly. "Or if you don't want to bring the kids in, that's fine too. We can just add a quote from them if you'll email us one. My number and email address are both on the bottom." He gestured to the business card still heavy in my hands.

The wife and kids...

It was one of those moments where I knew the truth, and I knew it was best to be honest. Follow the golden rule, yeah, yeah. But then I imagined the alternative. The thought of openly admitting that I was a more than single man who didn't have so much as a prospect of a girlfriend and certainly had no children running around was mortifying, though the honesty would be honorable. On the other hand, the thought of keeping my mouth shut and not technically admitting to having a family at home could lead this lodge into something big. Or at the very least get me a few new students.

I didn't consider it for another second before gritting out a quick "yeah, I will."

They smiled at each other and then back to me before walking away. "We look forward to hearing from you, Mr. Graves."

I waved goodbye and turned to the employee entrance of the lodge. Turning around the corner, I all but slammed my backpack down and pulled out my phone, going straight to Instagram. I typed in Family Matters Magazine, and a second later, a verified account popped up in the list of suggested profiles.

I stared down at the screen, at the logo in the profile picture that matched the one on the business card still resting between my fingers. The number of followers sat right beside it, calling to me.

2.8 million.

I clicked on the first post that wasn't pinned to the top of their profile, a picture of an older couple standing outside a large ranch over in McCoy. Over four hundred comments. Almost all of them stating how cute the couple was or how they couldn't wait to visit. Just booked a flight there, one of them said.

This was legit. Numbers that hadn't been fabricated from thin air. Numbers that could bring in the kind of exposure the lodge desperately needed for this tourist season. I could fix this. Change the script. There was a serious opportunity here to do right by Pops, by all of my family.

All I needed to do was find a wife and kids.

Chapter Four
Madeline

There were few things in life I enjoyed less than waking up screaming. Very few, though.

Standing at the edge of my bed, inches from my face, Piper stood, silent, at gremlin height, with a perfectly straight expression.

I reared back, gasping for air and clutching the tank top I'd passed out in. My laptop beside me groaned as I leaned on it. It was still there from the night before, when I'd fallen asleep attempting to finish studying a random Quizlet I'd found on the human nervous system.

"Gah!" I shouted before lowering my voice. "Piper, stop doing that."

The view from the window behind her showed that it was still dark out, the streetlamps casting an orange glow in the distance. Best-case scenario, it was six a.m. Worst-case, it was four.

Ever since she was five months old, little Piper had been an early bird. No exceptions. It was like her body had its own alarm clock, and when it went off, there was no convincing it to go back to sleep. No snoozes allowed. Once, I ran a test, thinking that if she stayed up till midnight, maybe she would sleep later. She woke up at four thirty, wide-eyed and yanking on my hair.

Piper pulled on the edge of my blanket, exposing my abdomen to the cool air. "Sham Jam?"

My arms stretched high above me, tapping against the fabric headboard, and shivers ran down my whole body as I yawned.

"MayMay?" She pulled the white comforter farther. "Sham Jam?"

I nodded; eyes still closed. "Yes, baby. I'll get you a Slim Jim."

Just like with movies, Piper had her phases when it came to snacks. Some months, it was fruit or a certain cereal. Other times, it was cherry tomatoes or a specific Pop-Tart flavor. This month, it was Slim Jims.

Forcing my body to catch up with my mind, I sat up and swung my legs over the side of the bed, following a tiny, very much awake Piper into our kitchen.

Slim Jims weren't the most nutritious thing to eat first thing in the morning, but I was all for avoiding tantrums when at all possible. Plus, when Charlie woke up, I would give them a real breakfast. This was just like pre-brekky. An appetizer.

With two Sham Jams in hand, Piper and I made our way to the couch, plopping down with a throw blanket and putting on Pocahontas for the one millionth time. I kept finding myself humming the background music as I cleaned yesterday. Thankfully, we were reaching a new transition time for her, and I was going to start pushing Brave or Finding Nemo this kid's way.

Piper happily settled into my lap and munched away at her meat stick, tilting her head back into my chest. I leaned forward to meet her and planted a kiss at her temple.

He left them for you.

I breathed in deeply, soaking in the toddler cuddles that I knew would soon be gone. They'd be replaced by cranky preteen hormones and a house reeking of Axe body spray and Bath and Body Works cherry blossom body mist. But for now, I had my little Piper, who went through her phases and her ups and downs but never once denied me a cuddle.

Polishing off both of her snacks, Piper begged for more—which was a long whining sound mixed with a shh and an mmm noise. She must have somehow sensed my lack of rest because she ended up settling with my sleepily mumbled in a little while.

My mother's comments still rested in my head. The ones that built up over time. The I've heard that causes development issues in kids. Should we check in to that? to the Are we giving her enough milk? As if something as simple as an extra cup of milk would magically repair speech delays.

She always said we as if we were actually a we. The word felt like a trick, like a way for her to plant her tiny anxious seed in my chest and watch it bloom into an oak tree, shading all the good things I'd accomplished in life. She knew if she said we in that way, it would come off more like concern and less like the whole I think you have no clue what you're doing and it's obvious thing.

To make matters more complicated, it wasn't that my mom was the worst person in the world. You could go a whole lot lower on the how shitty are your parents? icebreakers. All of the true crime podcasts I'd listened to warned me of that much. Some days Mom was wonderful. A beautiful beaming light that shone around you, and you thought hey, maybe she's not such a pain. Days where she plastered a smile on and was as polite as she could manage. I remembered days in high school where she would randomly check me out and open the door for me and say Let's go shopping! We would stroll through Target and buy entirely unnecessary items, then go back home, settling in on the couch and going over our haul like we hadn't just witnessed what the other bought.

Then there were the other days. Here and there, she would snip at you or make a sly comment that felt a little harsher than usual. But this whole we thing was a new development since Will and Savannah had passed. Or more so since she realized that they weren't leaving Piper and Charlie to my parents, but to me.

She was kind of like a fly living in your bedroom. As long as you were away and kept to yourself, you would never notice her. But when you lay down at night, finally able to relax, you'd start hearing that buzzing in your ear. A comment here, a remark there, and next thing you knew, you were up at two a.m. with an electric fly swatter and a crazed look in your eye. We.

I picked at my fingernails, frustration and yet a little bit of embarrassment burning in my chest. Since the moment these kids had become mine, Mom never stopped telling me how concerned she always was with their health. Despite the fact that when Will and Savannah were both still here, I'd never heard a single comment from her.

I mean, would my brother and his wife give them Slim Jims at five a.m.? Maybe not. Actually, knowing how many green smoothies Savannah drank when she was pregnant with Pipes, probably not at all. I doubted she even knew what a Slim Jim was. But they still left these kids to me. My name was written in bold letters on that will, and that had to mean something.

I was exhausted down to my bones. And nothing sounded better than meaningless scrolling for a few hours and a nice long, hot bath before slamming an entire box of oatmeal cream pies and taking a nap on the couch. But I hadn't been handed a life where such things were possible. So instead, I straightened my back a little and turned my head to Piper.

"You want to go to the playground, Pipes?"

Her tiny head bobbed up and down excitedly before she made a whoosh noise and curved her hand, waving it around.

"Yeah, we can do the slide."

She did it again, more exaggerated this time, eyes wide, hand moving faster, and her smile growing.

I snorted. If given the chance, this kid would gladly climb up to the roof and jump off to see whether she could fly. An adrenaline junkie, if I'd ever met one. "Yes, darling. The big slide."

As long as we stayed home and sat around, I was going to be even more exhausted. Knowing my bed was mere feet away made it tempting to stay in all day and put these babies in front of some high-sensory TV so I could hit some REM cycles.

Are we sure they're not having too much screen time?

I ground down on my molars. Might as well make the most of it and get these kids out of the house and somewhere where they actually have fun. "Maybe we could go to the library after, yeah?"

Piper slid down from my lap, not bothering to reply, and ran straight to the back entrance to grab her shoes. I laughed, and it felt like tiny flowers blooming in my chest. This little one had that effect on people.

"No, baby. We'll go after your brother gets up."

I didn't know how, but if there was a way for her to say screw my brother. I'm going without either of you with her eyes, I swore she did it then.

My tiny circle might have been pure chaos, but they were my chaos. And I loved them all the same.

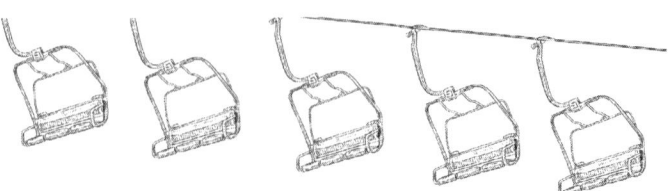

Chapter Five
COOPER

I balanced a tiny orange cone on my fingers, circling it around and around while pacing.

"Why didn't you just tell them you were single?" Finn asked, setting out flags near the cones I'd laid to prep the area for our classes.

After I'd found the account for the magazine, I didn't even look twice at the slopes. I raced straight home to sit down and start contemplating how I could pull this off. I ended up lying awake half the night, trying to think of anyone who might pretend to be my wife for a single lunch. Or heck, even a fiancée. I'd take a girlfriend who I simply had kids with at this point. Just something. But every idea came up empty-handed. Prospects of any previous girls in my life were out, considering the ones that weren't a dumpster fire were all married or states away.

"Did you not hear a single word I said?" I tossed up the cone, attempting to land it in line. "They need a family man. A husband. A dad. They don't need a guy who's just now getting his life together."

Finn shrugged and pushed the line of flags down farther.

Other than those I was related to, there were few women in my life that I was actually cool with. The dark-haired girl with gauges in her ears at the café in the lobby, who had memorized my order and refused to let me stick my finger in the gaping holes in her earlobes. The older woman at my favorite corner store, who hit on me regularly, despite her wrinkly husband working one register over. And...

I tilted my head back to Finn. "Can I borrow your wife?"

Without answering, my best friend ducked, grabbed a cone, stood up, and threw it with enough force to smack me in the face.

I spread my arms in defense when he picked up another one. "Not like that. Just for a single lunch. I'll treat her."

"I treat my wife. Daily."

"Come on. Just a couple of hours."

If that. I wasn't sure how long a magazine interview took, but I doubted they would need that much time. Where else was I supposed to find a girl to pretend to be my wife? eBay? Etsy? At some point, these code people needed to branch out of regular dating apps and start making fake-dating apps.

Finn's second cone hit my temple. "Something is wrong with you."

I groaned and put both hands to my eyes, digging into the sockets. "Help me out here, man."

"Get your own wife," he sneered.

"I'm trying to." I emphasized each word before straightening both cones he'd thrown my way.

We only had an hour before our first classes started, and I needed to sort this situation out soon. Chase had texted back yesterday and said he would prefer we meet in two weeks, when they had a break from their current projects. That left me two weeks to pull a prospect out of thin air.

Finn sighed, sticking his last flag into the ground and going to get the next set. "Just ask a friend."

"Olive is my only female friend." Other than the sandwich girl and the pervy old lady.

"Do *not* ask my wife."

"Well, then help me."

"I dunno. Maybe ask Madeline." He shrugged and dipped his head back and forth like he was weighing the options. "She's cute. Got two kids. Nice girl."

I racked my brain for any hint of recognition, but nothing came up. Names meant basically nothing to me until I saw a picture of the person. Hence, why all the male workers at the lodge went by Easy Money in my head. It got a laugh out of then 100 percent of the time and made me feel better for never remembering their names and not forcing it out by staring at their name tags. Madeline didn't ring any bells, though.

"Who the hell is Madeline?"

"Seriously, how unaware are you of your surroundings? I'm kind of concerned."

I chose to ignore that. "Who is she?"

"You just met her son a couple days ago. Charlie? I told you about him before he joined your seven- to nine-year-old class."

The new kid?

"Mini Coop?" I asked, pausing with a cone halfway to the ground.

Finn's nose scrunched. "Uh, I guess."

"You think I should ask the hot mom?"

Madeline. It fit her. All sweet and feminine, and yet had this twist that only made you more curious about her. Lavender sweater and soft honey-brown hair, with a smirk that I needed to see just once more.

Before Finn could answer, I had it sorted in my mind. She was perfect. Exactly what I needed. Beautiful, which wasn't even a requirement, but definitely a bonus. And she had a kid who wasn't a complete stranger. Not really anyway.

My mind raced back to the way we'd met. Despite the rigorous training I'd done to convince my frontal lobe that the embarrassing part of that story hadn't actually happened, it replayed often. I'd had plenty of humbling experiences in my past, but apparently my subconscious thought hey, why not add one more to the lot?

I know exactly who you are. What was that supposed to mean? That smirk, pink lips pulled up like she was holding back a laugh, said that whatever she knew about me was probably not great. Chances were, unless I could find one of those memory wiper things from Men in Black, Madeline was going to shoot me down because of whatever piece of my past she was aware of. I shivered at the thought.

But no matter what she knew about me—which I really hoped wasn't illegal and/or solid enough blackmail material to have me sending checks with lots of zeroes her way—I did need her. Or at the very least, if she said no, I could ask her if she had any somewhat attractive, breathing mom friends that could spare a single day for me.

"She's not his mom. She's his aunt."

My head shot up. His aunt? I guess that made sense. They had similar features, but I hadn't even considered them being related when I first saw her. Aunt would work too. She would work perfectly.

I nodded. "Hot aunt. Even better. So, you got her number or what?"

Finn shrugged. "I think it's in the emergency contact file on the main desk, or you could just go talk to her. She should be on shift later this morning."

"On shift?"

"Yeah, she's on the cleaning staff here."

Oh. This had to be fate. This was it. My luck was coming back in full swing. Maybe God had seen my year long hiatus from my previously reckless life and had rewarded me for my good behavior by sending me an angel. An angel with long wavy brown hair, wide hips, and a kick-ass nephew who was suspiciously good at skiing.

I laughed, mostly to myself, and shook my head. "This is about to be the best day of my life."

Finn's eyes lifted to the sky above us, awash in white clouds tattered over the light blue background. "And the worst of hers." He sighed. "Look, I feel like I should warn you. She's friends with Olive—"

"Perfect." I nodded. "Our kids can go on playdates."

Hypothetically speaking, of course. But it gave me more details to give the interview people. Ugh, yes, our rambunctious children spent hours with my coworker's kids, throwing dirt and learning TikTok dances and whatever else children do these days. Being a parent is so fun, isn't it?

"Settle down. Olive told me her brother passed away. She was the one to take in his kids, and I dunno. She's sweet but vulnerable. Just be careful."

He said this as if he wasn't the one who'd completely catapulted himself into his wife's life like a stuntman being shot out of a barrel. I distinctly remembered telling him to be careful years ago, and look where that got him. Married with a pregnant wife. See? Even when I was giving out terrible advice, it worked in my favor.

"I'm always careful."

Finn's eyes shot me a look along the lines of don't forget I have witnessed you crowd surf and fall directly into a trash can.

"I try to always be careful," I corrected.

"Try harder, especially for her. I'm not saying don't ask her, but don't expect a yes either. Trust me."

I really did want to listen and take in his advice, but my mind was doing this highlight reel that looked like little flashes of my potential future. Skiing. Interview. More skiing. Madeline. Work. Doughnuts. More Madeline. Skiing.

This was perfect. Every single thing about it was aligning with what I was desperate for. It almost felt like a little shoulder push from Pops up in heaven.

Finn and I finished setting up the normal kids' area, which was essentially two big squares that allowed for our classes to spread their skis wide and feel comfortable enough to move. The only downside was we had to set up one area on one slope and the other on the opposite side of the entire resort. It would be quickest if we each set up our own space, but then we'd probably never see each other, and despite Olive's incessant persistence, Finn was mine before he was hers.

We stomped the snow and dirt off our boots at the wire mat before heading back into the employee area, walking past the warmth of the tall heaters standing on the dark tile. Rows of "lockers" (a misnomer, considering they were more like multiple walk-in closets sitting side by side) lined the wall with our name plates nailed above their doors.

Mine and Finn's sat next to each other. His was filled with pictures of a certain pregnant blonde and ultrasound scans with giant circles on them in white Sharpie that said My baby! His all-black uniform rested on the hooks with his high-vis orange duffel bags below. Two old plane tickets were stapled on the opposite side.

Mine wasn't too far off from that. Except in place of just any woman's picture was a frame my mom had given me for Christmas last year with a photo of me, her, and my childhood hamster, Truman, when I was in fifth grade. She was squishing my cheeks with one hand while I laughed, and Truman sat in my cupped hands. There was a tall Christmas tree behind us, covered in homemade ornaments and multicolored light strands. I'd considered hanging the frame up in my house, but I didn't even own a stud finder, and I was at the lodge far more than I was home, so this felt more appropriate. My black uniform sat on the hook as well, next to my security badge and some artwork

I had saved from the kids. Not that I was the bragging type, but many of the mini-Picassos in my classes had made pieces that said I love Mr. Cooper, and one of them was a drawing of me in a red Superman cape, so I believed that said everything it needed to about me.

I reached for my uniform and my bags, pulling out the helmet and goggles and fresh socks, since mine were already soaked with ice. Sitting back on the bench of the far wall, I got ready for a day full of snow and screaming children.

After we were dressed and ready, Finn pursed his lips and nodded. Then he stood to grab his jacket and security badge. "You coming?"

We had a ritual of going to get breakfast in the lobby before our first lessons, but bacon cheddar scones were going to have to wait today. I looked at the time on my phone. I had an hour before I needed to be out there.

"Nah, I'll see you later."

I had a brunette to find.

Finn eyed me like he could see straight into my brain. "Remember what I said."

I walked to the door, swinging it open and pointing back at him. "Careful, careful. Yeah, got it."

Chapter Six
Madeline

"The leading risk factors for heart disease and stroke are high blood pressure, high low-density lipoprotein—"

I hummed along to the Siri-esque voice in my headphones as I dropped my basket of cleaning supplies softly on the rug in a room a good distance from the main lobby. I wasn't sure what the lodge technically labeled this room, but in my head, it was the fireplace room, since it was nothing more than a plain sitting room with a floor-to-ceiling fireplace that stood about twenty feet tall and a cathedral ceiling.

That was one of the nice things about my position. Mr. Graves, the OG one, had hired me for the bigger areas: locker rooms, lobby, office spaces, etc. Which was much nicer than going in and out of the same hotel rooms day after day. This at least gave me variety and allowed some flexibility in my schedule. It also allowed me to wear normal clothes and not an old maid's costume. It was a good thing too. Otherwise, I would rather work at the local Starbucks scrubbing toilets.

I pulled my vacuum away from where I'd left it by one of the forest green accent chairs and set it against the nearest wall. Unwrapping the chord, I bent down on all fours and ducked under one of the side tables that sat so conveniently in front of the exact outlet I needed.

"Over 877,500 Americans die of heart disease, stroke, or other cardiovascular diseases every year." The monotone robot lady in my ears kept on talking, clearly not caring a bit that I was on my hands and knees under a tiny table with my butt swaying in the air.

"And they say the mountains are Aspen's best view," a voice called out behind me. A non-monotone, non-Siri-sounding, very much male voice that rang a tad familiar.

My head shot up, and the back of my ponytail rammed into the wood above me with a loud thud. "Ow." I winced and slowly backed myself out from beneath the table, sitting on my feet.

"Oof, that looked like it hurt."

I looked up and saw Cooper Graves in his skiing uniform, minus the helmet. Messy brown hair all over the place, a wince on his all too handsome face. A scratch on the top of his right eyebrow that seemed fresh, and a set of keys in his hand. "Sorry, sorry. I was just trying to make my presence known so it wasn't like I was back here, and you were unaware..." He trailed off, staring down at me with a curled brow. "You know, 'cause your butt was kind of in the air."

I pulled out my headphones, disconnecting them from my Bluetooth. "Well, thanks for let—"

"Excess cholesterol can build up in the walls of arteries and limit blood flow to a person's heart, brain, kidneys." Siri's voice loudly blared from my phone in the cleaning basket across the room.

"What the hell are you listening to?" Cooper turned to the phone, his face twisting in disgust.

"I'm tryi—"

"Making blood sticky and more likely to clot, which can block blood flow to the heart—" The robot that was determined to speak over my every word somehow got louder, sharing facts about congenital heart disease and blood flow to arteries. One of the not so sexy diseases. If any were sexy.

I quickly trekked to my phone and turned the volume all the way down until her traitorous voice left us. Turning to Cooper, I forced myself to look him in the eye, despite the warmth pushing behind my cheeks.

"I have a quiz coming up on heart diseases. I was studying."

"A quiz?" His head tilted to the left.

I nodded. "For nursing school." My blood was rushing to my head, and my pulse pounded so loudly that for a moment I wondered if I had heart disease myself.

"You're in nursing school?" Cooper asked, and it was honestly embarrassing how little the man knew about me when I was aware of his entire bloodline's history. I knew this man's birthday, and he hadn't even known I existed until yesterday.

The first time I saw Cooper, he was ordering food at the café in the lodge. I immediately took in how attractive he was—as did the entire restaurant, with that golden-boy smile and eyes that practically shouted Warning: This man is way too charming. But at the time I was fresh out of a breakup—understatement of the century—and my confidence was at an all-time low.

I also saw him wink at the server twice and quickly decided that even if I was up to standard that day, my heart was best left for people who wouldn't have the potential to hurt it. People like my nine-year-old nephew, who I was pretty sure still thought babies came from moms' butts, and my almost three-year-old niece, who had an addiction to Sham Jams.

The other times I saw him were in passing, in which I briskly walked around him to avoid the gaze of those gender-swapped Medusa eyes. He was charming at a distance, and even more so up close. And he was far, far too dangerous. The one and only time I put myself near him was when Mr. Graves passed. It was clear his death hit his entire family hard, but something about Cooper seemed like it died away too. Like a dimmer switched turned down too fast, resulting in the entire bulb being blown. I felt bad for him, and looking back, it probably would have been best to mind my own business.

"Uh, yes." I set my silent phone back on the cart, placing my headphones directly next to it. When Cooper didn't elaborate, just sat there staring down at me, I cleared my throat. "Can I help you?"

I tried to imagine a scenario in which Cooper would seek me out, and none of them felt good. Either the check I'd written for Charlie's lessons had somehow bounced, despite how closely I kept track of my account, or I was getting fired—possibly for studying on the job—and the universe thought it would be hilarious to have Cooper do the letting go.

"Yes, actually, I need a favor from you."

A favor? As in he...would need something from me?

My nose scrunched. "Okay?"

"I need to borrow you...for like an hour or two." He swapped the set of keys back and forth between his fingers.

"Borrow...me?"

I swore if this man was going to ask me to clean his house, then I was officially done with life. This was going to be my new all-time low. No, this was lower than low. This was under dirt, under fossils, under those time capsules we buried in the third grade. Way down where the earth got hot. There I'd sit in my sad little bunker filled with empty oatmeal cream pie wrappers and half-melted iced coffees.

He nodded and gave me that terrifying smile that told me to watch myself or else. "Not for anything dirty. Well, not that kind of dirty."

"I am really not sure how to take this conversation."

"Look, I kind of screwed up something, and I need help fixing it."

A silent pause fell between us.

"And you need my help, specifically?"

He nodded and replied in that soft, low tone that sent shivers up my spine and butterflies to my stomach. "Only yours, Madeline."

Only mine? I raised my eyebrows at him. I wasn't one to assume such things, especially when I'd just been caught on all fours underneath a table, but let's say this man was hitting on me as good-looking and charming as he was, my only answer could be a strict no. If he was planning on having me clean up his house, my only answer would be a strict h-e-double hockey sticks no.

"Look," he said, clearly picking up on the unease that rattled through me. "The new lodge in town just opened. I know you can see our numbers are dropping. I signed up for this...thing to help us out, and by the time I finished, I realized that I'd essentially told them I was..." He took a sharp breath in. "Well, more like I didn't tell them I wasn't—" He threw his head back with a groan.

I shook my head as I spoke. "Cooper, you're not making any—"

"I need you to pretend to be my wife for like an hour."

"Your wife?" I practically shouted it. Might as well have held a megaphone to my mouth and said the two words for the entire world to hear. The heat behind my cheeks lowered to my neck and deepened.

"Or fiancée." He corrected himself with a shrug, as if that was any clearer. "Girlfriend may even work. I mean, this isn't the 1600s. We can have kids out of wedlock without the town coming together to burn or stone us."

"I—" Nope. No words were going to come across as remotely sane in this scenario. I just kept swinging my head from side to side like a pendulum that, instead of keeping things in rhythm, threw everything around it entirely out of rhythm and onto its butt. "I'm sorry. Let's go back to the beginning."

He shook his head too, groaning. "I don't know what it is about you that brings out the worst in me."

My chin pulled back at that. Any self-assurance I had was henceforth thrown out the window and forced to barrel roll into a cactus-filled ditch.

"I signed myself up for an interview with this family magazine. It's for the lodge. I'm sure you've noticed that numbers, tourists, everything, have been lower lately. I figured doing this little column would pull in more people. Anyway, they assumed I was married with kids, and I...didn't correct them."

"Why?"

"Because all I could think about was their 2.8 million followers on Instagram and how, if they posted a single photo of the lodge, it could change everything."

Well, that made a little more sense. More sense than him asking me to clean his house. But still...only yours, Madeline.

"Okay, so what do I have to do with this situation?"

"You have kids, and you know me."

I squinted. "Those are the only requirements?"

He nodded. "Plus, your looks, obviously. That wasn't, like, a real requirement, though. Just a bonus for my viewing benefit. Not that kind of viewing. You know what? I just need you to be my wife for a single lunch with these people. Or fiancée. Girlfriend. Whatever."

He said it like he was asking for me to spot him a dollar for a vending machine, or to hold the elevator for him while he waited for a colleague.

A humorless laugh bubbled up in me, spilling out of my lips. "You're joking."

His eyes lowered. "I assure you, I'm not." My laugh only grew further at how serious he'd turned. "I know I came across the wrong way the other day. I'm sorry. I really am not a creep, but to be fair, that lavender you had on really is your color and—"

"I know you aren't a creep."

"You do?"

"Yes."

I recalled how long I'd known of him. How long I'd thought he was far too handsome and avoided meeting his gaze. "I told you: I know exactly who you are, Cooper. I've worked here for over two years. We've met before. It's not like—"

"I'm going to stop you right there." He pointed a finger and waved it between us. "We have never met."

I knew he didn't remember me, and I couldn't blame him for that. But that didn't ease the sting. It wasn't like I had a huge crush on the guy. I just would have liked to not be disregarded, like I was chopped liver.

"We have, Cooper." My words were clear, matter-of-fact. The way his eyes darted to a far-off place and came back to me made me feel almost guilty.

"There's no way. Not in a million years would I forget meeting you."

I snorted, feeling my confidence building back up but still trying to keep myself in check for another blow. How often had he said that exact line to other women? And why did it even matter? Chosen guardian, model citizen. That was what I had to be.

So, I smiled and went on. "Well, you did."

"When?" he asked, a smidge on the defensive side.

"I brought you food after your grandfather died."

At that one sentence, any hint of that fun light in his eyes died, leaving this dull numbness instead. I recognized that kind of numb. It was the same kind I saw in the mirror each morning. At least he could turn his on and off.

His grandfather was the one who'd hired me officially. When I applied for a simple cleaning job, I never expected the owner himself to sit across from me at the interview table, a plate of cookies sitting between us. "Tell me, what's your go-to karaoke song?" he asked, as if my job was to DJ rather than to mop tiled flooring and dust fireplaces. I left that interview crying laughing with him, giving the man a hug as he whispered "see you on Monday" in my ear. He never stopped being that man. For the year he was my boss, he never once made me feel like an employee. He even wrote Charlie and Piper handwritten birthday cards with ten-dollar bills stashed inside them. I would go as far as to say that Mr. Graves was a friend. A friend when I desperately needed it the most.

"Oh." His shoulders slumped. "I didn't know."

I lightened my tone a little. "We're neighbors. I live one block over. Your cousin gave me the news, along with your address, thinking I might want to bring something by." She must have thought we were friends, because, foolishly, the first thing I asked when I heard was How is Cooper doing? "I didn't have Charlie with me, but I brought hamburger casserole and a giant pan of brownies."

"I remember the brownies." His gaze didn't lift from the far corner of the room. As if he was reliving the memory now. I knew that feeling so undeniably well, and it ate at me that I was the one who'd caused it. "I devoured them all in a single night."

"At least there's that."

His lips turned up slightly, but his eyes stayed on that corner. "Yeah, at least there's that."

I wiped a hand on my leggings. "You were grieving. I've been there. You pay little attention to your surroundings those first couple of months after. I get it."

At that, he lifted his eyes back to me. A vulnerable sweetness sat in there, and I smiled softly. Not in a pitying way, but in an I see myself right down that road even now, two years later.

"You do?" he asked.

I nodded. "I do."

He smiled back at me. It wasn't a 100 percent normal smile, but he was certainly getting there. He opened his mouth to speak, but I rushed to it before he could. "But I have to say no to the whole magazine thing."

His shoulders slumped again, this time less like it was instinct and more like he was a puppy begging for a treat. "Please, Madeline—"

"I would say no to anyone about that. It's not a you thing. I am a terrible liar, and I think it would make things uncomfortable for Charlie. You're his coach, and he likes you a lot. You'll find someone else, easily."

"I really, really won't."

"Then tell them the truth and say it's a family business so it still applies to their column. You're enough on your own, Cooper. You don't need a wife to get it done."

He tosses his head back with a sigh. "Fine. Well, thanks for the brownies. Sorry if I was an ass." He paused. "Again."

I chuckled. "S'fine. I'll see you around." Probably not, but it came out of me automatically.

"Yeah, see you around."

I watched him and his tight butt walk away before reaching for my headphones and going back to cleaning with the sound of Siri's voice discussing heart complications all over again.

Chapter Seven
Madeline

Even as I put both kids to bed that night, I still chuckled to myself, thinking of Cooper's offer. Or question? Or whatever you would consider it.

Brushing Piper's teeth, helping Charlie wrap up homework, starting a grocery pickup order for later this week. No matter what I did, I found myself smiling at the ridiculous notion. A man like Cooper with a woman like me. And on top of it, Charlie and Pipes being his kids. The thought made me giggle again.

If nothing else, Cooper had unknowingly brought a smile to my face on a day that I desperately needed it. I could be grateful for that.

As soon as I had a half-asleep Piper tucked into her bed—listening to "Colors of the Wind" instrumental on repeat—I slowly backed out the door and closed it. A deep sigh left my chest when I couldn't hear any rustling, and she hadn't broken into tears. Success. This was now what success looked like in my eyes.

"May?" Charlie whispered behind me, and I jumped, clutching my collarbone. What is it with these kids constantly scaring me? Was this an every kid thing or just one of those fun traits that only I got to experience?

"Yes, buddy?"

"Can...I sleep in your bed tonight?"

I sighed. Neither kid had slept all that well since I'd had them. Charlie's psychologist and Piper's speech therapist both assured me this was more than normal. That kids who lost their parents often clung to the next best thing, which, pity for them, was me. Nevertheless, I knew he couldn't sleep in my bed forever. Habits had to be broken eventually.

"No, bud." His shoulders dropped and his eyelashes lowered, pulling at every bit of my heartstrings. So, I compromised.

"But I'll lay with you in your bed until you go to sleep, all right?"

He nodded, and I followed him back to his room, which was covered in ski posters and sports memorabilia that I didn't understand. There were two framed pictures on his dresser: One of him, his dad, his mom, and baby Piper the day he first met her. The other of him, Piper, and me at Christmas. The difference in his smile in the two photos was night and day.

Charlie and I lay side by side on the twin-size mattress, him under the blanket and me on top of it, then I wrapped my arm around his neck.

His breathing was unsteady, and his chest shook like he was moments away from crying. So, I said, "Do you want to hear a story?"

He was nine years old. Maybe he was too old for story time and whatnot, but he'd never once denied me when I asked. So, I'd ask until the day he told me no. And even then, I'd probably ask some more.

Charlie nodded.

"Do you want funny, sad, or weird?"

"Funny." He smiled at me, and I thought for a moment before picking one.

Will and I were closer than most siblings. We rarely argued, we always shared, and we cared about each other until the very end. Our parents joked and said God had blessed them with two angels for kids. I thought it was more so that God knew he would take Will from me early, so he let us have the best memories we could for the short time we had.

"One time your dad and I went to a...friend's house"—a party—"and he ate too many hot dogs." Or drank too much beer. "We were sitting under this big deck with a couple friends." Who'd also had way too much to drink. "And he was all delirious...from eating too much. So, when someone on the deck started calling his name, he looked up and said 'God, is that you?'"

We both burst into fits of giggles, and he turned away from me, facing the window that looked out at the snowy mountaintop. Or maybe facing his dad's signed baseball jersey where it hung on the wall—as if he had been some world-famous player when he was in high school. Confident little thing.

"Hey, May," Charlie whispered. "Can we go get hot dogs tomorrow night?"

I sniffled through my laugh and decided hotdogs sounded incredible. "Yeah, bud. We can."

When his breathing steadied out and his movement slowed, I sat up and watched over my sleeping nephew with messy blond hair and long eyelashes just like my brother.

Maybe life was entirely unfair for not letting me have him a little longer, but maybe times like this made up for it.

When I was certain both kids wouldn't need me, I slipped out of Charlie's room and went straight to my own bedroom. I climbed into my fresh sheets and pulled my white comforter up to my chin before grabbing my phone from where it was charging on the nightstand. As soon as it lit up, practically blinding me, the first thing I saw was a text from Olive.

Olive: Just checking in. How's everyone's favorite aunt doing? :)

I smiled at the message. I met Olive through my brother a few years ago, when one of their mutual friends started a podcast and hired her. Through Olive, I met Finn, who convinced me to sign Charlie up for ski lessons to help distract him from his parents' passing. After Will died, Olive and I got closer. We bonded over how incredibly awful her family was and how mentally checked out mine was. Olive and Finn were the only real friends I had. The only ones who'd stuck around after everything. The deaths, the broken engagement, the kids. Those two were nothing if not persistent. They were the first friends that, although Will did introduce me to them, I made on my own. Kept them on my own too.

Me: Trying desperately not to fall asleep so I can enjoy some actual me time. How is everyone's favorite pregnant lady doing?

Olive: Large and in charge.

Me: Sounds about right.

Olive: Sooo are you busy this weekend?

Me: That seems to be a popular question this week.

Olive: Really?

I considered telling her about Cooper's proposition but decided against it. It meant nothing, and sharing it would probably turn it into a something.

Me: Long story, but no, not really. I work Saturday morning during Charlie's lesson, but other than hanging out with the kids and some schoolwork, that's it.

Olive: Want to go to dinner with me and Finn?

I loved going out with them, really. But, when your closest, and only, friends were a couple, it usually meant a lot of turning a blind eye to him groping her in the corner of a bar.

Me: Third wheeling doesn't sound ideal now.

Olive: Actually, I have another friend coming too. He's a really nice guy. I think you'd like him.

I almost laughed out loud. Of course she had someone else coming. She and my mom were each conspiring to get me "back out there." The problem wasn't that I didn't want to date. It had been a long time since I'd felt a lover's caress, and the last time I had, it was my ex, and the thought of him now made me nauseous. The problem was that I had higher priorities. And popping out more children—according to my mother—or letting loose a little—according to Olive—were not on the list.

Me: You sound like my mom. I can't date anyone seriously right now, though :(

Olive: This is the total opposite of serious. It's just us going to get dinner and maybe some drinks after. ZERO expectations whatsoever. I just want to get you out of the house!!

I sighed, looking down at the mound of laundry next to me on the bed—perfectly shaped like another human being—then over to the half-eaten bag of chocolates on my nightstand.

Me: I could probably get out of the house...

Olive: Then come with me! It'll be like girls' night, but with a couple extras. Come on, I'm way too pregnant for you to say no to me.

Me: I guess, but I mean it when I say no expectations.

I could agree to a single night out, a girls' night especially. But I couldn't agree to any kind of date. Not a real one, anyway.

Olive: No expectations at all.

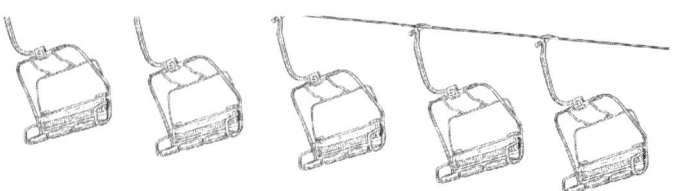

Chapter Eight
COOPER

The flowers in my hand looked awful.

In my defense, the last time I'd bought flowers was for my high school prom date, and even then, they were kind of ugly. How was I supposed to know what was "in" corsage-wise, though?

I'd spent the last three days trying to figure out another option for this magazine thing. Last night I stayed up imagining myself telling Brandy and Chase that I was indeed not married. But I just couldn't do it. Not after Chase had texted me and said Can't wait to meet the Mrs. and I had responded with She's a fine one to meet. How was I supposed to recover from that? I always did this kind of stuff to myself. Pops used to say it was a self-destructive mechanism. I couldn't even disagree with him.

I didn't have the time to find another girl to agree to the charade unless I went up to an absolute stranger. Madeline was still the best choice, since she technically had kids. Plus, she was a knockout. And she knew me.

She knew me. God, I felt so stupid. The girl had brought food to my house, food that I'd eaten every single delectable bite of, and I'd my memory had been completely wiped of her. To be fair, the few months after Pops's death were all one big, hazy blur of skiing, gorging on food, and self-hosted pity parties. Still, I was irritated with myself.

For the last two days, I'd hoped I would run into her at the lodge. I started looking around the lobby and extra spaces I knew she'd been assigned to, and still, nothing. Finn had one thing right. I could have grabbed her number from the emergency contacts list. But that felt even more stalkerish than my other interactions with her.

I'd already walked around the lobby, conference rooms, and locker areas looking for Madeline when I finally turned the corner into a little side area with a giant fireplace and floor-to-ceiling windows that highlighted the view outside. That same sage green cleaning cart she used the other day was settled on the far back wall.

I took a few steps into the room, craning my neck, looking for her, but I only saw a small toddler sitting on the edge of the windowsill. She had short blond hair and a soft smile on her face. She was holding an Elsa doll, making her jump from side to side while she hummed. I looked around for her mom, but as I got closer, I found a tall, curvy figure a couple of feet away, dusting the side of the fireplace.

I smiled to myself and cleared my throat, watching Madeline turn my way.

"You brought an assistant today."

Madeline looked down at the little girl, who was slowly moving away from me inch by inch, and sighed. "Yeah, my mom had a last-minute doctor's appointment, so the princess is with me today."

She had a niece too?

I turned to the kid, who was now standing, and took her in. She had to be younger than three. Maybe barely two. "What's your name?"

The short stack furrowed her brow at me and shook her head.

"She has a bit of a speech delay, and she doesn't really love people. But this is Piper," Madeline explained.

I hummed. I was used to being around kids with speech delays because of my mom's job. Nothing I couldn't work around. I usually talked enough for the both of us.

I bent down and grabbed a single flower out of the bouquet I'd brought before extending it her way like a peace offering. I smiled. "Here you go, dear. Never met a girl who didn't like tulips." Also never offered tulips to a girl, but that could remain unsaid.

Her tiny, chubby hand took it hesitantly before she backed up a couple of feet. My smile grew at that. "You're a tiny thing, aren't you?"

Madeline responded on her behalf. "Yeah, she's short for her—"

"I not tiny," Piper said, speaking up for herself. Rather loudly, actually. Madeline and I both pulled back an inch, her in amazement, me in terror.

"Wow, that was very good talking, Pipes," Madeline praised while she set down the little fluffy duster. "Let me see if I have an M&M for you." She turned to walk toward her purse and cleaning supplies in the corner. Madeline bent over at the waist and dug through her items with her round butt once again swaying directly at me, like it had a homing beacon to stick out wherever I was facing.

I turned back to the kid, fully prepared to make some kind of comment about the Elsa doll in her hand, but stopped when I saw a scowl on her mostly innocent face.

"I not tiny," she repeated in a low growl that sounded so menacing for such a small human.

I looked back to Madeline, who was still preoccupied, mumbling "I swore I put them in here" and "this bag is way too big" to herself.

I turned back to the toddler. "You sure?"

"You tiny." The nerve this kid had to point at me as she said it.

I reared back. "Listen here, half-pint—"

"No. You half-pi."

Speech delay, my ass. "Nuh-uh-uh. I'm six-five." I pointed back at her. "You are the half-pint."

"You half-pi," she insisted.

"Here they are!" Madeline declared before coming back with a couple pieces of chocolate for the tiny person in front of me. "Great talking, bug."

Piper smiled at her, an instant switch from the gremlin I'd just seen. And when Madeline turned to grab her duster again, Piper shot me another death stare and pointed from her eyes back to me. Holy crap, this kid was terrifying. Also, what is she watching to learn these things at such a young age? I would question her upbringing, but then again, her brother was an absolute delight.

As soon as Madeline turned back to us, Piper was back to playing with her Elsa doll.

"So, did you need me or something?"

I looked down at the flowers in my hands and shoved them toward her a little too forcefully.

"I just wanted to bring you these."

She looked at the array of white and pink in her hands and smiled before looking over at Piper anxiously. As if she was scared she would notice, she scooted a few feet away from the little girl.

"Oh, thank you. They're beautiful."

Good, I think so too. Let's pretend to be engaged for a day or two. What do you say? "I'm glad you like them."

"Is this because of the...magazine thing?"

I shook my head, but it turned into a nod. "Mmm, no..." I paused. "Yes."

She sighed and set the flowers gently on the mantel. "I am so flattered that you thought of me, really. But I meant it when I said no. My life is more than a little complicated right now. I don't really have space for anything like that. Believe me, my mom's been trying to get me to go out for years, and I just can't make it happen. Not like that." She looked at Piper and saw she was distracted, so she lowered her voice. "No dates."

"This doesn't have to be a date."

"You would tell them we're engaged, at the very least."

"Friends can get engaged."

"Cooper. I barely even know you."

"But you said you know exactly who I am."

"Fine." She fought a smile but lost, the corner of her lips lifting. "You barely know me."

I counted on my fingers. "I know you have a really cool nephew and a kind of terrifying niece. I know you are friends with Olive Branch. I know you smile when you are nervous, or actually, I think you smile like that all the time. It's cute." She smiled at that. "And I know you like tulips." I pointed to the half-wilted flowers on the mantel.

"That is barely scratching the surface—"

"Then give me more. Come on, shoot it my way." I jerked my chin back.

"Coop—"

"Fine, I'll start. My name is Cooper. I wanted to be an astronaut when I was little. I am awfully fond of the Shrek 2 soundtrack, and I love the smell of the post office. Your turn."

She sighed, but with that twisted smile that felt like she was holding back a bigger smile, then said, "Fine. My name is Madeline. I've always wanted to be a nurse. I am awfully fond of that soundtrack as well, and I love the smell of the lumber section in the hardware store."

"Nurse, Shrek, lumber. Got it. What else?"

She went back to dusting around the flowers she'd set down. "I think that's all you need to know, considering I'm not going with you."

"Please, Madeline. Come on. Give me one more round."

She squinted at me, and I kept going. "Fine, I'll give you one. I like the feeling right before I get a sunburn, when I'm all warm, and my skin is barely pink, but it doesn't hurt yet."

The chuckle out of her felt like triumph on my end.

"Give me one more, Madeline."

I smiled as her round cheeks blushed. "I like to be the first person to light a new candle."

"Oh," I nodded. "Candles, yes. Good one. Okay, next."

Madeline sighed. "Sorry, Coop. I'm swamped," She gestured to the room she was cleaning, then to Half-Pint staring at us both. "I mean it."

"Fine, fine. I'll keep looking. But if you change your mind, my number is on the tag of the flowers, all right?"

She looked back at the card. "I'll let you know if I change my mind."

I started to wave goodbye to the kid on my way out, but Half-Pint gave me the I'm watching you stare. I shivered and ran out of the room as quickly as possible.

Chapter Nine
Madeline

My life was incredibly boring. Boring to most, I would assume. As a thirty-year-old woman who was single, I probably should have been out in the world, traipsing down the streets of New York with my own Carrie Bradshaw and learning the promiscuous life lessons of femininity and friendships.

Instead, I lived a life on rotation. Every day the same, my routines never changing.

On Mondays I worked morning shifts and did online classes in the afternoon while Charlie was in school and Piper was with my parents or a babysitter if I was feeling less frugal.

Tuesdays were the same, except after my classes, I had to take Piper to speech therapy while Charlie sat in the lobby on his Nintendo Switch.

Wednesdays were slightly less crazy, with no classes. But I would force us out of the house by taking the kids to the five-dollar—toddlers watch for free—movies at our local cinema.

Thursdays were the same as Tuesdays, plus Charlie had lessons while Pipes was in speech therapy.

Fridays were the same as Mondays.

Weekends were mostly work and ski lessons for Charlie.

Repeat.

Again and again, over and over until the end of time. Or until these kids grew up, and it suddenly hit me that I indeed spent years with my head in the sand, taking it day by day. Sometimes hour by hour. Getting through life one Ghirardelli chocolate square at a time.

Not that I didn't like our routines or that I was miserable by any means. I liked our small, simple life. But it never felt all the way full. It felt like I was putting every piece of myself into these two humans that I loved with all the tiny centimeters of my heart.

I kept thinking, once I get through this semester, I'll be satisfied. Or once I can get Piper out of diapers, I'll be happy. Currently, I'd put my hope in the idea that once I graduated and could use my degree, then I would give myself and these wonderful tiny humans the life we deserved. If all went according to plan, then that was only a year from now. And in the grand scheme of life, a year wasn't that long, right? We would make it, slowly, surely. Maybe hour by hour, but I was going to get us there. If not for myself, for them. Possibly also for my nagging mother, who believed cleaning was about the most "humble"—she meant self-deprecating—job to exist on this earth.

"Piper?" the receptionist called.

Piper lifted her head from the tiny Pocahontas doll in her hands, looking back toward me for reassurance. Maybe I shouldn't like how much she hates people, but I couldn't help that it gave me a sense of security. No number of puppies or amount of candy in white vans would distract this girl.

I nodded to her and grabbed the diaper bag, walking with her over to the back area of the speech therapy office. Dr. Lora, who Piper called Lo-la on the days she talked, stood there with a bright, shining smile. She looked more like a cozy nanny than an actual doctor, and her "office" was like a kid's dream playroom.

I was hesitant to take my girl to any speech therapists at first. But I'd overheard a group of moms talking about how well their kids did with her, so I made an appointment, and from day one, she had been incredible. With long, smooth, white hair and the kindest smile, it was impossible not to love her. She wasn't one to rush anywhere; when she played with Piper, working on all the oohs and er sounds, she moved at this unhurried pace. Like she had all the time in the world for her. And when she talked, Pipes tuned in intently, like she was giving her the secret code to a vault of Slim Jims. Even I hated to leave by the time her sessions were done.

"Hey, Pipes!" Dr. Lora waved. My girl—who hated just about anyone she wasn't related to—grinned up at her with those tiny teeth shining and waved just as excitedly back.

I followed them to the toddler room in the back, taking my usual seat in the reading corner surrounded by fake food, squishy foam balls, and fluffy stuffed animals. The surrounding walls were adorned with vibrant rainbow murals and clouds shaped like different animals. My personal favorite was the elephant in a ballerina tutu.

Piper sat down at the same table she always chose, and Lora went straight to the Mrs. Potato Head in the corner, setting it on the table and smiling as my niece started pulling out the accessories one by one.

Dr. Lora turned to me next. "Madeline, do you mind if I have a word with you?"

She must have seen the unease on my face, because she held up two defensive hands. "Nothing bad. Just wanted your opinion on something." She gave me this soft smile that reassured me enough to stand and follow her out the open door.

"We'll be right back, bug," I whispered to Pipes, and she nodded without looking up at me.

The doctor and I turned the corner, and she whispered low to me. "I was wondering if this week, just as a trial, you would mind sitting in the lobby."

Alarm bells rang in my head in an instant, my self-defense mechanisms coming alive, ready for battle. "Do you think I'm...making her worse?"

It was my first assumption, considering my mom had made a comment on more than one occasion about me possibly stunting her speech by not correcting her more. But then again, Dr. Lora was the one who told me all speech was good speech. If she was saying new words, I shouldn't correct it the first time. Just praise that she said it.

Her brows dipped, and she shook her head, reaching a hand out to my elbow and touching it lightly. "Oh, no, no, no. Don't take it as an insult. I didn't mean harm by it. It's just..." She sighed and looked up before focusing on me. "I think you are her biggest comfort. Her safety net. That's a beautiful thing. You're blessed to have it. But often when kids are so attached to their parent—guardians," she corrected, "they don't try as hard. Again, not an insult. But I believe she doesn't feel like she has to push herself farther if you're around, because she knows you're there as a buffer."

Why did I feel like I was about to cry?

She continued, and I gnawed on my bottom lip. "I've noticed over the years that some kids do better when someone they love is near. But sometimes they hold themselves back. It's not uncommon, given her circumstances. Let's try it once, okay? You can sit outside the door and listen the entire time. If either of you hates it, I won't ask again."

I considered it for a moment before nodding. She smiled at me and went back into the room.

"Piper, your MayMay"—I loved that she called me that—"is going to sit in the lobby today, so it's just us for once, is that okay?"

Piper's green eyes looked from me to Dr. Lora and back, before she lifted her arm, Potato Head lips in hand, and waved goodbye to me. I waved right back, taking a few steps away, watching as she went right back to her toy. She rarely had meltdowns when I dropped her off at my mom's anymore. It wasn't like I expected her to fall on the floor, begging for me. Yet somehow, it kind of stung. My Piper, one half of the little gifts my brother had left me, was growing, becoming her own tiny person, and I could do nothing to stop it.

I sat just outside the door, a few feet away. Close enough where I could listen but far enough away that I wouldn't be seen.

An hour and ten tissues later, I had about twenty videos on my phone recording Piper's tiny voice coming from the room.

She wasn't reciting Shakespeare or prepping for a wedding speech, but that little voice was repeating words and sounds that I'd never heard from her.

When Lora would pull out one of those surprise eggs and asked if she should open it. Instead of just nodding, Pipes, in the tiniest, cutest, clear-as-day voice, said "yes" from the inside of that room, and I practically melted into the floor. She never told me yes, or yeah, or anything other than a simple head nod. The only words Piper spoke to me were the ones she felt were necessary. Sham Jams, Pokey, and Cah-lee (Charlie) being the extent. She always nailed down MayMay, but other than that, she was mostly silent or communicated with a scrambled batch of noises that I could piece together just enough.

It was selfish of me to cry, but I couldn't find it in me to stop. The floodgate was open, and the tears were pouring faster than ever when it hit me. She was at her best when I wasn't there.

You are valuable.

He left them for you.

I tried so hard to muster those words, to say them over and over again to myself, but they didn't feel true anymore. At the end of the day, if I wasn't MayMay—if I wasn't the one person these two kids needed most in their lives, then what was I?

It felt like someone had ripped out my heart, put a blond wig on it, and walked it right into that rainbow room. I knew these kids weren't going to need me forever, but that wasn't the problem. The problem was that I was so stuck in my own survival, in Quizlet cards and cleaning supplies, that I didn't even notice them evolving before me.

A deep fear of mine resonated in my chest. My mother was right. I was the one stunting her speech. I was the one who was undoubtedly causing the delays. It was my fault. And if she was right about it, how many more of the condescending wes that she threw at me were true?

It felt like my world had been turned upside down entirely. Like this entire time, I was living in only my point of view, but in the last hour, I had been lifted from my body and shown an outside view, and it was nothing like what I expected.

In the room beside me, Dr. Lora hummed a clean-up song, and Piper's tiny shoes clicked against the floor. The footsteps grew closer, and I did my best to wipe my mascara face, but the moment Piper locked eyes with me, she pointed right at me.

"May?" she asked in this tone that spoke volumes. This tone that asked me why I was sad.

I shook my head and slapped on the biggest, brightest fake smile I knew how to make. "Nothing, baby. Did you have fun?"

She nodded and smacked two closed fists together with a clicking noise in her mouth. Blocks, she was saying. I sniffed. "Blocks are fun. I'm glad you got to do that."

As I stood, Dr. Lora came out of the room, pausing abruptly at the sight of my face. I didn't even want to know what it looked like at the moment.

"Oh, Madeline. I—" Her eyes roamed me. From my watery eyes to the wobble in my lip to my cheeks pulled tight. Her brown eyes softened. "I'm so sorry."

I shook my head and waved a dismissive hand. "It's nothing."

"I had no intention of upsetting you—"

"It's your job," I said through a watery laugh. "You are so great at it that it makes me sad."

"I am good at my job, yes. You also have an exceptional child on your hands." A few inches taller than me, she squatted. "I didn't do that to make a point. I just wanted to see if she'd grown more in the last few months than she let on."

I nodded. "She did." I heard it all myself.

Dr. Lora nodded. "I do mean it as a compliment. You are a safe place for her. Don't let that get lost in the weeds. You two have a precious bond that is hard to find, especially given your circumstances." She looked from me to Piper.

I sniffed once more, feeling slightly more in control of my facial expressions and knowing tonight, when both kids crawled into bed, I was going to give in to the waterworks.

"Well, we should go." My fingers squeezed Piper's. "Can you tell Dr. Lora bye?"

"Bah, Lola."

Dr. Lora smiled at that, and a hint of amusement piqued in my mind at that. "Bye, Piper."

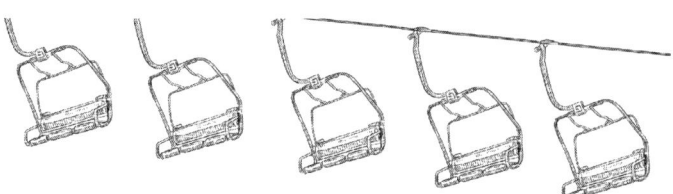

Chapter Ten
COOPER

F inn and I sat at our usual table, same as we had for the last several years—a two-person table near the entrance of the café—a breakfast burrito on his plate and my usual bacon cheddar scone.

I caught him up on the latest news of the upcoming ski competitions. We had about two more weeks to register our sponsored kids. I usually picked a random name, but after watching Mini Coop the other day, I had a feeling I already had a strong contender. It kind of felt like playing fantasy football, minus the fantasy...and the football.

Each year we hosted new judges. Some cared more about speed, others skill. Meaning, if one saw speed as a higher level of importance, we needed to focus on that further. So, each year I called my uncle for the scoop. And each year he ignored me.

After I told Ma I hadn't gotten a reply from her brother, she made an attempt as well, leaving him a voicemail that he never returned. So, then I texted him, saying Don't ignore me and my mother, you coward. And he responded with When did you become old enough to give me shit? Essentially, we would find out when everyone else did because my uncle had done this weird thing since he took over, saying that "Graves's don't get special treatment." To which I said, "Pops didn't die for me to be picked last for stuff like this."

I bit into my sandwich, speaking to Finn around it. "I need you to go out with me tonight."

"Married, but flattered."

I swallowed and groaned simultaneously. The interview was a couple weeks away, and I had yet to find a serious prospect. Madeline was out of the question, no matter how badly I wanted her not to be. And when I found one kind-eyed girl to ask, she laughed in my face. Didn't even say no. Just laughed. The whole kind eyes thing was BS, apparently.

"Seriously, I gotta find a girl to do this column with me, and I need my main wingman." More like someone to back up that I was, in fact, not a pervert looking for an excuse to ask a woman out.

"I would, but Olive and I have plans tonight."

I took another bite. "Let me third wheel. It's lame if I go out by myself, and maybe the waitress or something will take pity on me."

Finn squinted. "It would be more like a fifth wheel kind of thing."

"What?" I tilted my head. "Who's going out with y'all? When did you get new friends?"

Making new friends in our thirties, when we'd worked at the same place since we were teenagers, was a miracle in itself.

Finn snorted around his food. "It's a guy that Olive's brother knows. He seemed cool when we met him a few weeks ago at his house. And then—" He cut himself off abruptly, and I stuck my chin out.

"And then..."

"Madeline."

"What?" I asked so loud that the woman next to us reading a copy of Jane Eyre stood, grabbed her book and croissant, and scooted two tables over.

But she said she was swamped. Even the other day, when I left her my number, she acted like she was too busy for even a phone call. What did she call this? Was it just a me thing?

"That was a mistake," Finn mumbled to himself

I lowered my voice enough to not offend any more historical romance readers near us. "You mean to tell me—"

"I really shouldn't have told you."

"That my fiancée—"

"She is definitely not your fiancée."

"—is going out with another man tonight?"

"Didn't she reject you? Twice?"

Yes. For the sake of her schedule, not for lack of wanting. If she could go on a date with this random guy, why couldn't she do a single pretend date with me? I wasn't terrible to look at. She laughed at my humor. We both took joy in early 2000s movie soundtracks. What else was needed? Nicholas Sparks practically had the rights to our movie already.

I took an enormous bite, chewing feverishly. "This is absurd, I mean." I swallowed. "This is...this sucks. Where is he taking her?"

Finn finished off his burrito and wiped his hands on a napkin. "Well, he isn't really taking her. Olive and I are driving her to Zane's, to be safe."

Zane's was our restaurant. Where I regularly third wheeled—or I should probably say where Olive third wheeled Finn and me. Forgetting the rest of my food, I bent to the side where my backpack was.

"When were you planning on telling me about this?"

"I wasn't aware I needed to keep you updated on all things."

"Well, you should be. I want every update from now on. About everything."

Finn cut me a sideways glance. "I told you she was probably going to say no to you."

"Yeah, well, that was before I found out she was going out with some random guy. Why would she even say yes? Has she met him before? Does she know his favorite scent or what he wanted to be when he grew up?"

"No, they haven't met, and I'm not sure why that's relevant, but maybe she just wanted to get out."

"But I asked to take her out."

"Coop." He sighed and slipped his duffel bag on one shoulder before standing up. "You can come across a little...pushy."

I stood a little too quickly and got a head rush, but that wasn't stopping me. "No, I don't."

"You really do. And it's great, but sometimes..."

"You're one to talk, showing up at your fake girlfriend's family dinner uninvited—"

"Wait a second. That was different."

I scoffed. "Was it?"

"Yes." He was hissing now. "Olive needed saving from her wretched family members."

"Maybe Madeline needs saving too."

"She doesn't."

"M'kay."

"I mean it, Coop." He pointed at me with his spare hand. "She doesn't need saving. She's got enough on her plate."

"I'm not adding to her plate."

"Don't take from her plate, either. Leave her plate alone."

"I can't even lick it?"

"No licking."

My head dropped back as I groaned, my hands tightening on the shoulder strap of my backpack. "But she's perfect for what I need."

"Just don't do the magazine, or, I mean, you could tell them the truth."

I couldn't. I needed this column to work out. How was I supposed to let something my grandfather worked his entire life to keep successful just fail? New lodge be damned, I was going to find a way to bring our numbers back to normal. And Madeline Sage was still my best bet.

I had high hopes that Madeline would drop Mini Coop off today. I made plans of striking up a witty yet tasteful conversation, showing that I was excellent first date material, and whatever plans she had with this anonymous man could fly out the window.

Instead, I was met with the scary lady from last week. She eyed my badge again, squished the boy's cheeks, and patted him on the back toward me.

"What's up, Mini Coop?" I stuck a gloved hand out for him to slap, and he did it back with a smile.

"Hi, Mr. Cooper."

"Ready to have some fun?"

He nodded and ran off to the bench to put on his skis and helmet.

Since it was a Saturday, most of my regular students weren't here. Tuesday and Thursday afternoons were the fullest, and weekend mornings were the slowest, with an average of five to six kids. That meant my weekend lessons were a little more personal, giving me time to answer specific questions they have.

I lined the five kids up for the hill climber. We called it the magic carpet ride because it sounded cooler and usually made the kids slightly less terrified of it. Essentially, it did the job that a ski lift would, but on a much smaller scale. Kind of like an escalator up the snowy hill so the kids could take turns going down without the risk of a lift.

Mini Coop rushed onto it first, followed by two other boys, then the youngest girl. They'd all ridden it before, so there was nothing new there. The fun part was always on the way down.

The cool thing about teaching was that more often than not, the students were the ones showing me something new. Case in point, when Mini Coop jumped off the lift and immediately started racing downhill at full speed, letting his skis glide him in and out of these "french fry" waves that Finn and I had taught the week before. He didn't have a single doubt he couldn't do it, or if he did, he never showed it. It was something I noticed during my years here. The more I tried to help them, the bigger of a burden I was. Once you let them go, let them feel the icy earth beneath their skis, let them sense the rise and curves of the mountain, the way the wind blew against them...that's when they learned best. When they fell and got up faster and screamed again, again until they were begging to stay.

As an instructor, I honestly had very little to do with the whole ordeal. The skis themselves taught far more than I ever could. I was here for the push start, safety, and maybe a bit of guidance. But mostly they learned on their own. That was why it felt like more of a hobby than a job. I never felt the dread of a Monday or the groaning for the weekend. It was my escape as much as the kids'.

After they each warmed up enough, which usually meant me sitting at the bottom, watching them go up and down a couple of times and a whole lot of me screaming pizza!, I let them go wild. One by one, they raced down the hill and practiced the skills we'd gone over that week. Mostly just some tail drags and a couple one-eighties, but still, watching some of these kids go from barely being able to stand on their own to this? I felt like a proud mama bird who had just sent her kids to fly out of the nest.

By the time we were ready for breaks, Mini Coop had already made friends with the other class regulars. I turned to sit on the bench where we kept all of our essentials. This spot gave me a good view of our smaller hill and the bathroom entrances and exits, since the kids were in and out of there often. On several occasions, I'd had nightmares of my kids being taken from the bathroom, and because I was more than a little paranoid, I tracked each one of them like a hawk.

"May likes those too." Mini Coop pointed at the white chocolate Clif Bar in my hand, forcing my eyes to leave the bathroom signs.

My head tilted to the side. May? I tried to think of a kid in the program who went by that name, but I was drawing a blank until it hit me.

"Madeline?"

He nodded. "She says they taste like she's getting away with eating a cupcake for breakfast."

I took another bite with that in mind and nodded, totally getting it. "She's your aunt, right?"

He dipped his chin and took his own bite of an extra granola bar I packed. I wanted to ask more, to ask about his parents and just how he and his sister had fallen into Madeline's lap. But I imagined that would feel a lot like when people asked me about my dad. It was a story told hundreds of times, and it got a little older each time I shared it. A little staler and a whole lot more what's up with that guy?

"Is...Madeline going to pick you up today?" I went for non-chalant.

"Nah, Gram is. She's coming to our house with my sister."

"Your aunt's busy tonight?" I really, really hoped it sounded more casual out loud than in my head.

"She said she was going somewhere with Mrs. Olive. But I checked her Google calendar, and it said double date on there with a cake emoji."

I backed up. Cake emoji? "You checked her calendar?"

"Yeah, I always do." He shrugged and took another bite of the granola bar.

"Why?"

"So I know she's safe."

I stared at him for a second. This nine-year-old kid who looked out for his aunt, his only guardian, as if he was her tiny protector. I remembered going with my mom to get groceries and hearing a stranger hit on her from time to time. Usually, I shot them a middle finger behind her back while she politely said no. This kid really was a Mini Coop.

"Huh." I nodded with an impressed pout. We both ate a few more bites in silence.

Mini Coop finished his bar and looked at mine like he was still starving, so I reached in my bag for another. I handed him the bar and asked, "Does...she go on a lot of double dates?"

"Never." He opened the wrapper, discovering this one was chocolate, and his eyes lit up. "It's weird. Hope he's nice to her."

I nodded with a grit to my teeth. "Me too, bud."

We stayed like that a little longer, sharing a bench and both thinking of his aunt. The other two boys in our group asked for my permission before going back on the magic carpet ride.

"I don't want a random guy living in our house," Mini Coop said when they left, and I snorted.

"I doubt he would move in after one date."

"Whatever. May is too busy for that stuff, anyway."

"She is?"

"Yeah, she's gonna be a doctor."

My neck pulled back, and I looked from the kids going downhill to him a few feet over from me. "A doctor?" She mentioned nursing school, but a doctor? Out of your league, my mind sang.

He shrugged again. "Or a nurse. Something like that."

"Oh." That made more sense. *Still out of your league.*

He drank the last of his water, and I reached a hand out, gesturing for it. "I'll fill 'em up. Make sure those two don't kill themselves." I dipped my head to the two boys that kept slamming into each other. He laughed, and I took it as an okay.

Coming back with his water bottle and mine, I sat at the same spot on the bench.

"Hey, Mr. Cooper?" he asked, eyes still on his black water bottle with a blue ski logo.

"You don't have to call me mister all the time." I laughed. Especially since after so long, the kids usually found a nickname for me too.

"What do I call you, then?"

"My friends call me Coop."

"Are we friends?"

I leaned back, looking up at the snowy mountains and thought about it. "Yeah, Mini Coop. We're friends."

Chapter Eleven
Madeline

I severely overestimated my closet when I signed up for this outing.

I also overestimated my parents' ability to mind their own business. They weren't even here yet, and I was already working on the list of questions they'd have. When I asked my dad if they could watch the kids for the night, instead of answering me, he went straight to my mom, who, from the sound of it, dove across the floor for the phone and shouted, "Where are you going tonight?"

I left out the whole date aspect of it, considering I wasn't even certain I would call it that myself, and said it was like a friends' babymoon with Olive and Finn. She sighed and responded with "So, no prospects, then?" As if this was the 1800s, and I was to be auctioned off at my debut.

All of this led me to standing in front of my closet, staring deadpan at the same clothes that had been in there for the last few years. If this was a date, and it absolutely wasn't, then I'd probably go on the sexier side. But given this was more of a night out with my very pregnant best friend, and considering I really wasn't in the mood to be hit on the entire night, I just kept staring.

Olive was no help either, since I texted her What are you wearing tonight? and she responded with Something that holds my giant boobs and allows for baby movement.

I sighed at that and settled on some very tight jeans and a lavender sweater. They would have to do. And it had absolutely nothing to do with Cooper saying he liked this sweater last week.

Just as I was done getting ready, Charlie came running into my bathroom with a Lego box in his hand. "Can we open it up now, May?"

"Tanwiupupowmay?" Piper came running in after him, attempting to repeat his sentence.

All things considered after my breakdown earlier this week, Piper's speech had improved almost overnight. She wasn't exactly speaking clearly, and technically, she wasn't adding new words to her vocabulary. But she was repeating what Charlie and I said and picking up on new syllables. Plus she was no longer shrieking when we couldn't understand her. That felt like progress enough on my end. Or, technically, on Dr. Lora's end. I needed to remember to text her a quick thank-you and a sorry for leaving your office all snotty-nosed and ugly crying. You were right.

I eyed the Lego box with a mini Imperial Star Destroyer and a tiny Darth Vader to the side. I'd bought it for them months ago, during a labor day weekend sale, and I thought to myself there is going to be a rainy day where I really need this. It had been sitting in my closet ever since, and tonight felt like a good enough reason to whip it out.

"I guess so. Gram is about to be here, anyway."

I opened the Lego box and dumped the little baggies with instructions out onto the coffee table, then watched as the two of them got to work—Charlie organizing the bags in chronological order and Piper picking them up and moving them instantly. The back doorbell rang just as I was about to go put in my earrings.

"Gam?" Piper shot up, looking at the back entrance, and Charlie smiled at her. He'd noticed a big change in her this week too. He looked over at me, and I winked at him before heading to the door.

Standing on the other side of the door were my mom and dad, holding those reusable grocery bags filled with toys that neither of the kids needed but were going to be spoiled with anyway.

Dad stepped in first, opening his arms and hitting the floral plastic bags on the doorframe. "Look at you. Not a day over twenty. You've still got that little baby face." He used one bag-laden hand to squish my cheeks.

Mom appeared directly behind him, looking at me with this gaze that felt reminiscent of her seeing me in my prom dress for the first time. I held my breath, and possibly sucked in my gut a little, waiting for her approval. She opened her mouth, and for the first time in what felt like a decade, I honestly thought she was going to compliment me. Her eyes filled with this mix of wonder and almost a touch of sadness. The thought vanished, and as quickly as it appeared, it was gone. She moved her eyes from me to the kitchen behind me and said, "A bit more lipstick, love. That foundation makes them disappear."

They both walked behind me, over to the kids at the table, crouching down to see the Lego set with them. This was my key issue, right here. Not that my mom hated me or that I hated her. It was that neither of us understood the other. Not since Will had died. And when we tried, it all just crumbled. Could you still love someone without liking them as a person?

My eyes rolled, and I looked at myself in the small mirror with hooks where my keys hung. I could use some more lipstick, actually. So I scurried back to my bathroom, applied a thin layer, and tucked the tube into my palm for future applications.

I grabbed my shoes sitting by the door, a pair of thick wedges that I was praying muscle memory would help me walk in, and headed over to the table. Charlie was showing my dad the instructions, both of them eyeing it before I heard my dad mumble something like bunch of gibberish and who needs that? My mom sat with Piper as she waved her hands and made random noises similar to baby Tarzan. Mom just nodded and smiled at her.

Behind us, my phone buzzed twice on the counter, and I knew by the crunching of tires in my driveway that it was Olive telling me she was here. I spoke while bending down to tighten the straps on my shoes.

"There's a lasagna, salad, and brownies in the kitchen. Piper needs everything cut into small pieces. And if Charlie asks for grapes, cut them in fours. I don't care if he's nine. He can still choke. Also, bedtime can be pushed back to nine if they want to, but they usually like to be in bed by eight thirty anyway. Oh and—"

My dad held up a hand. "We've done this before, dear. Now go."

Mom nodded. "I spent two and a half years trying to set you up, and one text from your little Olive friend, and you go curling your hair."

I looked down to Charlie. His eyes were glued to the Legos in front of him, but his movements slowed, as if he was trying not to make any unnecessary noise. "I'm just hanging out with friends, and I wanted to get out of the house for a bit," I clarified, more for his sake than hers. I wasn't sure whether Charlie would care if I had a date, but I wanted to respect his wishes either way. He hadn't seen me with a man since he who shall not be named. "It's not really a date. Just a couple of friends and a plus-one."

"Well, bring the plus one-here if you can manage it."

I ground my teeth together. "Mom."

"I just meant to meet me." She clutched her chest and acted innocent before saying, "But you were blessed with a wonderful figure. It wouldn't hurt to show some cleavage."

"All right." Charlie groaned and covered his ears. "Enough of that please, God."

My dad rubbed at his own chest, avoiding my eyes. "It would too hurt. Gah, Eloise."

A honk came from the car outside, paired with another vibration from my phone. I bent down and kissed Piper's head. "Love you, bug." She gave a mwah sound back, which was good enough for me. Then I went to Charlie and rubbed the top of his blond hair, swaying the messy hair back and forth. "Love you, kiddo. Have fun, okay?"

His lips pulled a little. "Love you, May."

I smiled at that and grabbed my phone off the counter and my keys off the hook, blowing them both one more kiss and leaving through the back door.

Olive, Finn, and I picked a booth near the back of Zane's. The surrounding walls were covered with sports memorabilia and big-screen TVs broadcasting various sporting events. My eyes caught on the black drink menu with white text offering an extensive selection of beers on tap, including domestic and craft brews, but my hopes for something pink with an umbrella in it were slowly diminishing. On the TV facing us, there was a Colorado Avalanche hockey game going, and Finn and Olive kept stealing glances at it.

I looked at the daunting empty chair next to me, and a lump formed in my throat. I was so desperate to just get out of the house and see my friend that I hadn't even asked if this guy himself understood that this wasn't a date. Even if we hit it off, and it was some magical fit with a hot fireman or something, I didn't have the time to invest in a relationship. It was stupid of me to agree with in the first place.

Finn cleared his throat, and Olive spoke up, her hands resting on her belly. "I think Colton is supposed to be here at six. We're kind of early."

I glanced at the nearest clock. The hands of it were a half-naked lady's legs. Five more minutes.

Olive must have sensed my discomfort because she leaned across the table and spoke quickly. "Let me show you these shoes I've been dying to get our little Tater."

"Oh, you guys settled on a name?" I asked.

Finn shook his head. "Nope. She just calls it that because she knows I hate it."

Olive gasped and then shrugged, as if to say yeah, fair.

I giggled and watched her pull up the tiniest pair of Converses I had ever seen. So cute and so totally pointless. No baby needs shoes before they start walking. But I kept that to myself because these two were in pre-baby heaven, and I certainly did not want to pop that bubble.

"I love them," I cooed. "He or she will look perfect in them."

"I'm leaning toward he," Finn said. "I feel like as hard as the stinker kicks, he's got his daddy's skiing ability in there."

Olive rolled her eyes playfully. "Yeah, or she has Mommy's ability to kick Daddy." Finn guffawed at that and bent down to whisper something to her, making Olive giggle.

I refused to comment on how strange it was to hear your friends calling themselves Mommy and Daddy in the third person. But the PDA thing was cute. I couldn't blame them for riding the babymoon high for as long as possible.

"You got Piper when she was six months old, right?" Olive asked.

I nodded. "Five months."

"How was that?" Finn asked, taking a sip of water—he refused to order a beer around his wife, since they had made some kind of pregnancy pact.

I winced. Maybe it wasn't hard for most people, but that time, when Piper was a baby, felt like a fever dream filled with pacis, bottles, and a mountain of diapers mixed with all-nighters and lots of crying.

"Um...very little sleep and a whole lot of diapers."

Olive groaned. "I'm not ready."

Finn reached a hand over and rubbed her back. "You are ready. I bet there was a whole lot of cuteness too, right?"

"Oh yeah." I smiled. Even when she was screaming, you couldn't deny those sweet chubby cheeks. "The cutest phase ever. You guys are going to be incredible parents." I nodded at Olive when she eyed me like I was lying. But every bit was authentic. Even if they struggled, at least they had each other.

The bell hanging on the door chimed behind us, and a server called out "Welcome to Zane's." Then there was the sound of boots hitting the floor. A low, quiet thank you came out, and I turned to see a young man already waving at Finn. He was a little younger than I would have thought, somewhere around early to mid-twenties. But he was handsome—the kind of guy who looked like he opened doors for you and complimented your mother's earrings. Scruffy blond hair, a little bit of a dark beard, a kind smile. Nothing my heart went crazy for, nothing that made my pulse skip, but cute. Definitely cute.

He introduced himself as Colton, a land surveyor who liked to be outdoors at all times but appreciated a good nap, and at some point, he mentioned loving Hemingway and thinking bald eagles were "the shit." Not my type, if I even had one anymore. But if I had to sit next to anyone for the next couple of hours, he wouldn't be my last pick.

He smiled at me kindly, ordered a craft beer, and struck up a conversation with Finn about a local hockey team that they both watched. Olive looked at me from across the table, mouthing, "Cute, right?" I gave a timid smile and dipped my chin.

If anything, tonight proved I wasn't ready to date yet. I wasn't ready to bring a man home to my parents, watch him shrivel up at their loud voices, and expect him to stick around. Much less bring someone home to Charlie and Pipes. Just the thought made my stomach cramp. Maybe I wasn't ever going to be ready for that.

"So, Madeline." He turned to me at a lull in his conversation with Finn. "What do you do for a living?"

My pulse did pick up at that. Cleaning was nothing to be embarrassed about by any means. And truthfully, I loved my job. The satisfying vacuum lines on a rug, clearing dust from hard-to-reach places, wiping kids' fingerprints off the windows, their faceprints too, from where they stuck their cheeks to the glass to watch the snow fall outside. It was fun and easy, and I made enough money to pay the bills.

Yet every time I had to tell people what I did, I watched them flinch. They never realized they were doing it, and most recovered fairly quickly. Others, mostly old people, gave sympathetic looks afterward, as if I had a single thing to be ashamed about. That flinch, though, hurt. It felt like this little pinch in my side over and over again.

"I'm a housekeeper at the lodge." I said it in a cheery voice and wore a bright smile that said I love my job and not an ounce of me is ashamed. Even so, his pupils widened and this wave of sympathy washed over him.

"Oh, that's"—he paused to swallow—"fun. I bet you find cool stuff in the rooms."

"Oh, I don't clean the rooms." Not that it mattered whatsoever. "I do the main spaces. Lobby, movie room, kids' areas, locker room, stuff like that."

He nodded and didn't skip a beat when he said, "Ah, as long as you enjoy it."

"But I'm in nursing school," I tacked on quickly, as if I had to sell myself more. "I graduate next spring."

I hated that I added that anytime I told people what I did for a living. If I loved it and it wasn't harmful to myself or others, why did I care what other people thought? Specifically people I was willing to bet I would never see again.

"Oh, awesome!" He perked up at that, like I was a contestant on The Bachelor and I had just earned a rose tonight. The people pleaser in me revived itself at that. The dating part of my brain wrote it off as an ick.

We continued on with polite, simple, entirely boring conversation, and I was kind of grateful for that. Any signs of a spark would lead to complications.

And complicated was the very last thing I needed in my life.

Just as the thought entered my brain, the bell over the door chimed again behind us, and I watched as Finn's eyes went wide. His shaking head dropped into his hand. "Oh no."

Confused, I craned my neck and saw none other than everyone's favorite six-foot-five children's ski instructor walking our way, with snow on his boots and the widest grin on his face.

My mouth fell open as he strode to me in slow motion. His dark hair was scattered on his head like he couldn't be bothered to brush it before coming here. He wore a dark green Carhartt jacket over a gray hoodie and black pants, and every eye in this place turned to him. So chaotically Cooper.

"Do you guys know hi—"

"Evening, friends. Sorry I'm late," Cooper announced as he approached our table. He turned and looked at the old couple next to us, who were clearly on a date and wrapped his hands around the arms of their extra chair. "You two good-looking kids aren't using this, are you?"

They both shook their heads, blushing.

He nodded. "Thank'y," he said before turning it our way—my way—and setting it right between Colton and me. He pushed the chair so its legs tapped against my date's and said, with very little room for argument, "Scuse me, fella. Just gonna squish in here. Thanks."

He plopped his chair at the table right between me and the man, pulling up a menu, acting as though he had no clue that his armrest was pressed against mine. Or that his knee brushed my thigh.

My heart raced faster than it ever had.

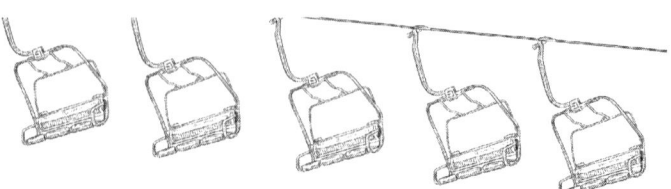

Chapter Twelve
COOPER

W as this my best idea? No. Was it my worst? I was about to find out.

If it was, then it was worth it just to see Madeline looking like this. Cleaning away in leggings and a T-shirt, she gave off pretty girl-next-door vibes. I liked it. It was cute. Here, seeing her confident smile—even if it hadn't initially been directed at me—and those painted-on jeans with that lavender sweater I first saw her in? It was like a lightning bolt to the chest. Tiny blips and zings of desire coursed through me. When she looked over at me and her pretty lips parted, her round cheek bones flushing and that crooked smile almost perking up, I knew it was going to be worth it.

I looked down at the menu, pretending as though I could focus on reading it when I was fighting the urge to stare at the woman sitting beside me. Or trying not to look at my best friend, who was diagonal from me. The one blatantly glaring at me from above his own menu.

Too late. I'd already licked the plate.

"Hey...Coop." Olive's greeting was more of a question than a hello.

"Hey, little Olive Branch." I looked up from my menu at her, watching as she pulled her lips in to fight a smile. "How's baby Finn?" I glanced at her swollen belly. I still remembered how they'd told me. Finn said he had a surprise for me. I was hoping he was going to tell me that I could have my favorite sunglasses back, the ones he stole months ago. But my World's Best Uncle shirt was pretty great too.

"Still baking."

"Glad to hear it. Do you guys want appetizers? I'm thinking bacon cheese fries."

A server with tight blond curls in a dark blue sweater approached us with a notepad. "Are we all ready to order?"

"I'm sorry." The man beside me, who looked like he still split his phone bill with his parents and had a dirty microwave at home, ignored our server and spoke directly at me. "Who are you?"

I stuck my right hand out to him, but I didn't look up from my menu. "Finn and Olive's best friend."

The guy watched my hand for a beat, and the server stared at us, mumbling, "I'll...give you guys a minute to decide" before slowly backing away from the table.

Eventually, Calvin reached up and shook my hand warily.

On my other side, I felt an elbow nudge my ribs. I turned from my menu to glance at Madeline. She looked up at me, those big brown eyes wide and her brows ducked down in confusion. She wore more makeup than she had the other times I'd seen her, and I loved that I could still see those scattered freckles beneath it. I smiled at her and dipped my chin. "Evening, Madeline."

She looked up at me, her nose flaring. I'd never seen angry Madeline. Didn't know that she existed, as much as she smiled.

Glancing behind me, she checked on her little date before looking right back at me and mouthing What are you doing here?

I shrugged and mouthed I had to check out your new boyfriend. I pointed my thumb to the far too young man beside me.

She shook her head, facing her lap, but I didn't miss the way her smile pulled when she did it. Even irritated Madeline smiled.

Eventually our server—now a redhead with a short bob and a pink I love wings sweatshirt—came around to take our orders. When Caleb beside me started asking about vegan options, I turned back to Madeline and saw her looking up at me.

"Hi." I smiled.

"Hello, Coop." She smiled back, a little timid. The same smile she'd given me when she said no to my offer.

"Have a good day?"

"Mostly."

"Good. Mini Coop and Half-Pint have a good day too?"

Her smile deepened at that, her eyes lighting up too. "Yeah, they did."

"Good." I turned back to the menu and ordered my own food.

Stacking all our menus together, I handed them to the redhead and took a deep breath, extending my chest. "So, Colter—"

"Colton."

"Yes, that's what I said." I stirred the straw in my drink. "Are you good with kids?"

He hesitated. "I think so?"

"How good?"

"Uh...I don't know."

I pulled my straw out, sucking the Coke off the end and letting it hang from my fingers like one of those long cigarette holders from the fifties. "So you have little experience babysitting, let's say, a nine-year-old and a two-year-old?"

"Oh, jeez." Finn groaned across from us as Olive giggled.

"Not exactly."

I stuck my straw back into my drink and stirred some more, Godfather style. "So do you feel you are qualified to be a dad?"

A nerve pinched in my side. It was actually Madeline's nails digging into me. I still stared at the guy next to me, waiting for a reply.

Cameron looked to Olive and Finn, as if he needed help to defend himself, before turning back my way with a lifted brow.

He glanced between Madeline and me. "Are you her brother or something?"

"Oh you wish I was her brother."

"All right." A set of hands clapped once beside me. "Cooper, let's go outside." Madeline set her fingers on the table and began to stand up.

Olive sighed across from her. "I'm getting déjà vu."

"I wasn't that bad, was I?" Finn asked.

"You were worse," Olive and I said in sync.

"I think I'm just gonna...go..." Coleman stood, grabbed his keys, and slowly backed away from the table, leaving his almost full beer sitting there.

"What just happened?" Madeline asked, settling back down in her seat and dropping her hands to her lap.

My arms crossed as I leaned back in my chair. "I just saved my friend from a terrible decision."

"I-I honestly do not know what to even say right now."

"I came on behalf of Mini Coop." My chin ducked. "He would want me to do background checks."

"Charlie?" She shook her head a little. Finn's and Olive's heads bounced back and forth between us like they were watching a tennis match. Or like they were dogs following a fish swimming from one side of the bowl to the other. "You came here on behalf of Charlie?"

"Yes. He needs a proper step-uncle. I don't trust just anyone near him."

"You've met him three times."

"We agreed we're best friends now."

"Oh my word." Her hands lifted to her hair, and a chuckle, possibly a nervous one or a pissed one—I hadn't quite been able to read those yet—fell out of her mouth. "You two are absurd."

"If Mini Coop can't be here to meet your future husband, then I will stand in his place."

"Future husband?" she squeaked. "I can't even date right now."

"That's what I thought you said, but here we are. On a double date."

"Is that what this is?" She gasped a laugh, this one sounding much more real and a lot less confused or distant.

"Yes, I am Colon's stand-in now."

"Colton."

"Sure."

Across from us, Finn draped an arm around his wife. "Ah, just like it was yesterday, huh, little grinch?"

Her head fell to his shoulder, and she let out a wistful sigh. "I kind of miss it."

Madeline laughed beside me, and I felt this giant ball of light bouncing around my chest, playing pinball inside me. It felt good, knowing I'd done right by my tiny friend. Felt even better knowing I was going to spend the rest of this evening not having to witness Colin sneak glances down Madeline's sweater.

Chapter Thirteen
Madeline

Maybe I should have been mad that Cooper had crashed this whole night. Maybe I should have gotten up and gone after my technical date. But I didn't. Instead, I stayed for the rest of dinner, laughing when Cooper made jokes at Finn's expense and discussing all things pregnancy and babies with Olive. Which was mostly her asking if newborn poop really was black and questions like you changed how many diapers a day?

For the first time in what felt like an eternity, I savored the sensation of reclaiming my individuality. It felt like, just for a couple of hours, my roles of aunt, student, employee, and even daughter were vanishing before me. I was cut back to the one essential task of simply being myself. Something I had entirely forgotten how to do. It was a rare moment of solace, where the weight of expectations and responsibilities melted away, leaving behind only the pure essence of my being.

I'd stayed up late just days ago, almost crying at one a.m., because reality had hit me—I didn't even know what my favorite color was. If I didn't have a favorite color, then who was I? Because yeah. I liked the color pink in those potted flowers in the summer. But I liked that burnt orange eyeshadow palette in the fall. And right now, I was particularly attached to the color lavender. But none of that made just one color my favorite. So was I even a person at all? Did I possess any originality? What made me...me? I practically panted in my bed just thinking about it, taking BuzzFeed quizzes, waiting for them to tell me who I was supposed to be.

But for these fleeting hours, there was a serenity that came with being myself. Of learning myself all over again. The Madeline who was entirely untouched by the demands of school or the constraints of her mother. The Madeline who was currently loving the shade of hazel in Cooper's eyes and the salmon-colored umbrella in her margarita.

I missed the kids, and I kind of wished they were here. Nevertheless, for once, the world beyond this table of four seemed to pause. Like it was allowing me to exist in my own space, unburdened and unbound.

I knew that the moment I stepped back into my house, the bliss of being my true self would dissipate and be replaced once again by duties that included potty trips, fourth-grade math homework, and trying to find a way to give the kids a good Christmas while on a budget that couldn't stretch an inch. Still, despite that, I clung to the laughter and shared smiles at this table like it was my job.

It felt like all those nights in middle school where I imagined my future brace-less and non-flat-boobs self hanging out with a group of friends. Surrounded by the warmth and light of easy conversation. The thought was so nostalgic that it felt as if Will were sitting right here beside me. It felt like I was having my cup refilled. Like every bit of energy that had drained from me over the last few weeks was being replaced.

An hour later, Olive leaned against Finn's shoulder, and he patted her leg. "We should get home. It's late for you, baby."

She groaned through a yawn. "I'm not even tired yet."

He smiled at Cooper and yawned right back. "Well, I am. Come on, let's go." Finn helped Olive and her big belly up and came to give both of us hugs goodbye.

I squeezed Olive around the neck and whispered a quick thank-you for the invite.

"Madeline, want us to take you home?" Finn checked.

I hesitated because I knew it was still early. But the kids were asleep, and selfishly, I wanted to feel free for just a minute longer. I wanted to cling to this version of myself until the last minute.

"Uh, I'll get an Uber." I decided before I could change my mind. "You guys are both exhausted. Go home."

"You sure?" Olive eyed me.

"I'll make sure she gets there safely," Cooper said before taking a sip of his drink.

"All right. Well, text me when you get home, okay?" Olive pointed to me as Finn guided her away. At the door, she shouted, "Don't talk to strangers. Love you. Bye." Finn pointed her off to his car as both of her hands moved to support her round belly.

I snorted as I watched them leave.

"They're entertaining," Cooper said with a chuckle, and I relaxed back in my seat.

"They are," I agreed, and we smiled at each other in utter silence. Well, minus the sound of hockey fans around us and the clanging of pints at the bar and the AC/DC song playing in the background.

"I'm glad I came tonight." Cooper's smile turned smug, and I gasped a laugh, feeling the effects of that last drink a little more strongly than the other two.

"I'm sure you are. Ruining my date—"

"You said it wasn't a date."

"Ruining my not-date," I corrected.

"I don't regret it." Cooper leaned back in his chair with that smug little smile and a Coke in his hand, looking like every woman's nighttime fantasy.

"I don't either. He was kind of young for me."

"Seemed like it. Unless you want a third kid to take care of."

I snorted. "I do not."

"He seemed like the type to be nervous to call and order a pizza."

"What does that even mean?"

He shrugged. "He wouldn't stand up for you. Wouldn't fight for Mini Coop. Not the best candidate."

Cooper trailed his index finger up the side of his glass, wiping the condensation off on the long digit before sticking it into his mouth. I honestly thought Coca-Cola should have been paying this man for endorsements.

"You know, you never finished my game the other day."

"Game?" I asked.

"Yeah. My you tell me what you like, and I tell you what I like game."

A laugh, a slightly flirtatious one, bubbled out of me, and I leaned toward the table, watching that smile of his. God, he had such nice teeth. It was a shame how hard it was to find nice, white, clean teeth nowadays. A trait overshadowed by perfectly quaffed hair and nice cheekbones.

"I didn't realize it was a game."

He nodded, eyebrows lowering and face turning a little serious. "Well, it is, and the winner is buying these drinks."

"How do we pick a winner?"

"I get to decide." He shrugged.

"What?" I gasped through my chuckle. "That is totally unfair."

"If I can't have you as my fake fiancée or wife then I get to pick the winner."

Well, I couldn't argue with that. Or maybe I could have if I hadn't ordered that last drink. I got too giggly when I drank. There weren't enough serious points to be made on my end.

"Fair. You go first."

He nodded. "I like—Wait. Should we set a timer?"

"What does a timer matter?"

"I'm not sure. This feels like a timer kind of moment."

I considered it, then nodded. "Yes. Timer."

Cooper reached into his pocket and tapped on the clock app on his phone, clicking the green stop watch button. "Okay. I like the sound that poker chips make when you put them together." He made a clanking noise with his mouth as if to demonstrate.

"Ooh." I cooed. "Good one. I like the smell of freshly cut grass."

Cooper groaned. "Lame."

"Fine. I like when I clock in at work, and it makes that little click-click sound."

"Ugh." He practically moaned—loud enough for the server to cut us a look. "I begged them to keep that. It's inconvenient, but I don't care. Give me the clicks and the hole punches."

"Right!" I agreed, also loud enough for the server to actually stop cleaning off the space, leaving dirty plates and half-empty glasses to move a few tables over.

He continued our game. "I like tool restoration ASMR videos. Sometimes I watch them to fall asleep."

"I like those houses at the beach that have dolphins or manatees holding their mailbox."

"Oh my God!" Cooper sat up so fast you would have thought I'd said something so revolutionary that we needed to call NASA right away. "I have wanted one of those my whole life."

I sighed, picturing a little ocean friend in my yard. "Imagine getting your mail from a manatee."

"Why even take Prozac? Doctors should just prescribe those things. Ten milligrams of manatee mail a day. Boom, done."

Despite Cooper not having a single drink tonight, only taking a sip of watered-down Coke here and there, he stayed right on my level as we kept playing. And if my words slurred a little, or I began talking a little louder, he pretended not to notice. Round after round, again and again, we found things we didn't even realize we liked in life.

He liked when peanut butter stuck to the roof of his mouth. I said ew. I liked the smell of puppy breath. He also said ew. He enjoyed bird watching. I enjoyed people watching. He also said he liked women who agreed to be his fake fiancée for a day, to which I replied, "good luck finding one."

After about twenty minutes, Cooper's hands reached out to stop the timer.

"What?" I asked, taking a look at the stopwatch. "Is it over? Did I win?"

He scowled at me. "No, it's not over. Also, I'm winning."

"Darn."

"You know," Cooper said, straightening his back and lifting his chest. "I think this isn't helping me get to know you better. I think I could take one look at you and know these."

My head tilted. "I look like a manatee-mailbox lover?"

Cooper's eyes trailed from my wedged boots, up my skintight flared jeans, to my hips and the cropped sweater with a hint of my skin poking out, then finally rested on my face. I don't know what he saw when he looked at me then, but his eyes lingered on my mouth for a second with this completely darkened gaze. A shiver rippled through the base of my spine all the way up to my neck when he said, "Oh yeah."

I wasn't exactly sure how that was the most erotic thing I had ever heard in my life, but it was. My skin erupted in goose bumps, heart pounding. My lips pulled into my teeth, and I fought back my smile. When was the last time I'd felt this flattered? Like my true self? Certainly not with my ex, and certainly never with someone who thought a specific type of mailbox was sexy.

"So." I cut off the train of thought that was quickly derailing into shirtless-Cooper mental pictures. "Should we stop, then?"

"No. We need to switch it. I think I can figure you out better if you say things you don't like."

I hummed. "Nah, I like way more stuff than I dislike." The words were mushing together more, and suddenly, it felt like I was the one with peanut butter stuck in my mouth.

"I think you want to think that. But humor me. I'll go first." He took a sip of Coke and popped his fingers like he was preparing to thumb wrestle Mike Tyson. He hit reset and started the timer again. "I don't like when people say it's raining cats and dogs. Freaks me out."

I nodded. Fair. "I..." I searched my brain, but everything that came up felt far too heavy for the moment. I didn't like that my brother had left me here alone. I didn't like my parents pretending it had never even happened. I didn't like that my heart kept racing every time I so much as heard the word Cooper. "I...don't like unnecessary small talk?"

Cooper gave me this look that made it known he was displeased with my answer. "No."

"No what?"

"No, I don't accept it." He stuck his hand out and curled his fingers into his palm in a gimme motion. "I want a better one, or I win the whole game."

"How is that fair?"

"That was like the golden snitch of this game. You pull the lame card, and I instantly win. Try again. I want something so controversial that if you posted it on Reddit, half the people would say 'same' and the other half would be enraged."

"Ugh, fine." I considered it for a moment, and honestly, what did I not like? It wasn't that I was this ball of ignorant sunshine who thought the world was rainbows and lollipops, but I certainly didn't just sit around all day and think huh, here are fifty things I do not like on this earth.

So I pulled the first one that came to my mind, an incident I'd experienced that morning.

"I don't like when fast food drive-thrus have two lines and merge into one so you have to awkwardly see if you can go next or if they should."

"It really shows the flaws of our society. I don't like the feeling of cotton balls."

"Cotton...balls?" My amusement was easy to hide in normal circumstances, but when I was three fancy-named pink-umbrella'd drinks in, things seemed to only become funnier.

"Yes, Madeline. Cotton balls." His lip quivered like he found it kind of funny too, but he couldn't let me know. "Is that a problem?"

I shook my head and mentally zipped my lips together to keep from laughing. "No problem."

We went through a few more rounds. He didn't like the feeling of sand on the beach. I didn't like hiking—the view was never worth the death climb for me. He didn't like books in third-person point of view. I didn't like movies with incredibly predictable plots. So the list went on, as did the drinks, until my stomach felt like a wound-up knot of coconut rum and bacon cheese fries. Or was it tequila that they put in these?

I swayed back and forth in my seat, enjoying how much it felt like I was on a boat swaying out in the sea with a slew of mermaids and hot pirates on board. I wasn't drunk. I mean, it didn't feel like I was. But there was definitely a gentle rocking in my head. And I had an awful hankering for a large Whopper. But I still felt like I had my senses. Enough of my senses to hear Cooper say that he currently had a hatred toward people who pretended like going to dog shows made them fancier than the rest of us.

I closed my eyes as he spoke and continued to bob along the waves in my head. Maybe it was his cologne wafting my way, the notes of marine mist mixed with kelp and amber wood. A cozy little pirate.

"All right." Cooper's hand tapped my knee. The one that was occasionally hitting his chair while I swiveled my seat back and forth. "I think we should head out." My eyes opened to see him grabbing his keys off the table and shaking them in his long fingers. "Let me drive you home."

I shook my head a little too quickly and then slowed it down. "I can get an Uber."

I just needed to download the app, but my phone wouldn't freaking unlock when I knew the password was right. Oh, never mind. I was wrong.

As I opened the app store, he tapped his keys—and the tiny, clearly homemade halfway decayed we heart Mr. Cooper keychain that looked like it was bound to fall off at any moment—on my wrist.

"Please, I won't sleep well tonight knowing I sent you off with a stranger. Plus, Olive might kill me later for it. You said I'm only a block away from you, so it's on the way."

Olive had been blowing up my phone since she left an hour ago, asking me if I was home, then whether I'd eaten enough, then a HELLO???, topped off with a message from Finn that said My wife is waddling back and forth in our bedroom. Can you please tell her that you are alive?

I fired off a quick I'm fine, call tomorrow text and turned back to Cooper. "Okay." I shrugged. Might as well take the ride. I was too tired and boat-y to argue.

Cooper tipped the server generously—probably for the excess shouting along the way—and guided me out the front door and to the parking lot.

"You can walk on your own, right?"

I pictured him carrying me in those lean arms for a minute and almost lied. But even a few drinks in, my lying had always been pathetic. "Yup." I popped the P and followed him through the rows of cars until he walked toward a large white SUV.

He opened the passenger door, exposing a clean interior with tan leather seats and a floorboard that wasn't engulfed with fast food receipts and empty Styrofoam cups that could possibly be growing mold as we speak. Not a single Pocahontas doll or Slim Jim wrapper to be found. Only a black tree dangling from his rearview mirror, hand sanitizer in one of the cupholders, and a phone charger facing the other side. Thank God we weren't taking my car.

Coop turned to me, offering a hand my way. That I refused to pass up on. My fingers interlocked with his. Warmth built in my palm, climbing through my fingertips and down to my forearm. His hand pressed firm against mine, and I had pink drink tingles coursing through me.

I avoided his gaze as I climbed into the seat. He squeezed my fingers once I got in. "Good?" he asked.

No, I wanted to reply. I am so starved for human affection that a mere five-second hand hold felt so sensual that my stomach did an Olympic somersault. "Yup," I squeaked, forcing my view to stick to the windshield, watching as snow fluttered down over the parking lot and onto the surrounding cars. Cooper pulled his hand away from me, using it to softly close the door. As his fingers drifted from mine, I knew that warmth was going to be there far longer than just this car ride. And I kind of hated myself for it.

A moment later, Cooper hopped into the driver's seat beside me. The car filled with his dirty pirate cologne again, and my pulse beat against the skin he'd just touched.

"On a scale of one to ten, how drunk are you?" he asked.

"I'm not drunk. Maybe a three. Just enough to feel comfortable talking to you more, but not enough where you should be concerned about my ability to take care of myself or the kids."

He nodded and started the car, switching the gear into reverse. "Gotcha, so the perfect amount, then?"

"Mm-hmm," I confirmed, leaning back into the headrest, closing my eyes and enjoying the smooth voice of Billy Joel around us on the way home. Even more soothing was Cooper's voice occasionally singing the words, but mostly just humming along like the sweetest lullaby. Reminiscent of a cat purring in the palm of your hand.

I smiled to myself, proud that, for once, I'd done something for me. I'd taken a few hours to be selfish and to spend time with people who actually enjoyed my presence—or seemed to, at the least, if Cooper's common guffaws were anything to go by.

The guilt was there too, deep down. Knowing I could have spent the time with the kids and instead chose to be selfish. It would hit me like a freight train at some point. But I refused to let it fully set in until I got back to the house and in my bed, with no one left to hear me having a pity party about my poor decisions. Rome wasn't built in a day, and finding out who I actually was probably couldn't be managed that quickly either. But it felt like progress, even if I lost it all again tomorrow. No number of personality quizzes with different results could replace the ground work I'd set tonight. Or I guess that Cooper had set, considering he was the one pulling out the game.

We pulled into my driveway, the headlights shining on my parents' car in front of us, over to the side door. The blinds in the window leading to the kitchen were suddenly pulled apart, and two incredibly nosy pairs of eyes appeared. I wished I could say it was the kids. But undoubtedly, that would be my parents.

I unbuckled my seat belt in a waving rush, pushing my door open and practically flinging myself out of the car. "Wellthiswasgreatseeyouaroundsometi—" I closed the door, cutting my sentence off.

My feet took off, and I was a little too tipsy to be worried that I looked like one of those birds on the beach chasing after a stray hotdog bun in the wind.

Cooper's door opened before I could get away from the car. "I'm walking you to the door."

"There is no need for that." I kept walking.

"I didn't mean it as a question, Madeline." His voice left very little room for arguments, and even if I felt like disagreeing, his feet were rushing to my side.

I looked from his long legs over to the door that was now creaking open, where my parents were now indiscreetly staring at us. By the way I paused, you would have thought I was sixteen again, getting caught making out with my boyfriend in the driveway.

"Goodnight, Cooper."

"Wait. Let me just—"

The door opened fully, and Mom stood there, eyeing us back and forth. "Were you not going to introduce us?"

I looked to Cooper, who was smirking at me, and to my mom, who looked like she was trying to do a mental recap of every crime show she'd watched in the last twenty years, wondering if he had been on any of them.

"Not really," I decided.

Cooper walked up behind me, his shoulder bumping against mine. "Evening, Mrs. Sage." He dipped his head in a hello to my dad. "Mr. Sage."

Any hint of alcohol and freedom dissipated from my body like the air itself had sucked it dry. I was going to be sober for the rest of my life because of this.

"Why does he look so familiar? Tom, doesn't he look familiar?"

"You think everyone looks familiar, Eloise."

She pointed a finger at Cooper beside me. "Well, he especially does."

"Cooper is Charlie's ski instructor," I explained. "You dropped him off last week."

"Yes! That's it. So you were her date tonight?" With the way she emphasized the word date, she may as well have been accusing him of robbing a bank or maybe putting salt in the sugar containers at various fast food locations. Because a man she hadn't set me up with was a man not worth knowing.

I opened my mouth to give a definite no just as Cooper spoke beside me. "Yep."

If this clueless man had any idea of the can of worms he'd just unleashed on us both, then I'd guarantee he would rewind the tape and shove that single syllable right back into his mouth.

Mom's eyes cut to me. "You're dating your nephew's coach?"

I hated that she made a point of calling him my nephew. He was. I knew that. It wasn't like I carried Charlie for ten months and popped him out myself. But still, nephew felt far too distant for what he meant to me.

"Uh..." I gave Cooper a look that essentially was a bunch of question marks. His eyes widened, and he replied with a long line of exclamation points. "Yes." No. No, no, no. I take it back, there were still remnants of coconut rum in my system. There was no other explanation.

"So, is it serious?" she asked, as if it was entirely sane to bring up within the first two minutes of meeting a date.

"Yes," Cooper proudly shouted as I muttered, "No."

I turned to him, and that lip quirked up when he said, "It's very serious."

The only expectation I had for that would be a ranting of how selfish I was for taking Cooper as my own or that I should instead find a "nice, reliable man with a steady income." I say this from experience, since my mom previously tried to set me up with a pharmacist. And a dentist. And men who all had jobs ending in -ist.

Instead, her lips pulled up a bit. Not a smile but not quite a scowl either. A...smowl. "Well, I don't know how I feel about you dating your nephew's coach, but I suppose at this point, any man will do. Someone needed to get you out of the house."

Dad was still staring at Cooper like he was about to whisk me away to the Netherlands to take my innocence and sell me CBD gummies—he still believes they're actual edibles. Meanwhile, Cooper was looking at me, and although I refused to meet his eye, I could feel the pleading.

He needed a fake woman in his life. I needed to get my mother off my back. He was trying to, for a lack of better terms, kill two birds with one stone.

One swell foop. No, that's not right.

"It's"—I lifted my eyes to Cooper, who looked like he was desperately waiting with this starving puppy look. I caved—"serious. But not serious enough where the kids know. We would like to keep it that way."

I was done for. Too much rum.

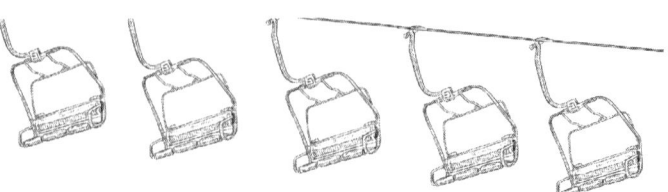

Chapter Fourteen
COOPER

Chase (magazine husband): Can't wait to see you and Madeline next Friday!

Cooper: we wouldn't miss it

"So you blackmailed her?" Finn asked as we set cones out on Monday morning.

As soon as I left Madeline's house under the eyes of her cautious family, I fired off a text to her.

Me: youre the best fake girlfriend ever

Me: whats your go to order at the cafe downstairs I'm bringing you breakfast every day this week

Madeline: I'm assuming this is Cooper?

Me: how many fake boyfriends do you have

Madeline: Not enough. You are not off the hook yet. You're lucky you didn't get the Spanish inquisition from my parents like I did the moment you left. Also: of course you're buying breakfast—a caramel macchiato and a bacon cheddar scone. Also: learn how to use punctuation.

Joke was on her, really, considering bringing her breakfast was an excuse to see her this morning. What I lacked in punctuation, I made up for in punctuality.

"I didn't blackmail her." I wasn't that cruel. She said so herself at dinner. She didn't like her mom trying to set her up with random men. I also did not like that. She had a problem that curved perfectly against my own, and boom, I'd solved both. "She needs me as much as I need her."

"Did she say that herself?"

I paused. "Not in so many words, but kind of, yes."

"Ugh, Coop." Finn groaned. "Olive doesn't have a ton of friends, and if you ruin this for her, I seriously might kill you."

My hands flew up in defense. "I am not ruining anything. She doesn't even like me. I am just doing both of us and this lodge a great service."

"I hope you know what you're doing."

I waved a hand. "Relax, I can do this."

My phone buzzed in the side pocket of my salopettes—French for ski pants, essentially—and I pulled it out to turn off my alarm. After she'd texted back on Saturday night, I said we probably should meet for breakfast in the mornings in the lobby. That way, we could hammer out the details of our arrangement for the interview. To my surprise and enjoyment, she agreed. Plans were already circling.

"I gotta go." I put my phone back in my pocket and scattered the cones in a somewhat straight—actually, not straight at all but would have to do—line.

"Where?"

"My first date with Madeline is this morning, and I refuse to be late."

I snagged my bag off the bench and slung it onto my shoulder, not waiting for his response as I trekked through the snow toward the lobby.

True to my word, I sat at a table in the back corner of the café, near the low hum of the speakers playing "Fly Me to the Moon," and the smell of fresh espresso being poured wafting around me. I had Madeline's order sitting in front of me while I waited for her to walk in.

Not long after, Madeline came in wearing a cream sweater with a thick scarf wrapped around her. I frowned at her lack of gloves and the red fingers wrapped around her keys. It wasn't the worst weather Aspen had seen—especially compared to last week—but still, she needed gloves.

She smiled all the time. I wasn't sure she knew how to stop, honestly. It was like a switch she had to force off.

I raised my arm and waved, showing her where our table was. The smile spread a tiny bit before locking into a scowl. She sauntered in and took the seat in front of me, staring at me as if I had spit in her coffee before she entered the room.

"What?" I asked, on the defense.

"I'm still mad at you."

I nodded. "Ah. Are you, though?"

"Yes."

"I did you a favor."

She opened her mouth and closed it again. "Not in the way I needed it. My mom is going to have our Pinterest wedding board planned out by tomorrow."

I shrugged. "You said you needed help. I helped—"

"No, what I needed was a mother transplant. Instead, you added stress to my already daily chaos. Now she's trying to watch the kids so we can do 'date night.'"—she threw her hands up in quotations—"once a week without them there, and I'm gonna have to come up with some crappy reason why I don't need that."

"Oh." I twiddled my thumbs underneath the table. "I didn't think about it like that. I'm sorry." I said it sincerely, lowering my voice and my gaze to match hers.

Madeline looked at me for a moment before taking a sip of her drink and sighing. "It's okay. I'm just overwhelmed right now."

I nodded. Made sense, taking care of two kids on top of nursing school, work, and her parents' pressure? How often did she actually get to come out of her shell like she had last night? How often did Madeline get to come up for air?

"Well, good news is this is just for a couple weeks. It will be done before you know it."

"That almost makes it worse." She stirred the ice around in her drink. "Because now, if we just randomly break up, then Mom is going to try to pull Charlie from classes to avoid you."

At that, my brows lowered. "Hell no. You can't take that kid out of classes. He's got more talent in one pinky than most do in their whole bodies. If anything, we could switch him to Finn's afternoon classes, right?"

I hated the thought of him giving up. I watched it happen to other students. Life got busy or their parents had to move, and you watched this raw talent shrivel up and die. It hurt from an outside perspective, and I couldn't imagine how bad it would hurt Mini Coop too.

Madeline shook her head. "He can only do mornings on the weekends. I have classes in the afternoon, and my mom has doctor appointments on and off throughout the week. It just wouldn't work. That was why I said no in the first place."

I nodded, considering. I was able to admit that I'd screwed up and had to fix it. "Let me think for a second." I hummed to myself and looked at the coffee shop around us like an answer would pop out directly in front of me with jazz hands, saying here I am, exactly what you've been waiting for! Contrary to my belief, the chatter of tourists around us and the aroma of freshly brewed coffee mingling with the scent of pine from the wood-burning fireplace did nothing for my empty head.

I turned to the large windows to my left that offered the perfect view of snow-capped mountains and small glimpses of skiers and snowboarders gliding down the slopes in the distance. Even that wasn't giving me any ideas.

"Let me keep thinking on it, but I will find a way to make this better for you."

She let out this sigh that said not likely, but it only made me more determined. I pulled a notebook and pen from my backpack and set them on the table.

"All right, for now, we need to talk business." I opened the notebook and tapped the corner of my gel pen to it.

"Business being...?"

"The business of Madeline and Cooper, super couple and ski extraordinaires. We should probably get a good couple name going for us too. I'm leaning more toward Cadeline than Mooper. Mooper sounds like a rejected member of the Muppets and doesn't exactly scream sexy."

"And Cadeline does scream sexy?"

"Sexier than Mooper."

She shrugged. "True. Or we could just not have a couple name."

The pen moved as I waved my hand. "Nah, we gotta sell this. For the actual interview part, it would be best if we knew everything about each other in case they ask you something specific about me."

Madeline nodded and took another sip of her drink, leaving a pink lipstick stain on the lid that I had a hard time pulling my eyes from. "Fair."

I clicked my pen and prepped it to write. "So go ahead and tell me everything about you, and we can go from there."

"Everything about me?" She scoffed. "I can't even remember what I ate for dinner last night."

"Then it's a good thing I didn't ask that."

"I can't just...tell you about myself. It's not that easy."

I crossed my arms, possibly marking my shirt with my pen, but I wasn't worried about that at this particular moment. "Is too. Watch this. Hi, my name is Cooper. I am a children's ski instructor at my family's lodge, Aspen Peaks. I enjoy spending most of my time on the slopes or with my friends and family. My favorite board game is Clue, and I think I look best in all black. When I was a kid, I had a hamster named Truman, whom I still miss. And I am totally on Rachel's side when it comes to her and Ross's whole 'we were on a break' moment."

Madeline stayed silent, staring at me like maybe I had more to add to that. I did. I could go all day long. I liked homemade Rice Krispies Treats way better than the packaged stuff, and I would sometimes think about eggs, and it would make me sick. I could fill every piece of paper in this notebook with things about me.

She muttered a soft and slow "how?"

I answered. "Well, technically, they were on a break, but I don't think that gave him any right to be with another woman. I mean, he waited like ten seconds to stick his tongue—"

"No, no." She shook her head. "How are you so good at that?"

"What?"

"That. Talking about yourself, knowing yourself. I had a meltdown the other day because I didn't even know what brand of cereal I like anymore."

She pulled at her hair, and in that moment, I noticed just how tired she looked. I hadn't seen them before, the heavy, bloodshot eyes and the yawning over and over again.

I didn't know how to answer that, not really. I just knew myself. I kind of figured everyone was like that. "I...I'm sorry."

She didn't respond, just slumped her shoulders a bit as her gaze zeroed in on the notebook in front of me.

"If it helps," I said softly, "I totally think you're a Cinnamon Toast Crunch kind of girl."

She snorted at that, and her eyes turned lighter for just a moment. "Maybe you're right. Doesn't change the fact that you had to tell me that. I didn't even know it myself."

I leaned back in my chair so I could take a better look at her. "I don't think you're giving yourself enough credit. Saturday night, you knew plenty about yourself."

"No. I knew plenty about obscure things I did or did not like in life."

"So?" I smiled a bit when she finally lifted her gaze to me. "Who says all those little things don't make you who you are?"

Madeline's head cocked to the side. "So you think if I just tell them I like fancy toasters, then that's all they'll need?"

I shook my head and tore a piece off my own croissant. "No, that's not what I meant. I just think you know yourself more than you think you do."

She didn't agree or argue with me, but the way her eyes darkened told me something about that didn't sit with her. I glanced one more time out at the window beside me and watched a guy on a snowboard gliding down the mountain, his board taking him in long, smooth, curved strokes. And that was when it hit me.

"I got it." I leaned forward, sitting on the edge of my seat.

"Got...what?"

"The solution to every problem you and I have."

"Not every proble—"

My hand reached out to hers, the short-sighted version of me thinking it would be a genius idea to hold her hand. She looked at our joint fingers, all warm and soft, before looking back at me. "Every. Problem. Madeline."

She squinted at me in disbelief but didn't move her hand either, so I kept leaning into the table, ignoring the edge stabbing my gut.

"Here's what we can do. You liked Saturday night, right? I'm not just making that up in my head?" It was worth asking, considering I had been known to make more of things than I should.

"Sure, it was nice."

"Let's do that once a week. Once a week, your parents can watch the kids, watch me pick you up and drop you off. And we can go somewhere to figure this out."

Her brows pulled down in confusion, but she didn't seem totally averse to the idea. "Figure what out?"

"You." I squeezed her hand, and we both looked down at our joined fingers. "We can meet once a week, and I can help you learn more about yourself to make up for whatever we're going to endure in the interview. It'll look like we're dating very seriously, and we can sort out your perfect LinkedIn/Tinder bio. An all-in-one combo."

"For how long?"

"Until you feel ready. Until you feel like yourself again."

I knew for a fact, mostly from yanking information out of Olive, that Madeline had changed after her brother's death. She hadn't explained how or provided details. When I asked, she simply said, "She isn't who she once was." Something I understood all too well.

I was fortunate in that my grief was the kind to knock you into reality. Like a punch to the face from life, but in a loving way. In a way that said you're better than this, and I turned myself around. Grief, for others, sometimes meant going in a downward spiral and getting lost along the way. I saw that in my cousins. In my uncle, who buried himself in work. In my mom, holding tears back at her father's funeral. Everyone grieved differently, and everyone grew from it differently too. Maybe this could be Madeline's growth.

"Why? Why would you do that for me?"

Because after the interview, I wouldn't have an excuse to see her anymore. And because I wasn't quite ready to let whatever that meant for us go. "Because I feel like I owe it to you, since I brought you into this in the first place." I started to leave it at that, but it felt cheap and all too fake, so I added, "And because I like you. I think you're cooler than you think you are, and about what it would be like if I could get you to smile like you did on Saturday all the time."

She laughed at that, and I laughed too before pulling my hand away from hers. Her smile died down a bit, turning into this soft, sweet grin when she said, "Seriously, my mom might drive you crazy. And I don't want Charlie to know, since none of it's real. He has a big heart, and he is already way too attached to you."

I held a hand up. "To be fair, he was my friend before I knew you well enough, so I agree. Bros before ho—" I caught myself midway. "No, I can't even say hos because that doesn't apply here. Bros before hot aunts. I'll stick by that."

Her cheeks turned the prettiest shade of pink when she said, "I can't believe I am agreeing to this."

"So you are agreeing?"

"I mean, not like I have much of a choice. Mom's breathing down my neck about getting a man in my life. She sends me the numbers of so many of her friends' sons that sometimes I just text them and say, 'If Eloise Sage happens to mention her daughter is interested in dating, please be advised that said daughter is not at all.'"

The thought of numbers being flung her way left and right made my palms itch and gave me this dreadful sense of unease in my gut.

"Perfect. What's your schedule like?" I asked because the alternative words—on average, how many men are reaching out to you each day?—felt like an invasion.

She hummed and muttered to herself for a second, mumbling about speech lessons and schooling and picking up groceries before settling on a day. "Friday nights would be best. I have online classes only on Friday, and it would be good for my parents too, since I think that's when they're most available."

I nodded and bit my lip. "Fridays, then? For our dates?"

"They're not dates."

"Fine." I rolled my eyes. "Fridays for our not-dates?"

She nodded and, without my permission, my brain immediately started rattling ideas off for the next few weeks in my soon-to-be-booked winter.

Chapter Fifteen
Madeline

T rue to his word, Cooper texted me on Thursday night after I picked up Charlie from the lodge.

Part of me expected him to be weird about the whole agreement. Actually, I expected myself to be weird about it. But when I left work early to grab Charlie, I caught them talking to the side. I couldn't hear everything they were saying, but Charlie stared at Cooper intensely as he spoke with his hands. Something about leaning back or maybe pulling back his skis? It was hard to understand, but I certainly didn't miss the way Charlie looked up at Cooper like he was standing next to an actual superhero. It made me feel just a little better about our arrangement. Well, that and when I asked my mom if she could watch the kids for me for a "date night," she practically squealed into the phone and proceeded to share details of how she "locked in" my dad early on. The words that followed would henceforth be burned into my memory like a painful scar.

Cooper: still good for tomorrow

He didn't include any punctuation, but I assumed he was asking instead of telling.

Me: Yup, where should we meet?

Cooper: ill pick you up

Cooper: dress warm

I contemplated that for over an hour, wondering why I would need to dress warmly, or at least warmly enough for him to mention it. I imagined the possibilities of what he would define as not-date material. More than likely skydiving in those squirrel suits off a snowy mountaintop, or maybe joining a flash mob dance downtown without knowing any of the dance moves. Either way, I had no idea how to prepare myself that night.

I stood in front of my closet and pulled out a pair of flared jeans. They paired well with my cowgirl boots—a recent obsession after Olive and I had watched The Longest Ride ten times in one week—and a sweater. I laid the outfits on the bed and turned to Piper beside me. She stood there, hands on her hips, a toddler-safe sucker sticking out of her mouth, and shook her head disapprovingly.

"What?" I asked.

She didn't respond, of course. She just looked from the outfit to me, and then proceeded to saunter out of the room, closing the door on me. So this outfit was a no. As I turned back to my closet, looking at the articles of clothing I'd worn over the last seven years, my door opened again.

Charlie popped his head in and clocked me in front of the closet before walking over and standing right beside me.

"Are you going on a date?" The way he worded it sounded like I'd signed up for a marathon or mosh pit in the middle of nowhere.

I didn't want to lie, but I definitely couldn't tell the truth. So I stared down at that sweet, freckled face that was quickly transforming right into his dad's. He still had that baby face a little. He wasn't looking fully grown by any means. No hint of facial hair coming any time soon, and he still had some of that squish in his cheeks. But the kid had grown a foot since I'd had him, and his once tiny boy nose was slowly turning into a pointy man nose. I just couldn't stand it. He was getting so big so fast, and I felt like I was missing something right in front of my eyes. Like I had been watching a movie, but left to get popcorn, and when I came back, poof, there went the credits.

"No," I somewhat lied, somewhat didn't. "Just seeing an old friend. Nothing fancy." Cooper was an old friend. Older than me, at least.

"Are they gonna...come inside?" he asked timidly.

"Uh, probably not. They're pretty shy."

The lies just piled up one after the other, like a credit card swipe or two, and suddenly, you owe ten thousand dollars, and you start to consider selling every pair of underwear you own on Etsy.

"Hmm," Charlie hummed, like he didn't believe me and walked up to my closet, grabbing a sky blue sweater that hit me at a weird angle and was the wrong kind of oversized. "Wear this." He laid it on the bed next to my pants.

"That sweater isn't very flattering on me." I hated that word, but I couldn't exactly tell my kid oh, can't wear that because the last time I did, someone at the pharmacy asked when my baby was due.

"I know." He shrugged and walked out of the room. I balled up the sweater and threw it at the door as his prepubescent laughter echoed down the hall. He was still my little boy deep down.

Deciding to stick more to comfort than looks, I picked my favorite cream-and-black striped sweater on top of a white undershirt for warmth and pulled on tight flared jeans with long fuzzy socks and Ugg boots. He said dress comfy, not dress like we were going to see the Queen of England.

After I dropped off the kids at my parents' house, I left with a whole lot of unsolicited advice and a condom slipped into my hand by my own mother, who said, and I quote, "Can't have any more running around right now." I threw it into the garbage outside, right where her camera system faced and faked a gag to the security device.

I pulled into Cooper's driveway, remembering which house it was by the greenish-gray front door and wooden shutters. The front porch was small, but not as tiny as mine. I remembered standing on that porch and glimpsing inside, seeing an extremely gray, immaculately clean living room behind the man with dull eyes. His large white SUV sitting out front gave me a hint too.

I parked next to his car and hopped out, unsure if this was the kind of situation where I should knock on his door or send a simple I'm here, come outside text. It wasn't like this was a date by any means, so I shouldn't have felt this uncomfortable and unsure of what to do. But still, when Cooper walked out of his front door with keys in his hand and a giant smile on his face, I felt a tsunami-size wave of relief flooding over me.

He looked down at my outfit and back up to me, smirking that wolfish grin that made me feel like I was meek prey.

"You said dress warm," I defended.

Cooper shook his head a bit. "S'cute. I like it."

My cheeks warmed at that. Cute. Like a cartoon duck or a bunny in a field of wildflowers, hopping around aimlessly.

We piled into his SUV, and I immediately took note of the new tree hanging from his rearview mirror. A green one this time. The aroma of pine and crisp and spicy outdoors. It felt like getting a hug from a buff, surly lumberjack wearing a red flannel. In the best way possible, of course.

"Where are we going?" I asked.

"It's a surprise" He put the car into reverse and began backing out of the driveway, turning his head past me and leaning closer to my seat to see. "But you'll like it, I think. It'll give us a good, clean palate so you can see what you do or don't enjoy."

I tried to think of what we could do in Aspen that Cooper would consider a palate cleanser but came up entirely short. "Well, you're right about one thing: it will definitely be a surprise."

He nodded. "It's not far. 'Bout twenty minutes." He stopped the car in front of his house and pulled out his phone, which was connected to the car's console. "All right, music. We can either do an early 2000s playlist or we can do my cowboy playlist. Pick one."

I shrugged. "I don't care. Either is fine."

"No, Madeline. This is all part of the find yourself experience. You have to pick. I chose the location; everything else is on you."

My curiosity was piqued at that, but I held my hands out and spoke through a chuckle. "I really don't car—"

"Pick one."

"No, you—"

"Now. Three, two, one—"

"Two thousand," I shouted and then pulled back, surprised. My bottom lip jutted out as I tilted my head. "Huh, I really thought I was going to say the other one."

Maybe he wasn't too far off with this whole find yourself thing. Although if finding myself was going to include any form of ritualistic sacrifice, jumping out of planes, or taking hallucinogens like any of the self-proclaimed celebrities said, I was out.

He turned the volume up and spoke around Maroon 5's "This Love."

"This is going to be fun." He smiled and took off down the street, leaving me wondering and all too excited.

"A drive-in?" I asked through a gasp-slash-laugh. "We're going to a drive-in when it's"—I checked the temperature below his speedometer—"twenty-five degrees out?"

"It was a part of my theory."

"Your theory?"

He nodded. "Yup, now pick between the two screens. We've got The Shawshank Redemption and Grown Ups."

I hummed. "I don't know, I'm fine with whate—"

Cooper clicked his tongue and shook his head with a tsk, tsk, tsk. "Come on, Madeline. I thought you'd catch on by now. I'm not picking a single thing tonight."

I smiled to myself and watched as he pulled closer to where the road split into two, where I had to make the choice between two movies. "Uh..." I drew out.

"Better pick soon."

"Fine, Grown Ups," I decided, then leaned back in my seat.

"Perfect. I had a feeling about that." Cooper grinned as he turned the car to the right side of the fork, following other cars packed into rows. We pulled in by the tiny hut covered in space heaters where a young girl was taking money for tickets. We bought tickets for one car and listened to her monotone spiel about their rules and regulations. Something she clearly had memorized and probably snored out in her sleep.

"One ticket for one movie. Space heaters are available in the front if you pay extra. Concessions are to the left of the main bathrooms. Hit the line of Porta Potties, and you've gone too far. Please remember this is a family establishment and should be treated as such. No smoking, alcohol, or inflatable houses are allowed."

I leaned past Cooper to look at the girl, who was chewing gum and playing with her acrylic nails. "Do people bring...inflatable houses?"

"You would be surprised at the things I've seen," she deadpanned.

I rested back in my seat. All right, then.

"Thanks," Cooper said to her. "We will refrain from bouncy houses, smoking, or public nudity."

She nodded at him and tore the ticket stubs, pointing with two fingers to the area we should park in. Cooper drove off with the windows rolled down.

String lights were hung on the gravel driveway, lighting a path to the parking lot that faced a giant screen with a countdown on it. Twenty minutes until the movie started. The smell of popcorn and cotton candy filled my nose as I watched kids bundled up in giant coats sitting in the snow, playing beside their cars.

I pulled my jacket around myself tighter; thankful I'd put on layers and had decidedly not gone with the ugly sky-blue sweater.

"I'll grab a heater when we get parked," Cooper said, as though he could read my mind.

I nodded. "Sounds good. I can pay for it since you got the tickets."

He shook his head and backed into the next available spot so the trunk faced the screen. We parked beside a silver Toyota Camry with an older couple sitting in their lawn chairs, heated blankets plugged in and sprawled across their laps.

"Nuh-uh-uh. That's not a part of this deal."

My fingers unbuckled the seat belt when he put the vehicle in park. "Well, I'll find some kind of way to repay you..." Eventually. I wasn't willing to say it aloud, but part of my worries in all of this was how I would afford whatever not-date he planned. I wasn't broke by any means. It was just that I had every penny accounted for, and when some five-hundred-dollar expense got thrown my way, it knocked me off my feet a bit.

He shook his head and unbuckled his seat belt too. "Try all you want, Madeline. You'll find cash in your mailbox the next day."

"That sounds like a threat," I joked.

"It's a promise. I got you into this, so it's only right." He grabbed his keys and turned the car off. "Plus, you've got enough to worry about with the kids and all."

I winced at that. Maybe it was ridiculous of me, but I hated how much that bothered me. That whole oh, you poor single mom thing. The pity-pouts at the grocery store when strangers asked, "Where's dad?" When I had the strong urge to strictly answer with "he's dead. Thanks for asking" just to humble them a bit. I hated the pity. The sympathy. As if me taking care of two of the most wonderful people in this world was such a burden.

Cooper paused with his door halfway open and pointed to me. "Don't take it like that."

"Like what?"

"Like I feel sorry for you or something." My breath hitched in my throat. "You scrunch your nose every time something offends you or upset you. You know that?"

My fingers instinctively reached for my nose, as if to force it to stop.

"I didn't mean it in an oh, poor you way. I meant it in a you have a lot on your plate and I'm glad I have a way I can help without overstepping way. That's all."

A slow, small grin pulled at my lips, and I dipped my chin. "Good."

He nodded. "All right, now let's get you fed."

We walked down the pathway to the concessions, two tiny buildings across from each other, one with pizza signs and one with hot dogs.

"You know the rules. It's up to you." He stuck a hand out, as if to say after you, and I followed in consideration.

"Hmm. Pizza."

He nodded. "Excellent choice. Noted." Cooper pulled out his phone and typed a bit before putting it right back in his pocket. I pointed to it. "What was that?"

"My notes."

"Your...notes?"

He nodded. "It's for me to worry about. You mind your own business."

I hummed in amusement and walked over to the pizza concessions. We stood in a long line filled with families young and old, waiting for our turn.

"How do you like your pizza?" he asked.

I shrugged. "Doesn't matter. I eat pretty much everything."

He scowled at me, but there was amusement behind it. Like he was fighting a smile. He was smowling. "Madeline."

"Fine, pepperoni."

Cooper nodded, typed a bit more on his phone, and then put it away. I imagined him typing a note.

Not-date #1: all too boring, Madeline has no personality. 0/10 do not recommend.

In which he would be all too right.

The young couple at the front of the line turned from the window to order, giving us a better glimpse of them. That was when I froze entirely.

"Did I tell you what Mini Coop called me this week?" Cooper asked. But I was entirely solid, unable to move. Unable to react. A statue. A dried-out clay model called Surprise stuck on display.

Short blond hair, stocky build, large muscles, with a baby on his hip and a Henry Plumbing logo on his back. A petite long-haired brunette by his side with a Barbie-shaped figure, smiling up at him.

I couldn't breathe. I couldn't think.

"Madeline? Did you hear me?" Somewhere in the distance, Cooper was speaking. Wherever he was, I wasn't there with him.

I watched as he leaned down to plant a kiss on a tiny blond head of hair. The baby leaned into his touch. I was going to be sick.

"Madeline?" A hand grasped my arm. Cooper. "You okay?"

No. No, no, no.

The couple grabbed the dinner they ordered, a diaper bag slung on the woman's back, and that all too cute baby on his hip while they gathered their things. They were going to see us. Oh my God. He was going to see me.

That was when my body leapt into action. "We need to go." I spoke low and fast.

Two hands fell to my shoulders, and Cooper stared at me. My eyes were still stuck to the front of the line. "Madeline, tell me what's wrong. Do you have low blood sugar or something? I have glucose tabs in my car."

I shook my head. "My ex is here. I-I can't—" I reached up to my chest, like I could rip it open and will myself to breathe in that way.

"Which one?" he asked, scanning the line in front of us.

I shook my head again.

"Which one, Madeline?" Cooper insisted, and I lifted a shaky hand.

"In the front. With the baby."

He turned to him and started to walk. "No—" I grabbed his wrist, catching him. "Please, he can't see me. I can't see him. Cooper, I'm begging you. I'm—" scared. Absolutely terrified that someone I put so much of myself into, who up and vanished in an instant, was going to turn around and see the shell of a person I was now. How empty I was. How...bland.

"Madeline." He stared at me with this look I couldn't read. And I wondered just how much fear he could see in my eyes. I looked back at them. At him and his beautiful wife and perfect baby, all turning our way. Cooper caught my stare and turned right back. "*CanIkissyou?*" he rushed out, squishing it all into one word.

"Yes," I said before thinking. I meant to say what? but apparently, this whole fast-paced decision-making nonsense had my brain in a whirl.

And before I could react, his lips were on mine.

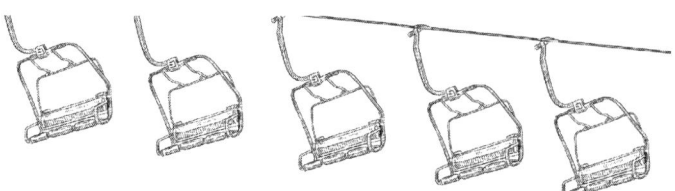

Chapter Sixteen
COOPER

S he was scared. That was why I'd done it.

Or at least that was what I told myself. But I knew in the back of my mind, in the same spot that held all those painful memories and secrets, that I'd done it for me too. That I'd set my hands on either side of her jaw, taken one look at those quivering pink lips, and leaned in without hesitation all for my own selfish reasons.

I expected her to pull back. A quick peck to the lips, and it would be done. Over and forgotten by tomorrow. A favor to a friend. That was all.

I was wrong. So incredibly wrong.

Madeline was sweet. I'd known it when I met her—or, I guess, the first time I remembered meeting her—and I'd known it even more solidly when I'd heard that those two kids weren't even hers, and yet, she'd taken them in as such. She had a big heart. A kind one. And maybe she didn't know how to describe herself, but I did. I did enough for the both of us.

Madeline Sage was sunshine itself. Not the kind of sunshine where, if you stood out of the shade for five minutes, you would have a sunburn. And certainly not the kind of sunshine that hid behind clouds and barely peeked out. She was the form of sunshine that showed up right after a bad rainstorm. The sun that made rainbows appear and made you look around and think there were a whole lot of good things in this life. Especially after you'd experienced all the bad ones.

I knew all of that, and yet, kissing her was anything but sweet.

Her lips molded against mine, the fullness resting in the curves of mine. Like two pieces of pottery perfectly pressed to fit together. I sighed into her mouth when her hands rested on my chest. She sighed right back when my hands on her jaw dropped to her waist and slipped down to the curve of her hips. My pinky slipped under her sweater and below her waistband, riding there. Gliding up and down until I felt goose bumps raise on her.

I opened my mouth, maybe to speak, maybe not. Maybe to tell her hey, pretty sure he's gone now. But either way, she took it as an opportunity to open her mouth too, slipping the tip of her tongue against mine. Mint from gum and vanilla from that ChapStick she'd anxiously applied the whole way here tangled between us. I wondered if there was some way to bottle this up. I was desperate for it, for her. For more.

So I kissed her, and kissed her, and kissed her some more.

I kissed her until we were nothing but tongues and lips and teeth. Her hands shifted to my shoulders, pulling me closer. I slipped my hands into her back pockets and squeezed. She gasped against me, like the sweet Madeline she was, so soft and gentle. I leaned in farther.

Was kissing always this way? Kissing. I wanted to laugh. What a trivial way to explain what we were doing now. Either way, I knew there was no way it had been like this before. All those times before felt like practice for this moment. Just for her. I could blame the relentless pounding of my heart on my abstinence, sure. It would be easy to chalk this moment up to a well, I haven't been with a woman in over a year branded excuse. But I knew this was entirely unrelated. This was me with something, someone, so good that it felt like the universe was rewarding me.

Somewhere back in the galaxy where we stood in line for pizza, I heard a few throats clearing. And I thought one mom told her kids to cover their eyes. But that was on Planet Earth, and I was nowhere near there.

A shiver rippled up my spine when I felt her hips wiggle against mine, lighting me up in ways I didn't know were possible. I considered it then, throwing a sweet Madeline over my shoulder, tossing her into my car—safely buckling her in, of course—and jetting us off to anywhere but here. But then she hummed against me in the prettiest moan, and I honestly thought no wonder the lady taking the tickets was so crass. This old field had some kind of erotic potion in its soil, and it was poking up through the grass and snow, right into my bloodstream.

"Excuse us." The guy behind us shuffled around us, moving closer to the pizza line. I probably should have stopped. But she didn't either.

A moment later—or maybe an eternity later, who could say, really?—a light flashed in our eyes, and a loud, thunderous voice spoke near us.

I pulled back to see a security guard, a stocky guy dressed in all black, with a badge swaying from side to side over his heart. I squinted at the badge. Gerald Simpson.

"This is a family establishment."

Yeah, Gerald, I wanted to reply. I almost made a family right here on this field.

Madeline spoke for me, clearing her throat. "So sorry. We will leave." She eyed me, holding in a laugh it seemed, and walked right past the line of people staring at us. She didn't once glance back to see if her ex and his wife were watching either. I was far too proud of that.

When we got back to the car, neither of us said a word. We stared down at the old couple in their blankets, sleeping and holding each other's hands, and then I think it hit us both. We slipped into my vehicle and I started the engine.

Madeline mumbled out a whisper. "We're horrible people."

"Downright vile."

"The lowest part of society."

"Right next to the two-lane drive-thrus."

She looked over at me as my hand gripped the seat belt, pulling it halfway over my body and then pausing. We made eye contact. A silent beat passed, then we both started laughing. I threw my head back against the seat, letting go of the seat belt and cackling.

Madeline's shoulders shook when she dropped her face to her hands, laughing with me. "So embarrassing."

My head shook from side to side, still laughing. "No, it was amazing."

"Do you think he realized it was me?"

I had forgotten about him for a second. My ex. That was all she said, but between those two words and the glimpse of fear in her eyes, it was all I needed to know.

"I'm not sure. If he stared really closely, then maybe. I guess it depends on when you saw him last..." I left that last part open-ended. An invitation for her to share more, though she could easily decline too.

She looked up from her hands, her previous smile slowly falling as she leaned back in the seat. "It's been a couple years."

"Oh? Have you...changed much since then?"

"Yes." A humorless laugh poured out of her lips. "I've changed everything and nothing at the same time."

I took that as my sign not to push any further. I could be reasonable when the situation called for it, even if I was desperate for more information. And just because I didn't push for answers tonight didn't mean I wasn't going to later.

"Hey, Madeline?" I asked.

"Yeah?"

"Do you remember the things we don't like game?"

She snorted. "Yeah."

"Well, I really, really don't like your ex."

Her laugh came back at that, a loud crack that fizzled out into a sigh. "Yeah, me neither. Sorry if I ruined the whole not-date thing. What other plans did you have?"

I hummed. Originally, my goal was to force her to keep making decisions so she would realize she was capable of finding herself, even if it wasn't in the way she expected. After we watched the movie, I planned to see if she wanted dessert, extend this night as long as possible and take notes of every little thing she did until I had my own full assessment. But now I knew any kind of whimsical surprises I had up my sleeve were going to be severely disappointing in comparison to defiling each other in the pizza line.

"Well," I started. "I was thinking we could sit in back and watch the movie." The one that had started when neither of us was paying attention to anything other than our mouths. "Or we could sit here and I can learn more about you. You know, for research purposes."

She smiled at that, a soft, slow one that felt reserved just for me. "Let's do that, then."

I smiled back. One only for her.

Chapter Seventeen
Madeline

Cooper: whats your email

Last night was...unexpected to say the least. I'd come home from the drive-in on shaky legs, with a fluttered heartbeat. I'd zombie walked down the hallway and straight to my room, flopping on the bed face down.

Maybe it was because I hadn't gone out alone with a guy in a long time, or maybe it was just because Cooper had that natural magnetism. Whatever it was, it had me laid out on my bed like a starfish, replaying the night until I fell asleep, dreaming of first kisses, apple cider, and cold winter nights on heated car seats.

After we'd agreed to stay at the theater, decidedly ignoring the film behind us, I learned more about Cooper than I ever thought possible. I learned more about myself than I thought possible.

I learned that he was closer to his grandfather than anyone else in the world. That they used to go skiing together. That Cooper never had to slow down for him. Even in his eighties, the guy could always keep up. I learned that his mom was a nurse before she had him, and that his dad wasn't in the picture—didn't get many details there. I also found out that he hates mayonnaise (What's the point of it? Also, did you know there's raw egg in that shit?), and that he thinks Oreos should only be eaten if taken apart and devoured in two separate pieces.

We played that game until it turned into less of a game and more like two people talking. Sharing things that I never knew I wanted to share. We didn't get super deep. We tiptoed around his dad's absence and my brother's death, understanding the topics were off-limits. But we talked about our favorite movies and food and desserts, and all the things we loved in life.

I asked him what Charlie was like during lessons. Cooper informed me that he was the star of the show. He was quiet when he needed to be, but when Coop wasn't teaching, he was off making friends and showing off. "He's extremely talented," he said over and over again. Telling me of mute grabs and "bonks," which I didn't really understand but which sounded cool. I was happy to celebrate for the kid.

Cooper asked about Piper too, calling her Half-Pint. It was really cute. I told him about her current Slim Jim phase, and how I know every line of Pocahontas start to finish. I also shared that I was pretty sure I had a growing crush on Kocoum, and why in the world did she choose the ugly white guy who, spoiler alert, abandons her in the sequel anyway?

We stayed like that until the lot full of cars emptied and we had to leave.

Truth be told, my favorite part of it was when I crawled into bed, because I thought to myself I have a new friend. A friend who'd kissed me like we were about to take things to the floor, but a friend, nevertheless. Something that felt impossible for me to make these days.

Then, this morning, I'd just finished getting ready to get the kids when I saw a text from him, asking for my email address. That only made my curiosity grow further.

Me: Why?

Cooper: consider it another surprise

I sent him my email address before walking over to the Keurig and setting in a new pod. I turned to the clock on the oven. It was 7:36 am. I still had time to grab the kids and take them to the resort for Charlie's class at nine, and then Piper could hang out with me while I clocked in for my shift. One thing I hadn't considered in this arrangement was that if I asked my parents to watch the kids once a week, chances were I wouldn't get them to babysit any other time. It didn't exactly make a difference, though. Neither kid seemed to mind hanging out with me at work. Charlie would usually be on the Switch, and there were enough TVs in the place that I could easily entertain Pipes.

I reached for my pastel pink mug with the kids' handprints painted on it—something I forced them to do in the summer when I was absolutely sick of being stuck in the house and signed us up for pottery classes. Just then, my laptop chimed on the counter, signaling that I had a new email. I bit my lip to catch a smile.

Mug in hand, I sat in front of it and opened a new email from skiingtothegraves@gmail.com. My eyes rolled a little at that, but still, my excitement was there when I opened it.

Madeline,

Last night was great. I'm looking forward to repeating a similar transaction next Friday. Please scroll to see the attached full evaluation.

PS Next time, there will be more than just apple cider and hot pretzels involved.

All the best,

Cooper Graves

My fingers rushed to open the attached document, a PDF file with Madeline Sage's Personality Evaluation in striking bold font. Just below it, in a smaller size, read Completed by personality professional and expert kisser, Cooper Graves. I snorted at that and then let my eyes fall down to the rest of the PDF.

For the series of multiple-choice questions, here is what we were able to find for Ms. Sage.

Musical choice: Early 2000s playlist. Consisted of Jesse McCartney and some Maroon 5. Took note of some particular foot tapping at "Hey, Soul Sister" by Train.

Film choice: When choosing between Grown Ups and Shawshank Redemption, Madeline chose Grown Ups. Maybe surprising to some, but I know she has quite the twisted sense of humor behind that polite smile.

Food choice: Pizza or hotdogs? She chose pizza. Nothing too shocking there, but what kind of pizza did she prefer? Pepperoni. I am aware that our test subject may consider this choice to be "boring," but little did she know it was one of the final things I needed in this evaluation.

Last, and, believe me, certainly not least, the kiss. This was a surprising factor on all counts. Still wondering how I pulled that off, but it was what topped off the assessment. A.k.a. sexy and somehow adorable.

Overall evaluation for not-date one: Madeline Sage is everything, and yet nothing, she appears to be. Madeline enjoys a stroll down memory lane. She is nostalgic from time to time. She has an excellent sense of humor and loves the chance to laugh. *Note to self: the chortle laugh is my favorite.* She is a fan of the classics. What she considered boring or dull, I noted, was simply archetypal Madeline. *Another note to self: google that word to make sure it means what I think it means.* She was a classic, herself. Like an incredible vanilla milkshake that'll rock you to your core or a vintage song that makes you feel like dancing in the kitchen late at night. She hides what a kisser she is behind those kind eyes, little minx. Honorable mention: She has an ex that I would love to have five minutes outside with.

OVERALL: Madeline is the highest level of intriguing, and I am looking forward to my next assessment.

PS Also has an excellent backside.

Scientific peace out,

Coop

I couldn't make it halfway through without busting out laughing alone in my kitchen. I took pictures of my screen, as if I would ever delete this email, and read it two more times. Classic. He was so stupidly charming, it honestly kind of annoyed me. No wonder he'd lived the life he had, with the experience he had. That amount of flirtation in one body was explosive. He needed a warning sign as much as I needed a security system that would alert me when my heart started beating a little too fast at the thought of him.

My life was too complicated for a relationship. I drilled that into my mind again as I walked to my car and sent a quick text to Cooper.

Me: That was entirely unnecessary but greatly appreciated. I'll see you at nine.

His reply came instantly.

Cooper: absolutely necessary but glad you appreciated it see you guys soon

I smiled at that and set my phone in the empty cupholder. See? Friends. That was all. Simple, easy, no-strings friendship with a man who kissed like it was his job.

When I pulled up to my parents' house, a tiny light-blue cottage with white shutters and award-deserving landscaping, Piper's face was glued to the window. Her mouth was partially open, sticky fingers pressed to the glass and eyes squinting. Trying to see who I was, like the strangest little guard dog. Until I opened my door, waving an enthusiastic hello at her. Then she popped up like an eager meerkat and let out a squeal that I could hear from outside. "MayMay!"

Piper jiggled the locked knob, shrieking random syllables she liked to squish together until my mom came up behind her and opened the door. Tiny, fuzzy sock–covered feet came barreling out into the snow right toward me. I couldn't even complain about it because every day this kid greeted me like I was coming home to a golden retriever with the zoomies, running circles around me and jumping up my legs.

I bent down, wrapping two arms around her body and lifting her to my hip. "Look at you!" I stuck a hand out and waved it above her head in a flat line. "Did you get taller since yesterday?"

Piper nodded before reaching toward the door again and letting her body go limp in my arms. "Cah-lee. Cah-lee." She stretched out.

I chuckled and used her momentum to swing her back and forth as we reached the door. "Is Charlie inside?" I asked. Piper nodded with her entire body.

We popped inside, and I dusted the snow off my boots on the harsh mat. In the living room, I could hear my dad shuffling through TV stations in an attempt to find reruns of Family Feud. He liked to watch the ones he already knew the answers to and would pretend like it was the first time he'd seen it. Like some kind of genius.

My mom returned to the kitchen, humming and starting the coffee machine that she'd had—and hadn't cleaned—for the last twenty years.

I announced my arrival. "Good morning."

Mom turned to me. "Good morning. How was last night?"

The innuendo in her voice made my cheeks color. How obvious was I? "Good," I said, keeping it short and sweet.

Mom hummed again, going back to her song. I looked around the kitchen and dining room for Charlie but found both to be empty. Mostly empty, anyway. My parents were "collectors." Borderline hoarders was more like it. Everything held value to them, and they proudly displayed all things around their house.

Except for pictures of Will and Savannah.

It was like once he passed, Mom didn't even want to pretend he existed. Last month, I tried to say we should do a two-year memorial dinner, and you would have thought that the ghost of my brother himself had burst into the room. Both of my parents turned as white as a sheet and quickly changed the subject to their upcoming medical appointments.

At first, I understood. The first week, month, even three months, I let them keep the silence. Let them sit in their bunker of a house and pretend nothing was wrong. Everybody grieves differently, I told myself. It's not personal. I said that for the first year. But now we were just over two years since that terrible night, and still, neither of them so much as whispered his name.

I bounced Piper on my hip, a reminder of who I'd dedicated my life to. These two kids who Will had specifically left for me. I didn't need outside validation. And I would repeat it until it was true.

"Where were you last night?" Charlie strolled in with a tiny purple line under his eye. He glared at me with crossed arms.

"With a friend." That felt a lot more honest this time around.

"What time did you get home?"

"What time did you get off the Switch and go to sleep?" I countered.

He backed up a bit and frowned. "Hmm."

"That's what I thought." I took a step with Piper and reached one hand down to mess up his hair. "Go get your bags. We gotta see Mr. Cooper today." And I had to try my best to seem entirely normal in the process.

Charlie perked up at that, then raced to the guest room he'd claimed as his own.

"When do you plan on telling him?" Mom asked around the corner. I couldn't see her face, but I could imagine it. The wince there, the flinch she always seemed to have in her eyes when she looked at me. It made me wonder how much of my brother she saw in me.

We didn't look alike. Not at all, really. I had long brown hair with hazel highlights, whereas Will had my dad's short blond hair and green eyes. He had a strong Greek nose—also from my dad—and thicker eyebrows. But for my whole life, I looked up to Will. Anything he did, I did too. Which was why I played soccer three years in a row, even though I hated it. Or why I followed him and his friends to the skate park when it actually scared me. I considered anything Will did to be the best thing in the world.

"Uh," I hesitated. "Not for a while."

Her sigh wasn't held back and had some weight to it. "I am glad you are out there again. You need a man in your life." I rolled my eyes, and she corrected herself quickly, as if she could see me through the wall. "For the children's sake. S'not good for them to have no father figure."

"Dad is a father figure."

"No, he is their grandfather. It's different," she specified, and that was when I turned back around to the kitchen.

I was caught between a rock and a hard place here. Stuck on either end. If I told Charlie this elaborate lie, it would get his hopes up far too high. He loved Cooper, and, unfortunately for him, he had my sensitive heart. If I never told him, it would send red flags to my mom that something was off.

I was just going to have to wait until Cooper and I "broke up" for mutual reasons, then tell my mom we were just friends. That I was "too heartbroken" to be set up with anyone else. That alone ought to buy me a few months before I had numbers thrown my way again.

"How much money does he make?"

"Mom!" I hissed and lowered my voice. "I do not know, but I guarantee it doesn't matter."

"It does matter if it's a serious relationship. You can't raise the kids on your sole income forever."

I reminded her, "It wouldn't be forever. I graduate next spring."

She stayed silent after that. I wasn't sure why, exactly, but I had this feeling that my mom assumed I was never going to get a job after graduation. She would never say it out loud, but anytime I mentioned how there were tons of local hospitals hiring, I saw her eye my dad and look away without an answer. We sat in uncomfortable silence until Charlie came barreling in with his boots halfway on.

"Ready." He handed me Piper's diaper bag, and I grabbed it with a smile. "Thanks, bud."

The three of us said a quick goodbye to my mom, put on our shoes, and left.

When I dropped Charlie off at lessons and watched Cooper give him a bright smile and a quick high five, my heart leapt. And when Cooper looked over at me holding Piper, that sweet gaze darkened ever so slightly before turning back to normal. I drank him in from head to toe in that all-black skiing outfit and a badge dangling from his neck covered in stickers from the kids.

"Madeline." He dipped his chin at me in a hello and scrunched his nose at the girl on my hip. "Half-Pint."

Piper glared at him, no surprise there, and we watched him walk back to the group of kids. It took me a while to finally force myself back inside.

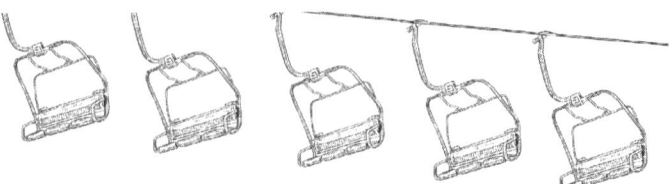

Chapter Eighteen
COOPER

When my Saturday morning lessons were finished up, I slumped against the bench behind me. Sweat dripped from my forehead onto my goggles as I lifted them up. It was barely over twenty degrees today, but my morning class usually kept me on my toes and required a good bit of moving around. Plus, I hadn't gone down any slopes solo in almost a week, so I made a couple of trips before the class began.

Today's lessons were supposed to be on grabbing the skis in the air, focusing more on consistency than perfection. Nailing each step of the process before moving to the next was imperative. Lifting a ski even a fraction too far one way or the other may not have seemed like a huge deal, but it could throw off the entire move and land you on your face in an instant. That being said, it was a lot of me repeating the same skill over and over again, using one muscle group in my legs until they were sore and tired, a dull and hot ache forming in my thighs.

"Water?"

I turned to see Mini Coop, not a drop of sweat on him, bouncing on his skis and holding out a black refillable water bottle to me.

I snorted and lifted my own, a bigger version of his. "Nah. Thanks, man." He smiled at that and sat next to me, watching the others practicing while they waited on their parents.

Something I noted early into these lessons was that these kids were just tiny versions of us. Tiny, uncorrupted humans who wanted to feel like they were bigger than they were. So I never talked down to them or treated them like they were babies—except for a couple of actual babies in a toddler class I held once. There was a lot of cheek pinching and baby talk from Finn and me both. They ended up hiring a woman for that position the following season. Apparently we didn't focus enough to actually get anything done. My grandfather told us we needed to zero in on work, to which I replied, have you ever seen a two-year-old try to ski?

Point being, I treated every kid like they were the same as me or any other respected adult in this place. And I thought it made them love me even more.

"Is your—" I almost said mom and had to catch myself. "Is Madeline coming to get you today?"

I kept my eyes on the rest of the kids while Mini Coop answered. "Nah, she's working this morning, so I'll probably just meet her in the lobby or something."

Instantly, a light bulb screwed itself into my brain, and I started talking before I could think. "Want me to walk you there?"

He was silent for a minute, and I looked down to see that his vision was glued to the hills in front of us. Specifically, it was glued to Faith, a sweet nine-year-old girl who'd been in my classes since the minute she turned four. Right now, she was struggling to nail control of the skis in her pink zip-up ski outfit. She was mostly quiet and kept to herself, but according to her parents, she was wild at home.

I looked back to Mini Coop. His lips were pulling at the edges, eyes never lifting. "You hear me?" I asked, but still, his eyes stayed glued.

Faith looked to the nine-year-old next to me and waved a gloved hand to us. I waved back. Mini Coop sat there. My elbow bumped into his side, and he looked up at me, confused.

Wave, I mouthed and lifted his hand up discreetly.

"Oh." He moved his hand and gave her a smile.

I watched as the two of them sat there, just waving for an absurd amount of time before I turned to him. "You can stop now."

Mini Coop dropped his hands but still watched as Faith staggered down the second half of the slope by herself. She was hesitant at first, looking down the hill and then to the people beside her. But she eventually tucked her blond braided pigtails into her ski mask and took it on her own.

"You like her?" I asked the nine-year-old beside me.

He practically jumped off the bunch. "What? No. Gross. We're just friends."

I snorted. "Do you stare at all of your friends?"

"No." He groaned in defense. "Stop. She's not even pretty. And I like girls with brown hair, anyway."

"Yeah, me too, bud." A picture of his aunt immediately came to mind. All wide hips and soft skin, freckles and the tiniest half dimple when she fully smiled. "But you know it's okay if you did like her."

The tips of his ears turned red as he squinted out at the snow. "I know that."

Faith approached the bottom of the hill, then she looked my way—or maybe at the short kid next to me—for approval. I clapped and attempted a thumbs-up, but these gloves were thick, so it probably looked like I'd raised a threatening fist her way.

Mini Coop stayed still, pretending like he hadn't been watching her. I elbowed him. "You should go say something."

He scoffed. "Like what?"

"I dunno. Tell her she did a good job, or maybe give her some tips."

I unzipped my bag to dig out another Clif Bar and tried to open it, but the gloves I really didn't feel like taking off got in the way.

We both stayed quiet for a while, the only sounds the distant talking of other students mixed with Christmas music playing toward the lodge. Occasionally someone would walk by, their boots or skis crunching the packed snow below their feet.

I got halfway through my bar when I heard Mini Coop's stomach growling beside me. It was reminiscent of a cat dying. Madeline said something last night about how much food the kid could put away. That she felt like her whole paycheck went to groceries because he snacked like it was nobody's business, despite being a scrawny little thing. I used to be the same way. I could pack away processed food all day long and not gain a pound, no matter how hard I tried. Now, I had one sleeve of

Little Debbie's, and I was looking more like a fluffy dad bod than a tight, toned washboard-abs guy. I guessed age did that to you.

I looked down at the second half of my bar and unwrapped it entirely, handing it over to him.

Mini Coop—maybe I should start thinking of his real name eventually—eyed it before grabbing the bar and taking a large bite.

We were silent as he ate. Only when he got to the very end of the bar did he speak up. "What would you say to her?"

"To who?" I asked.

"A girl." There went his pink ears again. "If you did like one. What do you say?"

It occurred to me then that this kid probably had no one to ask questions like this. Wasn't like he was gonna go to his aunt for girl advice, and I doubted his grandfather had much to say on the matter either. If he was anything like me, fatherless and relying on a mom/aunt for everything, his best friend for this stuff was probably Google. Or maybe other nine-year-olds, but I could guarantee they had no clue what they were talking about. Looking on Wikihow for tips on picking up girls didn't get me too far when I was a kid. It took way too much trial and error and a whole lot of rejections. Only advice Mom gave me was to have a big heart and be kind.

I hummed, trying to think of my best route here. "I would start small. Don't just go telling her you like her—"

"I don't like her."

"Just start complimenting her here and there. Maybe say you like her hair one day or her skiing or something."

"But then what?"

I sucked in a breath through my teeth, the cold air harsh against my gums. "Then, maybe when she's struggling, you could offer to help. Hold her hand or something. Just take it slow."

I was one to talk. The irony was not lost on me that I was telling my tiny friend to go slow when I had been hitting on his aunt just about every moment since she picked him up that day.

Mini Coop nodded. "Okay, then what?"

I understood curiosity, but he was still a kid, and I wasn't about to tell him to kiss the girl or anything. "Uh, just start there. See how you both do and go from there. You're young. You'll figure it out. You've got all the time in the world."

Jake's parents walked by us, grabbing his bags and waving. Mini Coop and I waved as Jake took off with them. Then another parent grabbed their kids, and another one. Leaving only us and Faith. She was at the bottom of the hill, a bit of a distance from us but close enough for us to see. She adjusted her skis so they popped off and walked over here. "Have you seen my mom yet, Mr. Cooper?"

"Nope." I popped the P and looked down at Mini Coop. He was staring toward the ski lift, the pink in his ears now turning bright red. "But let me go check around the exit. Sometimes parents don't see the signs. Faith, you can sit here."

She smiled at me, all crooked teeth and innocence. I didn't think of myself as a matchmaker, but they fit together pretty well. I grabbed my bag and began to walk away for a moment. But as I turned, a deep voice said, "Faith, you ready?"

Pig-tailed, pink-colored Faith stood and faced her dad in the distance. "Coming!" she shouted before turning to Mini Coop and me. "I'll see you guys next week."

We both said goodbye, or I did. Mini Coop just lazily lifted a hand and shrugged.

When she walked off, he turned to me, grabbing his things too. "That wasn't obvious."

I shrugged. "Can't blame a guy for trying."

I checked the time and realized I had over an hour before my next class, so I packed all the things I didn't want to leave outside for that long, which was pretty much everything except the flags and cones. When we were ready, Mini Coop and I took off to the resort, our feet pushing against the snow. The walk was one I took every day, but still, I never got sick of it. The sounds of laughter and skis cutting through packed snow. The tourists talking at the lift. The closer you got to the lodge, the more you felt the warmth radiating off the heaters outside by the patios.

We got to the lobby doors and dusted our boots off on the wire mat before stepping into the large room warmed by the thirty-foot gas-log fireplace to the left of the entrance. Immediately, a nostalgic wave hit me. I never got used to this place. It felt so comfortable, and yet new every single day. The scent of spiced apple cider brewing, the fresh baked goods from the café, and the slight hint of pine from outside wafting its way through. Bing Crosby's low, smooth voice crooned "I'll Be Home For Christmas" through the surround sound, and families, couples, and employees all spoke low and soft, conversations humming. It didn't matter to the workers here that it was only a week into

November. To them, Christmas started at 11:59:59 on October thirty-first.

When I was a kid, it kind of felt like Disneyland. How we would come here to trick-or-treat on Halloween night, the place covered in jack-o'-lanterns, with skeletons in ski gear hanging from the ceiling and all of the employees decked out in their costumes. Then, the very next morning, Mom would bring me up here for the sunrise opening. It felt like magic, coming in to see all hints of the previous holiday replaced by giant nut-crackers lining the walls, tiny villages with fake snow in every crevice, lights strung about, and a giant Christmas tree covered in colored lights and coordinated ornaments. Where love light poured out around us, and the skiing season truly began.

It still felt like that. Like pure magic. Maybe with a little less wonder. That and my imagination no longer pictured tiny elves jumping around the place, decorating it at midnight, but still, it was magical.

Mini Coop took a big breath through his nose, like he was trying to savor it too. "It always smells so good in here."

I copied him and savored the scent of clove, cinnamon, and pine. "Mmm, it does." I looked around us for a tall brunette or a sage-green cleaning cart but came up empty. "You know where Madeline is working this morning?"

He shrugged. "She's probably done in here by now. She usu-ally goes to the sitting room last so she can stare out the win-dows."

"Really?"

"Yeah, she likes watching people ski, I think. Or the moun-tains or something. She always sits there for like an hour."

I smiled at that. I'd always loved that room too. The lobby view was mostly of the mountains to the side, but as gorgeous as it was, the sitting room showed all the people. People on lifts, families gliding down the hill, young couples on first dates, holding hands and walking along the snowy trails. It was where I felt most at home. Plus there was always a candy bowl with butterscotch in there, and I always had a longing for old lady candy.

"Let's check there," I said, putting a hand on Mini Coop's shoulder and guiding him through the tourists. I was relieved that today seemed a little busier. The competition was coming in only a couple of months, and it was probably mostly due to people gathering to practice on the slopes. Still, it gave me some comfort.

We turned down the hall, passing the office, where there were rows of desks and computers for anyone who needed them. It was on the far left, along with a few of the employees-only rooms and the sitting room that faced the mountains. Before we turned the corner to the room, I heard faint humming and the distant noise of a movie being played.

The kid beside me walked right in as I took in the view of the room.

Cleaning supply cart pushed to the side, the dark hardwoods sparkling, and the cobblestone fireplace blazing. Madeline sat on the floor, facing the windows. With a blond toddler in her lap, chewing on a snack, Madeline hummed along to the song playing on the TV mounted above the fireplace. Some kind of vintage Disney movie that I didn't recognize.

She hadn't noticed we were here yet. She remained rocking Half-Pint from side to side while she sang softly to her and watched the view of snow trickling down and people laughing. Even as Mini Coop threw his bag on the brown leather couch against the far wall, she didn't flinch. Just kept her eyes on the view outside. Madeline was entirely unaware of how captivating she was.

"Hey, May," the kid said.

She jumped a little and looked back, relieved when she saw him and then curious when she saw me. That was when I noticed I was leaning my entire weight onto the doorframe, mouth slightly ajar, as if I didn't have enough willpower to force myself to stand correctly.

"Hi, bud. How was practice?"

He moved to sit beside her. "Good, got some snowplows nailed."

Madeline nodded at him and held out a hand that he smacked in a high five. "No idea what that is, but it sounds cool."

He nodded back, looking to the crisp mountains outside. "It was."

Madeline turned from him to face me then, smiling with that half grin and that hint of a dimple coming out to play. My heart raced. I watched as she lifted a hand from the tiny girl's back and patted the ground next to her twice in invitation. I bit my lip and grinned right back. The mountain view was worth a pretty penny in Aspen. But what I was watching—those freckles on Madeline's cheeks as she smiled with her eyebrows raised—felt priceless. How could you stick a price tag on something like that?

I took the invitation and set my backpack on the couch next to Mini Coop's before settling down on the floor beside them.

"Seems busy today," Madeline noted.

I took the silence from the tiny two as my cue to answer. "Everyone's practicing for the competition coming up."

"Oh, makes sense. It was pretty big last year."

Thank God. It, plus this magazine deal, was what I was riding on, hoping it would bring in enough people during the off seasons.

"Yeah, it always does well, thankfully." I leaned forward and looked past Madeline to the boy on her other side. "Speaking of, when are you gonna start private lessons?"

His eyes widened and he shook his head ever so slightly. His lips curled in, like he was making the universal sign of shut up, shut up, shut up. I lifted a brow at him in question.

Madeline looked to him, and his facial expression relaxed into a casual one. "Private lessons?"

Mini Coop shrugged. "I dunno."

"Are...you not signing up anymore?" I asked him, not sure what would be considered stepping on toes here. But when his aunt turned to me in confusion and he glared at me behind her, I knew I'd screwed up.

Madeline leaned back. "You're doing the ski competition?" Her voice was full of surprise and a touch of enthusiasm.

"I...no..." He trailed off.

I leaned in at that, Madeline and I both staring. "What?"

His cheeks turning pink. It was the first time I'd ever seen the kid look nervous. He was scared for no reason. "Bud, I told you

I'd give you private lessons. You're really good. I promise you could get at least top five in your division."

He shook his head. "I...not that." He eyed Madeline warily. "There's a hundred dollar sign-up fee."

Madeline's back straightened. It felt like all of the nice, calming energy in the room was sucked out by a vacuum. She shook her head at him. "Charlie, why didn't you just tell me?"

"Gram said—"

"Never mind Gram." She cleared her throat and took a lighter tone. "She's still in the olden days, bud. She thinks housekeepers like me work for like half a cranberry an hour."

Charlie and I both snorted at that, and she continued. "Don't you ever worry about money. We're doing just fine, okay? Please sign up. I want to come watch," she begged him.

Mini Coop looked at me, raising a brow, and I nodded. "Lessons are still on, all right?"

He looked back and forth at our encouraging faces and nodded at us. "Okay. If you say so, May."

Madeline pulled the toddler from her lap and set her down before standing up. "Go grab your bags, all right? I have two more rooms, and then we can go home."

I started to lean forward. "Have you taken a break yet?"

Madeline shook her head. "No, I'll just leave an hour early instead."

"Do you guys have somewhere to be?"

All three, Half-Pint included, shook their heads.

I leaned back onto both hands, looking up at Madeline towering over me. "Saturdays are free hot chocolate day at the café.

Want to go? We can watch people ski, and there's a basket of coloring books for Half-Pint."

There were no free hot chocolate days, but if I texted the lady working up front today and told her I'd come back to pay after my shift, she would probably keep quiet.

The tiny one muttered up at me. "You Half-Pi." It sounded like a threat. I smiled at that.

If I had to handpick a family to pretend was mine for just one day, I was extremely glad it was this one.

Chapter Nineteen
Madeline

Somehow, someway, Cooper and I were going to pull this whole interview thing off.

Every morning this week, whether we met in the café or he came to me before my shift, Cooper had gotten me an iced caramel macchiato and a bacon cheddar scone. In tow, he brought with him a list of questions for each of us to answer. From the mundane what brand of peanut butter do you reach for first? all the way to okay, but if aliens were real, do you think they'd know how to unlock a Tesla? We only had about fifteen minutes to spend together in the mornings, but we agreed we each had to tell one sad part of our lives to deepen the conversations that we'd previously had. When I said, "define sad," he said, and I quote, "I want to have wet eyelashes at least one day a week." So we did.

We still steered clear of my brother's death and his father's absence, which was fine by me, but we touched on other things. His first love had broken his heart right after they lost their virginity together. She ended up going out with his best friend the same night. He caught them in a hall closet at a party. I told him how sad it was that I'd only had one "love" other than family, and the guy had turned out to be a complete ass wipe. Cooper's words. Actually, what he said was "I should've made that ass wipe step outside with me so I could teach him a few things." To which I said, "We were already outside. Plus his baby was there." He responded with "good. Maybe it would teach the baby something too."

We texted periodically too. Not super often, since we both had busy lives, but when we did, it was always the perfect timing. When I was giving Piper a bath and was about to pass out from pure exhaustion. Ding.

Cooper: serious question do you think dinosaurs had feathers

Me: Serious question—did you know punctuation marks exist?

Or when I was up late the next night with Charlie, trying to help with math homework, but my eyelids were so, so heavy. Ding.

Cooper: can I pull this off

Attached was a mirror selfie of him in a local tourist boutique. One that carried mostly kitschy Aspen stuff, but occasionally had a good sale. He wore his typical jeans and snow boots with a black lodge hoodie. Sitting on his mop of brown hair was a tan cowboy hat.

Me: Is there anything you can't pull off??

Cooper: touché madeline dear

Things stayed nonchalant the entire time. We flirted here and there, both catching each other staring at times. But we knew what this was and what it couldn't be. More than anything, Cooper was a really good friend. He called to walk me through signing Charlie up for private lessons on the lodge's website, because I was "a geriatric" when it came to technology, apparently. And he called from time to time just to talk to "Mini Coop too." Every time they'd hang up, I would hear him say "tell Half-Pint I said hello to grumpy butt too." That always made Charlie and me laugh.

This morning, ten minutes before we were supposed to meet, I got a notification.

Cooper: so sorry madeline finn called in because olive's having those bracton hill contractions

Cooper: i have to cover for him this morning

Cooper: please dont hate me

Cooper: were still good for tonight right

I sighed and pushed down any thread of disappointment, reminding myself that we had lives to live. This wasn't the only thing happening for him. I was busy too. Too busy to be disappointed in something as simple as a justified excuse to miss our morning breakfasts.

Me: Totally fine. I'll see you tonight! Do you want to meet at your house or mine?

Cooper: yours

Cooper: go to cafe

Cooper: adele has your order

Cooper: not the singer

So I did just that. And sure enough, there was my order, along with a pink sprinkled strawberry doughnut sitting right beside it. The order was under Madeline, but in the notes, it said: sorry i messed this up with the cutest little frowny face on the side.

I texted him a quick thank-you while Piper and I snuck away to the lobby. We spent most of the day moving from room to room, her begrudgingly, while Charlie was at school. On Fridays, I focused more on the corners and crevices that weren't often seen, mostly dusting and wiping down blinds or near plugs and behind desks. It was the nice part about not being assigned to the staterooms. I had a more flexible schedule than anyone else in my position.

Piper kept quiet most of the time, at one point falling asleep while sitting up with a cheese puff in her mouth.

I finished up just in time to get Charlie from school, so I put all my supplies in the cleaning closet and carried Piper to the car. She screamed bloody murder the entire fifteen minutes to the school and through the car rider line, only slightly settling down when Charlie popped in beside her.

"What's wrong, sweet girl?" he cooed to his sister, hushing her a little as I pulled away. "You hungry?"

Piper's slowed cry quickly turned into an ear-piercing wail. Charlie and I both winced. "I got a Slim Jim in my purse, baby. Do you want that?" I asked quietly, but she only cried more.

The whole way home, Charlie made attempts to stop her tears. Wanna watch Elsa? Or Pokey? What about a piece of chocolate? I have crayons in my backpack. Want them? And when he started moving his hands, singing "Baby Shark." You would have thought he was stabbing her. Her screams were so loud that at a red light, the person in the car beside me looked our way to ensure no one was dying in our vehicle. I waved a hand in apology.

When we finally pulled into our driveway, I rushed out of the car to grab her.

"Shh, shh. It's all right, sweet girl." I picked her up and settled her on my chest as she pulled her legs around me and clung tight to my neck.

I reached a hand up to her forehead and winced when it was burning hot.

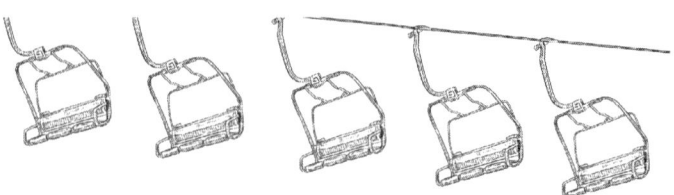

Chapter Twenty
COOPER

When I got home from work, I was still running on pure adrenaline.

With Finn being out, I had a good bit of slack to pick up and no breaks from skiing except during my older classes, where the students didn't need a ton of help anyway. By the time I was leaving, I was running on E. Until I remembered my date with Madeline tonight. Not-date, I guess. Still, I had tonight fully planned in my mind. Something fancy. A three-course meal at one of those places that never filled you up, bottomless champagne, and chocolate-covered strawberries in my car after. Appetizers with Gruyère cheese and entrées with tiny spreads of purple mash on the side of a ceramic plate. I'd break out the expensive cologne my uncle gave me last Christmas and probably put on that tie that had been wasting away since Finn's wedding. We could go back to the lodge after and go to the rooftop to look at stars or do something equally romantic that would give me all the fake boyfriend points. Maybe some music too. I'd make all of this worth it for her. I'd give her more of me; she'd give me more of her. And when I dropped her off tonight, I would try to snag one more kiss—for research purposes only.

I raced to the shower, jumping under the hot spray and taking every hygienic precaution possible, down to shaving my scruff and applying pomade. Just as I was getting dressed, my doorbell rang.

My eyebrows scrunched in confusion because:

1. I was picking Madeline up.

2. If she was here, she was an hour early.

I shrugged, assuming it was UPS dropping a package off, and ignored the ringing and went right back to getting ready.

Only then the doorbell rang furiously three times in a row, accompanied by pounding and a shrill "Cooper Graves, you answer your mom right now."

That made me snicker. Ma had this habit of showing up entirely unannounced. She liked to call them happy little surprises, but usually, they came at the worst possible times. Like when I was in the bathroom, or a couple of years ago, it seemed to always happen when I was entertaining a lady friend. She used to shout "You better be naked when I come in." We usually were. Now she knew better, though. She knew I was alone here a majority of the time. "You're all grown up," she always said now that I'd left every bit of that life behind me.

I walked to the door and opened it with wide arms. The brisk cool air fought its way in as I did. Mom walked past me and took off her coat, setting it on the couch. She stared at my getup—navy pants and a white button-down with a tie sitting loosely around my neck. She smiled a bit and shook her head, stepping over to fix it for me. Her hands reached for my neck as she undid and redid my tie correctly.

"You cleaned up for me?" she asked with this tone that I knew all too well was her way of asking her a question in different terms.

"Nope. Got a date tonight."

"Date?" She pulled back. "A real one?"

Err...no. But that situation was too complicated to explain to her. And playing pretend to one more person couldn't hurt. "Real as it gets."

"Who's the girl?" She hummed to herself and sat down, making herself at home on my tiny gray sectional.

"She works at the lodge. You probably wouldn't know her, but her kid takes lessons with me."

Ma pulled back to look at me with judging eyes. "She's a mom?"

I could have corrected her. Could have said "no, she's just an aunt." But I'd watched her with those kids enough to know, yeah, she was a mom. The way Mini Coop talked about her. The way Half-Pint stared at her like she was an angel who'd hung the moon. All other technicalities aside, those were her children.

"Yup." I combed a hand through my hair in an attempt to let this stupid pomade rest. "A great one too. Real sweet girl." Also a knockout. I didn't add that last part, 'cause I enjoyed my life and didn't want my mother to end it right there.

"Oh, Coop." I saw it in her face. The duality of being glad I was going on an actual date and the fear that I was dating a single mom too. "That's..." She trailed off, looking for the right words, and I snorted.

"It's great," I supplied. "Really, really great. You'd like her a lot."

She smiled a bit. "I'm sure I would, but I just...dating a single mom is a lot to take on, Cooper. That's why I mostly avoided it when you were little."

That and I sent death threats to anyone who tried. Mom and I were our own tight circle, one that didn't need anyone else. We had each other, so much so that I never really cared that I didn't have a dad. Other than the one instance. She devoted so much of herself to my life that anyone extra would have just ruined it for us, I think. I loved the way I'd grown up, and there was no way I'd ever change it.

That being said, I did understand where she was coming from.

"She's different, Ma. You gotta meet her to understand. The kids too. They're amazing." Well, Mini Coop was. That other little rascal left a bit to be desired, but Madeline adored her, so there had to be some good in her.

"I'm sure they're all lovely, Coop. I just worry about you raising any expectations for them and then..." She didn't have to finish her sentence. I got it.

Because there was one single instance that had broken both of us. Long ago, there was a guy in my life. A guy we both thought could be a dad for me. He played ball with me in the backyard and cooked dinner for us. Even let me sit in his lap when we went to see movies. It felt real at the time. Still kind of did here and there in certain memories. Mom and I both got attached, only for him to leave a year later. Mom never really said why, but I overheard my uncle once say he was a two-timing cheater, so that gave me enough of a clue. From then on, we understood that there would be no real father in my life. And after a while, we were okay with it. It went from an acceptance to a relief. All we had was us, but that was all we needed.

"This is not that, believe me," I defended. "I am nobody's daddy, and I promise no expectations are being set."

She nodded. "As long as she understands that too."

Madeline did, for sure. She was the one constantly turning me down. I was just along for the ride, and I was taking advantage of every moment I got with her.

Just then, my phone started buzzing on the coffee table. Madeline.

I picked it up and held up a finger to my mom, mouthing one sec.

"Hey, what's up?" I smiled to myself and tried to tamp down any excitement in my tone.

Immediately, things felt off. Madeline sounded out of breath, and there was crying in the background. "Hey." Her answer sounded more like a cry of defeat than a hello.

"What's wrong?" I started looking for my keys as the distant crying only worsened.

"It's...Pipes is sick. Really sick. Not sure exactly what she's got, but her fever has spiked and"—a hoarse cry came through—"we're a mess. But all the urgent cares that take her age are closed, and her pediatrician won't answer the dam—darn phone." She sighed. "I'm really sorry, Coop. I'll have to do another night."

I listened as she waited in silence for my answer. It sounded like a zoo had been let loose in her house between Charlie talking to Half-Pint and all the screaming. I turned to my mom, and she eyed me. What? she mouthed, and I spoke before even asking.

"My mom's a pediatric nurse, or she used to be." Ma was frantically shaking her head, but I kept going. "She came by to see me, but we could pop by and check on her for you?"

Ma had her hand raised to her throat, waving her fingers back and forth as she whispered, "Absolutely not."

I held a thumb up and mouthed please right back to her.

Madeline spoke up. "No, no. Don't do that."

"Why? We live right here."

"I know, and I won't have time to clean up the house. It's a disaster and—" I could hear water running. "I can't get her fever to come down, and I'm sweaty from running around, and poor Charlie—"

"Please just let us stop by really quick." The desperation in my voice must have been sign enough for my mom, because she slowly nodded. "We don't care about any mess or how you look," I pleaded as I listened to Half-Pint screaming in the back. "Please."

Eventually she gave up, and I dragged Mom out to my car. We sped down the road, taking two quick lefts, and pulled into Madeline's driveway. I was reaching for my keys when Mom's hand lay over my fingers.

"Coop, baby, when I said not leading them on or setting their expectations too high, this is the kind of stuff I meant."

"What stuff?" I asked in a defensive tone. "We're a block away. Her baby is screaming and crying. You used to be a nurse. And I'm supposed to just not come when she calls?"

Ma was silent. She knew I was right, but I saw her point too. She'd watched both of our hearts break when her ex left us. If anything, I should be thankful, since she was protecting Madeline. But then I thought about how ridiculous that thought was in the first place. Madeline had rejected me. Twice. Even when she'd agreed to this, it was begrudgingly. I was the one too caught up here. The one foolishly using some fake boyfriend excuse as reason to be near her. The one clinging to the fact that once this interview was over, I'd have nothing left to give or get from her.

So in my mom's silence, I said, "Believe me, if anyone is being led on, it's me."

I hated how true it was. How, just earlier that week, I'd watched all three of them in that sitting room, looking out at the snowy mountains touching the clouds. Feeling warmth spread in my chest, and not due to the lit fireplace on the opposite wall. My fingertips tingling, antsy to get closer.

I wasn't fit for fatherhood, believe me, I knew that better than anyone. But still, my expectations were far beyond my control already. All I could do was ride the wave out and see where it took us.

Ma nodded. "All right. If you say so. Let's go check on this baby really quick, and we'll leave as soon as we're done."

I didn't want to argue and say we'd stay as long as it took, so I kept quiet.

We hopped out of the car and walked to the front door. Mom stood beside me on the steps while I used the same knock I'd always used when I was entering a room with Madeline in it. One knock, a pause, and then three more. Whether she noticed it or not, it was our thing. She just hadn't had the chance to use it on me yet.

A beat passed before the door opened, and my heart lurched.

Madeline stood there, eyes watery and shadowed. She tried to greet me with a smile, but it was on a wobbly foundation, ready to crack at any moment. Her honey-brown hair was hanging in a loose ponytail, with fringe pulled all around it and a couple of uneven bumps coming out of the top. My eyes trailed down to Half-Pint in her arms, clinging so tightly that Madeline's skin was turning red where she dug into her. The sniffling cry that came out of the toddler as she buried her face in Madeline's neck only hurt my chest more. Madeline was at her breaking point. And I was the one to meet her there.

"Madeline, I—" I started to offer a hundred things. From pharmacy runs to Pedialyte and chicken noodle soup to a simple hug. But the word expectations kept lingering in my mind—in my mother's voice, specifically—so I stepped aside. "This is my mom. She—"

"Dr. Lora?" Madeline's eyes widened, and she stepped closer, like she was further trying to hide the chaos behind her door.

I turned back to my mom. She sucked in a shaky breath, mouth open slightly. It was the first time in a long time I had seen my mother shaken. Her hands seemed to gravitate toward me, brushing my arm like she needed something to hold on to.

"Madeline?" she asked with this voice that sounded so broken and scattered. "You're..." She looked back to me, and I dipped my eyebrows before turning back to the exhausted aunt in front of us. This time when she spoke, her tone was laced with soft sympathy, reminiscent of a mother finding out her son had suffered his first heartbreak. "Oh, Madeline."

Piper's cry turned into tiny sniffs as she turned to face us, lifting her head from her aunt's chest. She raised those tearstained eyes and snotty nose our way and said, clear as day, "Lola?"

My mom looked like someone had punched her in the gut, eyes wet and lips uneven, but still, she smiled. "Hi, baby. I thought I'd come visit you. Can I come in?"

Half-Pint looked at her and nodded, wiping the back of her hand over her eyes and reaching the tiniest little arms out for her. Without hesitation, my mom grabbed her, and we walked inside.

I sat with Madeline in the hallway outside their guest bathroom, a pile of dirty laundry to my left. We listened as my mom and Half-Pint were on the other side of the door, playing in lukewarm bath water. I could hear my mom scooping and dumping water with extra sound effects, and every now and then, you could hear a faint giggle from the little one. Charlie went to go grab towels from the laundry room, leaving only us.

"I had no idea you knew each other," I said. "Sorry if it's weird."

Madeline shook her head. "It's easier this way, really. Piper would never allow anyone else to check her temperature. She loves her Lola."

I snorted at that. "It's pretty cute. Lola. I need to start calling her that."

"She's great at what she does." Madeline smiled and wiped a hand over her face.

When we arrived, it seemed like she was on the brink of snapping. Like if three more minutes had passed, then we would have found her lying in a puddle on the floor. But when she saw my mom, who I quickly found out was also Piper's speech therapist, everything seemed to ease up a little. The tension slowly melted into dried tears and eventually comfort. Over the last twenty minutes or so, while Mom managed to get Half-Pint calmed to an occasional cry instead of the shrieking squall that was torturing all of us, Madeline and I sat against this wall.

Her house wasn't a disaster, but it was lived in. Much more so than mine. Almost made me dread going home in the first place. Various toys and stuffed animals spread across the vinyl flooring. Some small, faded purple markings on the light gray walls—presumably done by a tiny Picasso. Madeline's makeup bag open on the bathroom counter, mascara tubes and lipstick shades that I would love to see her in spread out in an array. An Xbox under the TV on a console table. Two piles of laundry half folded on a dark leather love seat. Framed photos were scattered around, mostly of the kids, but a few of young Madeline too. In the dining room, where I'd followed Madeline as she grabbed her phone after we arrived so she could make sure her mom knew there would be no date tonight, sat a large golden frame with a picture of a couple that I'd never seen before. The man with dark, almost black, hair and a strong nose held a tiny Charlie on his hip, and a tall blond woman at his side with a baby wrapped in swaddling clothes. Her brother and his wife.

It felt like I was given a glimpse into her life. Mini Coop's too. Like now, when I texted her and asked what she was doing, and she responded with simply washing dishes or helping the big one with homework, I could picture it. I could clearly envision Madeline living out her days here, and only just a block from me.

"You know," I said, watching as the woman beside me turned to give me her eyes, "technically, we're neighbors."

"We are." She smiled. It wasn't her normal one or the shy ones I'd seen her pass out. It was an exhausted, relieved one that felt like it was held together by WD-40 and duct tape.

"We could be like that Taylor Swift music video. Where they hold up signs to each other."

She snickered. "I can't see your house from here, though."

"It would be really big signs."

We both laughed at that and leaned back into the wall as Mini Coop rounded the corner. "I didn't know which towel you'd want, so I grabbed four of them."

Madeline smiled. "Thanks, kid. I think she's doing a lot better now."

"Sounds like it." He rubbed his ear. "Thought I was going to burst an eardrum."

"Me too," his aunt agreed. Then she sat a little straighter. "You can move the Xbox into your room tonight if you'd like."

Mini Coop looked shocked by the offer. "Really?"

She nodded. "Uh-huh. Just for tonight, since you helped so much."

"Sweet. Thanks, May!" He took off down the hall, and not three seconds passed before you could hear cords being ripped from their receptacles.

"Hey, Mr. Coop!" he shouted.

I answered. "Yeah?"

"Wanna come play COD?"

I paused and looked down to Madeline for permission. I was by no means a parent, not even a plant one, but I knew clear boundaries were important. And I would never step on the ones she put in place.

She shrugged back at me and mouthed sure.

"Yeah, man. Let me know when it's set up, and I'll join in."

He replied with a loud "'kay," and we listened to him shuffle to his room on the other side of the house.

In the bathroom, there was the sound of the plug being pulled and water circling down a drain. Madeline creaked the door open, dropped two of the four towels in, and closed it. Mom sang a song that I had been all too familiar with since I was Half-Pint's age too.

"You've Got a Friend," by James Taylor.

She claimed she sang it to me every night because we had more than a normal parent/kid relationship. We were friends. And sure enough, winter, spring, summer, and fall, she had been there through it all. All seasons of life, including this tiny one with Madeline and her two kids, short as it may be.

Madeline cleared her throat. "Thanks for coming by."

I nodded. "Thanks for letting us."

Mom emerged from the bathroom with a tiny blond gremlin passed out in her arms. Half-Pint was wrapped up in a purple hooded towel, one of those that had a character's face on the hood. A blond princess with a long braid and flowers in her hair. Her small chest rose and fell in steady breaths, and all signs of tears and snot had been replaced by rosy cheeks and a pink button nose awfully similar to her aunt's. The cutest Sour Patch Kid I'd ever seen.

"Want me to put her down in her room?" Mom asked Madeline.

She nodded. "I'll show you where it is."

They headed toward the other end of the house, and I followed. Mini Coop was there, softly calling for me from the doorway of his room. "It's ready."

I pushed off my knees to stand from my crouched position and followed the sound of an Xbox turning on and the main screen coming to life.

His room didn't have a specific theme. No matching set of curtains and comforters like I had growing up—my mom claimed that even if it was my room, she was going to have it looking like HGTV was going to randomly pop in one day.

A dark green comforter on his twin bed. A mahogany desk with an old clock. Sitting on it was a thick laptop and a wired mouse on a squishy red mouse pad that looked like it had been picked at by tiny fingernails. A bobblehead of Mats Zuccarello and some scattered homework papers with tiny doodles sitting beside it. Lumps of clothes in the corners—clean or dirty, I didn't know. There were a few hockey posters, one vintage comic skiing image that looked like Madeline had picked out for him, and a picture of him, his aunt, and his baby sister, all in a red booth at a restaurant, a birthday cake with lit candles directly in front of them. Last, a small beat-up teddy bear sitting on his bed that he swatted away when I entered the room.

Mini Coop–themed.

I gave an impressed nod. "Cool room."

Charlie walked from the console that sat on the floor since his dresser was too far from the TV. He handed me a spare remote, one with buttons that had sharp edges, like two tiny teeth had chewed on the knobs. "Here you go. It's our only spare. And Piper messed it up when she was getting her molars in."

I grabbed the controller without hesitating and tested my thumbs on the rough buttons. I hadn't played a ton of video games since high school, and even then, I was more of a PlayStation guy, if anything. The majority of my time had belonged to the snow and the mountains and girls. Though if I could sit my younger self down, maybe I'd tell him to stay inside a bit more.

"Thanks, kid. I'm a bit rusty, so go easy on me."

He only smirked at that and started the game without a word. I should have taken that as a sign that he was far more versed in Call of Duty than I was, but still, I got my ass handed to me. By a nine-year-old. Again and again. And then one more time.

Four rounds of creative mode, and my thumbs were sore from how hard I'd been pressing the buttons. As if the more I pushed, the more they would do the right things so I could put a child in his place. But that never happened.

I stood, gently tossed the remote onto his bed, and stretched. "Well, that was embarrassing."

"If it helps, I beat May every time too." He shrugged and started up another game, single player this time because me and my old-man fingers couldn't keep up.

It was easy to imagine Madeline sitting on the couch in their living room, Piper on her left, doing whatever toddlers do during the day, and Charlie fighting over winning status with her. I saw her pretending to be defeated, saying things like "one more time" and still never trying any harder. Always letting him win and always making sure he was proud of it. Because that was the kind of person she was. It was obvious that success for someone she loved meant success in Madeline's life too.

"I'm gonna check on your aunt and sis really quick." I walked down the hall toward the murmuring voices of my mom and the girl I was desperate to know more about.

Standing outside of a pale pink room, they were quiet enough to keep the tiny one asleep and yet still be able to hear each other.

"You think so?" Madeline asked, and my mom didn't hesitate to nod.

"I know so."

I creeped farther to listen in. If they turned around and caught me, I would have had no shame anyway, so I might as well lean into it.

"It's hard some days. A lot of days."

"It is." My mom nodded. "Even now, for me, it is."

"How did you do it?" Madeline asked in this tone that felt so flat, so defeated, that I wanted to pick her up and put my mouth on hers and blow it right back to that normal peppiness.

"I couldn't tell you. It's hard to remember a lot of times like this when you're living in survival mode." Mom sighed and kept her eyes on Half-Pint. "But I always trusted my gut, and it never steered me wrong."

Madeline hummed. "I didn't know you were a nurse before you became a speech therapist."

"For many, many years."

They sat in a moment of silence, and as I was about to step in, Madeline whispered low, almost to where no one could hear. "How did you know you wanted to quit nursing?"

I could hear the smile in Mom's response. "Someone came into my life and made me realize I deserved to do something I truly loved. Even if it meant sacrifice."

"You mean Cooper?"

Mom nodded. "Even as a baby, he demanded nothing less than 100 percent. He pushes you to be the best version of yourself."

"Yeah..." Madeline sighed. "He's good at that."

I bit down on my smile, pride shooting its way through my veins.

"You two seem good for each other. A good balance. Although, I am biased, as someone who is a big fan of both of you."

The way Madeline's shoulders slumped so quickly made it clear that wasn't the response she was hoping for, but she recovered quickly with a smile. One of the fake ones. "Thanks." A pause. "For coming over, and the bath, and the fever, and..." Another pause. "The Cooper."

I almost cackled at that. Mom snorted a little. "I can't take too much credit for that last one. Boy's a wild card. But I'm glad you two are friends." Friends came out wobbly and unsure, but Madeline didn't correct it, so Ma went on. "He needs someone good in his life. Someone strong and kind. It seems to me you're the right person for the job."

I smiled. She was.

"Thank you," Madeline whispered back, and I watched as my mom—the same woman who avoided high school reunions simply because she found physical touch so unbearable—wrapped her arms around my best friend. That was exactly what Madeline was to me, and maybe a bit more too. But for now, in this season, she was my best friend.

Finn would have an absolute fit. But I had a feeling the spot for best friend in his life was about to be replaced by a tiny squish ball of miniature fingers and toes.

I waited a moment and let them hug a bit before clearing my throat. "You didn't warn me that I was going up against a COD champion."

Both women turned around, and Madeline pretended like her eyes weren't watering. "I probably should have given you a heads-up. It's one of the reasons I keep the Xbox in the living room. If I didn't, we would never see him again."

"Probably not." I walked a little closer, careful of my boots making noise on the wood-grain vinyl below me until I could peek into the little one's room.

Tiny and covered in princesses and all things pink. A mini vanity with paint marks all around the side and two Slim Jim wrappers, and a half-empty cup of orange juice sitting there. A golden-framed picture of Madeline and both kids standing in front of Cinderella's castle, sweaty and smiling in matching T-shirts. Half-Pint-themed.

I hummed. "She's out, huh?"

"Baths always seem to make babies sleepy," Ma remarked.

"They make me sleepy too," Madeline said back, and every fiber in my being fought to not picture that very image right here, with my mother two feet away. A sudsy, sleepy, clothes-less Madeline in a tub of water was the last temptation I needed.

"Plus it's good for leveling out their temp. Just not too cold or too hot. Those can make it worse. Alternate Tylenol and Motrin every three hours until it goes away. You can do a tiny bit of Dimetapp for the cough. I know it says for ages four and up, but trust me. Two milliliters will clear it up."

Madeline typed the instructions into a note on her phone. Mom stuck her hand out for the device, and Madeline didn't hesitate to hand it back.

"My cell," Mom explained. "Day or night. Use it."

"Oh, I—"

"Use it. I know what it's like with one." She jerked her head to me. "Two is harder. Accept help where you need it. You have wonderful kids and a beautiful home. It's impossible to do everything on your own."

"Oh," Madeline's freckled cheeks turned pink. "Thank you. It's very messy."

"It is loved. Believe me, I miss my colored-on walls and scattered toys very much now." Mom looked my way with this sense of nostalgia. Like she was staring at a painting in an art gallery, something so beautiful it made you sad and a little proud for the artist too. I wasn't a parent, so I didn't know what it was like to look at your own kid when they were grown up, doing their own thing. But I imagined it was similar to passing by one of my favorite students from when I first started teaching. Knowing they could drive, go to college, buy their own deodorant. Proud. Sad. Nostalgic.

I smiled at my mom, apologetic. Sorry that I'd grown up on her. Sorry that I'd moved out and started my own life—one that felt like I'd hit reboot recently. Sorry I hadn't clung to our nights of eating pizza on the floor and putting together a one-thousand-piece puzzle in a single sitting. I hoped Madeline clung to her kids, and that they clung right back.

"Well, on that note, you ready, Ma?" I asked.

Mom nodded and reminded Madeline once more to call her if she needed anything. She then scampered off to grab her purse, leaving only Madeline and me.

"Thank you again," she said.

"You're welcome again," I replied.

We sat there in silence for a moment, just looking at each other. Watching our chests rise and fall. Watching her fingers twitch delicately, mine curled into fists by my sides. Watching her lips, luscious and so perfectly pink, part like she had more to say but couldn't piece it together. I did the same.

I heard Mom's footsteps coming closer and halting at the corner, where she was definitely listening in. I rolled my eyes and mouthed the word nosy to the girl in front of me. She smiled at that. A real, happy, Madeline one.

"Sleep good, all right?" I lifted a hand and pushed her shoulder a little. "Actually good. Not up-for-hours-watch-ing-New¬-Girl good."

She snorted. "I'll try. These are my me hours."

"What else do you do during your me hours?" I wiggled my brows and laughed when I heard a thud from the corner where Mom was. Served her right for listening in. There was no questioning where I'd gotten that from.

Madeline laughed and turned pink before my eyes. "Not thinking of you, that's for sure."

I raised a hand to my chest. "Gah, it hurts."

"Good," Mom said from down the hall.

We both snickered.

"I'll see you around, Madeline. Breakfasts and not-dates next week." I winked.

She nodded and bit her lip. "Breakfast and not-dates."

I pulled her into me, chest to chest. Heartbeat to heartbeat. My head rested on her shoulder as her arms wrapped around my neck. So easy. Like everything felt when it was just the two of us. A little more than friendly but nothing we hadn't done before. I breathed in to memorize her scent. Cinnamon, vanilla, and something extra sweet I couldn't put my finger on.

Mom and I both said a swift goodbye to Mini Coop on the way out the door, and when we got back in the car, she nodded. "You were right. She is different."

I smiled, and for the first time in a long time, I took my mom to get ice cream and watched a movie on my couch with her, soaking in our time together.

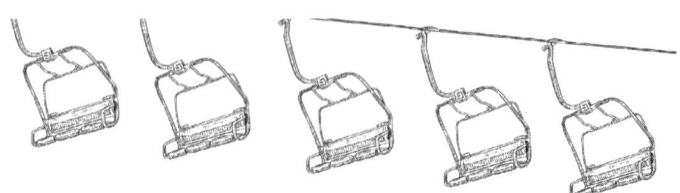

Chapter Twenty-One
COOPER

"H ey," I said, frantic and out of breath. "Is Elsa still in?"

"Is...Elsa in?" Finn asked, as if he hadn't heard every word I just said.

My foot anxiously beat against the tiled floors of the Target aisle I was standing in. Surrounded by princess dresses, fairy wings, and a Barbie Corvette that I pressed one single button on and now had alarm bells screaming at me. I had a feeling I wasn't as intimidating as I wanted to be. One hand on my hip and one hand holding a box with an Elsa doll with a tiny snowman beside it didn't help either.

"What the hell is that noise?" he asked before I could answer his first question.

I lifted the box to my head in frustration. "The alarm of Barbie's Corvette is more sensitive than you'd think."

A mom with a young girl turned into the aisle, staring at me, while the toy to my left obnoxiously shouted "let's go for a ride." I wanted to ride Barbie off the edge of the Grand Canyon at the moment. I dipped my chin in a hello, and the mom put a hand over her redheaded daughter's eyes, slowly pushing her away from the aisle without breaking eye contact and shaking her head side to side. Because clearly, in my socks and crocs, standing in the bright pink aisle full of Barbie Dream Houses and Rapunzel-themed Tiaras, I screamed "child-taker."

"Can I ask what you're doing? I feel like you think some things you say are easily translated, and I promise, they aren't."

I sighed and set down one Frozen set before grabbing the next one. Twenty bucks for a bunch of cheap plastic seemed ridiculous. "Half-Pint is sick, and I wanted to find something for her."

"Again, please use as many words as possible."

I put down that set and looked in the thirty-dollar range, which now also had a cool-looking blond guy with a reindeer. At what age did kids start putting Legos together? Two felt young...

"Half-Pint—Madeline's girl—she got sick on Friday, some kind of quick bug, but it was a mess. Mom and I went to see them, and you should have heard her crying—"

"Your mom met Madeline and the kids?" He might as well have said "you went to the moon and had a martini with a dog wearing a top hat?" in that tone.

"Yes," I said, firm and clear. I was about to give up on this stupid aisle and my phone entirely. "No more interrupting."

His silence let me know to press forward. "She finally went to sleep, but Mom and I stuck around a bit, and I..." I wasn't sure what to plug in to finish my sentence.

I...feel like Madeline needs extra help—besides her parents, who belittle her.

I...feel like these kids deserve more.

I...really, really like this girl, and I'm kind of praying Elsa will pull this together.

"I saw something in them that made me want to pitch in," I conceded. "So I'm now at Target with a cart half full of stuff that I think will help. I want to get both of the kids something exciting. So is Elsa still in? That movie came out like ten years ago."

"There will probably be geriatric women in white and blue dresses singing "Let It Go" at its hundred-year anniversary, and Elsa would still be in, Coop."

I nodded. "I figured." My hands reached out, and I looked between the two sets before grabbing them both.

"What else did you get?" Finn asked.

I looked at the half-full cart below me. How could something feel like too much and not enough at the same time?

"Some basics for the little one. Pedialyte, soup, a cup with a blue dog on it, candy, and an extremely large package of Slim Jims."

"Every two-year-old's dream," Olive chimed in.

"Thank you, Olive Branch." I moved on. "Got Mini Coop two small Lego sets and one Xbox gift card. But now that feels like a lot compared to Half-Pint ..." My eyes scanned the aisles, all the way down to that stupid Corvette still singing to me, telling me to come for a ride. A Tiana doll sat on the top shelf, and I shrugged before tossing that in the basket too.

"Madeline is getting a mug that says World's Hottest Mom. There wasn't an aunt one. A candle too. It smells like the resort"—or at least the closest I could find to it—"and two books—a sexy romance and a scary thriller."

"Ooh, good idea. In my experience, women love murder and high standards," Finn chimed in.

"Agreed." I nodded and moved those to my keep pile, right by the gummy vitamins that my mom mentioned to Madeline yesterday. But my keep pile was less of a keep pile and more of an entire cart full of stuff.

I walked down the aisle and turned where Christmas trees and decorative ornaments with little mice on them were on display. My hands instantly reached for the Hershey's chocolate peppermint bars, and I decided that one was for me. Those kids could rip it from my cold, dead body. Madeline could have one square.

"Does that seem like enough?"

"Seems easier to buy the whole store to me." Finn snorted, and he wasn't wrong.

Mom said gift-giving was my love language. A softer way of saying I buy my friends. An old habit that had stuck with me to this day. Even in preschool, Ma would send me with a toy, and I'd give it away the second we got there. She said it like I was some generous, noble kid, when in reality, I knew exactly what it was: a down payment on a real friendship.

In middle school, it turned into free ski trips at the lodge with kids who didn't even like me or hardly talked to me. In high school, I could afford to buy the forbidden alcohol from a couple of college sophomores. Or I could throw the best parties, get the best people together. And still, every night, with company all around me, I felt entirely alone. In what would be my college days—I dropped out midway through my first math class—it was buying drinks for the hottest girls, which usually meant the coolest guys being around too. Again, rooms full, heart empty. Over and over. Every single relationship I made that wasn't family was bought. And the more I did it, the more it seemed to dig deep.

Except for Finn. My one friend who didn't see a dollar sign or a new opportunity when he looked my way. My one friend who fought with me and laughed with me the way I always thought friends were supposed to. He got on my nerves sometimes, and I got on his nerves a lot. But it was real, authentic. A friendship that would stand the test of time. Marriage, babies, nursing homes—Finn Beckett was my first ride or die. Madeline Sage was a very close second.

I looked down at the cart in front of me and winced. It was a lot. Maybe too much. But it kept coming back to me. Why did I come here in the first place? Never once had it crossed my mind that doing this for this family would secure them in place. It didn't feel like a back-up plan. In the last hour, I hadn't once felt like a stray dog putting a dead squirrel on a back porch for a random family in hopes that they'd take me in. I'd felt like I was doing something they deserved and nothing more.

So I pushed my cart farther down the aisle. "All my money goes to me now. It'll be nice seeing it put to good use."

That made it sound like I was some billionaire or that I made enough money to fund a nonprofit organization, which I wasn't and didn't. I made the same amount as Finn, even when offered advances over the years because of my last name. But I had a good, steady income with a low mortgage, no car payment, and a 401(k). Alcohol was gone from my life, as were parties and women and any extravagant non-necessities that had taken up financial space in my past.

Looking down at the cart in front of me, I swore it was like the tiny white-haired princess winked up at me. This was different from all those other times. This felt like, for the first time in a long time, maybe ever, I had something good going on. A cart full of toys and candy and—Oh my gosh. I was Santa Claus.

"I'm proud of you, Coop." Finn's voice broke up my thoughts about how hard it would be to dye a beard white. "You seem like you're...you again. Like the real Cooper, not the old one."

There wasn't an ounce of me that felt offended at that, because I agreed wholeheartedly. "Thanks, man."

Silence passed.

"You *would* get a crush on Olive's friend."

I laughed a little at that. "I told you our kids would be best friends."

He snorted a little—Olive did too in the background—and sighed. "Yeah, yeah. They would be."

When I arrived at Target, it had been light out, the sun doing its best to melt the snow packed in the parking lot and warming my skin under my thick coat. When I left, it was pitch-black, the stars scattered in the night sky and the crescent moon shining over the half-lit parking lot. I didn't know what it said about me that I'd spent nearly three hours in the place or that I'd come in for three items, tops, and was now packing twelve bags into my trunk. But that's where I was.

On the bright side, it was pushing nine o'clock, so I knew the kids were in bed. I could drop this stuff off on their porch and run without making a huge deal of it.

Chapter Twenty-two
Madeline

It pained me to admit that my mother was right about anything.

And believe me, it was a rare occurrence. The time she said my obsession with spicy food was causing me to have IBS in high school? Embarrassing but very true. When she told me that her favorite drugstore mascara, an ugly brown tube with green swirly designs, was just as good as the forty-dollar one at Sephora? Painful to admit that one. When she told me again and again that I was stunting Piper's speech? Still not over that. And last, when she swore up and down that I needed a better security system for the house.

She was right.

It wasn't something I considered a necessity when I moved in. It required some adjusting, going from a sketchy apartment with a blind neighbor named Lewis who liked to tell me about the sounds of mice he heard in the walls and the orange oozing drip coming from my walls every time I took a lukewarm show-

er—since it could never get full hot—to a house in a neighborhood with an HOA. It felt a bit like being thrown onto Mars
and your pilot shouting good luck as you barrel rolled into a
crater.

It was Will and Savannah's house. They'd bought it
when they found out they were pregnant with baby Charlie—pre-marriage, which caused my parents to flail about the
living room when they found out—and turned the cheap fore-
closure into a dream house.

White-tiled showers with black grout, a sage-green front door
with a golden knocker in the shape of a hummingbird, dark
wooden kitchen cabinets, and white marble countertops. They
took it one room at a time, finishing every space except the
master bedroom. They never had the chance to finish that one.
They also never put in a more updated security system than the
one they'd installed almost ten years ago.

There was...some way to access it. I just didn't know how.
The only thing you could access was the driveway camera,
which was black and white and so entirely grainy it looked like
a sad teenager's Pinterest mood board after their first breakup.
But even trying to access that was a pain in the butt. You had
to reboot this dinosaur of a desktop in Will's old office and
re-download the software and do a whole bunch of other security clearance crap that honestly seemed like more of a pain than
just calling 911 the second you heard footsteps on your front
porch.

Or, in this case, the rustling of plastic bags on the front porch.
Prior to being a parent, I was a relatively go-with-the-flow girl.
Mostly because I had been engaged to an artist who claimed

that life was a never-ending movement, and you had to board the train before it left you. I didn't understand it at the time—I still don't—but I certainly was not a go-with-the-flow woman now. I was a baseball-bat-by-my-bed, pepper-spray-in-my-purse, self-defense-class-taking woman because my biggest fear was being caught in a position like this with my kids in the house.

I was currently perched on my knees over the couch, peeking through the blinds covering the living room window at what seemed to be a tall man in all black, hood raised, and...were those Target bags?

I shook my head. It didn't matter. My fingers gripped the bottom of my light-blue baseball bat, which was probably made for prepubescent boys and was more than likely taken from Charlie's donation pile. It didn't matter.

The threat was still there when I crept to the front door and said, "I have a weapon and I will use it," just loud enough for him to hear but not so loud I'd wake either of the kids. They didn't know my weapon was made of hard plastic.

"Good to know." A smooth, rich, warmed-honey voice poured through the cracks of my green front door, and my shoulders fell.

Cooper.

I cracked the door and hissed, fighting my smile but also attempting to keep myself upset, because who just drops by someone's house without a text or even a knock? "What are you doing?"

Cooper stood there in black jeans, snow boots, and a dark gray hoodie with an Aspen Peaks logo in white font pulled up over his hair.

"Playing Santa, and you're ruining it," he hissed right back.

"Playing Santa for who? Also, it's November." I didn't know why we were whispering, but neither of us stopped.

"You and your kids. Go back inside and pretend this didn't happen."

Wha—my kids? "Why?" My whisper was turning raspy quick.

"Because Half-Pint had a crappy day, and Mini Coop is my friend, and you're—" He paused, still holding a white and red plastic bag. "You."

"I'm me?"

"Yes!" His hushed voice was strained. "So go inside."

"No!" I whisper shouted right back.

If this was some poor Madeline, the single aunt and broke nursing student, then I was not letting this happen. I could accept help when Piper was sick. I could accept Charlie's private lessons for the competition next month. I could not accept Cooper Graves bringing by random gifts like some hot elf with a shopping addiction.

I opened the door a little farther and slipped out, tugging at the sleeves of my sweatshirt and ignoring the cold concrete under my fuzzy-socked feet. "Take it back."

Cooper looked from the bags to me. His eyes met something at the top of my head—probably the bird's nest in my hair—and he smirked ever so slightly. "I will not. You can't make me."

"Yes I can." I fought back, squatting down and picking up the bags. "I do not take handouts."

He shrugged one shoulder, and that smirk pulled further, the organ pumping in my chest pulling with it. "What makes you think this is a handout?"

"You're...handing things out..." I said each word slowly.

"No, no, no. I'm here on official fake boyfriend business."

I crossed my arms over my chest, now remembering that I wasn't wearing a bra, and narrowed my eyes. "You are?"

"Yes. You see, if I were your boyfriend, it would be a regular occurrence."

"It would?"

"Mm-hmm." Cooper dipped his chin and let his eyes do this slow, smooth drag over my body, making me feel entirely exposed in my oversized sweatsuit. "And since your parents are entirely aware that I am your boyfriend—"

"Fake boyfriend," I supplied. The smile in my voice was so evident that I couldn't hide my amusement anymore.

He waved a hand. "Technicalities. Since they believe that, I feel it's best to take on the role in all areas. In case they start looking deeper. You know, how like Jared Leto practiced for the role of the Joker."

"So you're the Jared Leto of fake boyfriends?"

"Precisely, Madeline. No wonder you're a nursing student." He reached one hand out and pressed his thumb into the dip of my chin, a perfect fit. "Smart as a tack."

"Do you mean sharp as a tack?" I smiled.

"Ah, see what I mean? My girl's got the brains."

A tiny pig-like snort came out of me at that. I looked down at the bags still in Cooper's hands before glancing to his face. That lopsided grin that I knew caused all kinds of trouble sat there while he shrugged his shoulders, lifting the bags. "I can bring them in if you want."

A dangerous invitation, considering the kids were in bed and out like rocks, so it would be essentially Cooper and me in a house alone. Cooper, who'd kissed me better than anyone else ever had. Cooper whose hands had roamed my hips to my ass and made me feel wanted.

No, my mind reasoned. No, no, no. You will not get out of this alive. It was fake. He'd said so himself. Friends or not, attraction or not, gorgeous, full lips or not, this part of our deal was fake.

"Sure," I answered, going against my mind. Because what did logic matter, really? "Not as a fake boyfriend, though."

He nodded in agreement. "Fake Cooper will leave as soon as I set foot inside."

I nodded right back. "Good."

My hand gripped the doorknob, and I opened it, not too worried about the mess because he'd seen far worse last night, and apparently just about all of my shame had gone out the window.

Cooper followed behind me and shook his shoulders off when he got inside, like he was transforming from a frog into a prince. "Friend Cooper is here now, with some stuff that a random guy left on your porch. You know, you probably should've kicked him out."

I chuckled. "I should've, but you know, he was just so nice, and I do love Target."

He shrugged and lifted the bags up. "Fair." He set them down on the old wooden bench against the wall beside him.

"You really didn't need to do that, you know."

"I told you: I didn't." He lowered his brow, and I swore if I took that face and bottled it up into some kind of pheromone booster, then women would be walking around in a trance all day long. "Go talk to that guy about it. I had nothing to do with these."

I hummed. "Well, I'll have to call him and say thank you."

"You could. Sounds like a creep to me, though."

I guffawed with my head tilted back. "Maybe he is."

Cooper smiled at me, that real one. Not flirty, not sneaky, just an authentic smile with those straight white teeth and the most genuine green eyes. I liked that one. Friend Cooper, I thought.

We settled on the couch with a smorgasbord of food on the coffee table in front of us. Half-eaten bags of trail mix with the chocolate pieces all gone, slices of leftover cheese from sandwiches, salami and crackers, a cluster of grapes, a couple of strawberries, and a chunk of brie with local honey. The ugliest charcuterie board to ever exist.

Cooper propped his feet up on the ottoman in front of him, a plate full of our buffet on his lap, and his cheeks poking out like a squirrel preparing for winter.

"Ready?" he asked, mouth full.

After I'd asked Cooper if he was hungry, and his stomach had growled in response, I didn't exactly have energy to cook. Not that I had the groceries to do it anyway. So pathetic charcuterie was the best we could do. As soon as we got settled on the couch, with his long legs stretched out in front of him, and his back pressed against my couch cushions, he asked if I wanted to keep up our game. It had become a ritual of sorts for us the last few times we'd seen each other—other than last night. The more we played, the more pieces of Cooper I got for myself. I liked that.

I nodded and tossed a cashew into my mouth. "You first."

"I don't like dark restaurants where you have to use a flashlight to read the menu."

"Those exist?"

"Mm-hmm." He bit into a thick slice of salami. "My mom likes stuff like that. She didn't do it much growing up, so now she's into all of that. Champagne, lobster, desserts with blow torches involved. You know, dark restaurants."

I pulled my legs up onto the couch, tucking my feet under my butt. "I..." I hummed a little, trying to think. "I don't like going on vacation, really. It kind of stresses me out."

"Where have you been?"

"Only a few places when I was little. We did a road trip to Vegas when I was ten, but a ten-year-old can only enjoy Vegas so much."

"You didn't enjoy gambling with an escort?"

"You know, surprisingly, I think I just felt too mature for that. The Grand Canyon was nice, though. We stopped on the way home, mostly for pictures."

Cooper nodded and threw a salty blue M&M into his mouth. "You ever been to the beach?"

"Nope. But maybe I would enjoy it when I know everyone in my party can swim well." The thought of Piper anywhere near a body of water made my stomach lurch.

"I'll take you sometime, when the kids are older."

He said it so matter-of-factly. I'll take you when the kids are older. Like he was telling me he was going to grab a drink for me from the gas station. So entirely casual, and yet it was a promise of sorts. One I wasn't ever going to hold him to, but still, it was nice.

Our game, which we still had yet to give an actual label, turned from I like to I don't like to I used to.

He used to watch anime in high school. I used to consider any Nicholas Sparks movie to be a masterpiece. He used to have an odd obsession with the color blue—like he wanted everything he owned to be blue. I used to bake when I got stressed. He used to eat when he got stressed. We went down the line, from favorite Pixar moms to what we considered to be the worst kind of show dogs. All the while eating nuts, cheese, and berries like a couple of squirrels.

It was Cooper's turn now. "I used to go to taco and tequila night with my mom and her friends."

I laughed through my response. "I can definitely see that. How old were you?"

"Old enough to know it was ladies' night, and I was definitely crashing the party."

It was so easy to imagine. Cooper at Charlie's age, surrounded by middled-aged women, all cockiness and innocent smiles, same messy hair. He'd probably had them all cooing over him, and the attention-lover he was, had probably soaked it all up.

"I bet they loved having you there."

"They did. Or they always said they did. To this day, Mom tries to get me to come on Tuesday nights."

"You should go. They'd love it even more now."

"No," He laughed in that Cooper way that I was growing so fond of. "Now they ask why I'm still single or why I haven't started working on a family. Not as fun as it used to be. But still, I take mom out at least once a month, and that seems like enough for her."

Funny to think that, this entire time, Dr. Lora has been Cooper's mom. Lora Graves. I should have put that together, but I hadn't even thought about it. She insisted everyone call her Lora, or Lola for Pipes. When she talked about her son being single or how he was still her baby, I assumed that the guy was either a thirty-year-old virgin or that he was living in his mother's basement, only breathing fresh air on the anniversary of Star Wars films.

The last thing I would have expected was a six-foot-five children's ski instructor with dreamy green eyes, a panty-melting smile, and a soft spot for single aunts. But that's exactly what he was proving himself to be.

"I still can't believe she's your mom."

The way she looked at us when we opened that door, Piper on my hip, with her nose running on my shirt, my eyes swollen and purple, on the verge of tears. She stepped behind Cooper, and for half a second, I felt shame. Until I saw her face. Until she spoke, soft and low. "Oh, Madeline." She didn't say it with pity or disappointment. Not even sympathy. She said it with understanding, because she had been right where I was. Alone and terrified, with no one to lean on. Our situations weren't the same, but the outcomes felt similar.

"Yeah, I'm surprised I didn't put two and two together. She doesn't ever talk about her patients, and she rarely talks about work in general when we're together. Mostly, she just asks me about my life." He took a sip of lemonade that he'd snagged from the fridge earlier. "She kind of projects that way. Doesn't like talking about herself at all. Even if something bothers her, I have to basically force information out. She once had a benign tumor removed from her breast, and only told me because she needed a ride home after. Never even told me she had scans done or anything like that."

"Oh, wow."

"Yeah, I tell her everything, though."

"Everything?" My cheeks flushed. No way did he tell her about our kiss at the drive-in. I mean, no parent is that close with their kids, right?

"Not that stuff, Madeline." He smirked as I tried to fan away the heat in my neck. "We're close, but not that close."

I nodded and looked at the table in front of us. Tells his mom everything. I wanted to laugh at that. I can't even tell my mom where I order our groceries from without an argument starting, much less anything deeper. Even if I brought up nursing school or work, it was like she flipped a switch. We had never been super close, even when Will was here. But ever since he passed, it seemed to only get worse. She didn't want to talk about anything except the kids, and even then, it was mostly about what I wasn't doing correctly with them. Or the occasional text exchange, where she attempted to hook me up with her friends' sons.

"Have you guys always been close?" I asked, foolishly hoping he would give me some magic answer that I had been missing.

"Yup." He threw a raisin up and caught it in his mouth. "I think 'cause it's always been just us; you know? She's all I knew, so it was impossible not to be close to her."

I sucked in a breath. "Right."

It was too late for me to attempt any kind of rekindling, I supposed. Our house was impossibly quiet growing up. The only sounds were Will and me playing in the backyard. If the TV was on, it was playing the news, volume low, and if music was turned on, then it was either a commercial or it was accidental. I guess it was why, when Will turned sixteen, he took me everywhere. Even when he worked, shoveling snow out of driveways, barely making anything, he would take me to Taco Bell and buy me ninety-nine-cent cinnamon twists when it was all we could afford. He would blast Taylor Swift in the car for me and drive me around as long as I begged him to.

What Lora was to Cooper, Will was to me. And I hated that I had no chance of ever having that again.

"But that's not the norm, you know?" he added on, clearly for my benefit.

"Think about Finn and Olive. Neither of them is super close with their family. I think Ma and I are the minority here."

"Do you think Charlie and Piper will..." How was I supposed to finish that? Stay close with me? Come see me after they have their first kiss? Not throw me into a nursing home when my time came?

"Yes." He didn't hesitate. "I don't know how to explain it, but yes."

My chin shot up, my eyes meeting his face. "Really?"

"Yeah, I just know it."

"How so?"

"When we're at practice, Charlie brings you up all the time."

I scooted closer in, gasping. "Really?"

"Yes," he laughed while he scooted closer to me too. "He talks about your favorite Clif Bars or how hard you work or how your favorite view is the sitting room at the lodge. It's not that you're all he talks about, but any chance he has to bring you up, trust me, he does."

My heart grew to three times its size at that. Imagining my sweet, funny Charlie still not being too cool for me, even when I was gone.

"Ugh. I love that kid so much." I was going to make him a leaning tower of chocolate chip pancakes for breakfast tomorrow and spend the entire time squishing his face.

"He is a really great kid."

"Is that why you call him Mini Coop?"

"Obviously."

"And Half-Pint?" I asked with a smile in my voice.

"Half-Pint 'cause she's so tiny. You know, half-pint."

"You do that a lot."

"What?"

"The nickname thing. You have one for everyone. Mini Coop, Half-Pint, Olive Branch, Finland. Even the waitress at the café. Adele. Blonde from Tulsa." I saw that one in his phone the other day and teased him relentlessly about an obvious booty call. A joke he didn't find funny, apparently, because he deleted and blocked the poor girl's number right in front of me. "Everyone except me."

"Huh." He bit his bottom lip and looked off to the far right, into my kitchen. "Guess I didn't think to give you one."

Cooper leaned closer to me, lifted one hand to my face, and closed two fingers and a thumb around my chin as he tilted my face from side to side in assessment. He squinted playfully, smirking at me, as if he was running some AI-style research to find me the perfect nickname.

He tsked and shook his head, letting the wispy ends of his hair fly around. "Can't find one. You're Madeline."

I gasped. "What? I don't get a nickname at all?"

"Nope." He leaned in close enough for me to breathe him in. Clove. Pine. Clean laundry. Cooper. I took a deep breath in through my nose, wondering how long I could keep that scent to myself.

And just when I felt like enough of a lost cause, he looked down at my swollen lips and spoke directly to them. "I like the way Madeline tastes in my mouth."

I snickered. "That sounds dirty."

"It does, doesn't it?"

It was getting so hot in this house. Heat pulsed in my palms, up my arms, puddling in my chest. Still, I leaned a little closer. He did too.

"I mean it, though." He picked right back up, as if our proximity wasn't causing his body to light on fire. "Madeline rolls right off my tongue."

"That sounds even dirtier." I didn't know why I'd whispered it like that, but not all of my senses were with me anyway. Not when his lips were only inches from mine and he was looking at me like I was his favorite dessert.

It had been almost two weeks since that first kiss at the drive-in. And instead of the memory happily fading away into the distant part of my mind that held on to things, like algebra formulas or my high school's alma mater, that kiss was all I could think about when he was around. The way we tasted together, how perfectly I rested against him, how his large hands gripped me. It was like I had been towing this line for days now, trying to avoid dipping over the edge and picturing him kissing me all over again. And now I was right on the line, wondering if I could somehow pull this off one more time.

So when his hand reach for me, resting on my knee pushing against his, I gave up any resolve that logical Madeline was holding on to.

"It does...doesn't it?" He repeated the phrase, and maybe it wasn't meant as an innuendo, but it sure felt like one.

We kept our eyes locked on each other when my hand trailed down to his, fingernails grazing over the back of his hand and up to his forearm to trace the veins exposed below his sleeve.

"I think it's just because we kissed before."

Cooper laughed, deep and throaty, in this way that felt erotic and entirely wrong. "Oh, is that what we're blaming it on?" His free hand lifted to the side of my face and tucked a tendril of hair that curled around my cheekbone behind my ear. "'Cause I've wanted this since way before I first kissed you."

The knowledge of that alone had me squeezing my knees together and the room temperature rising another five degrees.

Our lips met, careful and slow, in the softest kiss. Softer than the drive-in, softer than I dreamed of at night. Blissful, that's what this was. And, unfortunately for us both, as soon as things began to turn heavy, a cry came from Piper's room.

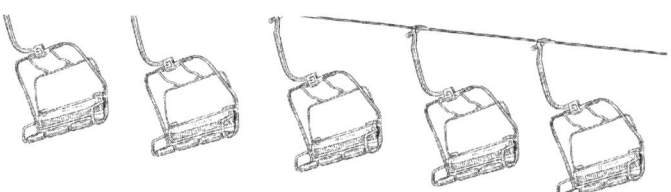

Chapter Twenty-three
COOPER

"Where are we going?" Mini Coop stood at the side exit of the lodge with his arms stretched wide.

I pointed toward the main entrance, down by the floor-to-ceiling windows and the fireplace. "We're not training at the normal spot." That was all I was going to give him for now.

I'd texted Madeline first thing this morning, avoiding the topic of what last night meant exactly. I'd gone straight to asking if her nephew was free today. It was my first full day off in the last ten days, and I felt no hesitation about spending it training the kid for the competition coming up in a little over a month. She responded with a quick and simple yes, so I swooped in to grab him. Part of me hoped I'd see her there, and the other part didn't, in case I'd see regret in her eyes. Luckily, I got both. Charlie was in the driveway with his bags, and Madeline stood at the window of their kitchen. She gave me this smile that was polite but reassuring and felt like enough. I waved, she waved back, and the two of us left for the lodge to start covering some ground.

His basics were down; Finn had laid that foundation well enough that I didn't need to correct any of it. His ski switches and nose butters were perfect. He was close to nailing a fifty-fifty on a box, and although his pop-offs needed some refining, pretty much everything he had learned up to this point was immaculate. All we needed to work on was some of the skills that would earn bonus points and let him practice on a steeper mountain than we normally trained on.

Our typical lessons were on the east side of the lodge, where we had enough of a curve to use the tiny escalator to guide the kids up and let them ski down. It was safer that way, not just because we could keep them all in a confined space, but also because if we didn't, we'd have to take them on the lift, and I didn't trust them to not fall out or jump off at the wrong spot and get lost forever in the mountains.

But one-on-one lessons were usually when I pushed them a little further.

"We gotta take the lift today." I jerked my chin over to the far right of the lodge's exit, where the bottom of the lift was located. In the distance, you could see a line forming in front of the waiting area. Rows of people decked out in their gear, snowboards and skis lined up, watching the light turn from red to green, signaling it was their turn to move.

"Seriously?" Charlie tried to hide his excitement, but his mouth was dropped open, and he was looking up at the lift area like it was a sacred place only accessible to the most honorable skiers and snowboarders such as myself.

"Yeah. Come on, man. We gotta beat the crowds."

The best time to ski was in the morning. The snow hadn't been churned up too much yet. It was still tightly packed and ready for you to make new paths on it. It was busy this morning, a relief after my lessons this week had been slow. But we should still be riding on new snow where we were going. We would have been here earlier, but I had a strict rule about sitting down and eating an enormous breakfast before taking the lift. There were few things worse than getting a couple of rounds in and dealing with hunger pangs that were so piercing you couldn't focus on anything other than the hole that was your stomach.

"O-Okay." Mini Coop readjusted his poles and followed me to the lift.

We got our skis tightened and double-checked our equipment, then we took off toward the small line.

Beside me, Mini Coop was bouncing on his feet, watching every person move in front of him. Studying the way they crouched when the seat came, how soon they pulled the bar down, and how they held their poles.

"You've done this before, right?"

I guess I should've asked before we were next to go up, but part of me had just assumed he had been with his dad when he was younger.

"No," he whispered back to me, and I felt like I'd cheated him on this already. Cheated Madeline too, considering she should have been here for this.

"No biggie." I shrugged. "Super easy. When the light turns green, we're gonna climb up like you always do, then a chair is gonna circle around, so just bend your knees a little bit and let it sweep you up. You've done a lot more difficult things. Trust me."

His cheeks turned pink right where his orange ski mask was pulled below his mouth, his matching goggles resting on his forehead. "Okay."

"I can ask the lift guy to slow it down if you want."

A gray-bearded man named Colbert was working it today. All I knew about him was that he hosted a Dungeons and Dragons meeting every Friday night and that his wife ran a pottery class on the side, but he seemed cool.

Charlie's face turned sour in an instant. "No!" he hissed in a harsh whisper, as if just the thought of talking to Colbert was mortifying enough.

I shrugged. "All right, if you say so."

When our time came, he did exactly as I did, eyes tracking my every movement and copying them. We settled onto the chair when it came around, and once I knew he was settled, I lifted up the bar and pulled it over both of us.

"See? No biggie. If you build it up in your head, you'll freak yourself out."

He nodded. "Like the mute grabs."

"Exactly like that."

For the first couple of minutes, we sat in silence as the lift pulled us farther from the ground. Our skis dangled below, swaying back and forth in tandem. Even after all these years, I still wasn't quite used to the view. Mountaintops covered in snow, the ground a brisk canvas of white and splattered with dark-green tree limbs off in the distance. The chatter of people on the lift, the wind whirling around us as we moved higher and higher. The sound of cables pulling, of skis rushing down the mountain. It was every bit as incredible now as it had been the first time I came up here.

"If you look all the way to your right, you'll see the airport." I pointed toward the area, my hand directly in Mini Coop's face.

He kept his eyes down, though, watching our feet rise farther and farther from the earth. "Mm-hmm. Cool." His hands tightened around the lap bar, and I was willing to bet his knuckles were turning white underneath those black gloves.

"You know," I said while Charlie's face was still tilted down, "I was terrified the first time I rode the lift."

Terrified was probably putting it lightly, considering I'd clung to Pops's legs, begging him not to make me go. I'd heard a kid at school talk about some great uncle's cousin's sister-in-law getting stuck on a lift at the highest point for hours. Which was completely unrealistic. If I had just mentioned it to Pops, he could've told me the resort had systems in place for things like this.

"Really?"

"Yep. My grandfather took me. Pops said if I just kept my eyes on the prize—he meant the ride down—that I wouldn't even notice how far up I was." It's funny to think about how often I used that advice now. Looking out at the final goals in life made day-to-day life a little easier.

At that, Mini Coop lifted his eyes to mine. "Your dad didn't take you?" The question was more than just one. It felt like he was reaching, asking for more. Wondering if my dad had passed like his.

"I don't know my dad." I shrugged.

"At all?"

"Nope."

"Not even his name?"

I shook my head. "Nuh-uh."

"So...it was just your mom?"

"Yep. I never really felt like I was missing out on much, though. Ma is great. She always felt like enough." I reached a hand over and readjusted where his helmet had slipped a bit. I needed to remember to pick up an extra from the locker room; this one was way too big.

Charlie stared at me for a while with clear curiosity, so I answered the questions I could see him thinking. "When I turned sixteen, Ma told me she could probably track him down if I wanted to meet him. But I chose not to. My mom worked hard to raise me, and I might be biased, but I think she did a good job. Pops helped a lot, though—that was her dad."

Charlie nodded and faced forward, eyes on the mountain we were approaching. "So you don't, like, miss him?"

"Hold up." I held a hand out. "Our situations are different. I don't miss my dad because I can't really miss someone I never knew. You—" I cut myself short from saying anything about his dad. I didn't know the guy beyond a golden picture frame and a couple of stories from Madeline.

I took a deep breath and approached it at a different angle. "You had a dad, and you lost him. That's different. You can and should miss him. It's okay to. It's a good thing, really. In a way, it helps keep him alive." It was the way I kept Pops alive and with me. Missing his wrinkled face and witty comebacks. Remembering how he took his senior coffee and how he looked at my grandmother like she was an angel, even when they were old and gray.

Charlie adjusted his mask, pulling it up his face a little before yanking his goggles down. "Okay."

He said it in this wavy voice that made it sound anything but okay. "Okay?" I leaned in, saw how anxious it made him to see the bar move, and leaned back to normal. "I'm serious, Mini Coop. Don't keep that stuff in. Have you tried talking to your May about it?"

He shrugged in this pathetic little way, like the marionette holding him up had gotten a finger cramp. "She's got a lot going on."

I nodded. "She does. But not too much that she can't talk to you about it. She'd probably love it, honestly." I backtracked quickly and felt like a traitor. "I would assume she would, anyway. I love it when my mom comes to me when she's sad about Pops. Feels like we're bonding over it in a way."

Charlie shook his head. "May's different. She doesn't like to talk about it a lot. Sometimes I'll get upset about...it, and she'll tell me a story that I didn't know about him. She seems almost happy at the moment. But then she gets all sad for a few days, and she gets stressed with school and stuff." Through the lens of his goggles, I searched his eyes. He turned his head before he continued. "I hear her cry sometimes at night. She thinks she's being quiet. I think she just wants me to think she's okay. But I know she's not."

And just like that, I was punched in the gut so hard, I thought I might throw up. I imagined Madeline lying in her bed, curled up with a blanket, trying to cry as quietly as possible, sucking in tight, short breaths, with her eyes bloodshot and heavy. I could see Charlie or Half-Pint checking in on her. She'd wipe those tears away, staple on that fake-smile mask, and nod. "Sorry, just watched a sad movie," she'd say, assuring them again and again. Repeating the night over and over. It was so easy to imagine because it was so Madeline. And I wondered then whether Madeline didn't have a sense of who she was because she'd been wearing a mask for so long and couldn't tell which face was real and which wasn't.

"Well, if it helps—" I cleared my throat, trying to toss any indignation out of it. "If you ever want to talk about your dad, you can call me."

"I don't have a phone," he pointed out.

"Okay, then write it down. Bring it to our lessons, and you can rant or—" I stopped before I said cry. I had the feeling that Mini Coop was still young enough to think crying was an embarrassment instead of relief flooding your body. Like a scientific reaction meant to comfort you. "Or talk about him as much as you want."

We were approaching the lift fast, and I wished we could ride on here a little longer to get another glimpse of this family.

"Okay," he whispered. "That sounds okay."

"Okay."

"He liked to ski."

That I wanted to hear more about. "Your dad?"

He nodded and adjusted his helmet again when it tilted. "Not like professionally. He wasn't as good as you."

I snorted.

"But he was good, from what I remember. My mom hated it, so we would stay back. But Dad would take pictures and videos of the views and stuff for me. It was cool."

I sucked in a breath. Any kind of pinch of sadness I had over my own father's absence immediately left my body. I never cried over the guy, never missed him. But I guessed a very small piece of me had wondered about what I was missing out on. Father-son stuff that I hadn't experienced. Things like this, I guess. My dad had chosen to leave me, and he'd done it gladly. Charlie's dad was ripped from this earth, probably clinging to his children in the process. Anything I had missed from that random guy my mom had married was abysmal in comparison.

So we sat for a little longer. Just two fatherless guys sitting on a bench, dangling above a blanket of snow, staring out at the kaleidoscope of blue and white around us. We rode the lift past the first stop, where we were supposed to get off, down to the second hill, and all the way to the third before looping back. Neither of us said a word about wanting to hop off. So we made a full loop.

A loop around the mountain and back, full of questions and answers, teaching and learning and references that seemed to always circle back to his aunt. And I sat there, soaking in every word about the Sage family.

He talked about his mom's dream of driving an ice cream truck around and how she always told him he would hang out in the back, in charge of taste testing each product. His dad would joke that there would be nothing to sell if the two of them were left alone in the truck. He told me about his grandparents, Madeline's parents. How they didn't like talking about his dad, or how, if he brought him up, they would immediately get busy. He talked about video games he wanted to try one day and his goals of having a job just like mine one day. I stayed quiet, beyond the random question here and there, and just let him talk. I nodded along with his discussions about his little sister. How she glared at strangers in grocery stores or how she had an odd love of water—always wanting to wash her hands or brush her teeth for an excuse to be near it. He thought she might become an underwater welder or something one day, and I couldn't disagree. I pictured taking them to a beach one day, and I imagined Piper hissing at random bystanders. I told him I was aware of her hatred for strangers—me included—and he shook his head. "You're not in the circle yet," he explained.

The circle, come to find out, consisted of Charlie, Madeline, and his grandparents. He also said that sometimes even his grandfather didn't belong in the circle, depending on Piper's mood. "Don't take it personally," he said at the sight of my half pout. "No one sticks around long enough to get in the circle. And if you do, it's kind of a miracle." That made me even more determined to crack the code that would allow me to squish in there without her noticing.

He spoke of Madeline too. Of how she loved the Beach Boys and coffee, even at nighttime. How she had a special place in her heart for limoncello cake and white cheddar Cheez-its. He told stories of her before his dad passed. How she would come to visit with containers of Nerf guns or Lego sets, claiming she was the best aunt. He would remind her that she was their only aunt, and she would say "No, in the whole world." She used to collect perfume bottles—still had a box of them in her closet, apparently—and Christmas was her favorite holiday.

I collected each fact like it was a precious gift and stowed it away for later. As if I was planning on writing some kind of Madeline dissertation and needed every single piece of her documented in my brain.

On the loop back, we talked about his crush on Faith—that he refused to label as a crush but didn't fight me on when I called it that. He told me he liked her smile and thought she was "super funny." Which, for some reason, made me laugh. In turn, that made him laugh, and everything we described after that was in partnership with the word "super." This mountain is super high. Your helmet is super big. Your head is super big. I am super at saying super. The list went on, both of us laughing when the other found a new super way to use it.

At one point we came to an agreement that we needed a super handshake, just for the two of us. It consisted of some high fives, fist bumps, and a few bird-flapping motions. It was a little long and a little awkward for a quick handshake, but still, it was something only for us.

"All right, we only do that if something really cool happens."

"Like what?"

"I don't know." I shrugged. "I'll tell you when it's time."

Eventually, we did jump off the lift. Both of us somehow changed when we skied our way down.

Chapter Twenty-four
Madeline

A fter the weekend I'd had, I forced myself to dive back into making studying a top priority. First thing Monday morning, I got Charlie to school and Piper to Olive's house—since she begged for "baby time," despite Piper turning three in a few months—and the minute I was alone in my car, I turned on an Australian male version of Siri and listened to him discuss examining various methods of soft-tissue intervention, the volume turned up as if I was listening to a newly released Taylor Swift album. I was a model student this week. I was going to get back to studying, back to focusing on the goal.

It wasn't like nursing school had taken a back seat for the last two weeks. I still attended every Zoom meeting and took every proctored quiz when the kids were asleep. It was still a priority. But so were my kids, and work, and paying bills. Along with other things, like Cooper Graves, who was slowly working his way up my list.

Every day this week, I listened to my Siri Aussie, who I learned was officially named Clyde, while I worked. I took notes in the spare minutes I found between dusting and wiping furniture down. I read chapter assignments during breaks and made so many Quizlet's that I had to start paying for a premium version of the app. I buckled down at night after the kids slept and zeroed in on all the subject matter I could.

By Friday, I could practically feel the burnout weighing on my shoulders. It sat there, waiting, taunting. Knowing it was approaching only made me dread it more. Finals were mere weeks away, and I was far from ready to make anything higher than a C in any class. And considering my two tiny but essential scholarships required at least a 3.75 GPA, it wasn't going to cut it. Most of my nursing school had been paid from a fund by a savings account my parents and I had been putting money into since I was sixteen and decided I wanted to be a nurse—mostly because I overheard a boy I had a crush on say they were admirable.

Working as a cashier in a local pharmacy that saw 0.5 customers per hour meant I'd saved a lot less than half of what I needed for nursing school, so my parents, who'd begun matching my deposits, increased their own. Still, over the years, with each job I had, I made sure the nursing school fund was still going. I even picked up odd jobs here and there—window washing, shoveling driveways, and babysitting; any extra buck I had went straight to that account.

If I'd had any control over it, I would have ripped it out when I found out that I was being thrown into the belly of parenthood without so much as an instruction manual. But the fact of the matter was, my parents were the main account owners, and it was clear that the money could only be used for school. Between that account and the tiny scholarships, I managed to make it through each semester with just enough funding.

So it was stupid to work that hard for that long and not enjoy schooling, right? Or if not enjoy it, then at least somewhat not hate it?

Still, knowing it was finally Friday felt like my only relief. Because that meant a not-date. Which meant a night of not learning about the human nervous system or other clinical health details that tended to make me feel nauseous. It meant a night with Cooper too, which I was craving in an almost mortifying way. We had only seen each other in passing this week. When I dropped Charlie off, he'd wink or smile at me with that smirk that felt like our own little secret. Or if we ended up getting coffee at the same time, he'd bump in line in front of me so he could pay. Or like on Wednesday, he came by at the end of my shift and caught me sitting by the big green accent chair with my feet curled up, watching the snow fall outside. I peered over my shoulder at him and smiled when he took the matching seat beside it and turned it around so he could watch with me. Neither of us said much beyond the typical how are you?, but it was nice. Comfortable. Like he knew I wasn't wanting a ton of conversation but still enjoyed his company. Like I'd pushed myself to the finish line, and he was the guy holding the sign at the very end. He was saying "push a little farther." So I did.

I did until Friday night, when I got a text from Cooper.

Cooper: tonight is still good right

Cooper: i can bring a thermometer in case someone gets sick again

I snorted and replied.

Me: Still good! Do I need to wear anything specific?

Cooper: clothes if you want

Cooper: but hey dont let me tell you what to do

Considering he hadn't told me to dress fancy or warm or any other adjective like he'd used in the past, I settled for simple. My favorite jeans, also known as the only ones, that didn't give me a weird, sagging crotch, a cream sweater, and a black jacket that I'd named my big girl jacket, since I'd gotten it when I decided, at twenty-three, that I was officially a woman and would own a legit coat, not just hoodies.

My parents were both under the weather tonight, claiming Piper had given them something even though they hadn't seen her in over a week, so Finn and Olive had stepped in. They claimed they needed practice. I felt like I was throwing them in the lion's den with these two, but they were the ones who offered, so I simply said okay.

"Why does the small one keep staring at me?" Finn pointed to Piper from across the room. She sat holding an Elsa doll that was almost as big as she was, clutching it tight enough that she was shaking whilst glaring at Finn with daggers in her eyes.

"She's plotting your death," Charlie answered behind him, making Finn jump.

"She doesn't like most people. She's sweet, and Olive does great with her, right?" I turned to my best friend, who had a bowl of bean dip resting on her belly.

"Yeah." She popped a chip into her mouth. "She kind of loved me by the end there. She even let me sit next to her."

"Is she going to stare at me the whole time?" Finn swallowed.

"Maybe. She hates men the most. She was always that way. Even as a newborn, if anyone other than Charlie, me, or her parents held her, she would scream."

Finn nodded and gave a wobbly half smile. "Great."

A car horn came from the driveway, and I craned my neck to see Cooper's car parked there, with his window down, smiling at me. I smiled back and turned to the other two adults. "Everything you could possibly need is on the note on the fridge. Neither of them is allergic to anything. Please call if anything happens. Piper is known to climb things, so watch for that, and Charlie mostly sticks to himself, but sometimes he will—"

"We've got this." Olive waved a hand and then flipped a piece of her long blond hair over her shoulder. "Go have fun with your ma—" She cut herself off, looking at the kids. "Friend."

I narrowed my eyes. "I will."

Giving both kids a quick peck on the cheek, I headed out.

Turned out that Cooper had more planned that I expected. He called it Tour de Aspen.

It included a stop for freshly brewed coffee in tiny pink ceramic mugs at Felix Roasting Co., where we sat next to each other in a blue velvet booth. He asked me what I was like as a child, a part of his experiment, he claimed, and I responded simply. I was a mini-Will. I did my best to do what he did, no matter how bad I was at it. I told Cooper stories about how I chased him and his friends around the backyard and about going to see R-rated movies way too young because I wanted to be where he was. How he never let me feel like a burden, even when his high school girlfriends clearly didn't want me tagging along on their dates. Cooper told me about the trouble he'd gotten into, which came as no surprise. He spoke about being prom king, a title he mentioned with a tinge of pink in his cheeks, and how he avoided anyone he went to high school with when possible. He told me about how he'd wanted a dog when he was a kid, but instead, his mom got him a hamster. He said he loved that thing so much that, one day, it fell over and didn't get back up. That they buried him and his mom performed a thirty-minute funeral in their backyard while he played the recorder. "Hot Cross Buns," because that's all he knew at the time. He also added that he found out a year ago that hamsters hibernate, and little Truman probably wasn't dead, but just in a deep sleep, so they more than likely buried him alive.

Our next stop was at a local place called Meat and Cheese. We ordered a flat wooden cutting board covered in salami and wheat crackers, slices of apple-smoked cheddar, a goat fig, and rose log. Tiny pickles with a sour kick that made me feel like a giant, and small orange sauces that seemed a little too adventurous to me. There he asked me about school, how I liked it, what my classes were like, and a serious question about whether gum really stays in your stomach for seven years. To which I responded with "eight if it's the Hubba Bubba kind."

I told him about how I was 90 percent online now, only going in person for labs or finals. I told him about how old I felt when I was on campus and how most of the nursing students I had met either resembled my high school bullies or were the nicest people I'd ever met. There was no in-between. I left out the part where I felt burnout creeping over me. Or how I cringed when I thought about the human circulatory system, imagining all my arteries and veins under my skin. I didn't tell him that the farther I got into school, the harder it got to accept that this was my future. Bloody gauze and coughing kids and vital taking. Instead, I asked him about how he enjoyed his job. "There's nothing I'd rather do," he said. "I'm good at it, and I love it." He spoke so confidently, so surely, that it felt like he had already watched his own life play out on a screen. Like he knew every scene that was to come. Not even an ounce of wonder there. Just knowing. I was honestly jealous.

When our board turned into scraps of pickles and half-eaten antipasto, we did a quick pop into Paradise Bakery for chocolate chip cookies—both of our personal favorites. We mostly stayed quiet there, considering we shoved our faces full the entire time. That was until we both looked up from our savage eating to see chocolate smeared across each other's lips. A splattered, melted brown mess on our hands and mouths and cheeks. Even a tiny droplet on Cooper's temple. We then laughed so hard that we snorted simultaneously, making us laugh even more until our laughter converted to wheezing gasps. The tourists around us stared until we wiped most of the chocolate off our faces. Except for that tiny drop on his temple. I kept that one to myself.

Last, a stop for fondue at the French Alpine Bistro.

We sat in a crowded room under the warm glow of antique light fixtures. The walls around us were adorned in historical paintings and portraits, one of a young girl holding a carving knife close to her, scowling, which Cooper said reminded him of Piper. I found it oddly endearing.

Our waitress took our orders, yapping on about expensive dishes like she was working on commission.

"You sure you don't want our raclette with homegrown potatoes? We get it from Ronniger farms. It's my favorite." The moules-marinière and tuna tartare were, conveniently, also her favorite.

When we both denied, agreeing that we were already stuffed from our previous adventures, she took it so personally that I feared she was going to somehow write a bad review on us as people and post it publicly. She said, more like enforced, the words homegrown potatoes about six more times before giving up.

As soon as we were alone again, I mumbled, "I think she was trying to poison us."

"Or maybe homegrown potatoes is a secret code meaning she was kidnapped by a local restaurant chain, and she hoped that if she said it enough times, we would get the hint."

We volleyed guesses regarding the waitress's obsession with potatoes as soft instrumental music played around us. We were clearly the least dressed up, considering our neighboring tables were draped in fur coats and wearing thin sunglasses on the tips of their noses. We both made assumptions, mostly by the vast amount of picture taking, that they were influencers.

"I'm feeling awfully influenced to wear sunglasses inside a restaurant at night, aren't you?" he asked.

I nodded. "Influenced to immediately start an Amazon storefront as a side hustle." We laughed over the melted Gruyère,

Beaufort, Comté, and Vacherin in the pot being warmed by an even fancier candle with white wax building up the side of it with each drop. Cooper said he had an urge to stick his fingers in it, and when I asked whether he meant the cheese or the candle wax, he said both.

The fondue came with a bottle of white wine, which I could only assume was also fancy, considering its label looked worn, and it smelled like excellence. Like the kind of stuff Rose's family would drink on the Titanic. When our waitress poured each of us a glass and set it in an ice bucket, you would have thought Cooper and I had just watched Return of the Jedi while high on extra-strength weed gummies by the way we both exhaled long whoas.

Cooper nudged his glass over to me and ordered himself something called les innocents, which, when I put my context clues together, I assumed meant nonalcoholic drink. An element of surprise came a moment later. Literally, that was what the drink was called. A sparkling water with elderflower syrup and a piece of fresh mint resting on top.

Cooper took a sip and winced. "I was too influenced."

"Can I ask why you don't drink?" I asked as I brought the glass to my lips. Maybe it was inappropriate of me to ask. But then again, I wasn't sure whether Cooper knew what inappropriate meant.

Cooper's hand paused as he was holding a piece of warm bread mid-dip. "I don't want it to change your opinion of me." He said it with such hesitation that it honestly made me like him more. To see someone so bold and confident suddenly a little raw.

"You don't have to tell me."

"I should." He finished dipping and set the bread down on his plate next to cut-up apples and roasted cauliflower. "It was a fallback for a while."

"A fallback?"

"Yeah, like...in high school, I never had issues getting drinks to parties. I could"—he looked up and hesitated for a second before continuing—"flirt with older women and convince them to buy enough for me and my buddies to have a good night. Then I got older, and I was twenty-one, and it was so easy to grab it and go to parties or invite people to the lodge after hours. So easy. For years, I told myself this was how it was supposed to be. That everyone in their twenties drank like this. I'd use the whole it's five o'clock somewhere reasoning. Or I'd hear about a group of tourists coming in for the competition, or a celebrity staying at the lodge, whatever the excuse was, I would go to the bar and have a good time."

I nodded even if I couldn't relate, not even a little bit. My twenty-first birthday was spent at a spa with Will's girlfriend. We got the kind of massages where people stand on your back, and I drank half of a sangria before saying it was "ew" and "spicy" and left it for Savannah to drink.

"Well, time went on, and I kept having these parties or get-togethers or whatever. And it was like the only way I could get people to come was if I mentioned there would be alcohol. Or women. Or anything extra that might grab attention. For years, it was like that."

I hummed and tried so hard to keep any jealousy swirling in my throat from rising up. Unfair, Madeline. He didn't even know you existed back then.

"So, one day I asked the same group of guys if they wanted to come to this bonfire in my backyard. It was kind of a test. I sent a text to a group chat, and the only responses came back with BYOB or are you covering? Or will girls be there?, like we were still seventeen. I said no to both and waited for their responses. They never came."

"No one showed up?" I whispered.

He shook his head. "Someone showed up, all right." He laughed in this way that built up from his chest. "Finn welcomed himself into my backyard. He sat in an Adirondack chair and talked my ear off for the rest of the night." He smiled as he spoke, recalling the memory. "'S how I knew he was a real friend. A long-haul friend, you know? He stuck by. And even though I went right back to alcohol and women and sometimes a few drugs, nothing crazy, Finn was right there. And he never asked for a thing. Well, not until Olive came into the picture anyway."

Then I smiled. "So, you've been best friends ever since?"

He nodded. "Ever since."

"When did you decide to stop drinking?" I asked.

"I stayed like that for a couple more years. Too long. Ma and Pops both said I was treating myself too poorly, that I was better than that. I kind of brushed them off until Pops passed. That was when it cemented. That I had to turn my life around. There was no other choice. It sucked for a little bit. I watched all of these people I thought were friends suddenly disappear from my life. But eventually, it got better. And I put 100 percent of myself into the lodge. I taught more lessons, started skiing again on my own. And somehow, it healed me."

"Whoa," I whispered, and it sounded like the white wine ice bucket situation all over again. "Cooper, that's..." Amazing. Sad. So heartbreaking. That you thought you weren't enough on your own. "I'm proud of you."

He smiled at that and took a sip of his drink. "Thanks, Madeline. I'm proud of me too."

We smiled at each other a little longer, lingering in this happy place that was free of responsibilities and worries. That was how it felt to be with him.

"I'm glad you told me."

His smile unzipped from one corner. "Doesn't make me seem pathetic?"

"I like this Cooper much better than the old one, if it helps."

Cooper groaned and stuck his palms into his eye sockets, rubbing. "I don't think I'll ever forgive myself for not remembering you bringing me dinner. Gah, it's going to haunt me."

"Well, not to rub salt on the wound, but I'd seen you before then too."

"You didn't." He shook his head feverishly. "Tell me you didn't."

"I've been working at the lodge for two years, Coop; chances are I was bound to have seen you. You're like a local celebrity. Everyone is drawn to you." It was true. Everyone basked in his warmth when he was around. A heater on a back deck during a cold night, drawing everyone in.

"Where? Where did you see me?"

I shrugged. "The coffee shop, talking with Finn in the distance, flirting with tourists."

He groaned into his hands.

"And I vaguely remember you dancing in a video on Olive's Snapchat stories."

His groan went louder before he lifted his head up. "No."

"Yes."

"Was I doing the worm?"

"I...think you thought you were doing the worm?"

Cooper shook his head. "How are you still here? Seriously?"

"I know how losing someone can change a person, and I kind of saw that from a distance. You looked healthier over time. Happier. I didn't stalk you or anything—"

"Bummer."

"But I paid attention after your grandfather died. He was my friend, and it felt like I was doing him a favor."

He smiled at that. "Then I guess you meant what you said. That you knew exactly who I was."

"I did." I smiled. "Which was why I didn't try to drop kick you for acting like you were Charlie's dad."

He shook his head. "That was not my finest moment. But to be fair, you broke my streak."

"Your streak?"

"My no women streak. I wouldn't even make eye contact with anyone under fifty unless they were married or clearly in my safety zone. I worked hard on that streak. Had a reminder in my phone and everything."

I snorted. "What did the reminder say?"

"It was in all caps. NO TALKING, NO TOUCHING, NO LOOKING. Worked pretty well for a long time."

"Did it?"

He nodded. "Until I saw a pretty brunette in a purple sweater, and I lost all inhibitions. I turned the reminders off that afternoon. You were the exception."

"Oh." It felt like someone was shrinking my rib cage when I sucked in a breath. "Well, I'm glad."

"Me too," he agreed, and we sat there for a while longer, gorging on apples, cheese, and freshly baked bread.

And when we left, fondue empty and bellies full, he helped me into my coat and rested his hand on my lower back. My spine relaxed into his touch, and when I looked up at him as we exited into the brisk Colorado air, he was already smiling down at me.

We'd had to park pretty far down from the actual restaurant, considering it was a Friday night and we were reaching peak tourist season. So we walked, swaying from side to side as our hips bumped, with his hand on my lower back. Somewhere in the back of my mind, I felt a tinge of guilt for not sharing this night with Charlie. For not inviting him or even just telling him who I was with. But it was washed away when a dry laugh came from Cooper.

"I still can't believe you like Planet of the Apes."

I gasped a laugh, watching my breath exhale into the cold night. "Man versus apes. It's classic. What's not to like?"

"Madeline, they're gorillas on horses."

"I was influenced!" I said in a wine-induced laugh.

"No amount of influencing should cause you to reach for that movie."

"Movies," I corrected. "Have you even watched them?"

"Meh."

"So, that's a no, then." We passed a club with people waiting in a long line to get in.

"No, it's a meh. Those movies are like...I don't know. Like a small hernia. Like it could be worse, but I definitely don't want it."

My laughter was mixing with the mint gum I'd stolen from the hostess stand. I guessed it wasn't considered stealing when the bowl of them was right there. But when we both reached for one and got some funny looks from the staff, it felt like stealing.

"You're comparing one of the greatest cinematic films of all time to a hernia?" I shrieked the last word, and a girl in a very small dress and almost blue legs looked at me in disgust as we passed by her.

"Just a small one." Cooper's pinky hooked into the belt loop of my coat and rested there, same as he'd done with my belt loop of my jeans when we first kissed. Heat licked its way up my neck.

He looked down at me with this smirk, the same one he'd worn right after he kissed me. The one that caused something warm to settle in my belly. It was freezing out, the chill pushing down to the bones in my feet, but Cooper's gaze was warm. Like I was on the beach of a private island, laid out on the sand and listening to the ocean roar in the distance. He made me feel like we were on vacation, like maybe he would one day take me to the beach, and I could feel his warm gaze all over me there too.

When we got to the car, I made a quick call to Olive to check on the kids. She said they were both passed out in their beds with brushed teeth and washed hair and that "Piper didn't kill

Finn, despite her best attempts," which sounded like a successful night to me.

I hung up and turned to face Cooper as the seat warmers slowly started doing their job on my upper thighs. "Sorry, I can be kind of paranoid about them."

He shook his head. "Don't apologize. I'm glad you called. I was wondering too."

"Really?"

"Of course. Mini Coop was my friend before you were."

"And Piper?"

"Well, we can't all be perfect."

I laughed at that. "She is just misunderstood."

"So are sharks."

When we pulled into my driveway, I curled my fingers around the clutch that I'd used as a wallet tonight—a pointless attempt, since anytime I tried to pay for something, Cooper would say "how cute" before slamming his own card down. That was when I came to learn that I did like old-fashioned dating standards.

"Thanks for tonight." I didn't mean for it to come out as a sigh, but I couldn't exactly stop it. "It was a nice break."

Cooper nodded with that smile that was reminiscent of a wolf watching its prey from afar. And I'd never felt more like a lone little bunny in the woods. "This was the best not date ever, hands down."

"How often do you go on these?"

He hummed. "Do dentist visits count?"

"Why would they?"

"Well, he has his hands in my mouth a lot. Feels kind of romantic, if you ask me."

"No, I don't think they count."

"Then you're my one and only, Madeline." He smiled.

I knew it was a joke. A cute little line thrown in there with a dash of flirtation, but still, it felt like someone had scooped out my insides and tossed them into a KitchenAid mixer, and I was watching myself fall apart. Maybe there was a medical term for that, and I just hadn't been paying enough attention in my classes. But that? That was what it felt like when Cooper said, "you're my one and only, Madeline."

It wasn't just that he looked the way he did, tall and messy-haired and so imperfectly perfect. Like God had made him, had taken one look, and was like "no way can we send someone that good-looking down." So he added extra quirks, like a slightly crooked nose and a curved upper lip, only to discover it made him even better-looking than before. But it was that he was sweet too. It was like someone offered you a free breakfast, and you were thinking you'd have a single piece of burnt toast and an undercooked fried egg. But it turned out to be a Dr. Seuss–worthy meal of french toast, chocolate-chip pancakes, ham, and delectable Swiss croissants. He was this bundled surprise. The more I peeled back to see, the more I liked.

"I should probably..." I pointed to the house. Go to bed kicking my feet and giggling. Relive this night over and over, as long as it takes to cement it in my brain. Take a very, very cold shower. "Go in."

He nodded and looked toward the house where Finn and Olive were not so discreetly staring at us. "Ah, I gotcha. I could walk you in?" he offered, and because I was still scared of Charlie finding out, I shook my head. "It's okay."

He nodded and gave me this understanding smile that made me feel like I had no more explanation to give him. He reached a hand out to me, grasping a honey-brown tendril of hair and tucking it behind my ear. "Next time."

"Next time, what?" I whispered back.

"Next time I'll kiss you like no one's watching." He stared right at my mouth as he said it, and I never wanted so badly to take a lamp and throw it at our best friends right now.

"O-Okay." I nodded. "Sounds good."

He snorted. "Good night, Madeline."

I exited the car on wobbly legs. "Good night, Cooper."

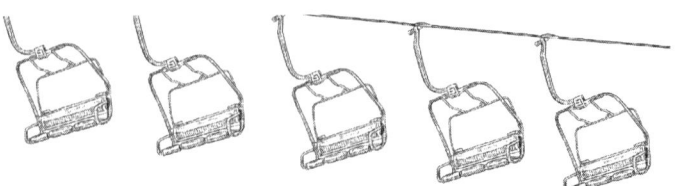

Chapter Twenty-five
COOPER

I remember when Finn first met Olive. How from that one plane ride back here, he was an entirely different person. I always thought it was so weird, and mostly terrifying, that he'd found a woman that made him want to change overnight. Then I met Olive. And she was sweet and pretty, although a little prickly here and there. But mostly, I saw how she looked at Finn when he wasn't looking. That, I thought, was pretty cool. So in my head from then on, I thought, wow if I ever settled down with a girl, she would be so lucky. She could look at me like that.

Because I was genuinely that self-involved, that ignorant about relationships that I assumed that was how it was. Because I had never met someone and thought that I would be lucky if I could have just five minutes of her time.

But now I knew better. Now, I stood in the ski lodge lobby, holding a coffee order that I had memorized, with three Slim Jims stuck in my back pocket, because I knew that whatever this was, it was something more. Something beyond not-dates and friendly flirting. This was a next-level, could very well be a real thing if I played my cards right kind of situation. And I had a very obvious two-and-a-half-foot tall elephant in my way.

I had one kid down—Charlie loved me, that much was clear—and one to go. All I had to do was bribe her enough to make her love me. Or actually, you know what? All I had to do was make her tolerate me. Because I had no plans of going anywhere as far as Madeline was involved, and little Half-Pint was going to have to get used to me without her death glares shooting my way twenty-four seven.

I got to the lobby an hour earlier than usual, clocked in over at the regular station, and set all my bags and gear in the locker room, waiting for eight o'clock to arrive. It was kind of foolish, considering time really didn't revolve around us, but I had nothing better to do, and I needed to go over the plan in my head one more time.

Last night, after I dropped Madeline off at her house, I'd driven back to my place and had sent Finn a text.

SOS. CALL ME AS SOON AS YOU LEAVE HER HOUSE.

The fact that I used any form of punctuation must've given a hint as to the gravity of my situation, because he called not even three minutes later.

"Are you okay?" He was panting.

Olive was practically shrieking beside him. "Do you need an ambulance?"

"No." I considered it for a moment, the fact that my heart was doing somersaults like it was Cirque du Soleil in there, but then decided against it. "No. I need help, though."

"With what?"

"Madeline."

"Oh Jesus," Finn groaned. "What did you do?"

"I tried not to fall for her, believe it or not. Just maybe not as hard as I could have tried."

Olive sighed. "Yeah, I get it."

"What am I supposed to do, seriously?" I ran my hands through my hair and tugged. "She has kids. Two of them. And we started this whole thing because I needed a fake girlfriend, and now everything is blurry, and I am so bad with kids and I can't be a dad, but those kids need a—"

"Cooper," Olive interrupted. "Slow down and breathe."

I tried to do what she said, but each breath I took in felt sharp, like there was a spear in my side, pressing into my lungs. "I can't do this."

"Yes, you can," she assured. "Let's start here: Coop, you are wonderful with kids."

Finn agreed. "This is true."

"Your entire life's work is being around kids. You are so good at it that all the parents brag on you."

"It can get out of hand sometimes," Finn added. "But it's true. Plus"—he sucked in a breath, and I could picture them both in his car with their hands tangled together—"we would trust you to watch our baby any day."

"You mean that?"

"Of course," Olive answered.

And I tried to really picture it then. Something serious with Madeline. Christmas mornings in matching pajamas, watching them open presents and watching Elf on a couch under fuzzy blankets with hot cider. Or summers in Aspen, when the snow had melted and the flowers had bloomed, and we could go to local plant nurseries. Or trying the drive-in again in hopes that they don't recognize us. It was easy to see. Except for one fuzzy little dot.

"But the little one hates me." I sighed.

"Piper hates everyone," Olive agreed. "But she's not impossible to get to. You just have to know how to work your way in."

"You're in the circle?"

"I...don't know what that means, but she doesn't stare at me like she wants to hit me with a piano anymore, so I'd say yes, I'm successfully in the circle."

"How?" I practically shouted. "What do I do?"

We stayed on the phone for an hour after that, Olive and Finn tacking on different pieces of advice until we formed a solid plan of attack. And I was more than ready.

Sure enough, when eight rolled around, I kept my eyes glued to that door until a curvy brunette swayed into the lobby in her regular work uniform with her blond niece in tow. Half-Pint had a familiar Elsa doll in one hand. The fact that I knew I'd bought it for her gave me a boost of energy, like maybe I could actually pull this off.

I watched as they sorted through the scattered crowd of early morning skiers and tourists. I stood and checked my back pockets one last time before following them back to the employee-only areas to clock in.

"Madeline!" I raised a hand and watched as she and Piper turned around, one with a bright, wide grin and the other sporting a scowl that seemed more like a threat than anything. Not today. Today, that was going to change.

"Hey, Coop." She set her purse on a wooden bench on the side and plopped the toddler who'd been on her hip right beside it. "What's up?"

I held the coffee in my hand, which now had a top layer of melted ice that we both chose to ignore. "Had to bring your coffee."

She eyed it. "You don't have to keep doing that. We're even now."

I shook my head. "Not quite yet. But we will be."

"Well, that's sweet but—"

Just then, right on time, a knock came from the door. "Hey Mad—Oh, hey, Coop." My best friend stood at the door with the least suspicious grin possible, knowing exactly what to do.

"Hey." I just dipped my chin, because my acting skills were far less superior to Finn's. He'd played a tree in a school play once.

"Madeline, I was going to see if I could borrow you really quick. I had a push present idea for Olive, and I need your opinion."

She looked over at me and back to Finn before shrugging. "Sure."

Madeline set the coffee beside Piper and turned to me. "Uh, let me just—"

"I'll watch her," I volunteered.

"Are you sure? She can be a bit—"

"I'm sure. Go ahead. We'll be right here."

Madeline looked down to the rabid chipmunk on the bench and back to me. "Okay...just...good luck. I'll be right back."

She and Finn walked out while he gave me a curt thumbs-up behind her back.

Once they were gone, I turned to look at the toddler. "Listen here, Half-Pint."

A half growl came from the back of her throat. "You Half-Pi."

"Sure." I reached a hand in my back pocket and wrapped my fingers around the thin meat stick. "Now"—I pulled it out, and immediately the growl from her deepened—"settle down, Cujo." I unwrapped the Slim Jim and held it out to her.

"This..." I paused. "What do you call this again?"

She muttered something to herself like shmjm, and I said, "What?"

"Sham Jam." Her growl was replaced by a whisper.

"Sham Jam. It's all yours, but I need a favor from you too."

The almost three-year-old stared at me, waiting. So I continued. "If you let me in on the circle"—her head tilted a little to the side—"you can have this Sham Jam."

"Two," she said.

"Two what?"

"Two Sham Jams."

This sneaky little... "Urgh." I groaned. "Fine. Two Sham Jams." I pulled another one out of my back pocket, glad I'd brought reinforcements.

"Here." I set both now unwrapped sticks in her tiny open palm. "But remember, I am in the circle now, got it?"

She eyed me like she had no clue what I was saying, but I knew one thing: kids were always smarter than they let on. She didn't smile, certainly not like she did with her aunt, but she gave me this half-quirked lip before taking a large bite and chewing. Her way of letting me know we were at a truce, I supposed.

I sat next to her and pulled out the third meat stick in my pocket, opening it up for myself. She made a garbled sound next to me that sounded more like she slammed her hand down on a keyboard than actual words.

"What?" I asked, tone lighter than before.

"Mmm!" She pointed at the snack in my hand. "My Sham Jam."

I shook my head side to side. "Nuh-uh-uh. You got two, Half-Pint. This one's mine."

Before I could react, her tiny ninja fingers reached up and snuck it out of my loosened grip. She took a bite off the tip for good measure and then sat there, smug as shit, holding three Slim Jims and leaving me with nothing.

"What?" I gasped. "What was that?"

"Half-Pi's Sham Jam," she said, like it was final. A judge banging a gavel, done for the day.

I leaned back against the wall and slumped. "You're lucky she's worth it."

Just then, Madeline and Finn turned the corner.

"I think she'd like pink more than yellow, but that's just me." Her voice, like petals blooming or snow melting, came in a soft wave until they walked into view.

Finn took one look at me, lifting a brow. How'd it go?

I jerked my head down, and he glanced at the toddler with three Slim Jims hanging out of her mouth. Then he nodded back in satisfaction.

Phase one was complete.

"Well, I gotta get my nine-o'clock class set up. Coop, I'll see you later?"

I lazily raised a hand. "See you later."

Finn went through the exit, back out toward the hall, leaving the three of us.

"Sorry about that." Madeline huffed a small breath. "He wanted me to pick what heart-shaped jewelry I thought Olive would want after pushing the baby out."

"And you said?"

"That heart-shaped jewelry was made for children to give to their mothers or for people you hate."

I nodded. "Noted, so what did he go with?"

I listened intently as she rattled on about bathrobes and candles and other eccentric items that I imagined I would want too, if I'd pushed a watermelon out of my asshole.

"But mostly, I think it was the heated blankets and unlimited Red Hot apple cider that would really tip the scale."

"Sounds like Olive."

She nodded. "So, what were you going to tell me?"

I hummed and stood, closing the gap between us. "Oh. I was going to ask if you were busy the week before Christmas."

Madeline hummed back in this singsong tone. "I don't think we have any plans. Other than the usual family stuff."

"So...you would be available to come to this with me?" I reached into my back pocket and whipped out the white envelope I'd stuffed in my not-Slim-Jim-full pocket.

Madeline eyed it with reservation. "What would I be saying yes to?"

"Open it." I jerked my chin to the envelope in my hands.

She reached slowly, like there was a bomb in there, and opened it with such ease that if I was desperate here, then I'd honestly be offended. When she pulled out the papers, she seemed to read them three times over before looking up at me—smiling—and looking back down. She fanned the papers out, counting each copy.

"We're...going to see Disney on Ice?"

I nodded and tapped the tickets that I'd ordered at Olive's suggestion. "Yup. Center seats too. Felt like I was securing courtside Avalanche tickets or something."

"Cooper." She glanced over at Piper, who had begun listening in at the word Disney. "There are five tickets."

"Yup."

"Why?"

"Me, you, Mini Coop, Half-Pint, and Mini Coop's friend. Or maybe my mom? I don't know. She gets freaked out by people in costumes."

"Why?" she asked in a small breath.

"I think it's because of the whole uncanny valley thing, where something somewhat resembles a human but not fully—"

"No, no. I meant why are you taking all of us to see Disney on Ice?"

"Oh." I smiled. "I thought it would be cool, all of us together."

She looked back down at the papers, and a slow smile pulled at her lips before tucking back down, like she couldn't show it. "This is a week after the interview?"

I heard the question in her voice there. The wondering about more. This was a week after the interview, where we would be pretending to be together and kind of the whole purpose of our not-dates. There was no need for any more after the interview. Except there was a need. Way down deep in my belly, I had enough need for more for the both of us.

I nodded. "It is. Consider it my formal invitation of our first not-not-date."

"Not...not-date?"

"Mm-hmm." My chin dipped.

"So a date, then?"

I held up my hands in defense. "If that's what you want to call it, then by all means."

The slow smile of hers transitioned into the bright, shining one. The one that made my heart feel tight and my pulse speed up. Like suddenly, I could feel every nerve ending in my body being heightened when that smile came around.

"So...you're asking me on a date?"

"Yes."

"A real one."

I nodded and matched my smile to hers. "Nothing artificial about it. I'll even buy you some Mickey ears if you're feeling influenced."

Madeline glanced over at Piper, who was no longer listening to us but was now down to half a Slim Jim left, and all her focus was directly on it. "You want our first real date to be with the kids?"

"You're a package deal, right?"

She bit on her bottom lip and kept that shy smile to herself. "I think so. Yes. But we should probably give Charlie a heads-up beforehand."

"Already on that." That was somewhere between step four and seven. I figured that during our next lesson, we could have a talk, man to man, and duke it out on a ski lift, where he couldn't run away mid-conversation and I couldn't chicken out.

Madeline pulled the tickets to her chest. "Well, then I'm excited." She turned to Piper. "Pipes, look we can go see Elsa!"

Half-Pint let out this high pitched squeal that was so cute it almost made me excited to watch a random woman dressed in a wig dance around on fake ice too.

Madeline turned back to me. "Thank you, Coop. That really was so sweet."

I shrugged. "It's not that sweet. I have selfish intent behind it."

"Really?" She raised a brow. "What kind of selfish intent?"

I looked up at the time and saw I only had ten minutes to change clothes and go outside. So I shot her a wink and said, "Wouldn't you like to know?"

Chapter Twenty-six
Madeline

I was officially only two weeks away from my finals.

Two weeks away from what had to be the hardest semester in the history of the world—yes, including aerospace engineering programs and rocket science. Two weeks away from having a break between semesters so I could lift my head from the snow, take a deep breath, and enjoy the view before diving right back in.

Considering I hadn't been able to dedicate as much time to studying as I probably should have; I texted my mom last night to see if they could watch Piper after my morning shift. Her response was an extremely dry sure, but I knew she wasn't feeling 100 percent after her physical therapy appointment. But as much as I loved Piper, focusing on any kind of work besides her while she was around felt nearly impossible, and I was crunching down enough as it was. If I performed poorly on any of my finals, and I was left with a GPA below a 3.75, then my scholarships would be gone. As would school. As would any hope I had of a future where I could provide enough for these kids.

I loved my job. But the reality was, I couldn't do this forever. Besides, when I was little, I'd always said I wanted to be a nurse, and once I finished up my last two semesters, I would get to achieve that goal and maybe find that piece of myself that I felt like I was missing.

Pulling into my mom's driveway always made my blood pressure rise a little. Enough for me to notice. Like all of the cells in my body were standing at attention in preparation for some form of passive-aggressive conflict bound to come spiraling my way.

"Ready to see Gram, Pipes?" I shifted to park.

Piper stuck her arms out wide, reaching outward in her way of saying up, while she actually said "peeeassse" in a long, drawn-out squeal.

I hopped out and rounded the car to her side, unbuckling her from the car seat and settling her on my hip since the snow was still pretty rough from last week's storm and Piper didn't have snow boots that fit her well enough. Her feet were still that of a one-year-old, so the boots I'd bought her in the summer on clearance in hopes that they'd fit her now were far too large.

I didn't bother knocking, considering they knew I was on the way fifteen minutes ago, and walked right in to the kitchen, where my dad stood by the counter. His palms dug into the sockets of his eyes while a mug of hot coffee steamed below his face. Various papers were scattered around the countertop that Mom started scooping up once she heard the door close.

"Hi, Gram!" I said in a toddler voice, raising Piper's hand and waving it for her.

"There's my girl!" Mom turned around and made grabby hands at the two-year-old on my hip. "Gram wasn't feeling good before, but I am happy to see you. I made you some dehydrated fruit. Yes, I did." She squished her cheeks and took on a baby voice. "Some bananas for that belly and strawberries for that nose." Mom continued poking and squishing all over her granddaughter before setting her down and patting her on the bottom twice. "I've got some markers and paper for you in the living room, I'll be right there."

Piper ran away without even a glance back at me. I snorted. "I think she's sick of me after all the time we've been spending together."

"Well." Mom wiped her hands on a spare dish towel. "Most kids aren't as close with their aunts as she is. She's probably just realizing it's normal to be this way with distant relatives."

She didn't mean it as a dig. I didn't think. Maybe Cooper was right, and I did tend to see the best in people, but I really did think my mom genuinely was unaware of her emotional surroundings. How I was anything but distant to Piper and how, even though I had never been pregnant and I'd never given birth, these kids were mine.

You are valuable.

He left them for you.

"Okay." I hummed, figuring it would be best to skirt right past that.

"So." I turned to my dad, who was still looking at the floor like he hadn't slept in days. "Thanks for watching Pipes. I shouldn't be too long, but I packed dinner for her just in case. I have four finals to go through, but I may just study for two today and two another day, if you're free again this week."

"Okay." Mom hummed right back.

Our dance began. The one where neither of us said how we really felt. The waltz of I think it's weird how you never processed your son's death, and you take it out on your only kid left, who was always more of a backup anyway and...well, I didn't know what her side of that looked like, because she'd simply never said it.

So again, I moved on. "Deadlines for next semester signups are on Wednesday." They both stayed silent, looking at me like I wasn't speaking English here. "I got my classes all sorted...just need"—you know, the money—"to make a payment for finalizations."

Mom's throat cleared. "Oh, oh. Right. How much by...Wednesday, you said?"

"Yeah, Wednesday. And it's seven thousand this semester, since we have labs that I'll have to attend."

I still wasn't 100 percent sure how I could handle in-person classes, but somehow, I would pull it off. Maybe Olive could watch Piper while she was home with her baby? Or if my parents would help out a couple of days a week to—

"I can't do this, Eloise. You have to tell her." Dad suddenly stood from his silent spot and turned the corner to the living room, where I could hear Piper jabbering random noises.

"Tell...me what?" I turned back to Mom, watching as she anxiously wrung her hands around her tea towel.

"Okay." She started to pace a little. "Okay."

"Okay?" I asked.

"Okay," she parroted.

"Are you going to tell me or—"

"The money's gone."

My ears began to ring. Like a gun had been fired from right beside me, and my body was mid-recovery. The money's gone. She didn't mean—I mean, there was no way. It wasn't possible.

"What money?"

"The...nursing school money. It's not there."

My tone turned sharp as I tasted copper in my mouth. Numbers started compiling in my mind. Hours of time worked. The perfect amount saved, down to the penny. All the times I'd wanted to buy new shoes or get my nails done but thought, no, this needs to go to the school fund. Years. So many years of my life had gone into that account.

"What do you mean it's not there? Twenty thousand dollars doesn't just fly away." My breathing was heavy and uncontrollable. No amount of counting or sensory intake was going to fix this. I couldn't—oh my gosh—I couldn't breathe.

"No." Mom took a deep breath, her hands still wringing as she paced. "No, it didn't fly away. It was taken out."

"For what?" I snapped.

She still wasn't looking at me. Meanwhile I was dissecting her like a high school biology class frog, waiting to find any idea of is this real or not in her.

"For my surgery last year...and the half bathroom remodel over the summer."

Last year? My chest felt tight. This room felt tight. I'd never been claustrophobic before, but I imagined it felt a whole lot like this. Like I could strip out of my leggings and sweatshirt and rip these boots off, then run out into an empty snowy field and still feel like the world around me was too small.

"Last year?" My voice croaked, and I hated that I was on the verge of tears. "You mean...you took the money out starting last year? Why? If you had told me you needed help, I could've—" I cut myself off, because we both knew I didn't make enough to cover twenty thousand dollars. But I could have figured something out. Spoken to insurance companies, talked to the hospital about getting on a payment plan. I don't know, something.

"I could have helped" is what I settled on. "You knew I was going to need it for school. You knew I would need it to finish out my last two semesters. Why would you—"

Again, I cut myself off. Because right at that last sentence, Mom stopped wiping her hands on the dish towel. She stopped pacing. And her eyes were dead focused on me. My ears suddenly stopped ringing.

"Oh my God." It hit me. "You didn't think I was going to finish school, did you?"

The guilt on her face was enough of an answer. Now I was the one pacing. "You, you...those times where I mentioned that Aspen Valley was always hiring, and you shrugged it off. When I talked about plans of bringing Piper to daycare when I started working. All of it...it wasn't because you thought it would be hard to get hired."

I felt like a detective in a cozy mystery who'd finally solved the last clue to why there was a hand in the librarian's desk drawer. Only instead of being cozy, it was just a nightmare replaying in my head that I couldn't wake up from.

"You didn't think I was going to ever graduate. Did you? That's why you took it out."

Now I was stopped, directly in front of her. Our eyes met for what felt like the first time in months. This was the first time in...a year, I supposed, that we were truly seeing each other. And whereas I'd always hoped that one day, mom and I could be truly face-to-face with no walls up, I'd never thought it would be like this.

"You...you just struggled so much in the first semester. And I know school gets harder with each class. Those were just your basics, and you were so stressed and tired...I didn't see it working out."

I didn't realize there was still a small part of me hanging on to the hope that maybe I was wrong in my assumptions. But hearing her confirm it...knowing that neither of them—Dad included, really—believed in me felt like a letter opener to my chest. They'd never believed in me. Not as a student or a guardian to Charlie and Piper. Hanging by a frayed rope, every fiber torn apart, the final thread snapped. And I fell with it.

"I struggled because I had a ten-month-old who cried all night long. Because I was learning how to mix formula and sing lullabies and change diapers and pack lunches and do home-work and work a job. All while trying to process the fact that my brother and my only real friend were dead, buried six feet under. And it felt like he took me right down with him." I was sobbing now. Fat, angry tears forcing their way down my cheeks and onto my sweatshirt. "And my fiancé left me mere weeks before school started because he wasn't ready to be a father, and yet was with another woman a month later." A woman he ironically had a baby with now. I digress. "And on top of it all, I had parents who criticized my every move and decision, but weren't willing to help. I was strapped into parenthood with duct tape and told to hang on while every single good thing in my life was ripped out of my grasp. Meanwhile, you were over here pulling money out of an account that I worked to build for ten years to remodel your bathroom."

Somewhere in the distance I heard a door close, and I knew it was my dad taking Piper to the basement so she wouldn't hear me in my hysterics. I could be grateful for that one thing.

Mom sucked in. "The tile was—"

"The tile?" I sounded like a raving lunatic, but I didn't care. All the times I'd avoided conflict, telling myself it wasn't worth it, that fighting back never amounted to anything good, they all piled on top of one another and fueled me further. "I can't believe you—No. You know what? I can believe you. Because this is something only you would do."

I reached over to the counter and grabbed my keys, turning to the door. I had to get out. I couldn't be in the same room as her. I couldn't breathe in the air around her. If selfishness was a disease, I prayed it never caught me.

"Madeline, please. I'm so sorry—"

"For which part?" I cried out, and I hoped she knew they were angry tears and not sad ones. She wasn't allowed to see my sad tears. "For lying to me, or for spending the money you swore would only ever go to my schooling?" Her mouth opened to answer, but I shut it down. "Or for never allowing me to even bring up Will, forcing me to process and grieve entirely alone? Or for putting so much restraint on me and my ability to raise the kids that I feel like I've been choking for the last two years? Or how about for never being there for me as a kid? For not showing up to science fairs or school assemblies or soccer practices?" My hand curled around the doorknob. "Or how about for wishing the other sibling had been the one in the car that night?"

The last one landed harder than the others. I could see it in how she winced, visibly pulling herself back two feet. Hurt slashed across her face with the ugliest scar. Good. Maybe she knew a pinch of how I felt.

She'd never said it aloud. Neither had I. We hadn't needed to. But I knew it as well as she did. Sometimes we both wished Will was here instead of me.

So I opened the door and let myself out, ignoring distant calls of my name.

I wasn't sure what it said about me that my first instinct was to call Cooper. But I was in no mood to dissect the meaning behind it now.

"Hey, I was just thinking about you," he answered, and at that alone, I knew I'd called the right person. The only person. I was just thinking about you.

"Hi." My voice was wobbly and uneven as I fought desperately to sound okay.

A pause. "Baby, what happened?"

His voice was so soft it made me cry even harder, sobbing and chest heaving as my gut twisted tighter. It was the first time he'd called me anything other than Madeline, and that made me cry even more too.

"I...I can't..." I can't even get the words out. Where did I even start? What was I supposed to even say? Everything felt so fuzzy, and my tears were blurring the road lines just recently scraped of snow, and the car next to me was blaring "Hey Ya!" as if the world hadn't stopped spinning just minutes ago.

"Are you driving?" he asked, tone soft but clear.

"Y-yes," I sniffled.

"Okay, come to the lodge. Finn can cover my class. I'll meet you in the lobby. Please don't cry while you're driving. I need you to get here safely, all right?"

My breath in was so unstable that I thought I was going to break into harder sobs, if it were even possible. "Okay," I practically wailed.

"Whatever is going on is going to be worked out, all right? Come up here safely to me, and we'll go from there."

I nodded, but then realized he couldn't see me, so I gave another sniffle and an "All right."

Maybe I should have cared more about the fact that my coworkers and people I see on a daily basis were going to see me walking into the lodge ugly crying. But I had a one-track mind, and it was strictly focused on finding Cooper, wrapping my arms around his thick frame, and resting my head over the steady beat of his heart.

By the time I pulled into the lodge's parking lot, parking directly next to Cooper's SUV, I couldn't honestly remember even driving here. I was so thankful for my autopilot turning on, because my mind was like a scratched record, repeating the same words over and over. School. Spent. Didn't think. Will. Kids. School. Repeat.

Cooper said he'd meet me in the lobby, but when I was halfway through the parking lot, I saw him pacing outside the main doors. And when he glanced up, he looked at me with so much concern in his eyes I really thought I might melt into the asphalt and become one with the snow. He practically ran across the parking lot, ignoring a truck that honked at him for getting in his way, all the way to me, those dark brown orbs looking straight to mine, searching.

Two strong hands gripped my upper arms, and he bent his knees so we were at level height. "What happened? Did someone hurt you?"

I nodded. "I—my mom."

His eyebrows dipped down in confusion, and I knew I wasn't making any sense, but I couldn't force it out, and gosh, he was looking at me with so much concern that I honestly couldn't take it. I didn't know if anyone had ever looked so worried over me, and somehow, it was healing all these little micro-cracks in my heart that I hadn't even realized existed.

"Let's go inside, okay? I'll get you warm and we'll talk."

I nodded, and he wrapped one arm around my shoulders, guiding me inside. The automatic door flew to the sides, and I was grateful it was somewhat busy inside, because no one was staring at us. They were focused on their own conversations instead. Good. Maybe no one would hear me sobbing in the employee break room.

Except Cooper wasn't guiding me to the break room. We were going straight down the hall to a separate set of elevators.

"Where are we going?"

"Alex has an office up here that he never uses. I have the door code, and I go from time to time if I'm stressed or need a break from people."

I sniffed and tried to muster a smile, but it was laid on a poor foundation, so it came out pathetic. "You need a break from people?"

Cooper seemed pleased at me making any attempt at humor. "Yes, I, of all people, still need breaks from society."

The elevator doors swung wide open, and we stepped onto the tiled floor. A gold railing pressed into my behind as Cooper pressed the white button stamped with a 17 in gold font.

"Even Mr. Charming needs social rest?"

He looked over and gave me this sweet smile. One that said so much more than words ever had. "Please, Mr. Charming is my father."

I snorted a little, which quickly turned into sniffles, which manifested itself into quiet sobs as I remembered why I was here in the first place.

"It's okay. I promise. Whatever she did, we can figure it out together, yeah?"

Unless he had a magical way of making seven thousand dollars by Wednesday, I doubted it. But his voice comforted me enough that I didn't question him when the elevator dinged, signaling our arrival.

The doors opened to a short hallway with a single door at the end. It had a silver door handle and a dated keypad resting above it. For the owner of an entire ski lodge, it seemed...simple.

Cooper let go of my shoulder just long enough to type in a code. I turned my head to avoid seeing it. Being here alone felt like an invasion of privacy. And whereas I'd never met Alex Graves and doubted he cared if a random employee knew a code to his unused office, I did know that this used to be Cooper's grandfather's space. And I respected him enough to turn my eyes away from the key code being typed in.

"We can go in here. I promise no one really uses it except me, and I'm 90 percent sure one of my cousins comes up here to use her weed pen before her shifts on Thursdays." Cooper opened the door, and I followed him in.

The office was less of an office and more of a million-dollar penthouse that would be featured in a Jelly Roll music video or used in the background of a Forbes "Sexiest 30 under 30" magazine.

The expansive windows were the first thing that caught my eye. How could they not? Stretching from floor to ceiling, they offer an unobstructed panorama of snowcapped mountains in the distance. Pristine white peaks, dusted with fresh powder, glistened under the soft winter sunlight. The slopes scattered with skiers gracefully carving their way down the mountain, tiny splashes of fluorescent colors making their way onto a white canvas.

The office space was sleek, modern, and masculine. Forest-green walls adorned with wooden bookshelves lining the wall to the left. A mahogany desk that sat facing the window with a brown leather chair behind it. A familiar laptop—Cooper's—sat on top of it. A well-maintained, or possibly fake, fiddle leaf fig sat next to it. To the side, plush, oversized cushions sat on a white couch. The perfect mix of cozy and fancy. Like someone would drink a glass of scotch here with one of those spheres of ice that take twenty minutes to perfect. A coffee table that matched the desk stood in front of the couch, holding a small, elegantly decorated Christmas tree with tiny white ornaments, a bowl of pine cones, and a few scented candles that filled the room with a gentle aroma of cinnamon and pine. Cooper. It screamed. Masculine, cozy, beautiful, pine. Cooper.

"Wow," I whispered. "I can absolutely see someone using a weed pen here." I trailed through the room, past Cooper and to the windows, to look out at the expansive view. If I thought the sitting room was the height of this lodge, I was poorly mistaken.

"Right. Aurora would use a weed pen in a gas station bathroom all the same, so I suppose it doesn't do the view as much justice." He sighed and shut the door behind him, locking it.

"It's incredible."

"Glad you think so." Our voices sounded so light, like we were standing on a frozen lake, unsure of what was going to be heavy enough to crack the ice and make us fall through.

"I can see your grandfather sitting here." I rested my hand on the leather chair, smiling at the worn area where someone's tush had spent years on it. "Suits him well."

Cooper nodded and walked over to the mini-bar—because there was a freaking mini-bar. Before bending over and pulling out two tiny Fiji bottles. "It does. I used to come up here with him all the time." He stretched out a long arm, pointing to the TV hanging above the couch. "He'd let me watch anything I wanted as long as I was quiet and still."

It wasn't hard to envision a tiny Cooper, dark hair scattered on his head, lying on his belly, staring up at the TV, with his grandfather at the desk behind him. It also wasn't hard to believe Cooper was the kind of boy who had to be forced to be still. Even now, he was constantly moving. Fidgeting, playing with the ends of my hair, bumping my knee. Never still.

"Thus his love for Belle was born." I sniffed.

"That's right, in this very room."

He moved to sit on the pristine couch and patted a hand to his lap, legs spread in invitation. I accepted, briskly walking over and sitting down on his thighs. If I hadn't been so upset, maybe I would have noticed how strong he felt underneath me. How someone could be so soft and yet like a freaking brick wall was beyond me. All I knew was that I'd never sat somewhere more comfortable than Cooper Graves's lap.

I audibly moaned a sigh when his hand went to my hair, tugging and playing with just the right amount of pressure. "You want to talk about it?"

No. Yes. I wanted to scream into a pillow but also cry and listen to The Greatest Showman soundtrack and eat fondue.

"It's a long story," I explained.

"I have nowhere to be."

I looked back at him over my shoulder as his chin dipped to rest on my upper back. We adjusted so I could see him better, and he pulled back so he could look me in the eye.

"Essentially, my parents and I had this joint savings account for my schooling. I've been saving since I was sixteen, and they would match whatever I saved, so that way I'd have enough one day. So we'd be paying for all of my classes that way and—" I sucked in a breath, shakily forcing the rest out. "They spent it all. All of it. Drained it entirely."

Cooper went still beneath me. "All...wha—why?"

"For their half bathroom renovations and some medical bills. But you know what?" I let out a dry, bitter laugh. "That part isn't even what hurt the most. There's always more money to be made. I could have figured something out, helped them out, gotten a different job, something. It was that they didn't even tell me. Didn't question it at all, really. Just took it out without a second thought, and you know why? Because they didn't think I'd ever finish school."

Cooper's hand on my thigh tightened while I talked, just letting me know he was there. It made it easier for everything to slip out.

"She said I'd struggled so much in my first semester, which was only a few months after everything went down. Said she didn't see me finishing the schooling out. So they took some out a year ago, then again this summer. They just never told me 'cause they thought I'd drop out by now."

My tears came right back as I said it out loud.

"Madeline, I...I'm so sorry. I'm struggling with words because I have a lot to say, but they're your parents, and I can't tell whether calling them selfish pricks makes me the asshole?"

I shrugged. "They are selfish. On top of a lot of other things."

He nodded. "That's true. What if, and don't say no immediately, what if I helped out? How much do you need for this semester?"

I did exactly what he assumed I would. "No."

"Madeline—"

"Cooper."

"Just let me explain. If it's less than ten thousand, we can make a deal. I'll write a check, and all you have to do is be my girlfriend. It's simple. No interest."

I snorted. "My value as a girlfriend is ten thousand dollars?"

"Don't be ridiculous. It's worth much more, but I have always been one to strike up a deal."

"Well." I wiped my nose with the end of my sleeve. "Even if I let you do that, which I never would, I didn't tell you the rest."

He dipped his chin to my shoulder.

"I think the worst part is...I was relieved." And just like that, a weight lifted from my chest.

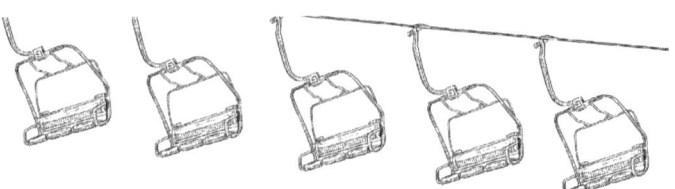

Chapter Twenty-seven
COOPER

"Relieved?" I asked in confusion.

Out of all of the things that had run through my head when Madeline called me with that broken, shaky voice, relief was the last one I expected. No, actually, the last I expected would be that her parents had spent her college fund on bathroom renovations and hospital bills.

"Yeah." She whispered it like a secret. Like we were two kids playing hide-and-seek, and she had to whisper something just for me. "Because I thought, finally, I don't have to do this anymore. The tests. The thought of labs next semester. The idea of having my nights back." She sighed mournfully. "And if I'm being honest with myself, that might be more selfish than what they did."

"It isn't," I interjected. "You are nowhere near them."

"How? How could I be relieved to drop out of school when I have an opportunity to graduate and make money at a job that could give the kids good lives? I could give them good futures, and still...I just want to be here."

"How long ago did you realize it?" I asked in a hushed tone.

"I think I always knew deep down. I just hoped they didn't know too."

"Well, then, maybe that means this is a good thing, right? A good thing in a really, really ugly disguise."

Madeline's face fell to her hands, and she groaned. "I think I just wanted to finish for the wrong reasons. Like, sure, money and stability would be great, but I think, more than anything, I wanted it to prove something." She shifted in my lap, and I moved my hands from her arms to rest on her hips. "Jake was one of the reasons I wanted to go to nursing school in the first place. Then, when he left, I was just so mad. Mad at the whole world, and I thought, watch this. Take everything away and see how I thrive. I thought I could graduate and get a big-girl job, and then my parents would see me. Then Jake would see me too and know they had been wrong the entire time. And instead, just like my parents knew I would, I hated it. I wanted so badly to be right about something. I wanted to be looked at and admired and prove the whole world wrong. And now I think I was just so relieved to have an actual reason to quit just so I can work here a little longer."

"That's some bullshit."

"What?"

"That. Is. Bull. Shit." I emphasized each syllable. "Madeline, respectfully, screw your parents." She huffed a little above me, but I made sure my tone was anything but amused when I continued. "No. Screw those girls who would look at this list of attributes for you and give you anything less than an absolute ten. Screw your douchebag ex who I honestly wish I decked that night at the drive-in. Screw anyone who makes you feel like you're less than what you are."

"You're just say—" She started, but I cut her off. Because there was no way I was going to let her excuse my explanation with an oh, you're just saying that. Because I didn't have to say anything if I didn't want to. I could've held her, let her cry it out, kissed her, and sent her on her way. But that would have made me exactly like him. And she needed to know I was the furthest thing from any of these people in her life.

"You don't have to prove anything. Graduating from nursing school, getting a crummy hospital job, or if you turned out to get your PhD and become a freaking doctor, who cares? You have kids, two amazing ones, that you take care of. You have a job that you love. You know you smile when you're dusting? This smile that is so bright it honestly makes me jealous, because I can joke with you all night, and still, I think you'd smile more while vacuuming or dusting." She smiled softly at that. "And you have me. And I don't care if you're a stay-at-home-mom or a housekeeper or a nurse or a damn aerospace engineer."

I don't love Madeline the mom or Madeline the nurse. I love you, Madeline, alone, I thought. With her kids, without her kids. Degree or no degree. I loved her so much that I couldn't even come up with a nickname for her. That's how down bad I was.

"You're enough on your own," I said. "Accomplishments, degrees, salary—all of that really means nothing if you're still miserable. We don't have a ton of time here on earth. So spend it doing something you love.

"And if you decide you want to go to nursing school, then I'll pay for the rest of it. We can do a loan if you want to pay me back. But I'll invest in your future gladly, because I know it's bright. And if you decide to stay at the lodge, I'll bring you coffee every morning and watch the view in the sitting room any time you want." She snickered, and I smiled back at her. "I mean it, Madeline. Whatever lane you're in, I'm right there behind you. And if you need to switch lanes, that's okay too. You have nothing to prove to anyone. Even me. Heck, especially me. You still think you don't know who you are?"

She looked up at me with this touch of confusion. A splash of misunderstanding in the hazel of her eyes. And it broke me to see it. Broke me so badly that I stopped holding anything left in me back.

"Madeline...you aren't who you were before the accident. You're not the you of after, either. You are...Madeline. You're not your hair or your eyes, though I love those. You're not what your ex did to you or what your brother and his wife left you. You're not what your parents make you out to be. This 'game' we've been playing?" I said, using air quotes. "It's not a game, Madeline. It's who you are. The music you listen to. The kind of pizza you order. You're the hater of two-lane drive-thrus and the lover of Planet of the Apes." She laughed a little through a choked-up gasp. "You're the fuzzy socks you wear at home. The way you sway your hips when you clean. You're the first to burn a candle. You are what you love. You are Madeline. Those are the things that make you, tiny as they might seem. They all build and push and make you you."

Madeline lifted a hand to wipe her tears on her sweatshirt before tucking her legs closer in my lap. I wrapped my arm under her knees and pulled her farther into me. Chest to back, warmth spread through my body, and when she whispered the tiniest thank-you, I kissed the top of her forehead and held her until her tears ran dry.

We listened as laughter and music poured from the windows outside. The sounds of a winter in Aspen. The ski lift workers, the yells of thrill rushing down the mountain, wind brushing around the lodge. I held her as we processed in the way we needed to, watching a view that we adored. Her soaking in my words, me soaking in the attempt to not call her parents myself.

After a while, Madeline hummed a little and then whispered, "Hey, Cooper?"

"Yeah?" A smile was in my voice when I answered.

"I like you a lot."

I breathed in her hair. Vanilla, cinnamon, warmth. "I like you more. I was thinking about it last night, and you know...you're a terrible liar."

She lifted up a little. "Oh?"

"Yeah. Like the worst. So if we do this interview next week, you know..."

Her lips tilted up at the corners and she bit down. "Hmm. I am a very bad liar."

I nodded. "Mm-hmm, the worst."

"So maybe I...should just be your girlfriend."

"Maybe." I smiled. "And maybe, for the sake of straightening blurred lines, you should've been since I first kissed you."

"No," she whispered and smiled up at me. "No, this is better. Waiting for you is better."

I shook my head. "It wasn't me you were waiting on, Madeline. I've been here a while."

Madeline leaned into me, her sweet smell wafting over me as I breathed her in. She was the first to tilt into me, but I was the one who sealed our lips together.

Our mouths mingled in tandem, pushing and pulling. Biting and sucking. Soft and slow one minute, with our hands in each other's hair. Then hard and fast the next, hips settling into one another, rubbing and moving till we were nothing but moaning, groaning messes.

I moved my lips to the crook of her neck, planting gentle, then playful, bites down to her collarbone. The softest moan left her lips right above my ear, and the sound was my undoing.

I growled as I gripped her waist, testing it in my hands and settling my hips into hers.

"I could just..." I searched for the right words. "Eat you."

"Yeah?" She laughed. "I'm flattered."

"So what are you going to do now?" I asked as my mouth trailed down her chest, pulling her sweater down with my crooked finger and kissing the exposed skin there.

She sighed, half in pleasure and half in dread. "Finish up this semester strong, in case I ever decide to come back and..." She hissed when I sucked on a small sliver of her skin. "Go out with a bang. Never tell my parents that they were right, and then see if, starting in the new year, I can work here full time."

"I like the idea of you here full time." I kissed her to emphasize the sentence, like a period.

"Yeah?" She smiled, hands running into my wild hair, and I bit her playfully.

"I like you right under my nose. Where I can sneak away and see you. And we can come here anytime we want. Just me and you."

I squeezed her backside and pulled her closer to me before looking up to her. We smiled at each other, and she gave me one more open-mouthed kiss before saying, "I'd like that too."

Maybe gift giving was my love language, but nothing could compare to the way I loved Madeline.

Chapter Twenty-eight
Madeline

From: skiingtothegraves@gmail.com

Madeline,

Friday night was perfect, as always. Please scroll to see the attached full evaluation. Next Friday will be perfect too. Different perfect, but still. Thank you for being a cooperative patient.

P.S. I told you there would be more food than just apple cider and hot pretzels involved.

All the best,

Cooper Graves

OVERALL EVALUATION FOR NOT-DATE 3 (2 was technically spent in the hallway floor outside a bathroom): Madeline Sage is, for lack of better terms, a keeper. Beauty is one thing, brains and humor are another. To keep this one sweet and simple: she is everything she thinks she's not. And it is a pleasure to show her otherwise.

I loved a good snowstorm.

For a few reasons. It reminded me of home. Not so much my parents' home, but the feeling of home. Nostalgia and comfort. Remembering December and January nights where snow and ice flew to the ground with such force that it should have been scary. The way it piled up in front of the door and the windows. As a kid, maybe it should have frightened me to see my parents rationing food in the kitchen, making sure we'd be fine. But for me, it meant a day of sitting in Will's bedroom, looking into the backyard and watching our half-broken trampoline get covered up by a white blanket. It meant pillow forts and watching movies and eating mountains of chips, knowing we had nowhere to be. Even when he turned sixteen and started working, it meant he wouldn't be going in to work. He would be home, so home felt like home, if that made any sense.

But also, snowstorms felt like God's way of saying "here's a new start." Something fresh. Something exciting. Enough to tempt your heart rate up a bit, but hint at some grand surprise outside the next morning.

I usually loved a snowstorm, I should say. I'd loved it until our power went out. Then it felt like I was playing Survivor. But instead of a tropical island surrounded by a bunch of hot people and camerapeople, we were on a frozen wasteland, where you might as well give up on life.

I was in the middle of a quiz when the lights flickered once. I heard a loud what the crap? from my nine-year-old, who must've picked up on the power outage when his TV turned off. Piper stayed on the floor; her legs positioned in a way that would probably make most yoga instructors jealous. "May?" she whispered into the semi dark room.

Charlie's loud feet thundered through the house to where we were. "I'm right here, baby," I announced.

I checked my phone. Seventy-eight percent battery was good. Plus it was already 6:50, so we weren't too far away from bedtime. We could make it along just fine.

"I'll turn my flashlight on. We can use it until we figure it out." I was sliding a thumb down the screen to click on the flashlight access when a notification fell from the top.

Cooper: your power out

If there was one thing about this man that annoyed me, it was his texting.

Me: Are you allergic to question marks?? Or any kind of punctuation?

The three-dotted bubble popped up and back down, and his reply came a moment later.

Cooper: deadly

Cooper: is your power out

Me: It flickered once a while ago, but it just went out completely a few minutes ago. Did yours?

Cooper: yea

Cooper: see you in a sec

I looked to Charlie, who was reading the text exchange over my shoulder, which made me incredibly grateful that the keyboard was still up. Otherwise, he would have seen a text from Cooper just yesterday asking me what I was sleeping in. Or my response of my grandmother's old night gown. To which he responded with vintage and hot.

"Mr. Cooper's coming over?" he asked with nothing short of pure delight in his tone.

"I...guess so?" I tried to tamp down on my own delight. "His power is out too, so I'm not sure why." Then it hit me. It was snowing like a freaking blizzard outside, and despite having snow tires on his SUV, there was no way he could drive here. Even if it was only a block. His driveway was also on an incline, whereas mine was a little flatter. Even so, I wouldn't be able to get out of here.

I texted him quickly.

Me: Are you seriously coming over?

Cooper: packing a bag

Cooper: does mini coop like cheezits

Cooper: do you

Cooper: i know what half pint wants

Me: Yeah we all like Cheez-its.

Cooper: white cheddar okay

Me: Cooper, it is snowing so hard I can barely see our drive-way. Please don't. drive

Cooper: i wont

Cooper: that was a question earlier

Cooper: is white cheddar okay

Me: It's fine, also, please don't come here if it means you getting hurt.

Cooper: honored you care that much madeline

I texted two more times about his absolutely unnecessary need to come here, but both messages were unanswered, so I could only assume he was busy packing a bag and somehow finding a way to fly over here.

"I guess he is coming, yeah."

Charlie didn't respond, but ran over to his room and closed the door. Then I could hear shuffling around. I turned to Piper, who was still plopped on the ground, aligning her dolls in a very specific Piper order.

"Half-Pi?" She phrased it as a question that I couldn't quite piece together, so I hummed a noncommittal response.

Unsure of how much time I had before a wild Cooper popped up on my doorstep, I frantically picked up the house. Or as much as I could in the dark. And then, because clearly, I had my priorities straight, I rushed to the bedroom to take off my oversized banana-yellow third annual oyster shucking competition T-shirt—that was actually Will's from when he'd taken a trip to Maine in college—and replaced it with the cutest matching pajama set I owned.

A long-sleeve lavender cotton button-up with matching bottoms and fresh socks.

Because, of course, my matching socks were much higher on the list of importance than, let's say, loading the dishwasher or deep cleaning our guest bathroom, scrubbing the sink from signs that a ravenous Piper had been in there earlier to brush her teeth.

I searched the kitchen for one of the two lighters we owned and pulled out three different candles. Peach Bellini, Christmas Wonder, and Mint Julip were all going to have to coexist in the same space, because I'd never thought of needing scentless candles until this very moment.

As I set the third candle on the coffee table, one sharp knock came from the door, followed by a pause and then three more knocks.

Piper raised both arms in the sky with a loud uh, signaling she wanted to be picked up. I reached down to grab her and settled her on my hip while she scowled at the door. Maybe we didn't need a better security system after all. If we ever did have an intruder, it was likely that this girl would bite some ankles if the time called for it.

"It's just Cooper." I bounced her on my hip as we walked.

She straightened. "Half-Pi?"

It didn't fully register to me until we opened the door to a snow-covered Cooper, who was standing on my front porch with a backpack on his back and something square wrapped under a black-and-white gingham blanket in his hands. His eyes drank me in with a dark, hooded look, from my socks to the ponytail my hair was pulled up in. That smirk that I'd grown so fond of quirked its way up, soft, slow, and then all at once. He looked at me like he wanted to eat me alive. Looked at me in the same way I was taking him in. In boots partially unlaced, dark gray sweats, and that same black hoodie with the lodge logo on it, he stood there smirking while I found myself entirely grateful for my sudden switch in pajamas.

And even after the way he'd taken me in, I wasn't the first one he addressed. "Hiya, Half-Pint."

Piper didn't respond, but she did a very tiny wave. That alone had my mouth gaping. And then she pointed to the bag on his back.

He laughed a little. "I got something for you, don't worry."

Cooper turned his gaze to me then, starting at my forehead and down to my lips, like his eyes were jumping from one freckle to the next. "Hi, Madeline" poured out like warm, sweet honey.

I like the way Madeline tastes in my mouth.

I slumped forward a little, eyelids heavy. "Hi, Cooper."

"Can I...come in?" He lifted whatever was under the blanket, and I registered just how cold it was out.

"Oh! Yes." I pulled back and cracked the door open farther for him.

Cooper passed by us and playfully pinched one of Piper's socked feet, to which she let out the tiniest smile before shutting it right back down.

He set down the blanket-covered square on the coffee table by the lit candle and then pulled his backpack off. Piper immediately started squirming in my arms, reaching desperately for the ground, and the minute I let her touch it, her feet started taking off, Road-Runner style, straight to him.

"I know," Cooper chuckled. "Here you go." He pulled out an extra-large Slim Jim, the kind you'd normally get at a gas station, and handed it straight to her.

By the smile that lit that kid's face, I swore you would think our living room had transformed into Disney World itself and that all the princesses she'd ever loved had made their way in, one by one. She turned to me and tilted that smile even farther, as if to say can you believe this guy?

I snorted. "You have an addiction." But because she was nearly three-years-old, she looked at me like I'd spoken an entirely different language.

Charlie chose that moment to come barreling into the living room. "Cooper?"

Cooper stood at full height from his crouch by Piper and smiled. "Hey, Mini Coop. What are you up to?"

"The power's out." He said it with the tiniest hint of sass, like don't you see?

"I noticed. I thought maybe I could help."

Like a magician pulling a bunny out of a hat, Cooper lifted the throw blanket from the square contraption and revealed a black rectangle with wires and a handle on top.

"A generator?" I recognized. "You brought us a generator?"

He nodded. "Yup, figured you could use it, and I noticed you didn't have one when I was here last."

"You drove—"

"Actually, I walked. Mercy doesn't do well during bad storms, and I was worried about taking it to the street."

I ignored the fact that he'd named his SUV Mercy.

"You walked...the whole way here...in a snowstorm. Carrying"—I pointed to the hefty box—"that?"

"It was only a block." He shrugged. "You guys needed it."

You like this man, my brain fired off. No, you more than like this man. I just might be falling in love with someone who didn't belong to me. Someone who would complicate an already complicated life. I knew that, logically. But that didn't seem to stop me.

Cooper must've caught on to the fact that I was coming close to spilling tears over a generator, because he spoke in a soft, testing voice. "'S just a small one. Nothing crazy. But we can hook up the TV so we can watch the weather until it blows over, or I brought my laptop. We could hook it up to my hotspot if you wanted to watch a movie."

I nodded and smiled. "Either would be nice. Thank you."

He smiled back, and I forced any hint of sadness about my future self, doomed to deal with a broken heart by the hands of this strong, yet so kind, man in front of me down into the depths of my chest to never be retrieved again.

Only twenty minutes later, Cooper and I had an entire setup in our living room. We couldn't quite get the TV going, since our signal was off, and it took a lot from the generator anyway, so we settled for movies on his laptop. I took the two nugget couches that my parents had gotten Piper for her birthday last year and set them up in a giant palette. Charlie and Cooper rearranged chairs and couch cushions, surrounding it, then they raided the linen closet for various throw blankets, muslin swaddles, and spare sheets. They draped the linens over chair backs and couch cushions, using chip clips to hold them on like the top of a circus tent. A perfect blanket fort, adorned with battery-powered string lights and LED candles that came with a tiny remote covered in buttons of every color in the rainbow, lighting the fort underneath in a pink glow. Piper's choice of color. It spread across half the living room and left one gaping side facing the fireplace.

Underneath, Cooper sat with Charlie to his left, leaning in so close I worried about the screen making him go cross-eyed, and Piper to his right a foot away, but still staring. "All right, guys. We got Shrek one and two, Finding Nemo, Beauty and the Beast—"

"Beauty and the Beast?" Charlie guffawed.

Cooper shrugged. "My first crush."

"Mine too." I smiled.

"The beast?"

"Lumiere, the candleholder."

Then Cooper guffawed. "You guys know you're related to a lunatic, right?"

Both of the kids giggled, but he kept scrolling through his previously downloaded movies. "Jackass one and two—don't repeat that one. Black Hawk Down—and you know what? Yeah, they just get worse from here. Pick from the top row."

Immediately, Piper's tiny pointer finger shot straight for Belle, whereas Charlie settled on Nemo. He let up, though, because he was a tiny version of his dad and seemed to always want what was best for Piper. "You pick first, Pipes."

Beauty and the Beast it was.

Cooper pulled out a few more tricks from his bag, a Nerds rope for Charlie, a bag of pre-popped popcorn for us, more Slim Jims and a tube of mini M&M's for the little one.

"You're like Nanny McPhee with that bag." I laughed as he brought a portable charger for our phones out and plugged them in side by side.

"Like when she becomes hot, though, right?"

"Of course."

Charlie's head lifted up. "Who's Nanny McPhee?"

Less than an hour later, both kids were passed out between Cooper and me. The kids talked, mostly Charlie, through the movie. Asking Cooper questions, wondering about what other movies he liked when he was his age. At one point, Piper shivered between me and Cooper, to which he sat up and said, "You know what this night needs? A bonfire."

"It's storming," I reminded him.

"You have gas logs, don't you?" He pointed to the cobblestone fireplace with a set of gas logs in there, never used.

"May can't figure out how to turn it on." Charlie huffed, making Cooper chortle.

"Hush." My cheeks started to warm. "I just haven't had time to try."

"Is your pilot light on?"

"I think so?" Truthfully, I hardly even knew what a pilot light was or its purpose. Homeownership was quite the adjustment when all you'd ever done was call your landlord when something broke or when your lightbulbs were screwed on too tight, and no, they weren't stuck. It was why I had Gary the super on speed dial for years, considering Jake had less experience in handyman work than I did.

Cooper paused the movie and crawled out of the blanket fort to go check it out, and within a few minutes, we had a fire going. Warmth spread through the house as we listened to the artificial crackles and pops. We never even turned the movie back on after that. Just watched it blaze in front of us, the flame transitioning from blue to orange to yellow tips, dancing in tandem waves.

"Can we sleep out here?" Charlie whispered, like if we talked at normal level, the fire would go out.

"Nope." I hummed. "Cooper's sleeping out here. We're all going to our own rooms." It was a reminder for myself as much as it was for them.

Still, though, not long after I said that, both kids were passed out, Piper's head resting on my chest, Charlie's head leaned back against a pillow, mouth wide open, snoring like an old man.

"Good God," Cooper whisper-yelled. "It's like a wood-chip-per is in his mouth."

"You should hear him when he sleep sings."

"Sleep sings?"

I kept a whisper in my chuckle. "Sometimes it's Mariah Carey."

He looked down to the nine-year-old beside him and snorted. "That's amazing."

We stayed like that a little longer, occasionally whispering to one another or glancing over to hold eye contact for just a little while before breaking apart when Charlie's snore would rise to a volume that shook the entire house.

"You carry the little one, and I can wake up the big one?" he offered, already sitting up.

I nodded and jerked my knee to Charlie's. "Come on, bud. Gotta get to bed."

He hummed back to me, something that sounded an awful lot like "Always Be My Baby." I raised my eyebrows at Cooper. See? He gave an impressed frown.

"Charlie," I whispered a little more sharply this time, and his eyes jolted open. "Come on. We gotta go to bed."

He grumbled a bit but eventually stood up and sleepily crawled out of the fort, Cooper's blanket in hand.

"Night, Mini Coop."

"G'night Mista Coopa," came back in this grumbled tone, and we both chuckled.

I slowly stood and carried Piper to her own bed, with Cooper following right behind me. I tucked her into the pink sheets and ensured the windows were locked—force of habit. I also reached to turn on her night light, then completely forgot the power was off, so I left and gently closed the door behind me.

Cooper and I lay under that fort, blankets folded over our laps, watching the fireplace glow in front of us, tired but unwilling to sleep. I didn't know if I'd ever had a sleepover like this, friend or otherwise. If I'd ever stayed up into the late hours of the night where secrets felt safe to spill. Where any walls around my past seemed to crumble and disappear into the snowy night sky.

We talked for hours. It started the way it always seemed to. The way Cooper always made it. "I like crab cakes," he said, and we went from there. Touching on subjects from our worst childhood nightmares to our favorite fonts—turns out he absolutely despises Comic Sans. We talked until our eyes felt droopy and our sentences started running together. I asked him if he wanted coffee, and he said, "If it means staying up and talking a little longer, then yes." So we each had two cups during the hours that were beginning to slip toward morning.

Cooper told me about his dad. Or his lack thereof. How his mom and dad were married and agreed they never wanted kids. Cooper was an accident, and when his mom saw the sonogram, she realized she changed her mind. She loved him instantly. His dad didn't, so they divorced, and he never heard from him. Neither did she, apparently. When I asked if he felt like he'd missed out on something growing up, he immediately said no. "My mom was enough for me. I never had to wonder, because she was always there. A built-in best friend." And I wondered how much it would take for me to be the same for my kids.

I told him how I was nervous about the semester coming up. How I had to pay for my classes by next week and how the end of every semester felt that way, crammed and stressed. Extra things to worry about on top of an already busy life. And when he asked if he could help, I told him I wished I could say yes, but that I didn't even know how to help myself.

"Can I ask," he said while I was mid-sip. "What were you like as a kid? You said you were like your brother, but you never gave me anymore. And you seem to, I don't know, flinch or something when I ask about high school."

I felt myself wince as he said it, as delicate as it was.

"School was never good to me," I explained, knowing how much deeper it went. Remembering the nights of staying up late, wondering what was wrong with me, felt like they were right behind me.

"You don't have to tell me if you don't want to. But I've been told I'm a good listener."

He didn't say it with any humor in his voice, but I chuckled a little anyway.

"It's kind of a long story."

"My whole night is yours."

I leaned back into the pillow that I had now turned to face the fireplace, watching the flames crackle and pop.

"When I was a kid, I struggled to make friends." It was an understatement, really. I had so many imaginary friends that my parents genuinely wanted to take me to a psychiatrist.

"I don't know if it's because I was shy, or because I just wasn't the girl people immediately ran to, but for so long, it felt like just me. Except when he was around."

"Will?" Cooper asked behind me as he settled onto the same pillow.

I nodded. "Will never made me feel like that. He would let me go everywhere with his friends, even when they clearly didn't want me there. Playing Xbox at midnight with seventeen-year-olds when you're twelve makes you feel wanted."

Cooper's hand snuck around to mine, and I didn't fight at all when his fingertips danced along my palm up, then to my wrist and back in smooth, soft swirls.

"When I got to middle school, some of his friends had younger siblings, and I finally started making my own friends. It felt like, for once, I was my own person. Like I was something more than just a random speck. My hair got longer. I started getting boobs. I was wearing makeup, and I felt like I was finally growing into my very own...someone. Someone beautiful." It was an innocent and blissful four months. A time where I was entirely unaware of the future and felt like nothing else bad could happen. All was right in the world.

"One night, we had a sleepover with some of the girls I'd met. And after watching Angus, Thongs and Perfect Snogging"—I turned to face him—"which really cemented my crush on dark-haired boys who could play guitar, by the way."

His brows lowered. "I already hate this movie."

"There was this game. You anonymously rate everyone in a circle out of ten. Their nose, eyes, hair, figure, everything. I gave out nines and tens left and right—"

"Of course. Because you are an angel incapable of hurting someone's feelings."

"No, because I truly thought that highly of everyone at the time. I really thought no one could not be beautiful. I still think that, really. Anyway, when we all got our papers back, I quickly found out that I wasn't what I thought I was." The memory felt like a sting in my chest that never healed. "That my nose was worth a three. My ears a two. My figure a one. All these little numbers started adding up, and each one seemed worse. And I realized then that my value was only worth what the people around me considered it to be. That even at my best, at what I considered my prime, I was a twenty-three out of one hundred."

"Madeline." Cooper's fingers laced through mine, and the pain eased a bit. "You're breaking my heart."

"I can stop?" I offered.

"Don't. I just. I wish I had been there that night. To give you every single ten you deserved."

My laugh was dry. "Cooper, we never would've been friends."

"Not true. Your love for manatee mailboxes would have made that clear."

He leaned a little closer to me, and I adjusted back into him until my head was on his shoulder, our palms pressed against one another.

"What happened after?" he asked, and I winced once more.

"Then I got to high school, and this new boy, this guy who had no preconceived notion of who I was, looked at me, and in an instant, liked me. He told me I was pretty." I was so, so easy to catch. "He was smart and funny, and it was like he filled every single crack in my heart. Maybe I loved him. Maybe he was just kind to me. It was hard to know the difference."

When you'd never heard someone call you beautiful other than your direct family, who basically had to, it felt more impactful than most would understand. How even in my most awkward, brace-faced, acne-scarred stage of life, there was a blond-headed boy who liked me.

"Will hated him—"

"Yeah," Cooper scoffed. "Me too."

I laughed a little. "That should've been the first sign. Will never hated anyone. But he was my first love, and I was so blinded by his words that I didn't really see his actions. Anyway, time went on, and we were great. For years. He went to college, I worked. We did everything together. And when he asked me to marry him when we were twenty-two, I didn't even second-guess it. He said he would work hard for me so I could stay home with kids one day. It felt like a dream life in the making. For years, it was so great. It felt like I was finally getting the life I deserved after time had screwed me over again and again."

I wish I could end it there. But then again, if I did, I wouldn't have Cooper sitting beside me.

"We would babysit for Will a lot. One night, we watched Charlie and Piper for their anniversary, and then…"

"The wreck?" His assumption was but a whisper.

I dipped my chin and felt my voice shaking. But there was no stopping it. "A drunk driver. He hit three cars, but Will and Savannah were the only deaths. The cops called me first, because I was listed as the emergency contact for both of them."

"Madeline." Cooper's voice was shaky too. "You must have been so scared."

I nodded. "I was. And I kind of shut down after." Maybe I should have explained it further, but I'd watched Cooper in his shut-down phase. I'd brought him dinner and brownies and watched as his eyes seemed like two broken orbs lost in space, wondering if there was any way back.

"You know how that feels," I whispered, like anyone else could possibly hear us.

He nodded.

"Anyway, Jake and I pushed through the next few days, weeks, up till a month. Then he kept saying I needed to open up. But I just wanted to be quiet for a little longer. I couldn't force it out yet. Then when he found out about Will leaving the kids to me for good, it was the breaking point. He said he didn't want kids yet. We were only twenty-seven, and we were too young to stay settled down like that. Our wedding was supposed to be two months later, and he said he couldn't do it. So we didn't."

"And you just handled it...all alone? The death of your brother and your only friend on top of losing your fiancé, in what, a month?"

I nodded and realized how stupid it was that I was ashamed of it. How could I possibly be embarrassed about something this tragic?

"Gah, Madeline." He squeezed my hand. "My heart hurts."

"I'm sorry—"

"No." Cooper leaned forward, put his hands on either side of my face, and squished my cheeks together until I looked like a chipmunk with very full cheeks. "Don't apologize for a thing. Ever. Especially not to me." He paused. "Except liking Comic Sans. That's still ridiculous."

"It's fun and whimsical," I murmured as much as I could with a squished face.

"So is LSD, I'm sure, but you don't see me using it."

He let go of my face and planted a light kiss on both cheeks where his grip had vanished. "I meant what I said, Madeline. You deserve to be surrounded by people who would never give you anything below a ten."

My heart felt like it was jackhammering against concrete by the way it took off without my permission.

"Your hair." His hand left mine to trail through it, gently yanking on my ponytail. "Is always a ten. I keep waiting for you to catch me staring at it when it swishes from side to side."

His fingers trailed back toward my face, cupping my jaw and pulling it closer. "Your eyes." He stared right into them, unwavering. "I think of them at night, when I can't sleep. You know I can tell exactly how you're feeling, just by these eyes? I swear it, Madeline. I could stare at them all day. They're hazel, but they have this light ring around the center like...I don't know. Like honey or something."

His hand moved farther down, fingertips trailing over my collarbone, down to my heart, where two fingers gently caressed above my pajama top. "Your heart. It's so good, Madeline. I'm honestly jealous."

I sniffled and realized my eyes were watering, and when I looked up to Cooper, I thought his might have been too.

"You think you don't know who you are? I think you grew up too fast and had no time to figure out what you liked. Not your brother, not your ex. You. And now you feel like you're racing the clock to make strings pull together and add up. I'll tell you right now who you are, Madeline."

I sucked in a shaky breath and felt a tear fall down my cheek, where Cooper met it halfway with his thumb.

"You"—he pressed his thumb into my half dimple for emphasis—"are everything. You're kind to a fault. You'd rather walk around in pain than say a word to anyone about it. You love everyone with so much fire, so much passion, that it pours out of you. You wanna know what my mom said about you?"

I looked back up to his eyes, watching them move back and forth between mine.

"Before we came to your house, I told her I had a crush on a girl, like I was fifteen again." We both chuckled a little. "I told her I was going on a date that night with a single mom, and when she heard that, she paused in her tracks. Gave me this whole speech about how I was in over my head, not ready for something like that. Then she figured out it was you, and when we left? We got back to my house, and she took it all back. 'Madeline's different,' she said. She warned me to take care of you. Of the kids. That you had a heart of gold, and she could see so much good in you."

I had always been a silent crier, or at least I tried to be. I kept to myself and licked my own wounds in a quiet corner, where no one could find me. But I was lying here, mentally bare in front of Cooper, giving him every piece of me as I cried away. And he didn't seem to mind. He seemed to only like it more.

"So yeah, this heart," he continued with his elbow propped up against my side, palm resting on my chest, "will always be a ten."

His other thumb moved to my lower lip, pushing and then pulling just enough to release it. "And kissing you? Is an eleven, all day, every day."

I smiled, despite my tears, because he always could pull that out of me, and lifted my face to his.

Our lips reached for each other, settling naturally like we had done this hundreds of times before. Like our bodies knew just what to do with each other. We kissed with every bit of teeth and tongue and lips that we could while managing to keep quiet enough to not bother the other two in the house. I had never been so grateful for creaky floors as I was when his hands and lips and pelvis all took their turns between my hips. I stifled my sighs and moans in my hand, and when he looked up at me from his crouched position with the most confident smirk and said, "give me one more," I genuinely thought I was going to pass out.

I wasn't sure how long we moved like that, taking our turns exploring and guiding each other. Learning and teaching. Growing together, moving closer to a cliff that we were both unprepared to fall over. We whispered each other's names over the low murmur of the music from his computer and eventually settled under one throw blanket together, with happy-drunk giggles erupting around us.

When I woke up, the weight of Cooper's arm resting over my waist, curling into me, comforted me. I was engulfed in the smell of clove and cinnamon on the blanket we had spread over us. Light poured outside of our tiny fort, our tiny getaway. Wait...light?

I shot up from where I was lying down, the blanket falling to my waist. Piper was always up before the sun. Always. Especially during winter. I was scrambling out from under the covers frantically when a deep, groggy voice spoke behind me. "Mmm. Stay."

"Why isn't Piper up?"

"What?"

I turned to face him so I could rephrase but stopped once I caught a single look at his face. Piper was up. I knew so because there was dark purple evidence on Cooper's forehead. And some blue on his cheek. There were swirls of markers all over his face, and a tiny red dot on his nose.

"Why are you looking at me like that?" He groaned.

"I, um..." Was really, really praying those were the washable kind. "Here." I opened the camera app on my phone, and he turned it around, looking in horror at himself.

"I look like a...human doodle pad."

"It's pretty bad."

"The worst," he agreed.

We both crawled out of the blanket fort and stopped halfway, on our hands and knees, when we saw Charlie and Piper sitting in the kitchen, shooting us looks full of glaring disappointment.

"Wha-What are you two doing?"

"Having breakfast," Charlie pointed at the cereal in their bowls. "What are you two doing?"

I ignored that. "Did you let her color on his face?"

Piper was grinning from ear to ear, knowing she'd been caught.

Charlie shrugged. "You should've told me you guys were dating."

Cooper and I shared glances that looked equally embarrassed and guilty. "Well, it's complicated, bud—"

"You never know how to handle these things—"

"I don't consider myself a fatherly type, so—"

We spoke over one another, excuses falling out one after the other.

Charlie went back to his cereal. "I kind of figured it out when May talked about how good the fondue was with Mrs. Olive, and then you started mentioning it to Finn at practice the next day. Plus your Google calendar is easy to access."

"My what?" I asked.

Cooper and I stood up and walked over to them. Piper walked over to me and reached up, so I picked her up and settled her on my hip.

"We okay?" he asked Charlie.

Charlie nodded. "Remember what we talked about, though."

Cooper nodded back. "I've got you, Mini Coop."

Then I wondered if I was still dreaming, because Cooper suddenly asked him, "You ready?"

Charlie smiled, and his eyes widened. "Seriously?"

"If this isn't a time for it, I'm not sure what is."

And just like that, Charlie and Cooper stuck their hands out to one another and did what could only be described as a minute-long handshake.

"What was that?"

"Don't worry about it."

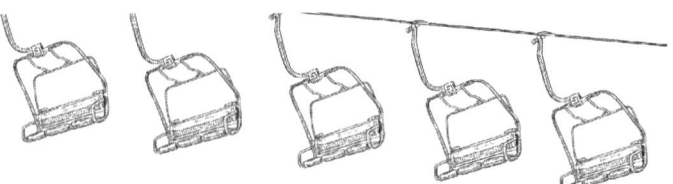

Chapter Twenty-nine
COOPER

M agazine interviews were more extravagant than I'd expected.

Madeline and I had walked into the Family Matters magazine's facility only ten minutes ago, and we were already drinking costly champagne out of flutes and had a cheese and meat tray with arranged fruits, jams, spreads, and wheat crackers on a golden coffee table in front of us.

"Do you think this came from Meat and Cheese?" she whispered, popping cubed cheddar into her mouth.

"Do you think they have the homegrown potatoes?"

"I still feel like we should check in with that lady. Make sure she's still in one piece."

I shrugged. "I still feel like it was her attempt at poisoning me."

"Best not-date ever."

"I'm gonna miss the not-dates," I admitted. "I like surprising you."

"We could keep doing them, you know? Hear me out...we'll call them dates."

"That, my dear, is revolutionary." I took a strawberry and bit off the end before turning it around and lifting it to her open mouth. The tip of the strawberry painted her lip slightly red. Those big doe eyes peered up at me through long lashes, and I felt a shiver up my spine when she took a bite. "You must've been inspired," I teased, and she flushed under my gaze, the prettiest shade of pink.

Admittedly, we were the most annoying couple to probably exist in Aspen right now. Besides Olive and Finn. I stood by that. But still, I couldn't get enough of her. My fingers in her hair, my hand on her back, a kiss here, a back-seat make-out there. We were the literal definition of PDA. I felt like I'd been given permission to enter a cave made of gold. Or like I'd been stuck on the hardest level of a video game, and then the coder themselves sent me a compiled cheat code and said, "have at it." We were hungry, frenzied. She'd pinched my butt on the way in here, and I'd had to visibly shift in my chair fifteen times since I'd sat down just from looking at her.

It felt like everything added up now. Like I had an answer for my past mistakes. Because if I hadn't made those mistakes, hadn't found out what it cost to make a real friend, then there was no way I would've nailed Madeline. I needed growth, and a little heartbreak. She needed to find her own way. And now we were here, just the two of us, feeding each other strawberries and laughing under golden light fixtures.

Madeline and I decided to stop our "practice" meetings after our talk last week and figured we would take a fresh start on things. I still took the time every morning she was working to bring her a caramel macchiato and a bacon cheddar scone. She still sat with me for twenty minutes while we played our regular game, plus a couple of new ones. But now, instead of feeling like I had to take every second in while we talked, I could relax, knowing I knew exactly who Madeline was. No need to mem-orize favorite colors or cereal brands. No faking our affection toward each other. It was a weight lifted off.

Plus, she really was a terrible liar. I was comforted knowing we would be going into this interview with nothing but 100 percent truth. Something we were entirely ready for.

Unless they asked us how long we'd been together. We agreed that I would answer that one, and I could push the numbers a little, for the sake of the lodge, anyway.

Neither of us tried to define everything between us right away, and I was grateful for that. I had a girlfriend. A real one, the best one, and maybe our situations were more complicated than most, but we could make it work. I distinctly told her I wasn't a great fit for fatherhood, or uncle-hood, I should say. But she brushed it off, kissed the corner of my mouth, and let me know we didn't have to have it all figured out right away.

Good thing too, because I couldn't look Charlie in the face at practice the next day. I was making some attempt at warm-up drills consisting of knee raises and toe touches, and the whole time, I tried to turn away from him so I didn't have this en-tirely guilty I was with your aunt last night and I'm the worst friend ever look on my face. Somehow I think he knew anyway, though, because after practice was over and I was sitting on the bench, watching parents pick up kids, Mini Coop came right up to me.

He sat next to me on the bench, same as before, and said, "Remember how I told you May would cry at night when she thought I couldn't hear?"

I hesitated a nod.

"Well, she hasn't...in a while. Since she started going out, I think. It's been nice."

I knew what he meant. I also knew that, for a nine-year-old, this kid was all too perceptive, and I wasn't convinced he wasn't some undercover CIA agent.

"I'm sorry I didn't tell you before," I said. "You were my friend first. I meant that." I waved to a dad in the distance who was picking up one of the students.

"Yeah...I know." Mini Coop gave me the smallest, crooked-teeth grin. "I'm glad May is your good friend too."

I smiled back and split my Clif Bar with him, and we left it at that. Every lesson since had been normal, and I thought maybe this was possible.

The tiny one was still unsure of me. She didn't hate me, but she definitely hadn't let me into the circle yet. But that was going to change next week. I was confident that princesses on ice and giant popcorn buckets would allow me in. I was all done buying my friends. But this kid was my only exception.

"They're ready for you, Mr. and Mrs. Graves," the receptionist that had guided us to this black leather couch announced. I did tell Chase that we were just kidding about Madeline being my wife, but that I was going to rectify that eventually. It wasn't far from the truth. But when we came in for our appointment, and the receptionist with short black curly hair looked at us and said "oh yes, the ski couple, you two have a seat. I'll be right with you, Mr. and Mrs. Graves," I didn't have it in me to correct her.

I stood and held a hand out for Madeline. She took it and brushed past me, the side of her hip grazing mine.

"After you, Mrs. Graves." I said it teasingly, but the words felt so warm on my tongue that if I thought Madeline alone tasted good in my mouth, Mrs. Graves felt ten times better.

She looked back, sporting a blush and a smile as always, and walked right in front of me as I trailed behind her.

We followed the short woman down the hall, passing areas scattered throughout the office furnished with whiteboards, hand-shaped lounge chairs, and colorful bean bags. The walls were painted in vibrant waves and adorned with inspiring quotes and past magazine covers. Families on farms, at sporting events, and a few famous faces.

We stopped at the end of the hall, and a door labeled the heart room opened to show a spacious room with stand-up light equipment surrounding a conference table in the middle. A large window in the back lit up the entire space.

Behind the camera setup, next to a guy with multiple lenses, there were Chase and Brandy in their matching pantsuits. This time they wore light blue, and somehow, it worked.

"Cooper! Madeline! There are our star guests." Chase did a little jog to us and shook both of our hands before guiding us to sit at the conference table.

"So nice to see you again, Coop. Madeline, you are nothing short of what Cooper said you would be."

She blushed at that. "I hope it was nothing bad."

"Nothing but the truth." I winked, and when she smiled at me, all warm and soft, I felt like melting right into this chair.

Brandy turned from the camera guy standing to the side. "Phew. Sorry, guys. Crazy day. Okay, let's get through some quick questions, and we can do pictures after."

They sat across from us, a laptop in front of Chase while Brandy interviewed.

"So, how did you two meet?" she asked, and without skipping a beat, Madeline cackled. Literally guffawed right next to me.

Brandy's lips quirked. "Please, tell us your side, Madeline."

I turned to face her. "Yes, Madeline. Tell us your side."

She smiled and dipped her chin a little. "It was cute. He was teaching my nephew, and we hadn't met yet. Well, we kind of had, but he didn't remember it—"

I tapped twice on the top of Chase's laptop as he was typing. "Redact that, please."

Madeline giggled and pulled my arm back. "No. It was perfect. He didn't remember me, but I remembered him. So when I passed by, and he didn't realize I was picking a kid up, Cooper decided to pretend like he was Charlie's dad. He did this whole 'poor me, a lost single father in need of a female presence' act, and I swear it took everything in me not to laugh." Only I thought she did laugh a little that day, a small chuckle that sometimes she didn't even realize when she did it.

"Hold on, wait a second." I held up a hand, and Chase stopped typing, looking over the screen. "She's making it sound worse than it was."

"Mmm, nope. It was pretty bad. He had his hand resting on Charlie's head, and my sweet boy, he never wants to bother anyone, so he just went along with every word Cooper said. Until I finally announced that I was there to pick up Charlie."

I tsked and shook my head. "Not my finest moment. But I'd just seen the most beautiful woman I'd laid eyes on, and my wits weren't about me." Madeline's lips quirked up, and we looked like two love-drunk idiots on their honeymoon. Like we'd both gotten shot in the butt by Cupid's bow twenty minutes ago, and the effects still hadn't worn off.

I kept my eyes right on Madeline as I talked, every word coming out true. "My God, though. You should've seen that smile. She was all bundled up in this big purple sweater, and her hair was down and messy. Freckles sprinkled all over her. She looked at me with this grin that said, "I know more than you," and I think I knew I was gone for her then."

We smiled at each other, and she shook her head. "He got me pretty quickly. Too quickly."

"Nah, you made me wait plenty."

"It was worth it."

"Yeah." I bumped our elbows together. "It was."

The rest of the interview seemed to fly by. Questions like "what can we expect from the younger divisions in this year's ski competition?" to more personal "tell us more about your future plans as a family" popped up left and right. I answered most, but Madeline stepped in occasionally when she felt it was more so directed her way. No one had yet to ask us if we liked the Shrek 2 soundtrack or how we felt about dark restaurants, but still, I was glad we'd spent all that time preparing. It wasn't the interview we were preparing for. It was our future. One with each other in tow, whatever that was going to look like.

At the end of their list of questions, they stood and directed us to the man with a camera in the far corner, a simple green backdrop in front of it. "We just need a couple quick pictures for the column. We can send them to you once they're finalized and let you pick your top three favorites."

Chase walked us over, and just before we reached the camera, I pulled at the hoodie I was wearing. "I'm sweating. Let me take this off."

I reached behind my shoulders and peeled my hoodie off, revealing my long-sleeve white T-shirt that said I LOVE MY GIRLFRIEND in bright red letters. I turned to Madeline and wiggled my eyebrows, hoping she would pick up on exactly what I was telling her.

I'd bought it a little over two weeks ago, after I'd seen an ad on my Amazon account. I bought three variations. The basic I love my girlfriend, the more unique Don't look at me, I have a girlfriend, and the classic My girlfriend will kill you. It was originally my plan to wear this shirt into the interview, and as we left, I was going to show Madeline that the shirt was my way of asking her out for real this time. Only time beat me to it, and last week at the office in the lodge felt more right than now would have. But I did want to tell her I loved her. And I couldn't let a good shirt go to waste.

"Oh my God," Madeline guffawed. "Your shirt!" She pointed at it with pure delight, and the smile that grew under her nose was everything to me. Playful and sweet, a touch of flirtation. A real Madeline smile.

"You like it?" I pulled the bottom of it to stretch out the words for her.

"I love it."

"It's true," I winked at her. "I do love my girlfriend."

She smiled and shook her head. "I'm gonna have to get these framed, you know?"

Chapter Thirty
Madeline

F inals days always felt like an out-of-body experience. Like I'd spent all this time prepping for this day and still, after all those hours, I wasn't prepared enough. Like the movie scenes where, in the brisk morning hours, sun rising slowly in the east, the two villages prepared their best for war, having no clue what's on the other side. No clue if they'll make it out alive.

Logically, I knew it was nothing similar, but for someone who avoided any and all conflict, it felt close enough.

I'd been up since four thirty, mostly on account of Piper's staring waking me up, followed by her request of A Bug's Life ("bug," as she called it.) But it ended up being perfect because that left me with two hours to cram.

My other three exams were less taxing than this one was going to be. They were all proctored online tests that I was able to do at home while Charlie was at school and Piper was at Olive's house, and with the three I'd taken, I managed a high B and two low A's. I'd take it. As long as I finished strong, I was determined to be proud of myself after this was done.

Not to prove my parents wrong, but to let myself accept an accomplishment for once.

I still hadn't talked to either of them since the fight. Cooper had come with me to pick up Piper after we left the lodge, and although I couldn't see them, I rolled down the window in my car and heard him say a short "I'm here for Half-Pint, and that's all." Which made me smile. He came with us to pick up Charlie from school, and we all went back to Paradise Bakery for almond croissants and gelato. He sat next to Charlie in a booth as they talked about the upcoming competition while I bounced Piper on my knee, causing her to burst into fits of giggles. Cooper and I shared flirty smiles and occasional winks, our knees sometimes bumping under the table. It made up for everything that had happened that morning.

And sure enough, a week after our interview, Cooper pulled into our driveway, his mom in the passenger seat, and we all drove off in his SUV to see Disney on Ice at the Aspen District theater. I'd told Charlie he could bring a friend, assuming he would hate the entire affair and would probably need some kind of emotional support. But he just shook his head and said "no thanks. I'm fine." So we invited Dr. Lora instead, who now insisted I call her just Lora. It was still taking some getting used to.

Piper informed me, in her own words, that she wanted Lola beside her in the car. So once we got her car seat in and adjusted, Charlie, Piper, and Lora all squished in the second row. For the entire drive, both kids were laughing at Cooper's mom and the various toys or snacks she pulled out of her purse. Goldfish were being passed around in a circle like this was That Seventies Show and Lora was Hyde. Occasionally the "Dr. Lora" would show up, asking what color something was or annunciating her syllables. "Is this blue? Bluh-bluh-bloooo," which made the rest of us snort.

When we pulled into the parking deck and took the elevator down to the event center, there were various off-brand carts lining the closed-off streets with bubble wands, princess crowns, light-up jewelry, and other merchandise with cross-eyed characters and misspelled names on them. Piper, in Cooper's arms, dove straight for a bubble blower with Elsa's face on it.

We'd come here last year, and I already knew the drill, so I reached for my toddler. "No, baby. They don't let you bring them inside."

"Bub, bub, bub." Piper did her impression of a bubble blower, and I sighed. "Yes, but there are bubbles inside. We'll get those."

"Dis bub bub." She pointed to a unicorn one that looked close to falling apart.

"Good job, Piper!" Lora said behind me. "Such good control of your speech! Can you say 'bub—boool'?"

Cooper shook his head. "Why would they sell these out here if we can't bring them in?"

"They're not connected to the venue. It's like a third-party merchandise rule. We learned the hard way last year when I spent fifty bucks out here, and then we had to go put it all in the car because they don't allow it."

"Hell nah." Cooper shook his head and pulled out his leather wallet, taking a twenty out of it. "She's bringing in the unicorn."

Piper squealed and clapped when Cooper handed her the bubble blower, then proceeded to blow bubbles directly into all of our faces. I turned to Charlie. "I can get you something too," I offered.

He shrugged. "No thanks. You can get me a game or something after."

I snorted. "Right, because a ten-dollar bubble blower and a fifty-dollar Xbox game are on the same level."

"Hey," he said in defense. "You asked."

We got in line for security to check my bag and Lora's, and sure enough, three security guards told Piper and Cooper they couldn't bring in external merchandise. To which Cooper said, and I quote, "You can take my life, you can take my freedom, but you will never take this damn bubble blower." Only they did forcefully take it and throw it in the trash directly in front of Piper, causing the meltdown of the century. She cried and wailed over "bub bub" until we got inside the arena, where there were dozens of concession carts, cotton candy stands, and giant stuffed Disney characters as far as the eye could see. And Cooper, the suck-up, bought her every single thing she pointed to. Lora and I stood back, watching in amusement. I turned to Charlie. "As much as he's dropping on her, I'll have to buy you three Xbox games to make up for it."

"You do what feels fair, May. I won't hold you back."

I snorted and wrapped an arm around him, ruffling his hair and giving him a quick squeeze.

By the time we sat down, center stage, we all had our hands full. Cooper with a giant stuffed Minnie Mouse, Piper with two bags of cotton candy and a plastic princess crown on her head, Charlie with two corn dogs and an Avalanche hat that I found for sale at one of the far kiosks. I held an enormous bucket of popcorn, enough for a group twice our size, and Lora held her phone, taking a million candid photos of us like we were a family on vacation and she was our hired photographer. Photos that probably felt cute in the moment but when looked back on, would be nothing but double chins and squinted eyes from laughing so hard.

Cooper and Piper shared the seat to my left, Charlie on my right, and Lora next to him. We watched as characters were revealed one by one, gliding in on their skates and dancing along to the popular movie soundtracks. When Elsa came out, you would have thought Piper had died and gone to heaven. The lights danced around us, bubbles flying left and right. Cooper's hand reached for mine about halfway through, lacing our fingers. He lifted my hand and gave the back of it a quick kiss, squeezing it tight. I smiled at him and thought to myself that I loved him probably more than I'd loved anyone before him.

Which had been practically all I could focus on for the last week. Every time I sat to study for this last exam, memories of bubbles and lights, Piper and Cooper singing while Charlie and I laughed at them, and Lora shaking her head, came pouring to the front of my brain.

Today's exam was different from those others because I'd have to go in person. Most of the classes allowed proctored tests from my laptop, but occasionally, the more strict ones meant going to one of those strict test-taking facilities that meant putting your phone, keys, wallet, everything into a locker, then being forced to take the test in a tiny cubicle under harsh fluorescent lighting. The closest one was thirty minutes away, and it took another thirty minutes to sign paperwork and set up.

Which was why I now had only an hour until Olive was supposed to be here to watch the kids for me, since it was a Saturday, and I was certainly not asking my parents to watch her.

So when my phone buzzed with Finn's name on it, I could only assume the worst.

"Hello?" I answered.

"Get this thing out of me!" Olive screamed in the background as Finn casually said, "Hey, Madeline, so uh—"

"Olive's in labor?" I assumed. She was only thirty-five weeks along, but at her last appointment, the doctor did say that baby Beckett was pretty large for her gestation period, and early labor wasn't unlikely.

"I'm gonna die."

"Baby, please don't say that. You know I can't live without my grinch."

"Shut up. Everyone in the entire world, shut up."

Finn whispered low to me. "So, we won't make it this morning."

I smiled at the thought of Finn rushing them to the hospital and Olive gripping his forearm until her knuckles were white and his skin was bruised. "It's fine. Go have a baby. Thoughts and prayers. Tell her she's gonna do great."

"I would, but I'm supposed to shut up. I'll do that later."

"Send me all the updates. I want to hear everything!"

"Will do," Finn whispered.

"This is my nightmare."

"Okay, gotta go." My phone beeped, and I called Cooper. He answered on the second ring.

"Morning, Madeline, my studious girlfriend. My soon-to-be all-free, all-mine girlfriend." The smile in his voice made my cheeks hurt from grinning.

"Good morning," I answered. "So, Olive's in labor—"

"What?" he shouted, and I nearly dropped my phone. Piper, who was on the other end of the couch, crawled to sit in my lap and listen in. "They called you before me?"

"Well, to be fair, they were supposed to watch Piper while I took my exam, so that's probably why."

He let out a humph. "Excuses."

"Well, I was calling to see if you were super busy this morning or could you possibly come watch the kids so I don't have to—"

"Talk to your parents, who we've agreed to shun until Piper graduates from high school."

"Precisely."

"Of course. Give me like twenty minutes, all right?"

Ten minutes later, he was at the door, three Xbox games in hand, including one with Disney characters on it. When I eyed it curiously, he shrugged. "Seemed like the best way to please both of them." He lowered his voice. "I also have a whole bag of Slim Jims in my backpack."

"Oh good, so you don't even need to know CPR or anything."

"Nope. I'm qualified enough."

Charlie and Piper followed Cooper around like two newborn ducks that had imprinted on the first thing they saw after hatching. He'd walk to the kitchen, and they were right behind him. He set up the video game, and they watched his every move from two feet over.

"You ready for it?" Cooper asked, standing over me as both kids were busy on the couch.

"I think so. I crammed as much as I could this morning. Even if it doesn't go well, I really do think I tried my best, you know?"

"You did, and I'm so proud of you."

I didn't know what it said about me that the words proud of you were a turn-on for me. Probably that I had mommy and daddy issues—a double dose, if you will. But either way, I wrapped two arms around Cooper and squeezed him tight, planting a kiss on his cheek. "Thank you so much," I whispered. Not just for saying he was proud and not for agreeing to come watch them. But just for...everything.

I pulled back enough to look him in the eye as I said. "I don't think I realized how badly I was running on E until I met you."

He squinted down at me. "Madeline, I was the one on E. You've given me a new purpose. Made me a better man in every way."

He bent down as I lifted up, and we met halfway, his lips pressing to mine in the sweetest, slowest kiss. Like molasses being poured. His mouth brushed mine a moment longer than we probably should have before he backed away, hands resting on my waist.

"I love you. Go kick some nurse ass." He reached one hand down to squeeze my bottom, and I giggled, grabbing my keys.

I gave both of the kids quick kisses and goodbyes, but neither of them even glanced up at me, entirely focused on their newest Cooper gift. He claimed he'd stopped trying to buy into friendships, but these two kids had been more spoiled in the last month and a half than they had been their whole lives.

And it made me love him even more.

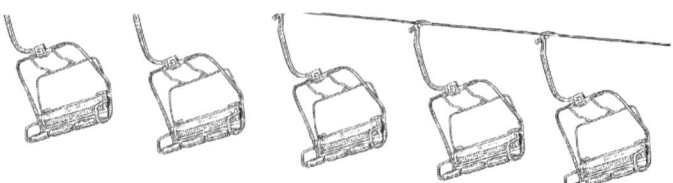

Chapter Thirty-one
COOPER

W atching kids at a ski lodge—where there were hundreds of witnesses if something were to go awry—and watching kids entirely alone in your girlfriend's house were very, very different.

It was like as soon as Madeline closed the door behind her, I became hyperaware of every sharp corner and potential height danger, and I was extremely curious as to where all her medications were and if they were locked up securely enough so the tiny raccoon wouldn't find them.

But Mini Coop was here too, and watching a nine-year-old with a two-year-old felt slightly less daunting than watching Half-Pint on my own, knowing that if I escaped for two seconds to pee, there was a high chance she was climbing an un-anchored piece of furniture.

Luckily, in the last thirty minutes, there had been no attempts, and if anything, it was almost...boring. Mini Coop was focused on the TV, playing multiple rounds of first-person shooter games, and Half-Pint was on the far corner of the couch in a tightly wound-up ball.

I brought snacks, pulling out my Nanny McPhee bag that Madeline still liked to joke about. Charlie ran straight for anything sweet, chocolate granola bars, fiber brownies—because gut health matters—or the tiny gummy bear packs I had left over from passing out Halloween candy this season. Every year, I assumed we'd be flooded with children in our streets, and every year, I was greeted with teenagers far too old for this with zero costumes, and a visit from my next-door neighbor, Rhonda, who brought me squash bread. It was more like a lump of cat hair with a side of squash bread, but the gesture was all that mattered.

Next year we could take the kids to the lodge for trick-or-treating. I hadn't gone in years since I never had a kid to attend with, and it felt odd for a thirty-year-old man to walk around an event entirely based around children. But it was all too easy to imagine next year. Madeline was the type to go all-out on costumes. I envisioned all of us in matching costumes. The Adams Family. Wizard of Oz. Oh, no, Star Wars–themed. I could be Anakin, obviously. A tiny Luke and Leia in tow beside us.

All of the "next year" events came flooding to me. After the New Year's competition, we didn't have a ton of events at the lodge for a while, but we could find something. Make up something if we had to. All I knew was it was so incredibly simple to sit here and picture what life would look like from here on out.

After Charlie rifled through my bag, stealing half its contents, I turned to Piper.

"Half-Pint." I shook the bag her way. "You hungry? I've got Sham Jams. Oh, and those Cheez-its you liked last time. And—" I paused, because her face looked strangely pale, and she wasn't looking anywhere near me. Her eyebrows were furrowed, and she was sniffling so quietly that I could barely hear it over the TV. "Half-Pint?" I scooted a little closer, and because I had no idea what to do with a two-year-old, I patted the top of her blond head. "You okay?"

She shook her head in response, and my mind came out with a roster of things that could have gone wrong since Madeline had left. A brown recluse had bitten her, and the venom was kicking in fast. She'd stubbed her toe on the leg of the couch when I wasn't looking. A bug had climbed into her ear, and she didn't know how to tell me it was taking over her brain. That last one was far-fetched, but my anxiety over children's health knew no bounds, apparently.

"Is it 'cause you miss May?" Charlie asked, using a more logical approach.

Piper shook her head again, and her hands kept circling her stomach, tightening her grip on herself and then shifting. The fact that she turned down a snack alone was scaring me, but now she was holding her abdomen like the favorite side character in action movies did right after you found out they'd been shot during the big scenes and they just never said anything.

"Hold on. I'll call your aunt and ask her, okay?" I petted the top of her head a few more times and felt sickly when she just sniffled and nodded.

I called Madeline twice. Both times, it went straight to voice-mail. I checked the time and winced. She was already in the testing area, and her phone was probably turned off and locked away.

"Okay, let me call my mom," I mumbled and turned back to Piper, who was now curled into an even tighter ball, with her eyes shut, her sniffles converting into heavy panting and fast-falling tears. "I'm gonna call Lola, okay? She can help."

Thanks be to God, Mom answered on the second ring.

"If you're calling to borrow my copy of Beauty and the Beast again, I am not—who's crying? Is that Piper?" She rushed out the last bit, and there was a sound of keys jangling in the background.

"Yeah, Madeline had to go take a test, and Olive is having her baby, so I was the next best thing and—"

"No, I was the next best thing."

"Of course you were." I rolled my eyes. Even in times of desperation, the woman always had to make a point. "Look, there's something wrong with Half-Pint's stomach, and I think she needs some kind of medicine, but I don't know what, and Madeline can't answer."

Mom hummed and was quiet for a minute. "Try five milliliters of Tylenol and call me back in thirty minutes."

I did as told, following Charlie to where the medicine was kept and getting a baby syringe out for her. Piper happily downed the Tylenol—thankfully, because I was not sure what I would do if she started flailing around and I was going to have to force it like I was wrestling a wild alligator.

Not even fifteen minutes went by, and Piper's sniffled cries were now ear-piercing wails. I picked her up, cradling her like an overgrown baby, and rocked her back and forth, bouncing on my toes. We tried different movies, different toys. Snacks, games, songs. We did an entire dance routine at one point. Every single thing you could possibly pull out to cheer up a toddler, Charlie and I did.

"Does she do this often?" I asked him, winded from all the bouncing and rocking.

He shook his head. "Never. Not like with her stomach."

I looked down to her face, scrunched up and red like she was in excruciating pain. I asked the one thing I really had no clue how to handle. "Do you think she needs to use the bathroom?"

Charlie shrugged. "I think she already did once this morning?"

I wasn't well equipped with the knowledge of a toddler's BM schedules, but twice in one morning felt like a lot.

Just then, Piper screamed out, unable to catch her breath in my arms, and the panic was settling deep inside me. This was wrong. Something was just...wrong. Not one bit of this felt right. Even that night that she had a fever and—wait, a fever.

"Where's your thermometer?" I asked Charlie. His eyes widened when he realized that neither of us had even considered that. Then he darted to the kitchen sink cabinet. He pulled out a white first-aid kit and a newer-looking thermometer, tossing it my way. Only both of my arms were being used to hold a twenty-something-pound child, and I couldn't catch for shit. So it fell to the ground, and the screen went haywire.

"Nice catch," Charlie retorted.

"Nice throw," I argued.

In a frantic haze, I called my mom again.

"This isn't working. Something isn't right."

I could tell by her paused silence that she knew it too. Mom never freaked out. She was the most level-headed person I knew. But if something were to go wrong, you could always hear it in her hesitations.

"Okay, this is an odd request, and I highly doubt this is it, but it's important to check."

"Oh God, tell me I don't have to put medicine in her butt." That was a thing, right? I started sweating bullets. I needed to take my sweatshirt off, but I was too scared to even set her down.

Piper's screams turned louder.

"No, nothing like that. I need you to ask her to jump. If she falls over in pain, we'll go from there."

"Uh, okay." I looked to Charlie and set Piper down next to him. She cried, holding her hands held out to me, but Charlie covered by saying. "Pipes, look! Look what I'm doing." He made a show of jumping obnoxiously up and down, and she refused, so I did the same thing. We were shaking the house entirely, but after a couple of moments, Piper did one single hop before reaching to her gut and letting out another wail.

I lifted my phone in an instant as I scooped her into my arms. "Okay, yeah. No, there's no way she can jump. What does that even—"

"Go to Aspen Valley now."

"Like...the hospital?" I swallowed the boulder in my throat.

"Yes. Now, Coop. No time to waste. Drive carefully, but take her to the ER. I'll meet you there. I need to make a few calls. I have some connections up there and can get her a room faster than you might be able to. But go ahead and leave now. Do not speed. You understand?"

No...not me. I was not the driving to the hospital guy. I was the buy you a bubble blower wand and ice cream guy. I wasn't—I couldn't. My breathing started growing frantic, my rib cage shrinking three sizes too small. This wasn't supposed to go this way. We weren't supposed to—

"Cooper. Baby, listen to me. You have to focus on her right now. Get both kids to the hospital. I'll meet you there, okay?"

I nodded and shook my head. Pull it together. Whatever is going on, you can't fix it on your own. You've got to get her to a hospital. I hung up on my mom and started reaching for any essentials. When Piper's screams only deepened, it hit me that there was nothing more essential than taking her to the ER. Now.

I looked at Charlie. "My keys are on the counter. Go start the car and get buckled in the back seat." His eyes were watering, but I couldn't find it in me to console us both other than to say a simple "Go, Charlie. Now."

He nodded and ran out of the door in his pajamas.

"Okay, okay. Think. We need insurance cards—" Piper's whole body was shaking against me. "No time for that. Uh..." I started looking around me for any kind of emergency item we'd need, and my eyes landed on the notepad Madeline had left, where she'd written her parents' phone numbers. She wrote on the very top NOT UNLESS SOMEONE IS DYING, and considering I felt like I was, I ripped off the top paper and raced out the door to the car.

Charlie was buckled in the middle seat, right next to Piper's car seat. My windshield wasn't iced over, thankfully, so I was able to buckle her into the seat as fast as I could while Charlie cooed in her ear. "It's okay, bug. Coop's got us. We're okay." I felt like he was saying it every bit as much for me as he was for her.

I double-checked the tightness of the straps just like Madeline had taught me to and gently shut the door before rounding the car. The whole world felt like it was spinning. Like I was spinning. My blood was pumping. My heart felt like it was going to give out. My own stomach started twisting and turning, and when I could hear Piper's pain-filled screeching outside the car, a wave of nausea hit me square in the gut. Two hands on my knees, I turned away from the car and emptied my stomach right on the driveway, pissed at myself.

I'd once said I thrived on adrenaline. Turned out I was wrong.

I jumped in the car right after, not bothering to waste any more time and speeding out of the driveway despite my mother's directions. Good news was Aspen Valley was only fifteen minutes, and traffic was light. If I pushed hard enough, I could make it in ten.

My foot forced the gas pedal to the floor as we crossed our neighborhood. I made the mistake of glancing in the rearview mirror once at the two blond kids in the back of my car. Charlie had his hand over the car seat, making shushing noises and rubbing the snot and tears from her bright red, almost purple, face. "It's okay, bug. We'll be there soon." I watched in horror as tears freely fell from his own face and then realized they were dripping down mine too.

I overestimated myself. Madeline did too. I couldn't do this. My stomach lurched like I was going to throw up again, but I had no time. I had to get her there. And if it meant throwing up in my car, which I really hoped it didn't, then so be it.

Seven minutes later, I whipped into the ER parking lot, ignoring the Do not park here signs and running around the car to the back seat. I unbuckled Piper and scooped her into my arms, asking Charlie to grab the note with their grandparents' numbers on it and my keys. I owed that kid a lot of thanks when things settled down, but for now, I was too busy running.

I raced inside at full speed, and my eyes met with my mom's as she stood there, talking to the receptionist.

"Here they are," she announced. There was such panic in her voice that it only drew mine up higher.

"Mr. Graves, follow me. We have a room right back here for you."

I followed the older woman in blue scrubs to a curtained-off area and sat on the bed with Piper in my lap as she dug her face into my neck. The cries from her never stopped, never let up. They only grew deeper and louder. Enough that the other two nurses that quickly popped in both were wincing.

"We need to know if she's allergic to anything," one mentioned as she started taking her temperature.

"No. Wait, I don't know. No food allergies but..." I looked to Charlie, and he shrugged, unknowing. "I can call her grandparents and ask."

I handed Piper off to my mom, who was gently rocking and shushing her on the crisp white bed while I typed in the nine digits and hit Call.

"If you're trying to sell me a car warranty, you can go to—"

"Mrs. Sage!" I shouted. "Does Piper have any allergies?"

"What? Who is this?"

"Madeline's boyfriend. Does Piper have any allergies?"

"Uh, latex, I think? Tom," she shouted. "Was it Piper who's allergic to latex?" Some silence fell. Well, not total silence, because our baby was still screaming, and the nurses were throwing out medical terms left and right with my mother.

"Latex," I told the nurse. "She's allergic to latex."

"Okay, we need to get her to a scan immediately," one announced, and Mom stood up, handing Piper over to me.

"Scans?" I asked.

"Scans?" Mrs. Sage yelled into the phone. "What is going on—"

I growled in the back of my throat and shouted into the microphone. "Your granddaughter is sick, and I'm working on it. If you care about these kids, then show up to Aspen Valley and quit asking questions." I hung up, wishing I could have thrown a handful of curses into that sentence but figured I'd get there soon.

"Why do we need scans?" I asked. "What's going on?"

"It's rare, I mean, less than 10 percent rare, but we think she may have appendicitis."

I threw up again, this time on my mother's white tennis shoes.

Chapter Thirty-two
Madeline

I came out of my test feeling pretty good. It wasn't the worst final I'd had—that was probably my first chemistry class last semester—but it wasn't the easiest either. Overall, I felt accomplished. I'd done something that even my parents had never thought I would, even if my grade was worse than I felt it would be. I wasn't going to graduate. I knew that. But I felt this new level of relief now. This form of a new start. A renaissance.

I stood from my tiny cubicle and exited through the heavy door, walking to the woman behind a desk at the far end of the hallway by the lockers where my phone was.

I smiled down at the gray-haired woman who had a half-eaten strawberry-banana yogurt cup by her equally gray mouse. "Last name?" she asked, her voice a stale monotone.

"Sage." I bounced on my toes. "Madeline Sage is the full name. It's a microbiology set—"

"It's printing," she said, like I was personally tearing her apart from the yogurt cup, but I didn't care.

I turned to face the printer, watching as three warm sheets with fresh ink came sliding out. I took a deep breath through my nose and out of my mouth. At the end of the day, the results didn't matter. I wouldn't tell anyone but Cooper. I certainly would never tell my parents.

Still, my hands shook as I pulled the papers out of their slot. My eyes scanned the first two pages, where each question was broken down, all the way to the third page, where, in big bold lettering, was Results: 82/100.

"Eighty-two?" I squealed, pulling the papers to my chest. "Eighty-two!" I shouted.

"Shh!" yogurt lady behind me hissed. But I ignored her, heading straight for my locker. Cooper was going to be so excited.

I pictured driving home to him in my living room, me waving papers excitedly back and forth and him lifting me off the ground and spinning me in circles. Maybe we could all go out to eat tonight. Or go get ice cream at Paradise Bakery. Heck, right now, all I needed was to hear his voice and to let him know I'd done it. I'd gone as far as the world would let me go. Graduation, no graduation. I was seriously proud of myself, for once. It felt like Will and Savannah were walking right beside me to the parking lot as I waited for my phone to turn back on.

This was the beginning of something new. Something unknown and beautiful, and we were going to find it together.

My phone turned on as I reached my car. I plugged it into the sound system and immediately searched for Cooper's contact. Only I froze as notification after notification flew across the top of my screen.

I tapped the phone icon and saw sixteen missed calls from Cooper—the latest one from twelve minutes ago—five missed calls from Dr. Lora, and two from my mom.

My blood ran cold as I stared at the red numbers. Missed call after missed call. My hands were shaking, my fight-or-flight response kicking in like a shot to my chest. I chose fight and immediately put my car in reverse to back out.

Everything in me went back to that night.

I'm so sorry, Ms. Sage. There's been an accident. We're at Aspen Valley ER.

One last text popped through.

Cooper: call me as soon as you get done.

He'd used a period. Somehow that made everything worse. My hands shook feverishly as I tapped the button to call him five times, the delay in my device only growing my anxiety.

He answered on the first ring, and I spoke before he could even say hello.

"Coop." My voice was as shaky as my hands on the wheel. "What's going on?"

He sounded just as shaky back, causing my blood pressure to rise higher. "Okay, so everything is okay. Everyone is safe now."

"Now?" I was shrieking, tears flowing from just the thought. "Where are you?" I was already pulling out of the parking lot.

"We're at Aspen Valley."

My chest started heaving. "Was there a—" God, this was not the time to get choked up. "Was there an accident?"

I couldn't lose anyone else. Not my babies. No one could take them from me, not even death himself.

"No. God, no, Madeline. I'm so sorry. I didn't even think of that. Baby, I'm so sorry. It's Piper...she had appendicitis. She's almost out of surgery now, though, and—"

"Appendicitis?" I cried out. "What, how? Toddlers don't just get appendicitis? She was perfectly fine this morning."

I thought back and realized she wasn't fine. She was more reserved. She didn't eat her breakfast. She wasn't squealing with excitement like normal. She wasn't herself last night either. Could barely eat any chicken nuggets, and when Charlie tried to play with her, she brushed him off. Maybe she wasn't fussy, but she wasn't herself either. And I was so focused on myself, on my tests and my giddy texts with Cooper, that I hadn't even noticed that she was in pain.

"I know, Madeline. It's okay now. Just come up here when you can. Drive safe, please. I know you're upset, but we caught it in time. Mom's back there ordering everyone around. She's in the best hands. I have Mini Coop sitting with me, and he's okay too. We're okay. Your parents are here too. Everything is going to be okay."

It sounded more like he was trying to console himself than console me, which only made me speed up.

My thirty-minute drive crunched into a fifteen minute one. When I walked into the ER, I practically screamed at the petite blond receptionist, who stared up at me with fear in her eyes.

"Piper Sage. Two years old. Tiny. Blond. Appendicitis."

As the poor woman opened her mouth, a hand rested on my shoulder, and the familiar scent of clove hit my nose. "Madeline." I turned to Cooper and sucked in a breath. "She's in here.

She's okay. They just brought her back from surgery. She's still passed out, but she's okay."

With our hands intertwined, Cooper led me down a bright, sterile hallway. We passed room after room, each one with sick or injured people laid up in hospital beds on top of white sheets. It smelled just like the ICU had two years ago. It made me nauseous.

He led me to a room on the far right, opening the door softly. Six chairs lined the wall. Everyone stared at me. My parents, Lora, my Charlie. But my eyes landed on my girl.

My tiny toddler, all signs of wild and crazy drained from her body, lying on a sterile bed in the smallest hospital gown I'd ever seen. My stomach lurched. Her tiny frame was so pale it almost looked purple. The skin under her eyes sagged despite the deep sleep she had been forced into. Her face was scrunched, like even in rest, she couldn't truly relax.

Guilt coursed through me. I should've been there. But then again, would I have even known what to do? Would I have gotten her here in time?

Horror stories over my time in nursing school came flooding back. Stories of kids who had appendicitis, and their parents had brushed it off as a bad tummy ache, the results lethal.

Lora was the first to break the silence beyond the steady beeping of the machine showing her vitals. "She did perfectly." She rounded the bed and raised a hand to my shoulder, rubbing up and down in the most comforting manner. "Cooper caught it at just the right time. The doctors said everything went just right, really." She rubbed slow circles on my back, the way I imagined most moms would in this scenario. Though my mom was in a far corner of the room, staring at me with guilt in her eyes. Lora patted me twice on the back. "It's okay, Madeline. She'll be up as soon as the medicine wears off."

I reached behind me and pulled a seat to the bed, stroking her blond hair and waiting for her eyes to flutter open. Everyone in the room stayed quiet, watching and waiting with me.

After a while, both of my parents stood and walked closer to me. Mom touched my shoulder, tried to recreate the comfort that Lora had given me, but it was counterfeit and unwanted. I shrugged it off.

"Madeline," she started. "We are so sorry about—"

"Not now," I snapped. "Not here."

From the corner of my eye, I saw them look at each other and nod, taking their seats in the corner.

On the other side of me, Cooper sat, playing with the ends of my hair, whispering comforting affirmations in my ear, talking to Charlie too. I felt at fault for not giving him much of my attention, but I thought he understood the severity of it all too well. We'd have our time to talk soon. A time when I could give him my undivided focus. For now, Cooper let him watch movies or play games on his phone.

I expected some kind of peaceful awakening when the anesthesia wore off. Like in the movies, when someone is coming back to their senses and they start piecing things together one by one. Not my Piper. Piper woke up crying, screaming, wailing. In the driest little crack of a voice, she cried out again and again. The same word over and over. Hafpa. Hafpa. Hafpa. She said it like she was breathing, like it was the first thing to come to her.

Only when she didn't get hafpa, she cried harder and said the word I'd only heard her ask for on the rarest of occasions.

"Dada," she cried out. "Da, da, da, da, da." The same syllable over and over as her eyes squinted in the bright room. "Dada, Dada!"

My heart broke in two. I reached for her hand and softly rubbed my thumb over the back. "Dada's not here, baby. May's here. May's got you." Her eyes attempted to flutter open, but the lids looked so heavy for her tiny body. "Charlie's here. Your Charlie, all yours. He's right here, baby." Charlie reached over and grabbed her other hand, whispering softly to his sister. We only pissed her off more. She pulled her hands away from both of us, looked right past me to the six-five brown-haired man behind me and said it one more time with her arms stretched wide for him.

"Dada."

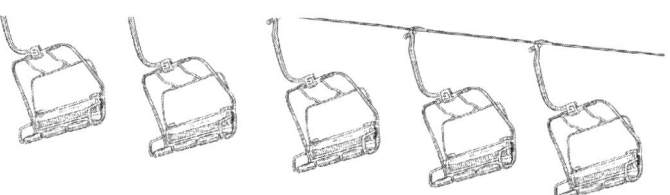

Chapter Thirty-three
COOPER

All eyes landed on me.

"Dada." The word rang in my ears, like the after sound of a gong, echoing in the walls of my brain. "Dada."

"I..." I lifted a hand to my chest and looked around the room. Charlie, with this expression that seemed like he was close to bursting into tears. My mom, watching me with soft, gentle eyes. Mr. and Mrs. Sage, covering their mouths with their hands in shock. Piper, red-rimmed eyes and tearstained cheeks, reaching out to me with both arms. And last, Madeline. Madeline, who looked at me with fear and sadness. And I just couldn't take it.

"I'm not..." I shook my head. "She's not my..."

Time felt stopped as the room seemed to spin. The walls closing in, my chest cramping tight. My eyes starting to water. I was about to cry. Oh, God. I was crying.

"I'm sorry," I whispered, and like a coward, I bolted out of the room.

"Cooper!" Madeline called after me, and I turned over my shoulder, refusing to meet any of their eyes. "I can't...I'm...Just stay here. I need a minute. Stay with her."

I pushed the hefty door open and passed two older nurses that I'd seen my mom talk to.

"You did a great job, dad." The short, gray-haired one smiled.

The taller, younger of the two, nodded. "Brought her in the nick of time too. She's blessed to have a wonderful father."

Dada. Dad. Father.

My stomach clenched tight, nausea rising in my gut, my mouth sour.

I was going to throw up. Again.

I ran past them to the nearest bathroom and rushed into the open stall, emptying anything left in my stomach. Dada. She'd reached for me. I threw up some more. Dada. I'd ruined her. Dada. Her own dad was six feet under dirt, and she'd found the saddest replacement and had stuck the golden name badge on me.

An unpaid intern with a CEO nameplate on his desk.

I emptied my stomach further, not holding back any of the pain it caused me.

After I pulled myself together, however long that was, I left the bathroom and looked down the hall to where Piper's room door was propped open. I wanted to check in, wanted details from nurses and surgeons. Honestly, I wanted a hug from my own mom. Because I was still running on pure adrenaline, and nothing in the world calmed me like the soft voice of my mom. I wanted to kiss Madeline. I wanted to be the one to comfort her. To apologize. To let her know everything was all right now. But

I...just couldn't. So I hopped into the nearest elevator, halfway shut with an older couple in it, and pressed lobby.

I sat in the hospital's coffee area for a while. I hadn't brought my phone with me. Honestly I had no clue where it was, and since, apparently, no one thought wall clocks were useful anymore, I had no clue how long I'd been down here. Enough to watch at least ten people order at the register, receive their drinks, take a seat, and leave with their families, friends, or spouses.

"Hi, Charming," a voice called out to me, soft and feminine. Like pink-painted nails scraping along my neck and down my throat. Like the tiny kisses she'd planted on my cheek just this morning. Like her hugs, so light, no matter how hard she tried to squish me. She was always so soft.

I looked up and saw Madeline taking a seat across from me. Her eyes were a little brighter, the mascara underneath them now wiped away, and she looked more relieved than when I'd seen her last. A weight had lifted from her shoulders.

"Hi," I mumbled.

"You ran out on me." She didn't say it in a defensive, accusatory way. Just like she was stating facts. Like she was recalling the last memory. "I was worried about you."

I puffed out a breath of air. "I lost my phone. I was going to text you that I was down here, but—" She pulled a black rectangle out of her pocket and set it on the table in front of me.

"I found it in Charlie's seat when you left. Figured you needed some time to breathe."

I nodded. "I did."

She sucked in a breath, one dainty hand reaching over the table to land over mine. "And?"

"And...I can't do this, Madeline." I shook my head. "I'm not fit for...that." I waved my hand, gesturing upstairs. "I love you. A lot. I love those kids. I don't think I realized just how much until I looked in my rearview mirror and saw them both crying in my back seat." The memory alone brought bile up my throat. My hands felt shaky. "I want you in my life so bad. I want all of you for myself. But I'm not...I'm not strong enough for this, Madeline."

I looked up, expecting to see her crushed. Waiting for her eyes to water and for her to tell me to screw off or go to hell or some other typical shouted break-up phrases. Instead, she was smiling. I should have known; she was always smiling.

"Cooper." She squeezed my hand. "You know what the doctor just told me?"

I didn't respond. Just looked down at our joined hands. The tiny bracelet I'd given her weeks ago rested on her wrist and grazed mine.

"He said that you saved her life. That if you hadn't driven her here...we could have lost..." She took a deep breath in and squeezed my hand, not quite able to say the words. "I owe you everything, Cooper."

"No." I pulled my hand back, and when my eyes looked up, she was still smiling. Only it was that sympathetic kind of smile. She saw right through my hardened shell, straight to the gooey center.

"Madeline...I threw up in your driveway."

She snorted a little. "Gross."

"So gross. I didn't even clean it up. I'm actually mortified about it."

"Coop—"

"I threw up because I thought she was dying. I thought I was dying for a minute too. The way she was screaming, how she clung to my neck...I'm haunted, Madeline. It was the single most terrifying moment of my life. And I have jumped off the side of a mountain with only skis and no parachute."

"Please never do that again."

"It was my early twenties. I felt invincible. Either way, I want to be what you need. What those kids need. I just don't think I'm cut from that cloth. I'm not your brother. Or Finn. Or any other great dad in the world. I didn't even have my own dad growing up. How could I possibly be someone else's?"

Madeline sighed and scooted her chair a little closer. "You know, when I first got the kids, I was terrified." She picked my hand right back up, and I didn't fight it. "During the first storm that came through, I thought of everything bad that could happen. I stuck them both in the bathtub with pillows and put helmets on their heads and made them sleep like that while I stayed up all night propped against the toilet, listening to the weather station. It was just a small thunderstorm. The power didn't even go out. But still, everything felt magnified with them. Every time Charlie fell and scraped a knee. When Piper was teething. When they missed their parents, and I was the most pathetic excuse of a replacement. At first, it all felt so big to me. Terrifying. But then, time went on, scrapes happened, colds happened, and slowly but surely, we made it. We're still here. And whereas I am not their mother, I think I'm a pretty good aunt. The best replacement there is."

"Yeah, but—"

"Cooper. Parenting isn't just the fun stuff. It's not just the ice cream trips, the Disney on Ice adventures, or staying late, watching movies in a fort. You've got to take the good with the bad."

"But I'm not—"

"You aren't a dad, no. And I'm not a mom. You're a Coop, and I'm a May. Those kids look at us with so much love in their eyes that I know they wouldn't want it any other way. And if you ask me, that's enough."

I lifted my head so I could see hers. Her spare hand reached out to my chin, fingers lightly scratching the stubble there. "Parenthood, or aunthood and unclehood, doesn't come with a book. And there are going to be times where we throw up in the driveway, unfortunately—"

"Hopefully not more than once."

"Maybe twice. But"—she squeezed my chin—"we can do it together, yeah? All the good, bad, and ugly. You and I can tag team it."

I straightened a little. "I want to. I do, Madeline. I meant what I said. I love all three of you. But I know myself. You do too. I'm not made for these things."

"You know what?" Madeline pulled my phone closer to us and tapped the screen. "Someone wise once told me that who we are isn't defined by our abilities but by who and what we love around us. You love those kids so much, I think you'd go to jail for them. Your value isn't in how well you can handle the bad times. It's in the amount of love you pour out into this family."

I looked up at her, knowing she was probably right, but I couldn't admit it quite yet.

"Finn texted you something. Maybe you should read it."

I gave her a curious look, but she just winked and pushed the phone closer to me. My notifications were flooded with missed texts and calls from the people I loved. But a more recent one sat at the top, from Finland.

I opened it first. Attached was a picture of a tiny blue-swaddled bundle inside a clear basinet. A pink head poked out of the burrito, peacefully asleep with shut eyes, long eyelashes, and what had to be the tiniest nose in the entire world. A little Finn. My eyes moved the wooden cut-out circle with fancy drawn-on font.

Eli Cooper Beckett

My lower lip wobbled all over again, and I zoomed in to make sure I wasn't seeing things from my lack of hydration.

Eli Cooper Beckett

I closed the pic and read the text from Finn that followed it.

Finland: Say hi, Uncle Coop.

Finland: Wish I could've told you in person, but I heard you've got some chaos with your own baby girl, so I figured I'd leave you to it. We love you, brother.

Uncle Coop. Your own baby girl.

I glanced up at Madeline to see she was crying already, with that same tilted smile. "I told you." She sniffed. "You were already made for this."

My fingers reached to lock my phone, and I pulled Madeline's chair closer to mine, our legs intertwining and my arms wrapping around her midsection, squeezing her tight against me. Chest to chest, heart to heart. Our breathing matched each other's as we cried.

Madeline's gaze warmed me up, first inside and then all the way out. And when she leaned up to kiss me, letting me give her the tiniest nip on her bottom lip, everything felt right in the world. Like a new start. A refresh on something familiar and cozy.

"Come on." I laced our hands together. "Let's go get our girl."

Chapter Thirty-four
Madeline

I had never screamed so much in my life.

And my boyfriend was Cooper Graves, so that really said something.

Still, I stood in the snow in front of my fold-out chair, holding a bundled-up Piper in my arms as we shouted, giggled, and squealed, waiting for her brother to come down.

Cooper and Finn stood on the other side of me. They cupped their hands to their mouths, either whistling loudly or yelling, "Come on, Charlie," or Cooper's loud and proud "Show them how we taught you, Mini Coop!"

The crowd this year was larger than ever. There were hardly spots for us to put down our chairs, causing Cooper and Finn to claim they were VIPs and that we deserved front-row seating. I wasn't sure if the number of tourists was due to the column or not, but I knew one thing: I owed that magazine everything.

"This is so exciting." Olive bounced in the chair next to ours. "Much more exciting than Ms. Rachel and Sesame Street back home."

I smiled over at her. "You're missing him already, aren't you?"

"So much I could die. But we are here for you and my nephew."

My nephew. She so proudly proclaimed it without a hint of doubt.

Across the way from us sat my parents in their own chairs. We hadn't quite gone back to normal. There were still some gray areas between us. But instead of dissecting them, pulling those unknown answers out and trying to figure out the big why of it all, I let it be. Not for their sake, but for my own. I'd told them I needed space. To figure out whether I had it in me to forgive them, to let it all slip away. Realistically, I knew it would be too hard to pretend it had never happened. But could I eventually try to snap back into place and be civil? Probably. Today just wasn't that day.

The light turned from red to yellow to green, a horn blaring, and shouts erupting all around us, signaling their take off.

Charlie's skis carved graceful arcs in the snow, sending up sprays of powder with each turn he made. We all stared in awe as he navigated the course with surprising control, his movements fluid with confidence. Just like his Cooper.

Parents, friends, and families of all competitors cheered and clapped around us, their voices mingling with the sound of skis slicing through the snow. "Come on, buddy!" Cooper shouted, and the encouragement rippled through the crowd. He hit a series of small jumps, catching brief moments of air before landing smoothly, his form impeccable.

My fingers were so tightly wound around Cooper's that I was probably cutting off his circulation.

Charlie approached the final stretch, the crowd's excitement reaching a fever pitch. With one last burst of speed, he crossed the finish line with two other boys on his tail, and the crowd erupted in applause. All five of us were jumping up and down, screaming at the top of our lungs.

"Did he win?" I asked, still kind of unsure about how this whole thing worked.

Cooper leaned down and spoke in my ear. "We don't know. He was the first for time, but sometimes points can be added or deducted, so it's hard to say. It'll be close."

What felt like an eternity later, they finally announced the winners.

"In third place: Carter Jenkins."

My palms were sweating like Niagara falls.

"In second place: Justin Tyler."

The crowd roared, but we stayed entirely silent. Time stopped, Cooper squeezed my hand. My heart raced, Piper gripped my shoulder. Everything felt entirely paused in this moment.

"And last, in first place, with a time of three minutes and thirty-eight seconds and a score of sixty-three out of seventy: Charlie Sage!"

The crowd erupted into cheers, but none louder than our group. All five of us jumped up and down, screaming at the top of our lungs as we watched my boy accept his ribbon and trophy.

He climbed onto the winner's platform with this cheesing grin that felt bolder, brighter, than I'd seen in years. Our boy. Our Mini Coop.

Cooper raced past security guards and judges and volunteers, ignoring all of their arguments and you shouldn't be back here, sirs to run straight to Charlie. He gave him a tight hug, arms wrapped around his shoulders before lifting him up as high as he could and shouting loud enough for everyone to hear. "That's my boy. Look at my Mini Coop!"

Charlie cackled in the air as Cooper showed him off like a trophy.

After plenty of gloating, hugs, and squished cheeks from all of us, he went over to a group of friends off to the side. Cooper and Finn assured me they were kids from their classes, but still I watched in curiosity. Even more so when one tiny blond with braided pigtails wrapped her arms around his neck and pulled him in tight, leaving Charlie standing there with pink rushing up to his ears.

"Who's that?" I asked.

"Your future niece-in-law." Cooper smiled, and I elbowed his side.

"Stop, I just finally accepted that he'll be ten next month. Don't rush it."

His arms wrapped around my waist and squeezed me. "I'll never rush a thing with you, my Madeline." I smiled against his lips as he spun me in a circle.

You are valuable. He left them for you. I squeezed Cooper's hand and added one more affirmation in place. *You are Madeline.*

Epilogue

Family Matters Magazine Presents: One Family, One Lodge.

Ten years ago, we wrote our first column on Aspen Peaks Ski Lodge and were blessed to get to know Cooper Graves and Madeline Sage. They spoke of their first meeting, clearly still in the honeymoon phase of life. We learned about the upcoming annual ski competition and how they and their family were involved.

Now that we're back in town for the newest ski competition, we thought it would be fun to take a trip down memory lane and catch up with Aspen's favorite ski-lodge power couple.

"Give us details. Tell us what's new with you."

Madeline Graves chose to answer this one. "Well, baby number two is on the way." She placed her hands on her swollen belly. "A girl this time. Hopefully not as feisty as our first girl."

Cooper interjected. "Hopefully just as feisty. Our Piper is a spitfire."

"Tell us about the kids," Chase said.

"Let's see...Mini Coop—"

"Charlie," Madeline supplied.

"Is my apprentice. He's taking over our third position as children's ski instructor at the lodge, focusing more on the younger groups. He always wants to be out on the hills. Our Piper is now thirteen, and she is very busy in dance lessons and overall just being Piper. She has her first boyfriend too—"

"Cooper threatened him when we took them to the movies."

"She's a smart kid, but still, I don't like it. Then our first Mooper baby—"

"We don't call ourselves that, by the way," Madeline assured us.

"Grant is seven, and he is very into skiing, just like his brother was. And now we've got baby Lola on the way."

"And the lodge?" Chase asked. "How is it going?"

They laughed simultaneously, and we had a feeling there was something there that only the two of them knew about.

Madeline chose to answer. "Thriving." She smiled. "Never better. Two new onsite lodges have been added since we spoke last, and I don't think I've ever seen the mountain so busy."

"So you two are keeping busy, then?"

"Mostly," Cooper answered. "We've kept our positions all this time. Just with a little more flexibility now. With three kids and one on the way, we need light schedules. But the lodge is our second home. We're always either on the slopes or in the sitting room by the fireplace."

"You two seem so lucky to have found one another," Chase remarked.

Cooper nodded. "She's my Madeline." He squeezed her hands and looked into her eyes. "I owe her everything."

We are looking forward to interviewing the Graves family in ten more years, excited to see how their family and their love continues to grow beyond all bounds.

THE END.

Hi friends!! You made it!!

So, here's a little secret between us: sometimes being an author isn't all cupcakes and rainbows. *Gasp*, I know. Don't get me wrong, I love my job! But, it is a job. And sometimes that means burn out, boredom, or imposter syndrome.

After finishing my latest book (at the time it was For the Record), I was EXTREMELY burnt out. My motivation to write was out of the window and I knew I had two more books to complete this year and I felt just useless. If I couldn't write, then what could I do? It lead me down a bit of a spiral and finally I settled into Snowed Under.

Something happened in this book that I can't fully explain, but I got lost in it. I fell deeply in love with Madeline and Cooper. I had so much fun that I literally *CRAVED* writing. Even late at night all I wanted was to write. I finished this book in 34 days (insane for me) and I loved EVERY SECOND OF IT.

That being said, it wasn't just me who got this book completed!

First, as always, I have to thank my family. My Justin and my Saylor (also known as my little half pint)! My every inspiration for Madelines niece was FULLY based off my sweet toddler. They were the same age as I was writing and although my daughter doesn't have a speech problem she did have an adoration for 'sham jams' and all Disney princesses. I had so so much fun recreating her in a character, especially considering she is literally my fav human on the planet. Well, tied with my husband. Love you, boo bear!!

A big, big thank you to my very best friends: Madison Wright and Kelsey Whitney. I literally would never have wrote a thing beyond my first book without you two and your constant inspiration. I love my little silly gooses.

Thank you to both of my editors: Beth and Mel, you are so so excellent to work with and it is always a pleasure to see you (professionally) spin my crap into gold hehe.

AND ALWAYS: thank you to YOU! You, reading this! I adore you, whether we have met or spoke or not, you mean so much to me!! I can't thank you enough for being here and taking a chance on my characters!!

And lastly, thank you to the agent who absolutely ripped this book (and my writing career) apart. You turned out to give me quite the inspiration. :)

Juliana Smith is an author in a small town in Alabama. When she is not hanging out with her book characters, she is with her family. Juliana writes heartfelt romance filled with laughter and warm fuzzies. She can usually be found in a Chic-fil-a drive-thru or listening to Star Wars theory podcasts, often at the same time.

Printed in Great Britain
by Amazon